BELLAMY

G. Bradley Davis

TELEMACHUS PRESS

Cover art and design by Bayley Ramos

Publishing services by Telemachus Press, LLC
7652 Sawmill Road
Suite 304
Dublin, Ohio 43016
http://www.telemachuspress.com

Visit the author website: www.GBradleyDavis.com

ISBN: 978-1-956867-67-1 (eBook)
ISBN: 978-1-956867-66-4 (Paperback)

Version 2023.12.11

Bellamy - English and Irish (of Norman origin), French: literal or ironic nickname meaning 'fine friend', from French beau 'fair', 'handsome' (bel before a vowel) + ami 'friend'.

Source: Ancestry.com

For my butterfly, Carolyn

BELLAMY

CHAPTER ONE

When a child knows they are truly loved, it allows for a multitude of parenting mistakes.

I have been told that I am a Welsh storyteller at heart. Well, do I ever have a story to tell, the likes of which have never been told before now.

They say that the motives behind most murders are love, money, power, or revenge. The motives behind a love triangle ending in murder is simple enough. Scorn, rejection, embarrassment, and revenge all come to the party, but this murder had none of these. Many murders are committed in the act of another crime. A holdup, a drug deal gone bad, or an argument, are the highest statistical culprits for murder. But all those reasons for snuffing out a life are generic, lacking the intent of the one culpable.

The murder that happened in this small Pennsylvania hamlet in the fall of '74 was complex. So much so that everyone missed the minutiae; like skipping several chapters of a novel. Not because the details were hidden from sight, but because there was a convenient conclusion. *Conclusion.* People like things wrapped up with a pretty bow. An alternative meant not wasting time with the details but rather, jumping to the *inevitable* ending to the story. *Inevitable.* Funny thing about the inevitable. Everything looks obvious when looking back.

When it came to this murder, it was a falsehood that everyone bought in to. The entire town never knew who the perpetrator was and the motive behind the killing. They believed the story *had to* end the way *they wanted it to end*, and as a result, the truth was never told. Facts were replaced with assumptions and assumptions led to fallacy. In a small town like North Hills, a mystery cannot be left unresolved (another reason for *creating* a conclusion). It was a sterile town. A town that would not, could not, tolerate loose ends. Everything and everybody had its place. Every piece of the puzzle *had to fit*. A community that was barely a mile from one side of town to the other lent itself to rumor and innuendo with both traveling faster than a fire through a barn packed with late August hay.

I guess I could leave sleeping dogs lie, but for years the events of that day have gnawed at me like a porcupine at a hemlock smorgasbord. The more I try to smother the recurring memories, the more frequently they resurface, often with fresh nuances. I had even thought of seeing a therapist or psychologist, but the fear of confirming that I really may be crazy has kept that idea at bay. I mean no harm to anyone that falls within these words I write, nor do I seek your sympathy. My intent is simply to document exactly what happened, why it happened, and to expose the truth; the truth which has been buried beneath years of discarded fears and misconceptions.

I left North Hills soon after that dreadful event and never returned. The murder left its marks on me like pock marks from chicken pox. I needed to breathe. The air in that closeminded town left me gasping for breath. The suburbs of Philly seemed far enough away but, after my divorce, I exiled myself to the mountains of northeastern Pennsylvania. Just me and my dog, Blake. We are isolated in the woods and surrounded by nature that speaks quiet truth. Sometimes I do not see another person for weeks, and that is more than fine by me.

Before I continue, I must throw out a caveat. If you agree to continue reading this work, understand that my story is not to be rushed. You, then, will take a journey back to my childhood and with it share in my less than smooth ride. My early childhood was, as it is for us all, that which has transformed me into who I am today. Good memories often wrestle with bad ones in a futile attempt to land on top.

I have never told this story before. Since *talking about it* is what any good therapist would say is the best medicine, I am more than ready for any prescription that will help me find peace. The origins of this fiasco go back many years before that fateful day. Any psychologist would advise patients to return to their childhood to find answers.

⚛

I had curled up in a fetal position so to limit the target size for the beatings. The problem was that when you are curled up in a ball the back of your shirt rises, exposing skin just above the beltline. That is exactly where the leather strap landed. Any amount of clothing softens the sting of the lashes, but bare, taut skin tears easily at the end of the whip. I remember reading somewhere that 40 lashes were considered deadly, thus the often-reduced sentence of forty minus one. Although they often felt like forty, I seldom received more than a dozen strokes.

The leather belt struck a second time, but this time lower, finding the well-cushioned expanse of my derrière. The flogging continued. The third and fourth lash were higher on my back and hurt, somewhat surprisingly more than the others had.

My stepmother was convinced she could beat the bad out of me but, apparently, she was wrong. Though there were four kids in my family, somehow, I consumed her attention and received most of her cruel corporal punishment. She had no tolerance for people who were not compliant. So, it was I who received the status of homo sacer for my repeated disobedience. I was the black and bloodied sheep of our family.

It was the result of the fifth crack of the belt that made my stepmother stop the beating. Ostensibly, she needed to regrip the torture implement. To do so, she had grabbed the end of the belt allowing the brass buckle to strike my back, tearing both my shirt and flesh while exposing a three-inch gash. I fell flat on my face from the surging pain that shot through my injured back. Reaching back, I felt the back of my shirt wet from absorbing the blood flowing from my wound.

Had my father been there, he certainly would have stopped my stepmother from her abuse. He would have allowed the beatings, of course, but would have stopped them when they crossed that line between punishment and torture. But my father worked endless hours so we would have just a little more. Those long hours provided the extra money needed for my brother's music lessons or my sister's braces.

🚲

My friends call me Cal. I was a disappointing child that never lived up to expectations. I was inquisitive, to a fault. I was the type of boy who would pick up a hot coal just to see how it felt in the palm of my hand. I was seldom interested in the mundane, and if the truth be told, I often lived within a fantasy world I created to make reality more palatable. I would become easily bored at school and tended to fantasize about my teacher if she were attractive and younger than my stepmother. Why I experienced sexual obsession at the tender age of six years old would be one of the things I would love to ask a shrink, but that will remain an unanswered question.

In college I had to take a psychology course to fulfill the social-science requirement for my degree. Right or wrong, I have always felt that my early childhood problems and my lifelong obsession with breasts stemmed from my mother not having breast fed me. Life is hard enough without having to be force-fed the nourishing juice from a Guernsey. Drinking milk from a cow instead of your mother? That does not even sound natural. Without a doubt, I believed that was the reason why I was a late bloomer. Clearly, there were far-reaching psychological effects having not suckled at my mother's breasts which impacted both my cognitive and socio-emotional development. For example, I could not tie my shoes when I entered kindergarten. It took forever to learn how to ride a bicycle. I wet the bed till I was 7, and I sucked my thumb even longer! I've always known that I was...well, different!

But I have always felt guilty blaming my mother. She died while I was but an infant. I have no recollection of her and no memory of what she was like. Her photographs displayed a beautiful lady with an olive complexion and high cheekbones characteristic of Eastern European women. She had dark, curly hair which flowed past her shoulders, deep beckoning eyes, and a figure that would rival Bettie Page. She was first generation Ukrainian and grew up in the eastern European neighborhood of Pottstown, an hour's drive west of Philadelphia. Whenever anyone spoke to me about her, their face was transformed into a captivating smile as if describing their finest birthday party. She was much like my father, in that she could do anything she set her mind to tackle. She was renowned for her seamstress skills, as she made most of my sibling's clothes. I received their hand-me-downs. Her baking was legendary, and she was prudent with the family finances and generous with those who were less fortunate.

Her name was Maria. I would often retrieve a dog-eared photograph of her from a cigar box where I kept my most treasured possessions. Later, I would find a more secretive place to store the things I did not want anyone to find. Having no recollection of her, I would take the photograph of her and roll my thumb over it trying to imagine the texture and softness of her soft, flowing hair. In truth, I longed for her to return to me and give me the one thing no one else could, motherly love. Cancer had been found in her left breast and from the bits and pieces I was told, she suffered terribly for well over a year until the disease completed its filthy work.

I hated school and academics did not come easily for me. I was short for my age and my attention span far shorter. Stupid I was not, but I did have a speech impediment. I had difficulty pronouncing words that had an R in it, often bringing mocking laughter from listeners when speaking those dreaded words which only added to my academic challenges. *Furst. Ulsa. Burd.* Simple words were just not that simple.

When my mom passed, our two paternal aunts took turns helping their younger brother care for us by cooking and cleaning. That is, until dad remarried when I was four. Big mistake! Dad met Dasha at a Bible study at church and curiously, like my biological mother, she was Ukrainian, having emigrated with her parents, sister, and brother when she was five. Being the youngest, my stepmother insisted I call her mother, even though my older siblings were not held to the same criterion.

I heard repeatedly from Dasha, to the point of noisomeness, that the youngest child was always coddled and spoiled...*like it was my fault!* She would tell me the youngest are underachievers having had the road paved by the blood, sweat, tears and spankings of their older, pioneering siblings. The proverbial bar of expectation had been lowered, she would say, so that the youngest child could easily skip over it. *The youngest have it the easiest!*

I could not disagree more! My understanding was verified by my own life experience that the youngest was perceived to be less intelligent than their older siblings, lazy, and carelessly willing to take *unnecessary* risks, which resulted in a lack of confidence in the child. Perhaps the risk-taking thing is true, but I also experienced unrealistic expectations that were placed upon me being the youngest which often came in the form of wishful cloning. *Why aren't you more like your brother...your sister?* Individuality was frowned upon in the Lloyd household; conformity encouraged.

In our home we had a collection of cherished family photographs, mostly of us children. There were hundreds of photos of the first born, Olivia, and scores of photos of the second born, Audrey. When my brother Ted, the first son and heir to the Lloyd throne, entered the scene, the cameras flashed like the red carpet at the Oscars. But when I, the fourth child, wandered into the domestic tranquility, there never seemed to be film in the camera or an extra flash bulb in the drawer. And don't even start with the hand-me-downs. Other than underwear, which was a perennial Christmas gift, I never received anything new. So please, do not tell me that the youngest have it the easiest. Being the youngest, from my perspective, had its own unique set of challenges.

With all that said, I was the one piece of the Lloyd jigsaw puzzle that just did not fit. I always had difficulty staying within the lines of my coloring books. Like a white boxer puppy who is surrounded by its fawn and brindle counterparts, I was clearly different.

CHAPTER TWO

*Love and discipline in child rearing should be balanced as
carefully as you would juggling nitroglycerin.*

C hildren and dogs seem to have the same innate ability to distinguish good people from ones they should avoid. Even when a grown-up offers them a wide smile with an expanse of large, fairly white teeth, their instinct is to be cautious. Sure, the promise of ice cream or candy can cause a child to make the wrong decision, but their first intuition is to raise the proverbial red flag. Their vision is not clouded by mature philosophies and political correctness that cloud an adult's vision. This poor visibility often causes grown-ups to suffer from a deficiency of observation. Adults often see and hear what they want to, as if their minds were made-up about people before they even have an initial conversation with them. Regardless of how obvious things appear to a kid, grown-ups often see things differently. Though I was but a child, I instinctively knew that I should be wary of our family's pastor.

At the ripe age of five, my observation of Reverend Bartholomew Michael Markey could not have been more spot-on. Now, looking back many years later, I could not tell you what it was exactly that made me fear the reverend like I feared no other grown-up. But make no mistake, there was something peculiar, if not sinister about this ordained figurehead. The clergyman did not like dogs and dogs did not like him. Perhaps that was my first indication that something was off about him.

The Reverend Markey was a tall man, 6 foot 5 or so. He had narrow shoulders and a soft pouch in his mid-section that exemplified an undisciplined life. Still, adults were calmly manipulated by his gift of persuasion, and the authority he presented as a "man of God." His hair was unkempt; a mousy brown color which had grown long enough to be combed over to cover his ever- disappearing hairline. He sported a trim, pencil-thin mustache just like the ones I would see on villains in cartoons, like Boris from the Rocky and Bullwinkle Show. The few times the good minister came over to our house, Jackson, who never growled at anyone, snarled, and barked endlessly. He had a habit of stroking the hair on the back of kid's heads and gently rubbing our necks which made that same hair stand at attention and cause me to breakout in a cold sweat.

Maybe it was the way his eyes were positioned; so close together that they crowded his long, pointed nose. And they were black as coal; so dark that you could see your reflection in them when he would bend his towering frame over to talk *at* me. And that breath; hot and filled with a stale, musty odor that resembled the basement of an old, deserted house. Then again, it could have been his enormous hands that had five long and thin arthritic protrusions that resembled the rods from my tinker toy set. The Rev's fingernails were a half inch too long and when he extended his arms, I could have sworn he was the Grim Reaper reaching for those whose time had come.

But it was the minister's smile that made me most apprehensive of him. It wasn't that his smile was that odd as it was how *often* he smiled. He *always* smiled, as if it had been painted on his face, like the large plastic clown at the entrance to the kiddie rides at Willow Grove Park. It was as if he could smile even with a tear in his eye….as though a smile was the necessary camouflage to hide something else…something he did not want you to see. It made me want to hum the Smokey Robinson & the Miracles' song I would hear from my sister's record player, *Tears of a Clown.* Camouflaged Clergy. *No one smiled all the time. No one!* He smiled when my brother got stung by a bee at the Sunday School picnic. He smiled when Charlie Dauterman, the church janitor, broke his ankle on the front steps of the church one icy February day. For crying out loud, he even smiled at funerals!

My stepmother volunteered on Mondays and Thursdays in the church office. On Mondays she would take the flower arrangements from Sunday's service over to the old folks at Green Meadows

Community; a place grown-ups called a retirement home, but one I called the waiting room to heaven. One Monday, Dasha took me with her to the church office. As I was sitting in the large hard-back leather chair in the office, my feet dangling high above the floor, my eyes were glued on to the church secretary, Mildred White. She was a whale of a woman with full, puckered lips and cheeks so plump it made her eyes squint as if she were Asian.

"Oh no!" Miss White cried out. The phone wobbled as her hand quivered against her ear. I watched as a tear rolled down the secretary's round cheek, frozen, immobile for just a few seconds before dropping onto her large breast.

"When?" she asked. "I'm so sorry. Okay. Okay. I'll tell him. What can we do for you, John?" I was always pretty good at figuring out what was being said on the other end of phone conversations I could not hear. Dasha was always on the phone, and I could tell what the remainder of my day would be like just by the way she responded to the mystery person on the other end; that is, unless she was speaking in Ukrainian.

Miss White ended the phone call and slowly hung-up the phone. Reverend Markey had come out of his office in time to hear the end of the conversation and looked at Miss White for an explanation. "Reverend, that was John Robie on the phone. Betty passed away this morning."

The Reverend walked over to Miss White and placed his hand on her shoulder. "She's in Glory. She's at peace now." And there he was...smiling as if he had scored the final run in the annual North Hills/Ardsley Fourth of July baseball game. At five years old, I did not know much about dying, but I knew it was not something to smile about. It made me wonder why your cheeks tend to promptly hurt quickly when you force a fake smile, but never seem to hurt when your smile was genuine. I figured it must be hard work to hold a smile you did not mean.

Growing up, it seemed as though my family lived at church. Church of the Rising Son was not any mainstream, organized, traditional sect of Christianity. It was a cult, a hybrid of several religions. In fact, its own laws were reminiscent of the Middle Ages which embraced a warped legalistic theology that applied to everyone but the minister. It was more Rev. Markey's unique sect. The church preached that the 12 disciples... Matthias had replaced Judas the betrayer... transcended time and never died. From generation to generation, they took new physical forms and were scattered throughout the earth to evangelize to every corner of the earth. Like many false religions and prophets, Reverend Markey plucked scripture out of its context to serve his "theology." For example, he used the apostle Paul's words "to bring to light what is the administration of the mystery which for ages has been hidden in God, who created all things; in order that the manifold wisdom of God might now be made known through the church." Another favorite verse to support this warped doctrine was his interpretation of Matthew 16:28, when Jesus told his disciples "Truly I tell you, some who are standing here will not taste death before they see the Son of Man coming in his kingdom." Pastor Markey even claimed he was one of the original disciples, Bartholomew.

The church would routinely hold exorcisms. That is, until one teenage girl died when blankets were held tightly over as she was beaten during this ritual. That happened when I was just an infant, and no one would talk about it. However, I am convinced that I would have been subject to something similar if they had not suspended this heathen practice. What did not cease was the parental thrashings that were encouraged to purge evil from a rebellious child. A severe form of corporal punishment was more than encouraged. If a child would not willingly change his behavior, and cease sinning, you would have to beat it out of him.

Dasha was a pious woman, and she took church and her faith seriously. On more than one occasion I would peek through the slightly opened door of her bedroom as she was down on her knees, praying for my salvation. In her eyes, my soul was in great jeopardy.

We seemed to *live* at church. We would go to church on Sunday mornings; first to the Sunday school, then to worship service with the grown-ups. Most of the kids went to children's church but my stepmom insisted on me and my siblings *assimilate* into big-people's church at a young age. I assumed it was like teaching a puppy how to do their business outside when they were young rather than waiting till it was a couple of years old. They learn faster when young.

The church building was a converted women's silk-stocking factory that went under when the owner failed to see the transition to nylon stockings. It was made of red brick and if not for the steeple with a fish on the very top and one large stained-glass window that couldn't be seen from the street, it could have passed for any office building in town.

The church and its congregation were originally located in the Nicetown neighborhood of Philadelphia. The church joined the urban mass-exodus and moved to the *safety* of the suburbs when people of color started moving into that area of the city, giving credence to the phrase "the most segregated part of America happens on Sunday mornings at 11 o'clock." I guess grownups thought the neighborhood wasn't very *nice* anymore. A few years later, racial unrest burned hot in North Philly when the accelerant of brutality inflicted on blacks by white cops resulted in three days of rioting.

After the morning worship service, our family would go home to a cold lunch, normally consisting of sandwiches made of luncheon meat and processed cheese on margarine-spread bread. We were not allowed to play with the other kids on the block on Sundays because we honored the Sabbath. It truly was a day of rest for the Lloyd family. I was not allowed to watch TV, play football, or whiffle ball in the yard or do basically anything that involved exerting any energy, and the possibility of getting dirty or having fun, was out of the question. The only good news was that I did not have to do any chores on Sundays. What I could do was homework, which I found strange because that was clearly *work*, just as the name suggests, read the Sunday funnies, take naps, or play board games. Then, we went back to church for the evening service. I guess I resented the forced adherence to the Sabbath back then, but now I can appreciate it much more, not that I know anyone who strictly observes it anymore.

On Wednesday nights they held classes to study the writings of Reverend Markey. Friday nights were youth night, where the teens would have a place to hang-out; a place where their parents would allow them to go and know they were not trying to have sex, smoke pot, or drink a six-pack of PBR.

Sundays were mostly uneventful, but there was one Sunday morning I will never forget. It was mid-July and the church was filled to the rafters, which just added to this steamy sanctuary that lacked air conditioning. The four ceiling fans pushed the hot air around so it would not sit thick in any one row of seats. Our family always sat in the second pew, just behind Mrs. Pompton and her fox stole whose beady eyes would stare at me all through the service like a snake focused on an unsuspecting frog.

Our self-assigned seats were just to the left of the pulpit and nearest to the stained-glass window that depicted a white-robed, red-sash Jesus with a staff in one hand and a little lamb cradled in the other. The window faced east so that by 11 o'clock the sun would hit the stained-glass and make the colors explode like fireworks. By 11:13 the green hillsides of the shepherding scene could be seen vividly on the organist's white blouse and by 19 minutes past the hour Jesus' red sash hit her wheat-blond hair.

On that specific day, the choir director, an aging man with poorly dyed thinning hair, walked up to the pulpit and asked the congregation to turn their hymnals to page 271. I could tell by the organ and piano's prelude that it was my least favorite hymn, *In the Garden*. It had funny words like *tarry* and whenever we came to the word *dew*, I would look at my brother, Ted, and try to get him to laugh, as long as our wicked stepmother was not watching. But apparently it was someone's favorite song because we would sing it three Sundays out of four. *I come to the garden alone, while the dew is still on the roses*, the congregation sang. Mrs. Townsend, in her operatic, falsetto voice was standing right behind me (we always stood when we sang or when scripture was read). My eyes would squint when she would bellow out the shrieking high notes.

Meanwhile, Reverend Markey sat in his cushioned, high back chair; his legs loosely crossed. He wore a starched, white shirt, gray and white striped tie, and a plaid jacket…and he was smiling as he walked to the pulpit.

"Good morning," the minister declared.

"Good morning," the congregation recited back.

The reverend repeatedly stroked his thin mustache as he surveyed the congregation, making me think a goatee would have been more appropriate. *Then he would "look" like Satan, too.*

"Today we have reason to rejoice. A sheep that was lost has been found."

What the heck was he talking about? I wondered whether this had something to do with that painted glass window I loved so much.

"One of our own...one of our flock was led astray, but this morning the transgressor will come before us to publicly repent and to ask for your forgiveness," the minister stated.

Oh crap! I felt a hot sensation throughout my body which made me increasingly anxious. *Is he talking about me?* I had been trying to squelch a guilty feeling about a petty larceny I had committed a few weeks earlier. In preparation for *Missionary Sunday*, every family in the congregation had been given a small cardboard church that had a slit in the roof for depositing loose change. The first Sunday of the following month they would collect the cardboard church banks and give the money to some missionary evangelizing in Africa. I had *borrowed* some of the change to buy a butterscotch sundae at Jack Frost, the corner ice cream shop. *I swear I was going to put the money back!*

"Public confession is powerful and effective, and it brings the much-needed cure from God. Spiritual weakness results in the indulgence of earthly, sinful pleasures," the minister added.

Crap, how did he find out about the money? Did Dasha and Dad know?

Reverend Markey continued, "One's infidelity to God affects others in the congregation. It is a cancer that so easily spreads...a root that produces such bitter poison. We must purge this sin from our congregation."

My eyes became as large as yo-yos and I could feel sweat begin to exit from every pore of my body. My starched white short-sleeved shirt was soaked, and my clip-on bowtie was half choking me to death! I forced my index finger between my neck and shirt collar and slid it around my neck in hope of giving me a little breathing room.

"In order for the sinner to confess their sin, they must call it by name and I'm going to ask them to come up here in just a minute to do just that."

It was then that it happened. I could feel the warm and wet sensation spread across my shorts and trickle down my thighs. In a strange way, it felt a little liberating, that is, until I realized what was happening.

"Taking responsibility and seeking reconciliation is welcome and I'd like you all to give Naomi Baker a hug after this morning's service," the reverend said. "Naomi come on up here."

I had not seen Naomi anywhere around church for months. By the time she reached the second step to the platform I saw her enlarged belly that caused her dress to stick out nearly a foot. *Heck, I didn't even know she had gotten married.* I could not help but wonder what she had done wrong. I did not think Naomi could ever do anything wrong.

I had always thought Naomi was the best teenage girl in the entire church. I found her beauty mesmerizing. She had a pretty, round face with shoulder length hair the color of pecans and full, red lips. Her breasts were large for her frame, and they would always force the buttons on her one-size-to-small blouse to spread ever so slightly so I could catch a glimpse of her lovely lace bra and beckoning cleavage.

"In order for Naomi to confess her sin, she must admit guilt and acknowledge her sin. Asking for forgiveness is a prerequisite for reconciliation with the church body so that she can be readmitted into our congregation," the minister explained.

Just then a small yellow trickle ran down the pew, like water down a hog's feeding trough, heading straight for my father's backside. I was not sure whether my father had felt the wetness or smelled the stench of urine, giving new meaning to the phrase "church *pew.*" Before I could give a detailed explanation, my dad and Dasha looked at each other, then to me as each grabbed one of my arms and dragged me, stiffed legged, up the center aisle so that my toes left two impressions in the thick, sky-blue carpet like the train tracks that lie behind the local Kenyon Diner.

CHAPTER THREE

*Imaginary friends never leave until we find a real friend
who can take their place.*

After a thorough beating, I had been exiled to the far reaches of the gulag, or my bedroom, if you please, after the church ordeal. I had been banished from the populace, which included my two sisters, my brother, my wicked stepmother, and my father. Time always passed glacially in Dasha's purgatory, as there was no one to offer me any empathy or sympathy, as I sat sentenced to rot in solitary confinement for a week. The expectation was always that isolation from the populace would result in some type of attitude adjustment, but it never did.

They say necessity is the mother of invention, and I had a desperate need for a friend, a confidant, someone I could talk to and trust. Enter Bellamy. Feeling overwhelmingly alone in the gulag; alienated from the world around me, Bellamy simply *appeared* in my room. The door had never opened, and the windows were too high for anyone to have climbed into the room. I was not really surprised at his appearance. I guess that is why I was not the slightest bit afraid of him. In fact, quite the opposite.

"What's your name?" I asked.

The boy put his arm around me and pulled me close to himself.

"Bellamy. Listen. It's alright. It wasn't your fault."

Bellamy? What an odd name. "It's always my fault. I don't do anything right and I'm always getting in trouble. No one likes me."

"I like you, Calvin," Bellamy said. "I am your friend. I'll never leave you. Never! Please don't ignore me. You won't want to introduce me to your family and friends. I get that. That's okay. They won't even

see me, because they won't *want* to see me. When you need me the
most, I'll be there for you."

I looked up from my curled position on the floor, my eyes wet as
I looked into Bellamy's eyes. He was about the same age as me, but
with an air of maturity that was difficult to explain. There was a
confidence, but with the absence of arrogance, and a face of empathy
that seemed trustworthy, an alter ego that was everything I was not.

I thought about having a best friend, the kind that both my sisters
and my brother had. The kind of friend you could hang out with,
laugh with, build memories with. I had no idea how long I sat there
on the rug, mesmerized, as if off in a dream, sucking my thumb, when
I heard my stepmother calling me to wash-up for dinner. When I
looked around the room, Bellamy was gone.

My stepmother was the contemporary Cheka. She morphed into
becoming the secret police who investigated and dealt with any
threats to her regime by attacking her enemies, both internal and
external enemies. But to her defense, she was a product, if not a victim,
of her own childhood. Her father, Misha, while working in the Russian
city of Orel, escaped to America the winter of 1914 by a route which
eventually took him through Austria-Hungary. From there he sailed
to America from the port of Rijeka on the Cunard at the cusp of World
War I in 1914, just before the port closed. His brother, who remained
behind, would be killed in the October Revolution of 1917.

Misha was a Ukrainian immigrant who quickly became a
successful real estate salesman in Pennsylvania. He used his magnetic
charm, handsome good looks, and shrewd business sense to balance
his dealings between the traditionalists and the roguish. Misha's
business agreements were all handshake deals. He believed that a
handshake was more binding than anything that could be written on
paper. Unfortunately, he and three friends were killed in a drunken
automobile crash, all his debtors seemed to dissipate, like rain drops
on a hot car hood, leaving Dasha's mother and siblings penniless.
Literally, they went from prosperity to poverty overnight.

Dasha's mother only knew a few words of English as she found herself stranded alone in a foreign country with three children under the age of seven. Through a neighbor acquaintance, she got a job scrubbing floors and cleaning bathrooms at affluent homes on Hanover and King Streets in Pottstown. Pottstown was an industrial town bounded on the west by the Manatawny Creek and on the south by the Schuylkill River.

Desperate, Dasha's mother simply settled for the first available suitor. He was an authentic swine who qualified as a potential husband simply because he breathed and had a steady job with the railroad. She married him out of necessity for stability and mere survival. Nine months to the day after their wedding, they had a girl of their own, Olena, whom he treated like a princess. As much as he loved his daughter, he despised his stepchildren just as much and treated them like second class citizens. He saw them as nothing more than irritating little gnats that would circle around him as he agitatedly shewed them away.

Every Christmas he would buy his little princess several presents from the Ellis Mills Department Store. But there would never be anything under the tree for the children who were bred by another man. That was Dasha's cold reality. The world was painted black and white. It was a sad childhood, but as she escaped the vault of hell by leaving home to marry my father, she carried with her more of her past than she ever realized.

My stepmother simply did not like me and, to be quite honest, I did not like her. At that young of an age you instinctively know that you are *supposed* to like your parents...*love* your parents. Talking about guilt? I felt like I was hands-down the most terrible son the world has ever seen. Now, many years later, I still do not get it. I was a little kid. What is there not to like about a child? It is not like I deliberately did things to upset the witch. We were polar; she was negative, me, positive, complete opposites. One of us would say calm, the other windy; one bitter, the other sweet. Dasha was determined not to be undermined by some little shit. Our relationship was a constant struggle of wills, both of us being as hardheaded as a statue of Chang and Eng Bunker. The only thing that connected us was my father.

This was the milieu of what would become a lifelong struggle for me, a struggle with conformity verses individuality. As people's expectations and demands of me grew, I tended to retreat, running in the opposite direction as fast as a rabbit. No matter how fast I would run, those expectations would inevitably catch-up, casting a shadow over me like a descending bird of prey.

I became familiar with the merits of self-denigration. If your expectations of yourself are low, you will never disappoint yourself. If other's expectations of you were low, then you would be obliged not to disappoint. Apparently, I had disappointed any and everyone who had such high expectations of me. Of course, some of those expectations were based on my siblings and not on my abilities. My stepmother wanted a Calvin that could be created by placing my three siblings into a blender, pureed for a few minutes, and then a much more palatable version of the Calvin she wanted could be poured out.

I found myself slipping into depression even at that early age, but I figured out a way to survive. I owe a lot of that survival to Bellamy. Fear had been my only other faithful companion. True friendship is rare. It is laughable when I hear people say they have dozens of friends…. Hundreds of friends. Those *friendships* are fragile. One misspoken word or misconstrued sentence can shatter those relationships. One is fortunate to have one true and loyal friend. Bellamy was a *true and loyal friend*. He was the only person who encouraged me to be who I was, not who others wanted me to be, that is until Perry and Simone came into my life. More about them later. Bellamy was a genuine friend, my guide and confessor. It was because of him that I could escape the adult persecution that haunted me.

Strangely, I would often find myself in a dark pit that eerily morphed into a familiar place that I eventually did not fear. When you visit a place often, it becomes *normal*. Some things you cannot change. Some things you eventually accept. Though it always brought inner pain, the pain hurt *good*, if that makes any sense. It became that friend you really do not like but, for some godforsaken reason, you *let him* stick around. Self-doubt could always be counted on to offer some choice words of discouragement; words I would grow accustomed to. I would get sucked into a warped mentality that I could not dismiss for fear that I may end up alone. *A bad friend is better than no friend at all.* And so, I learned to live with it, like a wart you know you should have removed, but after a while you become oblivious to it. You just do not care. It becomes part of who you are. It becomes an appendage. Maybe that explains my need for Bellamy. He wanted nothing from me. He only had my best interests at heart.

🚲

I would get into trouble without intent. A perfect example of that was the naked-behind-the-couch story. Saturday nights were mandatory tub nights in the Lloyd household because the next day was Sunday, church day, and that meant putting on your Sunday white shirt, a tie that choked the life out of me, and dress slacks. For that you had to be "Dasha" clean. There was a personal hygiene check-off list which had to be followed very carefully. Brush behind your ears, check. Wash behind your neck, check. Scrub every little crevice until your body was the cherry-red color of a strawberry Twizzler, scrub your fingernails with a brush and make sure your arm pits are washed twice; check, check, check.

One Saturday night I remained in the bathtub playing with my favorite grey battleship and destroyer until the soap bubbles had all but disappeared. As I was drying myself off, I looked down at my male appendage and could not help but think of my stepmother's absurd words she would create for anatomical body parts, the penis being a prime example. Dasha had taught my brother Ted and I from an early age that our male organ was called the "Johnny," which completely baffled me since I had a cousin named Johnny. No wonder I was a confused little kid.

Still wet on my back, I ran naked into the living room to make a brief exhibition to anyone who might be present, normally strumming my Johnny like it was a six-string while singing some inane song. After receiving some much-needed attention and laughter, I would trot down to my bedroom to put on my pajamas. On this occasion, and to my disappointment, the living room was empty. I could hear chatter in the kitchen, so I peeked around the corner to catch a small glimpse of the kitchen table. I saw a teenage boy whom I did not recognize, dressed in dark slacks and a solid baby-blue button-down shirt, talking with my parents. I was just about to retreat to my bedroom when everyone stood up from the table and headed my way.

My escape down the hallway was blocked and, to say the least, I began to panic. Without hesitation I scurried behind the living room couch just in time to see my parents walk down the hallway toward their bedroom and my sister, Audrey, along with what appeared to be her date, enter the living room. I was trapped!

Minutes seemed like hours as I sat motionless behind the couch listening to the two of them talk about ridiculous things like final exams, the senior prom, where they planned on working for the summer and how the boy feared the draft and going to Vietnam. *Heck, couldn't they talk about these things in his car? How long would they be camped out on the couch?* I knew that time was running out and that sooner or later Dasha would check to see if I was in bed. It was then that I heard Dasha asking my older sister if she had seen me. I knew I had to make a run for it, but my options were limited. Audrey was sitting closest to the entrance into the living room, with her back away from the hallway and towards her date. My only hope was that the boy would be too engrossed with my sister to notice me, and that Audrey wouldn't turn around. I made my move.

Crawling on all fours, I slowly, with military-like stealth, made my way to the hallway. The problem was that my exit would force me to crawl nearly to the center of the entrance before making a U-turn for the hallway. Every few feet I would look over my shoulder to see if I had been made. So far, so good. It was just when I thought I made it safely out of the living room when, quite unexpectantly, I let out a malodorous air biscuit. With whip-like quickness, both Audrey and her date turned their heads just in time to see my two small, white, round cheeks and a crack scuttling out of the room.

Thankfully, I heard nothing more about it and, for the time being, escaped the wrath of Dasha.

CHAPTER FOUR

*Youth is to all the glad season of life; but often only by what
it hopes, not by what it attains, or what it escapes.*
                                    —Thomas Carlyle

P hysically, I took after my mom much more than my dad. Unfortunately, I was a late-bloomer, and it did not help that I was always one of the younger kids in my class at school. I was shorter than most of the boys, reached puberty later and got my driver's license later. All of which were more than a little challenging for a kid who was already struggling with confidence and acceptance. Thankfully, Bellamy was always there to help me navigate the difficult times.

I had a few sprinkled freckles on my upper cheeks and caramel, light brown hair, cut straight across my brow, which would turn three shades lighter in the summer sun. When I look at photographs of me as a kid, there is always a memorable smile; forty percent mischievous, forty percent innocence, with a splash of a born skeptic thrown in. I was a kid who never took things at face value, which did not work favorably for me in my academic endeavors.

Why should I believe anything someone tells me? Blind faith? It may have played out differently had I believed that these grown-ups had my best interest at heart. When proven repeatedly that that was not the case, everything an adult said was suspect. It is not that it was not necessarily true, I just had to prove it for myself. This type of mindset does not play well in academia. You are told to take every word from teachers and authors of textbooks as fact. I was especially suspicious of history. Anything older than a century can only be known through unreliable whisper down the lane.

I was named Calvin after the French theologian, John Calvin, which partly reveals the religious, fundamental upbringing I received. I always found it odd that my parents named me after a Frenchman since my father had disdain for the French; partly for how quickly they turned and hightailed it from the Germans in the Great War, and because my dad despised De Gaulle. After reneging on France's agreement to pool their gold resources with the rest of Europe, De Gaulle demanded that the U.S exchange gold, rather than treasury debt paper, for the dollars they earned from French export.

When I was young it never dawned on me that I was named for the theologian's surname, not given name. Nonetheless, as I said, religion was an important element in the Lloyd household, and its legalistic thick smoke would strangle the life-breath out of me. It would fuel a life-long wrestling match of truths, questions, and wavering faith. My spiritual journey would take me from an inherited faith to a nonbelieving infidel, and finally to a posture of acceptance of God and the Bible's teachings. Sometimes you need a shock to your system to change your perspective. For me, it was that murder which shook me to my core. But I am getting ahead of myself.

I wanted to grow up to be just like my father, Thomas Edwin Lloyd. He was a man with street-smart wisdom, unquestionable integrity, and the ability to learn and master just about any skill he put his mind to. My father's frugality came from having experienced the Great Depression firsthand, and it was obvious that that event influenced many of his decisions in life. I have always believed that my father had limited his life experiences. His decisions were calculated, and he was not a gambler. After the war, instead of going to college, he got a good paying job. He did so out of some sense of responsibility to his family and the fear that one day the depression would return, making money not only scarce, but worthless. A good job in hand was worth more to him than delaying a steady income while spending four years attending college. It was a shame, because he was a brilliant man.

My dad felt no need to prove his masculinity, unlike me and my friends, and he never felt the need to join a "Big Boys Club." Mr. Dean tried to get my dad to join the VFW, but Thomas Lloyd could not have been less interested. It seemed to me that just about every man I knew belonged to some type of club. There were the country clubs and the American Legion or VFW. There were the Masons, and the Knights of Columbus (for the Catholics), the Elks, the Moose Lodge, and the Fraternal Order of Eagles. Yikes! Old man frats. If a guy did not have an official club, he made the local bar his club where he would attend "meetings" just about every night.

My dad fought with the 1st Marine Division at Guadalcanal as part of the Pacific theatre during World War II. That was enough to prove to me that my dad had *courage*, something I yearned for. Dad's work ethic was legendary and my respect for him, immense. He worked long hours and took advantage of any overtime that was available.

Dasha was a stay-home mom, like most of my friend's moms. Other than how strict she was and the frequent beatings I received for not conforming to the Lloyd expectations and my disobedience, which came naturally to me, I thought our family was fairly normal. Nonetheless, I continued to experience an increasing disconnect when it came to me and the rest of the world. I would have embraced Henry David Thoreau's "On the Duty of Civil Disobedience," that is, if I had ever read Thoreau. My literary repertoire consisted of *Mad Magazine*, *Sad Sack* comic books and Ray Bradbury fantasy novels.

I was an accident-prone kid, mostly because there was not a tree I wouldn't climb, or a mound of dirt I wouldn't jump with my bicycle that would result in a broken arm, stitches, etcetera. Once, Dasha told me that my injuries were the "bad" coming out of me. In retrospect, I guess I did not get hurt enough.

There were ways I found to express my creativity that was seldom appreciated, or even understood. The way I acted and reacted to life were often viewed as bizarre, not just by my family, but by others as well. It was more than traveling to the beat of a different drum; I was viewed as a weird kid. I saw the world differently than everyone else. *Everyone!* Taking risks was more than acceptable simply because the possible consequences of my actions were seldom a deterrent. The ability to comprehend simple concepts was difficult for me and I could not, for the life of me, understand why people could not see things through *my* lens. This helped launch my creative drive which was necessary to craft a world which was both safe and effective for me. When I was young, I hated my inability to conform, but as I grew older, I realized that I really did not want to be like the masses.

I was the youngest child of four, and although my stepmother desperately wanted her own biological children, it was never to be. Dasha manipulated me and my siblings, as well as our environment, in an attempt to mold together four progenies to be clones of each other. She was only successful with the three older children. I had trouble being compliant, and I exhausted extensive energy and time attempting to find myself—yet find myself I would. I understood that there was a vast world outside of my home, and I heard it calling me to live life fully and to do so under my terms.

I was six when my grandmother, Mom-Mom died. It was the first death I had experienced, having no recollection of my mom's passing. After the memorial service, I walked to the car with my father to take the ride from the church to the cemetery. A cool afternoon breeze assisted the leaves on the tall elms to bow ever so slightly as if to honor the deceased.

I spoke first. "Dad?"

"Yes, Calvin."

"Can we visit mom's grave after the burial service is over?" I said as I scanned the hundreds of gravestones neatly patterned like a checkerboard as far as my eyes could see.

"Today's not a good day to do that, Calvin. I'll take you another day."

"Why? Isn't she buried here?"

"Yes, but it might be better if it's just you and me who come. It wouldn't be fair to Dasha," responded his father. That did not make a lot of sense to me, but I did know that Dasha didn't approve of her stepchildren dwelling on her predecessor, or should I say, her competition. We walked to the car and waited for my stepmother, brother, and sisters. It was a short drive to the cemetery and my thoughts were sobering. *When will my dad and Dasha die? I hope Dasha dies first...and soon.*

My family was seated in the first row at the gravesite, directly in front of the coffin and the large 3 x 8-foot hole in the ground. Desperately needing to ease my nerves, I reached deep into my pants pocket and retrieved my prized Bullwinkle Pez dispenser. With a flick of my index finger, I pushed back the antlers and pulled out the little rectangular grape treat. It just so happened to be the precise moment Dasha decided to look at me, witnessing the crime. Without warning, Dasha slapped my hand that held Bullwinkle causing the rectangular treat to fly, end-over-end, kicking off Mom Mom's casket and into the grave. Reverend Markey abruptly stopped reading from his black Bible and, as if in slow motion, the reverend, and every mourner present, turned slowly and stared disapprovingly at me. Bellamy was laughing uncontrollably.

A few months later the Grim Reaper paid a visit to my great-aunt Gertie. My paternal grandfather's sister had always been old and wrinkly, at least as far as I could remember. Aunt Gertie's furniture and household possessions were divvied up by Dasha and my aunts and to my horror, I received Aunt Gertie's bed, *the one that she died in*. Sure, I had wanted a big boy bed for months now, but not one handcrafted by the Angel of Death. My brother, Ted, smiled as my father and Uncle Ron reassembled the deathbed in my bedroom.

"Aunt Gertie died of an incurable disease which is highly contagious," my brother told me. "You're not going to make it to third grade." When I tried to protest to my parents about me having to sleep in the open coffin, I was given the "just grow up and stop being an ungrateful brat" speech. For the next couple of weeks I would stay awake long into the night wondering if every shadow and creak in my dark bedroom was the messenger of death coming to escort me. The shadow of the old oak tree limb outside my bedroom window looked exactly like a boney arm of the Prince of Darkness with his long index finger bent ninety degrees toward where I lay. Bellamy would lay next to me, but I got the feeling he was just as scared as I was.

The morning light was especially welcomed in those first few weeks of sleeping on the deathbed. I would wake-up in the middle of the night from a dream starring Aunt Gertie. The dreams would differ from night to night, but it always included a scene where I would be in bed asleep. In my dream I would awaken just in time to see Aunt Gertie bending over to give me a good-night kiss. Her fake eye lashes were on crooked, and her fire engine red lipstick extended well above her lips. Her lips puckered and just when she was inches away from my lips, her skin and flesh dissolved, dripping onto my bed sheets, exposing a skeletal face with fake eye lashes and red lipstick in tack.

It always ended the same way, with me screaming like a cat who had its tail crushed by a rocking chair, my parents running into my room, and my brother terrified and shaken from a sound sleep in the bed next to mine.

CHAPTER FIVE

Youth, which is forgiven everything, forgives itself nothing:
age, which forgives itself everything, is forgiven nothing.
—George Bernard Shaw

Summertime was always special growing up because there was no school. One of the highlights of summer was the third Saturday in July, the day I would leave for camp. But this was not just any ol' camp, it was Camp Wackasack! Camp Wackasack was the greatest, most incredible, fun-filled, action-packed camp in the whole world! The site was constructed like a huge stockade, positioned just an hour outside of the fifth largest city in the U.S. of A, but it could have been located in the Wild, Wild, West, as far as I was concerned.

Dasha had spent the week sewing little pieces of cloth with CALVIN LLOYD printed on them in my shirts, shorts, bathing suit...even my underwear! *Who in the world would want to steal a pair of my undershorts?* She packed my suitcase in geometric shapes; shorts folded in perfect squares; t-shirts in rectangles, and underwear in congruent triangles. There was an orange container for a bar of soap and a pink toothbrush travel kit which belonged to my sister.

"I can't take this toothbrush case to camp!" I begged.

"What's wrong with it?" responded Dasha, without lifting her head from her packing.

"It's pink, mom. All the guys will make fun of me!"

"Well, just ignore them. There is nothing wrong with a boy having a pink toothbrush case, and I'm not buying another one when this one will suit you just fine."

I had already made up my mind that once I started unpacking in the camp cabin, the pink case would remain in the gathered pocket of his suitcase. I would also leave the toothbrush on the windowsill near my bunk, risking being a dance floor for cockroaches. Bottom-line, nothing was going to ruin my week at camp!

After Dasha had finished packing my suitcase, there were a few precious necessities that I knew had to be added. I scoured around my room and started throwing things into my ditty bag; one Swiss army knife, Sad Sack comic books, the May issue of *Argosy* magazine, Ludwig Von Drake Duncan World of Color Yo-Yo, the coonskin cap I had found in someone's trash, and a handful of Bazooka bubble gum all were going to make the trip to camp. Heck, these were all things a guy needed for a memorable week at camp.

As our '61 Brookwood station wagon pulled up to the entrance of the camp there was a line of cars dropping off 6-year-old boys, sleeping bags and suitcases, I was surveying the camp's perimeter. The tall fence surrounding the camp was made of hemlock boards placed side by side vertically with the tops sharpened to a point to prevent Indians from scaling the walls. The near corner had a watch tower with slits where, no doubt, guns could slip through to shoot any attacking enemy. My thoughts went immediately to finding a way to get inside that watch tower for a closer inspection.

Being a little naive and needing little help with my fantasy world, I thought the camp was impenetrable. Only pre-approved station wagons transporting new campers were allowed through the gate which was guarded by some skinny man with glasses and a clipboard who looked remarkably like Barney Fife. Camp Director, no doubt. The whistle around his neck gave him away. "Death's head on a mop stick," Bellamy whispered. The man had on a Camp Wackasack t-shirt and cargo shorts that were an embarrassingly eight inches above his knees. They were more like hot pants than an explorer's frontier shorts. Trying to make sense of this fashion faux pas, it dawned on me that frontiersmen never wore shorts! *This guy was a fraud!* He did not look like the bearded, weathered, frontiersman who should be wearing a fringe suede jacket and carrying a Kentucky long-rifle that

I had dreamt about for weeks. But nothing was going to ruin my perception of the camp. No Sir-ee Bob!

The anticipation of archery, canoe races, fishing, catching frogs and snakes were all enough to send a young boy into some kind of altered state. The wonderful nuances of the camp were endless. The snack bar was open every day. The thought of having ice cream every day was enough of a reason to want to go to Camp Wackasack. Being away from the watchful eyes of parents and knowing that camp counselors could hardly be expected to have complete control over their charges at all times offered countless adventure opportunities beyond what my mind could conceive. Ahhhhh, the possibilities.

My Dad patted me on the back and said goodbye. Dasha turned her cheek as she bent down towards me, expecting a kiss. Now, it is not like I minded kissing Dasha, but there were guys all around me that I had yet to meet. I had to establish my moxie and coolness. A kiss from "mommy" would not exactly help me accomplish that.

"Thanks! See you next week," I yelled as I ran toward the bell tower.

I grabbed a smooth round stone off the ground and headed toward the tower tossing the stone from one hand to the other. The bell tower stood twenty feet tall, had four thick wooden legs and a steeple-like roof over the bell. Between the legs were bench seats made from oak logs that were cut lengthwise. I sat on one of the benches and sized up the situation. I was rocking back and forth on an unstable board when the bench seat pivoted just enough to throw me backwards and onto the ground. Amid the fall, I inadvertently threw the stone up in the air, hitting the bell which alerted the campers that it was dinnertime. Problem was, it was only 3 o'clock. The hungry campers stampeded the mess hall from all directions like a colony of ants attacking a Jolly Rancher. It was true camper mayhem. Expecting a feast of meat loaf, canned green beans, and powdered mash potatoes, they were turned away in ravenous disappointment being told to wait for the *official* bell to ring.

When I tried sitting down again there was a sharp pain in my left keester. Reaching down to my butt-cheek, I discovered a tear in my shorts and realized that I was the first casualty of the week. A

5-inch splinter had pierced my left cheek causing a stain of blood on my shorts. Reluctantly, I walked over to the First Aid hut to have it removed by nurse Betty, a thin, unattractive, flat chested woman who looked and spoke remarkably like Jane Hathaway of *The Beverly Hillbillies* fame.

By 1600 hours my cabin was full of its assigned campers, and we had been introduced to our counselor, Rick. He went around the cabin having the boys state their name and why they wanted to come to Camp Wackasack. Just before chow time the campers decided, collectively, that we needed nicknames, and nicknames are what we got. Larry was "The Hunchback" because, well, he had this weird bulging in the back of his upper shoulders. Lonnie was lean and tall and when he would run, he would take huge awkward steps. We decided to call him "The Healthy Animal," taken from a Kellogg's Special K commercial that featured a polar bear standing on its hind legs. Edward was short, fat and had a serious problem with flatulence. He received the name Zeus, because when he farted it was like thunder and lightning. Someone asked Billy Bates if he ever received any letter from a grown-up addressed to "Master Bates," as in *masturbates*. The place broke up and Billy got pretty pissed off but the name "The Master" stuck. Huan's parents were from Taiwan and strictly practiced Mahayana Buddhism that prohibited the killing of *any* creature, even a mosquito. As a result, Huan became a smorgasbord for every mosquito at camp and began looking like a human blackberry and so we campers gave Huan the nickname "Skeeter."

The ever-studious Kevin who wore coke-bottle glasses received the title "Professor" and Bobby got the nickname "Muskrat," simply because he looked like one. Nate was at least 4 inches taller than the rest of us, skinny, with wiry, curly hair. He adopted the name "Boner" for obvious reasons. Art proudly showed the rest of us that he only had 4 toes on his right foot, so naturally he was called "The Freak." Don's mother was French and when she was dropping him off at camp, kissed him goodbye, saying "Au revoir ma petite mouche." We drilled Donnie for hours until he told us that petite mouche meant "Little Fly." That seemed pretty humorous to the guys, so from that point on he was known as "the Fly." They called me "Mayhem" because of what happened at the bell tower earlier that day.

Like Muskrat, Hunchback and me, Charlie was from North Hills, but had arrived at camp with a nickname in place, one he could never escape. The previous August, Charlie was playing stick ball with some neighborhood kids when a fast-rising summer storm arose from the southwest. Without warning, Charlie was struck by bolt of lightning. Although he was hospitalized for only a few days with burns on both his hands and feet, he never was quite the same after that. The name Choo-Choo was coined when he started wearing a blue and white stripped train conductor's hat and repeatedly sang the Good and Plenty song about Choo-Choo Charlie.

The next morning Counselor Rick had recruited another counselor for a hike up to Sunrise Lake, a lake at the top of the mountain. Rumor had it that this lake had never been fished before and it was teeming with trophy-sized trout and largemouth bass. This other counselor was a megalomaniac suffering from allusions that he was creating his own government where he, and he alone, would be the authoritative dictator worthy of allegiance and obedience. The campers did not see it quite that way. His name was Ted, but he demanded that the young campers address him as "Colonel."

The hike was long but uneventful. When we returned to camp, Counselors Rick and Ted snuck behind the camp's laundry facility to catch a smoke. We campers were told to take showers and wait in the cabin until the counselors returned to discuss the next day's scheduled activities. What happened next is up for interpretation and years later I would swear that I had no idea how the whole thing started but, to the best of my recollection, it went something like this ...

... we were getting undressed when, for no apparent reason, Muskrat started strumming his bald-headed yogurt slinger as if it was a Les Paul 8 string. He started singing his own variation of Shocking Blue's *Venus*. "I'm your penis, I'm your fire, your desire, do-do-do-do-do-do-do-do-do-do-do!" The entire cabin positively howled in laughter. The Professor fell off his cot and cut his forehead on the sharp corner of bunk while the Freak leaped off his cot, as uninhibited as Muskrat, and joined in the band. As the two were playing with their pork swords, they became erect and, as if on cue, they began to swashbuckler each other. There they were, one hand on their hip, arched backs, one attacking forward while the other retreated, all the while striking the other with their purple headed soldiers. It was not 30 seconds before the entire cabin was in a commotion as 14 young lads celebrated their boyhood with skills that would have made Errol Flynn proud. The Fly received points for style while Master decided to make the rounds, advancing towards one opponent, then, within seconds challenging another. He would lunge, spin, and attack the blindside of another rival while shouting "En guard!"

The squealing and laughter could be heard a good way up the hill and apparently reached the laundry cabin where the Colonel was folding some underwear. Had we posted a guard at the door we may have had time to gather ourselves in time, but this was such a spontaneous act of unadulterated innocence that any idea of strategic planning was preposterous.

The Colonel barged through the door, stopped, and for a split second had a look of complete stupor that made *him* look simple.

"I'm going to contact each of your parents and have them pick you up tonight, you little pre-verts!"

"Don't you mean "perverts," Colonel?" the Professor interjected.

"Don't you correct me, you little weenie whacker!"

The young fencers put away their now softened sabers and sheepishly retreated to their bunks. I knew this was not going to be good. Just the thought of my parents having to pick me up in the middle of the night sent chills down my spine. Turning to the Hunchback I whispered, "When my parents find out that I was using Mr. Winky for anything other than relieving myself, there's going to be hell to pay!"

All the campers were sitting on the edge of their bunks with a sense of dread when Master spoke first. "My parents are going to kill me."

"I'll be grounded till I'm 100 years old," the Healthy Animal chimed in.

The Freak turned to me and said, "My Dad's never going to let me come to camp again, and there is no chance he'll let me visit my cousin in Florida. I'm screwed!"

That is exactly how I felt, screwed, that is until Boner spoke up.

"Hey, I got it! The Colonel swore he'd beat the shit out of me if I told anyone this, but we're pretty desperate, aren't we?"

Everybody shook their heads in agreement.

"What is it?" the Fly asked. "Come on, tell us."

Boner stood up and walked to the center of the cabin. He had everyone's attention.

"Yesterday, during free time, I took a walk out to the gravel pit just to check it out. There's a little dirt path that goes off to the right, where those big blue spruces are."

"Yeah, go on," Skeeter said.

"Well, I heard some giggling and so I moved closer to investigate... and guess what I saw?"

"What?" We all asked in unison.

"There was the Colonel with that redheaded girl from the kitchen crew. She had her top completely off and her culottes down to her ankles. Her bra was hanging on a limb from the hemlock tree they were under. The colonel had his jeans off and he clearly had a chubbie"

"How'd her tits look? Master asked.

"What's a chubbie?" asked the Fly.

"You know, a hard-on, a woody, throbbing gristle, the full salute, a boner, right Boner?" Muskrat asked.

"Right you are, my little rodent," responded Boner.

My eyes grew bigger than hub caps as the solution to our problem dawned on me. Looking at Boner with a shrewd smile I said, "We can blackmail the Colonel!"

"Exactly!" replied Boner. "When that stinking weasel comes back into the cabin and we'll give him the news. He tells, we tell."

"He'll keep his mouth shut," shouted the Hunchback.

"You betcha," I said with a smile.

ڲ

Our plan worked perfectly. For the remainder of the week, the cabin gang would refer to the incident as "The Enlightenment," but after we went back home, the matter was never discussed again. The incident did not leave me quickly, however. The humiliation Bellamy and I felt at the hands of Counselor Rick gnawed at me. Had my stay at camp lasted longer, I would have found a creative way to seek revenge. I can accept a lot of grief, but being humiliated is something I never would tolerate.

CHAPTER SIX

Bullying comes in a variety of forms: physical, intellectual and emotional. We all are bullies.

B
ellamy had not made an appearance for several weeks. It seemed as though he appeared only when I was lonely, bored or, most often, when I had been punished, embarrassed or humiliated, which was often enough. When things were going fine, I guess I did not need him.

September 8, 1964, the day after Labor Day arrived and with it, the first day of school. Every year I began the school year with the same mindset, that this year would be different! I would pay attention, do my homework, and get good grades. The way Dasha treated her step kids was directly related to how our performance reflected upon her. If you *performed* well and she was able to boast about our accomplishments, the better your treatment. Better yet, if you were fortunate enough to shine on a public stage, like my brother did by being a brilliant pianist, you received the queen's favor.

I so wanted to be in that inner circle that I was determined to do well in school that year. If I was a good student, people would compliment Dasha and life would be infinitely better for me. If I did poorly, it would be another year of beatings and time spent alone in the gulag. My rationale was that I was a lot smarter than I was the previous year and had outgrown my speech impediment, thanks to several years of being pulled out of class for an hour with the township speech therapist. *This year I'll get all A's. Dasha will be proud of me! Heck, I might even move up in her pecking order!*

That September, the Phillies were in first place with a 5 ½ game lead over the Cincinnati Reds on the first of the month and the dream of a championship seemed real. As far as I knew, the Phils had never been in first place in the month of September. The year before the Phillies won 87 games…87 games!! *But this was 1964. This would be the year the Fightin' Phils would go all the way.* That past summer, Jim Bunning had pitched the first perfect game in the National League since 1880! It was an omen! *They will cruise to clinching the pennant.* My Aunt Anastasia subscribed to the TV Guide and there, on the front cover, was a photo of Connie Mack Stadium and a preview of the World Series. It was going to be a great year!

As went the Phillies, so went my academic year. On Labor Day, the Phillies split a doubleheader with the Dodgers while the Reds lost 2 to the St. Louis Cardinals. That increased the Phillies' lead to 6½ games with 25 games left to play. I had gotten several quizzes back and received an "A" in both. All was going well, until things did not.

The Phillies got hit with a string of injuries. Frank Thomas broke his right thumb sliding into second base, pitcher Ray Culp started to have problems with his right elbow and things began to look dubious. By the 20th of September the Phils still had a 6 ½ game lead over the Reds with 12 games to play. Easy peasy!

A few days later, when Chico Ruiz stole home to steal the win from the Phils, it was an ugly omen. It just happened to be coincided with the appearance of my first "F" of the year on a math exam. I began to feel edgy. Phillies manager Gene Mauch was getting nervous, too. Mauch decided to pitch his two best pitchers, Jim Bunning and Chris Short on only 2 days' rest, and the result was devastating. The Reds were not taking advantage of the Phillies woes and after the Phil's seventh loss in a row, the St. Louis Cardinals took over first place. The Phillies would finish with a 92–70 record, the best season since the 1950 pennant-winning Whiz Kids, but there would be no World Series for my Phils. The ten-game losing streak to end the season did them in and my academic year followed suit.

My third-grade teacher, Miss Angelo, was a creepy old maid who made my teeth itch and my skin crawl. She dressed like the Amish and smelled like Ben Gay and, for the life of me, I just never could get *comfortable* around her.

Most of the children in my class thought they *knew* me; after all, how much was there to know about an eight-year-old boy? You knew his skill sets in athletics. You knew if he was a goody-goody, a bore, a bully, a fighter, or a coward. You knew how bright or senseless a kid was. You could also tell a lot about a kid by his parents. How strict were they? What kind of job did their dad have and what type of expectations and pressure did they place on their child? Did the kid enjoy school, despise school, or simply tolerate it? But there really was only one person who truly knew me, who understood me, and that was Bellamy. In retrospect, he was the only one I felt safe and comfortable with. I did not have to put on one of my many facades with Bellamy. I could always be transparent.

North Hills Elementary was just about like any other grade school in 1960s America. Due to an overwhelming national fear of communism and the increasingly aggressive Soviet Union, we had mandatory bombing drills. An alarm would sound throughout the school, and we would have to briskly walk, single file, to the basement of the school where we would be safe from the inevitable commie bombs.

There was only one way to teach back then and there was only one way to learn. If you, by some chance, did not learn that way, you had purchased a one-way ticket to *Dunceville*. It was clear that I had already boarded that train. I hated the "clone" mandate at school that required a Pavlov dog's mentality. Besides the fact that it bored me to death, it never ended with a tasty treat. The bell would ring and the clones would respond by walking into the classroom. Sitting at the same open desks with the same laminate top and the same black lacquer edge with the same groove to place the same number 2 pencil in so that it would not roll away. The same 5 desks per row. A perfect square. They would look at the same white, chalk-smeared blackboard, the same teacher's desk, the same 4 windows and the same metal cage that protected the heater. The first hour of class, English. "Class, open your *Words Work for You* to page 24." Second hour, math. Then recess, history, lunch, science. How dare I think autonomously. Conformity was certainly not my strong suit.

One day, as Miss Angelo began with her lecturing, I began my daily daydreaming, spotting a monarch butterfly dancing with the wind outside the large window to my left. I followed the orange and black ballet high into the trees and watched it disappear. New beginnings, I thought. New school year and a new teacher, anything was possible.

The first grading period arrived and Miss Angelo handed out the report cards alphabetically, thank God, with short comments like "Well done, Richard. Exceptional, Judith," and "much improved, Robert." Miss Angelo always used the children's proper names. The report cards were 5 x 7 cards slid into a manila sleeve with the pupil's name handwritten on the front. When she handed me my report card, she lowered her eyes and mumbled, "I expected more out of you, Calvin."

Yeah, so did I.

Walking home from school, I took the long way, through the black section of town. I wanted to go to Pep Boys to pick-up a lock for my bicycle, and it was shorter than walking the long way around. I knew I was risking getting beat-up by Ricky Maddox, a black kid from my class who was a head taller than me, but I really didn't much care. I figured that I *deserved* getting beat-up for simply being so stupid. *I'll get that beating when I get home and Dasha sees the latest edition of the "Disappointing Times."* That is when I saw Simone sitting on a swing in her side yard.

Simone was in my class at school. A pretty little thing with a kind heart who always seemed authentic. She did not see me as I stopped to watch her dress blow high in the air exposing her dark thighs and white panties with little pink flowers scattered on them. I was totally mesmerized as I watched her swing back with bended knees, then extending her legs forward as she pointed them toward the sky. There was a sense of dance in her swinging as if she were leaping gracefully in a ballet performed for only one spectator, me. It was in the downswing that she turned and caught me staring at her. I felt sudden heat on my face as I turned quickly and started walking down the street, but Simone took the momentum of the upswing, flew off the seat and ran across her yard in an angular path to cut off my stride.

"How long were you watching me?" She said as she cut off my exit route.

"I wasn't watching you. I mean, I saw you, but I wasn't staring or anything."

"I like that you were watching me, Calvin. You know you don't have to be afraid of me," she said with a curious smile.

Yes, I knew that, yet there was an uneasiness that came over me.

"Where ya going?"

"Nowhere. Home, I guess."

Simone's skin was the color of almonds, and her hair was the color of dark cocobolo which had a thousand little ripples like tiny waves running from a thrown pebble. She had large, dark brown eyes that were both bright and welcoming.

"Did you get your report card?" She asked.

Of all the things we could talk about, she brings up my grades?

"Yeah," I answered reluctantly.

"How many A's did you get?"

This wasn't going well. I really didn't want to talk about my grades.

"I don't know."

"You didn't look at your report card? Let me see." Before I could conceal the envelope, she grabbed the manila sleeve from my hand.

"Give it the hell back!" I screamed.

Holding the sleeve above and behind her head, I leaped toward her. As I came dangerously close to her cheek, I smelled the aerial notes of jasmine and the woody tones of a freshly cut cedar. As I pushed forward my hand for the report card I brushed fleetingly against her breast, not that a third-grade girl had anything to speak of. I was prepared for her reaction, but none came.

"Here," she said as she handed me the report card. "You didn't have to get so upset."

I jerked the manila jacket from her hand, turned my back to her and headed home.

Before I reached the corner of our property, I got a whiff of something coming from Dasha's kitchen. Stemming from a passion for food and the capability to consume large quantities of it, I had the uncanny ability of being able to catch a whiff of her cooking by the time my foot hit the corner of Hawthorne and Locust and be able to tell exactly what was for dinner that evening. Dasha was a good cook, not in the Lobster Thermador sort of way, but in the well-rounded salad, meat, starch, veggie type of way, sometimes with a Ukrainian flair. Lifting my nose toward the north-northeast to get a better sniff, I decided it was pork chops and fried onions. Another good dinner option, but I knew the meal would be anything but pleasant.

As I approached our driveway, I noticed a colony of ants devouring a grasshopper. It gave me the feeling that I was about to be the grasshopper. Dasha was anxiously waiting for me at the kitchen door, expecting some cosmic phenomenon to occur where I would get straight A's which, of course, would reflect well on her. Three out of four of her children were model students and a real blessing to be around. Unfortunately, for both of us, the planets were not going to align on this day. When she saw the list of C's and D's, her blood pressure shot to her head like a steaming geyser and shouted, "What's wrong with you? Why can't you be like your brother and sisters?

Indeed. Why can't I be more like them. I knew what was coming next. She walked down the hall to her bedroom and reached into my dad's side of the closet retrieving a thick brown leather belt. She knew that the belt would have greater impact on my skin than a wooden spoon. Thankfully, I was wearing pants and not shorts. When I was younger, I would have to pull down my pants and undershorts to get my beatings. As I got older, she would simply aim for the legs if I was wearing shorts. Dasha was the very definition of *insanity.* She would continue the thrashings every marking period even though, for some inexplicable reason, the beatings never seemed to improve my grades.

The first whip was always the worst. Dasha cocked back her arm and hit me just above my waist, in the soft area just beneath my right arm. That tender skin which never receives sun when you are at the beach. It hurt. It hurt bad, but I was determined not to give her the satisfaction of even a single tear. I would simply stare at her expressionless. The second blow was supposed to land in the same spot but caught my elbow, and it hurt as badly as the first. She would normally swing until she got tired which, depending on the day, consisted of seven or eight lashes. I took the beating and never did cry.

"Go to your room!" Dasha shouted.

Gladly! And to my room I went. Sitting on the thick green rug at the foot of my bed, I felt Bellamy's warm hand against my shoulder.

"I know what you're thinking, and you're not stupid." Bellamy spoke softly, in almost a whisper.

"Then why do my grades suck?" I asked.

"I don't know, but what I do know is that you don't try to do poorly in school. It's just so damn hard to pay attention."

I said nothing for a long while. Finally, I turned to Bellamy and said, "I hate her. She doesn't love me. Isn't a mother supposed to love their kids no matter what? I swear to God, she hates me."

In retrospect, I now get Dasha, although it took a few decades. Hurt people, hurt people. It really is that simple. No one is born mean, but a pitiful environment for a little kid can really scramble their psyche. Things happen to people that tear at their heart. Often, time will help heal the heart, but when that tear is deep, it leaves a scar. Scars never disappear. Scars are reminders of a painful experience.

In retrospect, I am sure that I was aware of this, but I would never cut Dasha any slack and, perhaps, rightly so. I knew that Dasha had been treated very poorly as a kid and, like me, she never outgrew the pain. What was confusing was, if she knew how badly it feels for a kid to be deemed worthless, why in the world would she choose to inflict that kind of emotional pain on her husband's kid?

I was never told that much about my stepmother's childhood. I would pick up tidbits here and there, mostly when Dasha and her sister got together. There were, however, questions that no one could answer, and I never asked. Questions like, why is it that those who mistreat their own children often extend a warm and inviting love to children that *aren't* theirs, presenting a kind and loving facade that these children would find alluring? Why could they extend this love and acceptance to other children but not their own, albeit stepchildren?

I wondered if some people were just born nasty or if one's environment was the culprit for their evil ways. *What about that article in the paper I read about that son of a judge who cheated on his wife and when his mistress got pregnant, killed his lover and unborn child and buried her*

*body in a shallow grave behind his Daddy's cabin up in the Poconos? Now
that boy had a good upbringing, but he turned out rotten. Or the boy who had
watched his alcohol-loving daddy use his mommy as an anvil too many times
and told his son he was a worthless as a tit on a boar hog? That boy grew up
with a mean streak the size of Montana. He went down south somewhere and
was executed for raping and killing 3 women. Clearly, his environment
scarred him, but would he have turned out differently if he grew up in a
nurturing and loving home?* Nature or nurture? It truly is a paradox. I
wondered how my childhood would impact me when I became an
adult.

"Yes, Cal, she is supposed to love you. It sucks, but it is what it is.
Look at it this way, the day you reach eighteen you can leave and never
look back," Bellamy said as he put his hand on my shoulder. Eighteen
seemed like a lifetime away. "What we really need is to find a way to
handle her. We cannot continue to take this crap! You're nothing more
than an old, dusty rug that she throws over the clothesline and beats.
That is how she views you. With each whack she actually sees the dirt
coming out of you. If we put our heads together, we can come up with
something that makes her think twice before laying a hand on you.

It is a shame that kids simply lack the wisdom that age and life
experiences bring. I have found that life really is all about a few
decisions. Not whether you should order chocolate or strawberry or
whether you should steal second base. Life is about three or four,
maybe as many as a half dozen, decisions that will drastically alter
your life, depending upon how you choose. They are forks in the road,
and if you choose the wrong road, you may never get back to the
original course that *was* heading in the right direction.

In my late forties I began climbing glaciers, which has provided
many life-lessons. Life is much like mountaineering. As you climb the
glacier of life, you take along sixty pounds of past experiences in your
backpack. All those experiences are necessary to reach the summit, but
critical decisions need to be made as you labor along. A climb is not
easy. Neither is life. Taking the time to do a Rutschblock test to
determine the stability of the snow is imperative, but ignoring the
likelihood of an avalanche and continuing to climb is foolhardy at best.
Doing the little things also improves the chances of summiting. Things

like staying hydrated and consuming calories that are being quickly exhausted by extreme physical exertion are as important as using an ice axe to knock excess snow from your crampons.

When you are absolutely spent and do not think you can go on, you have options. You can quit and head back to where you started, to the safety of the past. You can press forward, despite the discomfort and difficulty, because your eyes are on the prize, something you believe is obtainable. Or, you can remain where you are, afraid to go forward, afraid to go back down the mountain. That decision is always fatal. You will end up starving, or dying from exposure on the mountain. In life you die a slow death of boredom and lack of stimulation. *That is how many people exist.*

These decisions are so crucial that they will decide the direction the remainder of your life takes. Certainly, the person you marry and what career path you want to pursue are two of those decisions, but there are always a few unexpected ones. My fear growing up was that, when faced with a life-changing decision, I would select the wrong one. Of course, you can avoid making the decision entirely, but that often ends up being as costly as making the incorrect one.

I had no idea how long we had been sitting there in solitude. It must have been a while because I had forgotten Bellamy was still there when he finally broke the silence.

"She's pretty and so nice to us."

"Who?" I muttered, ignoring Bellamy's use of the plural.

"You know who I mean. Simone."

"She's alright, I guess."

"She likes you," Bellamy added. I ignored the comment but wondered if that could be true. *Does Simone really like me?*

I wonder why it is that so many of us think that if someone *really* knew us there would be no way they could *really* like us? Is self-loathing that comfortable that we feel no one can love us since we don't even love ourselves? Is it really that unbelievable that someone would love us? Actually, for some of us the answer is *yes.*

"But she's colored," I added.

"So?"

"I can't have a colored girl as a girlfriend."

"Why not?" asked Bellamy.

"Yeah, why not," I mumbled. "Because you know the crap I'll get from dad, Dasha…everybody!"

"If they expect the worst from you, what does it matter?" asked Bellamy.

Bellamy had a good point. I got up off the floor about the same time I heard Dasha calling me to wash-up for dinner. I could not stop thinking, or rather, obsessing over Simone. I kept telling myself that it was crazy, absurd, yet I could not get her out of my mind, that is, until I heard Dasha call everyone to supper.

Dasha had prepared a meatless dinner, but one that I loved: fried eggplant, sweet, white Jersey corn-on-the-cob, fried tomatoes, and tomato gravy. The tomato gravy wasn't traditional spaghetti sauce, but rather a sweet sauce made with whole milk and sugar, thickened with flour and poured over white bread. All throughout dinner I felt guilty, not so much about the report card, but that my thoughts were consumed by a *colored* girl.

After dinner I went outside with my dog, Jackson, following close behind. Laying on the ground, I felt the cool grass on my back. I looked at Jackson who laid next to me. She cocked her head to the left and stared at me with that inquisitive look as if she were wondering what kind of "game" I would invent for the two of us to play. In the past I had invented "Here come the bad people so we have to hide behind the rhododendron until it is safe" game." There also was the "You are the outfielder and I'm the batter" game, as I would throw a tennis ball as hard as I could against the stucco wall that made up the side of our house, so it would fly over my head compelling her to leap, catch, and return with eagerness to repeat the game.

As I was lying on my back, Jackson wondered, *"What kind of game could this be?* It was the "look at the clouds and find a face, an animal, or even a huge bag of popcorn" game. Jackson did not like that game much at all. I looked at the puffy cumulus-formed marshmallows and stared. It did not take long for me to find a sea turtle that changed into a rhinoceros when the clouds moved and finally into a large, arching bridge over an ocean of foamy water. I wondered where the bridge went. Wherever it was, I wanted to go there.

CHAPTER SEVEN

Choose your friends wisely, then cherish them forever.

T he house I grew up in was a brick-faced ranch house on the corner of Hawthorne and Locust Roads in the eastern edge of North Hills. The other three sides of the house were white stucco with its sharp scalloped points that I found difficult to bounce a tennis ball off. Rhododendrons grew in front of both the living room and the bedroom I shared with my brother Ted; ewes grew in front of the dining room. A breezeway separated the house from the 2-car garage, and there were three tall oak trees in the front yard, the tallest which stood at the corner of the yard where no grass would grow. There, I would play in isolation with my matchbox cars, creating roads and tunnels in the large roots, entertaining myself for hours with some imaginary rural road trip. Imagination and loneliness were attached to my life like ticks on a wild turkey.

The backyard had a cherry tree, a peach tree, and a pear tree; the pear tree never produced fruit, which always reminded me of the Bible story I had heard in Sunday School of the barren fig tree that Jesus cursed. The backyard butted up against Mr. Slaven's expansive property where he allowed my friends and I to play football. Mr. Slaven sold the adjoining lot to my dad in 1960, which is when we built our family home.

Flowing from the windows of my home were sounds and smells that were warm and inviting, like the late August waves at the seashore. Arriving back home I would often be greeted with waves of fresh baked bread or the sound of my brother Ted playing the piano or cornet, or my sisters, Olivia, and Audrey, practicing their clarinet or flute. Ted was a gifted musician, and it did not go unnoticed by

Dasha or my father. Ted would skirt chores for the sake of practicing his music and, since I lacked any obvious talent, I was relegated to assume his chores as well as mine. In retrospect, I guess that made sense. No matter how hard I tried playing the piano or cornet, it was futile. Somehow the music-gene that my siblings possessed skipped over me, just another confirmation that I did not belong to this family. It was like a *Highlights for Children* magazine that often had some drawing and would ask the reader to find those items that did not belong in the picture. There might be a picture of a sailboat on the water and in the clouds at the top of the picture you would discover a pitchfork. I was the pitchfork.

Ted was not an "outside" kind of kid. He ran like ink from a fountain pen; deliberately and slow. I, however, was as fast as an arrow from a bow. I once won a 100-yard dash when I was in second grade. The race was for first, second, and third graders and the boys who placed second and third were both third graders. I only tell you this because I come from a long line of non-athletic people, and I am very proud of that accomplishment. Athletics was never encouraged in the Lloyd household; academics and music were.

My frugal stepmother, having grown up poor during the Great Depression, knew how to make a dollar last beyond its life expectancy. Meatless dinners were common, and Dasha would find creative ways to be economical. I would marvel at how she would collect the small pieces of soap which had become unusable until she had nine or ten of them and then sew them in an old washcloth to create a sudsy cloth once wet.

North Hills was an archetypal, all-American town. There were the railroad tracks on the east and southside of town and a country club which bordered the westernmost edge of the sleepy hamlet. Penbryn Park, nicknamed by the local kids *Chollie Mollie's*, sat on the east side of town, just behind the row of houses lining Edge Hill Road. The town had two penny candy stores, that is until Kline's closed, leaving Plockies as the lone tabernacle of cheap treats. Chernoff's pharmacy,

Joe's Market, Jack Frost soft ice cream stand and a taproom that sat next to the fried seafood joint, were all on the perimeter of town, allowing the rectangular grid of homes to occupy the interior of the town.

On any given summer morning, you could get whiffs of scrapple, pork roll or other salty breakfast meats escaping from the screened windows of working North Hills kitchens. Freshly washed laundry would hang with wooden clothes pins in the early morning summer air. Bicycles sounding like wannabe motorcycles by securing a baseball card of a perennial .220 hitter onto the frame of the rear wheel with the same wooden clothes pin could be heard along the scuffing of sneakers as young girls hopscotched their way to home base.

Caddy corner to where I lived was the home of Mr. Krauthammer, commonly called Mr. Crap-hammer by the local teenage establishment, due to his refusal to allow kids to retrieve balls or stray frisbees that found his yard. Rumors were that he would confiscate any ball that was hit into his property and any kid trying to retrieve them was never heard from again, but I never knew a kid that had disappeared behind the forsaken land. Large oak and maple trees created a darkened domain and a 15-foot untrimmed Arborvitae hedge formed a green wall which gave the property more than privacy, making it the darkest house on the block. The sun struggled to make its way through the shaded trees which enabled thick moss to cover the dark grey asbestos shingles. Every time I would look at Mr. Krauthammer's house I would see imaginary gargoyles with sharp elf-ears, bat wings and gnashing teeth leaning over edge of the roof waiting for a wandering youngster to devour. My imagination was not always a good thing. Growing up, fear never seemed far off.

I would hang around with some of the other boys from my class as there were always six or seven kids you could gather for a pick-up game of whiffle ball or football. Usually, I hung out with Larry and Bobby, who we called Hunchback and Muskrat, as I have said. The nicknames they received at Camp Wackasack stuck. Often, when you could find the three of us together, Charlie "Choo-Choo" Cardin would tag along.

Sometimes I would wonder where each of them would land twenty years later. Hunchback, would probably be a carpenter or electrician. Muskrat might become a doctor or dentist. Choo-Choo's future would be less promising. I expected him to end up as a gravedigger, or trash collector. Me? I wasn't quite sure what I was destined to be, but I would dream about the possibilities. Fueled by television shows like *The Lone Ranger, F-Troop, Gilligan's Island, Get Smart, Batman, The Wild, Wild West, Bonanza, Hogan's Heroes, The Man from U.N.C.L.E., Mission Impossible,* and *Sea Hunt,* I had wanted to be a cowboy, an Indian, a farmer, professional baseball player, sailor, an Indian again, a herpetologist, a spy, a professional football player, President of the United States, an assassin, and a scuba diver. It was not until I realized that an Indian was an indigenous American, an ethnicity rather than an occupation, that I gave up that dream.

After a breakfast of *Sugar Pops,* I had some chores to do; empty the dishwasher, collect the trash and take the cans out to the curb, and mow the lawn. Once completing the tasks, I went to my room where Bellamy and I began inspecting a box of animal skulls I had collected from my many explorations in the woods when Dasha walked into my room. I had been grounded for the better part of eternity for breaking a garage window with a homemade slingshot.

"This came in the mail for you," Dasha announced.

My eyes grew as large as hubcaps when I saw the box wrapped in brown paper and tied in twine.

"I've been waiting for this! Thanks, Mom!" I said, using the title Dasha preferred.

I would often send away for novelties and tricks I found at the back of *MAD* magazines or *Sad Sack* comic books. Three weeks earlier I had sent away for some unbelievable treasures I found advertised in one those comic books. The ads were more than enticing.

Enter the WONDERFUL WORLD of AMAZING LIFE

SEA-MONKEYS

Own a BOWLFUL OF HAPPINESS—INSTANT PETS!

What really sold me on ordering the Sea Monkeys was the promise that they were so eager to please. Heck, they could even be trained, so the advertisement stated. Instant pets, instant friends!

I pulled the bag containing the Sea Monkeys out of the box. I would have to explore my treasure chest of novelties in secret since my dad told me not to order anything from the back of a comic book because it was a colossal waste of money. I reached into the box feeling around for the other things I had ordered, pulling out a pair of X-Ray Spex. For only a dollar I would be able to see right through the clothes of the beautiful sixth grader, Mandy Breyer who lived down the street from me. The last item I found in the box was a packet of itching powder which, little did I know, was actually finely ground finger nails and toe nails shipped from somewhere in China. I would need a naïve and oblivious volunteer to try that new gag gift on and I knew that my older brother, Ted, would do just fine.

My brother and I had nothing in common but our last names. Ted was a more serious specimen of teenagerhood. Serious about his studies, serious about his stamp collecting and serious about getting into State, where he planned on majoring in music. I was the anti-Ted, and I lived to torment my all-too-serious-and-boringly-studious brother, if for no other reason than because he was at the top of my stepmother's pecking order. I found him at the bottom of that ladder and I despised the whole idea of a family social hierarchy, but that is the way it was.

There were also those occasions that I accidently made my brother's life miserable, like the time I convinced Ted to play *David and Goliath*. Ted was Goliath, of course. I mined a puppet from deep in the corner of the large wooden toy chest, placed a nicely shaped stone in it, twirled it around my head and let it fly. No one was more surprised than me when it hit Ted squarely on his temple, knocking him silly and to the ground. The easy flow of blood from Ted's forehead immediately brought fear and shock as my brother sat on the driveway in a painful stupor. Thankfully, and most likely because Ted had yet to gather his wits, my brother begged Dasha not to take me to the woodshed, and so I miraculously escaped what seemed to be the inevitable corporal punishment.

With the itching powder in hand, I slipped down the darkened hallway, past my parent's bedroom, to the last door on the left. Ground zero! Ted had laid out a light blue, long-sleeve sweater-shirt on his bed that he was planning on wearing to a piano recital that evening. *Perfect!* Reaching in my pocket, I pulled out the small white envelope and noticed some Chinese writing on the front of the packet. For a split second or two, I wondered if the writing was a warning of some sort as I sprinkled the powder around the inside of the pullover. *Too late now.*

Ted had been in the shower, and I listened carefully for the water to stop. *Time to exit the bedroom and look inconspicuous.* Passing by the bathroom, I saw him come out with a towel wrapped around his waist and headed down the hallway toward the bedroom. I knew Ted would take at least a few minutes to comb his hair and glue it down with half a can of hairspray. My brother's hair had to look perfect. I decided to wait in the living room for the show to begin. It would be another 10 minutes before Ted would come into the living room and I thought it best to lay low in the company of my parents.

Ted entered the room wearing the rust-colored dicky that laid tight against his neck and already had made small gestures of discomfort as he scratched his rib cage and again on his elbow. It wasn't long before he was itching as though he had been trapped in a wool straight jacket with disturbed ant hills in the arm pits. It was only a moment later when Ted screamed that something was alive and crawling all over his body. He pulled the sweater up over his head in two seconds flat, still screaming something unintelligible as he ran into the kitchen.

I tried stifling the hilarity that was building up inside of me, with little success.

The Chinese itching powder was as advertised and worth every cent. Now howling uncontrollably, I had not noticed my parents who had left the living room to see why Ted was screaming. Within minutes, Ted was back in the shower trying to remove that which was torturing him. My reaction told my parents everything they needed to know; that I had done something to make Ted's afternoon unbearable.

The beating and time I spent in Dasha's gulag was well-worth the punishment!

CHAPTER EIGHT

*It is true that many creative people fail to make mature
personal relationships, and some are extremely isolated. It is
also true that, in some instances, trauma, in the shape of
early separation or bereavement, has steered the potentially
creative person toward developing aspects of his personality
which can find fulfillment in comparative isolation.*
—Anthony Storr, *Solitude: A Return to the Self*

I had finally slept an entire night in Aunt Gertie's death bed. In
fact, it was a Saturday morning and I had slept past eight o'clock;
highly unusual for me. I was always an early to bed, early to rise
kind of guy. Saturdays were the only day unadulterated by
grown-ups, at least for the most part. When my stepmother would get
into one of her moods, chores would be dished-out and the prison
work crew would not have free time until noon. By that time, it was
nearly impossible to hunt down the gang.

I did not want to waste any time by sleeping in this specific day. I
had been saving money for months so I could make a special purchase
at the pet shop located across from the railroad station at the edge of
town. I threw on some jeans and my patriotic red, white, and blue
striped shirt, and ran into the kitchen. I opened the fridge, drank the
concentrated orange juice from its container and plopped a slice of
Wonder bread in the toaster. I saw a pork chop left over from dinner
on a plate in the fridge and the longer I waited for the toaster to pop
up, the more I could not get that hunk of meat out of my head. The
refrigerator door opened at the same time the toast jumped out of its
slot. Grabbing the pork chop by the bone and putting the toast in my

mouth, I raced out the kitchen door. Within seconds I was on my bike, flying down Hawthorne Road and turning on to Locust.

Down the street I peddled turning right on Hazel Avenue and then a left down busy Edge Hill Road. Crossing the road, I went into the parking lot at Chernoff's Pharmacy for a package of vanilla wafers, and across Jenkintown Road to the pet store, where Muskrat was waiting for me, looking a bit pensive.

"What's the matter?" I asked. "Today's the day we've been waiting for. I've saved up for this for months. I've taken on more lawns to cut and even washed Mrs. Lawrence's windows!"

"Yeah, I know," Muskrat said with an expression of apprehension on his face. "Something's wrong with my dad."

"What do you mean?"

"I dunno. He's just acting different. The other day my mom called him at work because the washer went on the fritz, but his secretary said he took a personal day. He never told my mom he was taking the day off. When my mom asked him about it, he just said he had to run a bunch of errands and didn't want to waste a Saturday. Then, he started growing a beard. My dad with a beard? Are you kidding me? You know him. He's not the beard type. Heck, he even shaves on Saturdays."

"Ah, it's probably nothing," I said as I propped my bicycle against the side of the weathered, whitewashed building, the paint peeling in large flakes, silently pleading for a fresh coat.

A bell announced our arrival as I opened the door. The proprietor always struck me as a person who disliked animals, which really made no sense to me. He was a smallish man with a belly too large for his frame. The man was bald, except for a pushover which did not cover a third of the area where hair had long before abandoned him. The store reeked of animal turds and dirty cages, but I knew we would not be in there long. I had waited for the "25% OFF ALL REPTILES ONE DAY SALE" which was today. I maneuvered down the aisles crowded with charcoal air filters, sacks of feed and carpeted cat trees, to find what would be my new pet, a 3-foot green iguana. There were a few smaller ones in the next aquarium, but I wanted the big boy. Thirteen dollars seemed to be a fair price for an exotic trophy like this, and I had already selected a name, Mabel, assuming the green prehistoric friend was a female.

I have always been driven to do the opposite of the masses. In that regard, I strove to be *different*. I knew no one who had an iguana as a pet; that was one of the attractions of owning one.

"I'll take the green iguana," I said to the store owner.

The man's back was to us as he was bent over stacking cans of dog food into a giant pyramid.

"The big one?" the man asked.

"Yep, the big one."

The man's eyebrows raised as he grabbed a nearby shelf to help steady himself as he rose from a squatting position. The iguana had been for sale for a year and a half and the man thought he'd never sell it, but now that the price dropped, it entered my sweet spot.

Digging into my right-front jean pocket, I pulled out ten one-dollar bills, some balled-up into a tight little orb, and a fist full of change. Accompanying the money was a flattened piece of Bazooka bubble gum and a blue-grey piece of lint. Carefully I counted out the thirteen dollars and gave it to the man.

"You're 78 cents short," the man exclaimed.

"What do you mean? I thought it cost thirteen dollars since it is on sale," I replied.

"It is. Thirteen dollars plus six percent tax."

My heart dropped. It figures. How could I have forgotten about the stinkin' tax? I looked at the iguana, then to the man, then back to the iguana. I started to gather the cash I had laid out on the counter when the man said, "Go ahead and take the lizard. I've had him for over a year, and I don't think anyone else is waiting in line for him."

"Gee, thanks Mister," I said with eyebrows raised.

The man pulled out a flat piece of carboard from behind the counter and began folding it at pre-creased points. Quickly, a box with handles began to take shape. Gently, he lifted the iguana out of the glass aquarium and placed it in cardboard box.

"What do I feed him," I asked.

"Lettuce and insects. Crickets, flies, mosquitos."

"We can catch tons of crickets down at the ballfield," suggested Muskrat. "I've gotta get home. My dad's mounting a basketball hoop on our garage roof. I'll see ya later."

The man handed the box to me and, almost immediately, I began to contemplate how I was going to sell the idea of a 3-foot pet lizard to Dasha. When I opened the door to exit, the bell rang once again, signaling the beginning of this junior herpetologist's fascination with reptiles.

I grabbed my bike and rode home with one hand on the handlebar and the other holding the cardboard box, up Locust Avenue to the corner of Hawthorne Road, where my home stood. In the corner of the garage, I found my old aquarium, dirty and dusty, but without a crack in the glass. I had bought it a few years earlier when I went through my tropical fish phase. Now it would house the mother of all pets, an iguana. I knew no one who had an iguana. I would stand alone in my quest for "Pet Individuality."

After cleaning the aquarium, I collected some gravel, a rock I had found in Chollie Mollies, the local enchanted forest. I also found a twisted stick and positioned both in the aquarium so it looked like the lizard's natural habitat, or what I imagined it would have looked like. To my bedroom I went, the box containing the iguana under one arm and the aquarium under the other. When I got to my room, Bellamy was sitting on the bed.

"An iguana?" asked Bellamy.

"Yeah! Isn't it great?"

"It sure is! No one has an iguana."

"I know, right?"

"What are you going to tell the commandant?"

"I don't know," I responded.

"Well, maybe we should figure that out, 'cause she'll be home soon."

"Well, I think I'll tell her that I'm really getting interested in science and studying a live lizard can only help me in the classroom."

"Brilliant!" shouted Bellamy.

It was after four when my stepmother got home from the Food Fair. With groceries in her arms, she rushed about knowing she had little time to prepare dinner.

"Mom," I said. "I need to show you something."

"Not now, Calvin. I've got to get dinner going."

I went back into the bedroom I shared with my brother and crouched over to get a closer look at my new pet. Pressing my nose against the aquarium I went eye-to-eye with the large, green reptile. Lifting the screen from above the enclosure, I gently lifted the iguana out of its glass home. I laid on back on my bed and placed the iguana on my chest so I could study its face up close.

"Your name is Mabel," I said matter-of-factly.

I did not realize that I had fallen asleep, nor how long I had been out. Startled, I looked around the bed for the iguana, but she was nowhere to be found. Quickly I jumped on the floor and looked under both my bed and my brother's, but no Mabel. Under the bureaus and in the closet, I searched, but to no avail. While the rest of the Lloyd household went about with life as normal, I searched high and low for the miniature dinosaur. Not finding him anywhere, I retreated to my bedroom. When I opened the door, I saw my brother lying on his stomach reading a book, and Mabel hanging on the curtain behind his bed.

Before I could say anything, the iguana lurched forward and landed on Ted's back and began slowly walking toward his neck. Feeling the gripping nails on his back, Ted turned his head only to see the prehistoric green face staring back at him.

"Ahhhhhhhhhhhhhh!" Ted screamed as he leaped from his bed to the hallway in a millisecond.

I heard Dasha's footsteps running down the hall as I grabbed Mabel, who was clinging to the bedspread near the floor, and placed her back in the aquarium. When all the commotion died down and I had explained to my parents the "no returns" policy of the pet store, I quietly accepted the 2-week grounding penalty and went down the stairs to the rec room without turning the light on. Bellamy was there waiting for me.

"Well, that went well," Bellamy said with a belly laugh.

"I can't do anything right. Everyone hates me."

Looking directly at me, Bellamy said, "You are incorrect on both accounts. You can do plenty of things right. The problem is that you are misunderstood."

"I want to be understood," I said as he looked down at my feet.

"It's not the end of the world. Actually, it was pretty funny, don't you think?"

Once I gave it another thought, I had to agree with Bellamy. The whole thing *was* pretty funny.

"Look," said Bellamy, "we are not going to keep taking abuse forever. I promise you that. There is going to come a time when we will respond, and when we do, the world better watch out! A volcano can only hold back the pressure for so long! When it erupts, all hell breaks loose!"

What I did not realize then was that most people have no idea how much they really do not know. They live in a movie where everything is scripted for them. They act how the script tells them to act. They move stage left, stage right, house left or house right. They cry when the script says cry and laugh when it says to laugh. They are robots who, the longer they play their assigned role, become numb to the sensitivities of the world. They live an entire life without swimming outside the fishbowl and, if they ever do realize that they have been duped, it's too late and the curtain falls.

My desire was to dance to the rhythm of a different tune; it was who I was. Instinctive. Most children yearn for conformity; however, I have always been suspicious of conformity, even more so as I grew older. Conformity insinuates that the masses are correct. As the years turned its pages, I began to see the plot of the story that had been written for me. Conformity is more than boring; it is a life killer. Not the longevity of life, but the *experience* of life. A life worth living.

Although I may not have realized it, I was a modern-day Lewis or Clark. I pioneered through the wilderness. Bears and lions, and storms, drought, and floods tried to throw me off course, but I would not have any of it. I was going to be just fine. Heck, even Bellamy agreed with a beaming smile!

CHAPTER NINE

*A good youth ought to have a fear of God, to be subject to
his parents, to give honor to his elders, to preserve his
purity; he ought not to despise humility, but should love
forbearance and modesty. All these are an ornament to
youthful years.*

—Saint Ambrose

D own on Ivy Lane lived an odd little bachelor by the name of
Perry Strathmore. I had heard the fathers at Indian Guides
refer to Perry as "a little funny" but I never found him very
funny at all. Yeah, he was odd, but funny? Not so much.
Besides, these fathers always joked around. Why would they criticize
a man offering some comic relief?

Mr. Strathmore was frequently seen wearing a paisley ascot, bell-
bottom slacks with buttons at the fly instead of a zipper, and sported
a peridot ring on his pinky. Strathmore was always on the cutting edge
of fashion. His wavy blonde hair was long over his ears and combed
to the side where he would use a bobby pin to keep it in place. I had
never seen a man wearing a bobby pin before. Perry was never seen
outside without wearing his signature horn rim sunglasses and would
ride around town in a canary yellow Triumph Spitfire, which I thought
was more than cool; a California look in the suburbs of Philadelphia.
He was a florist and shared a building with his brother who was also
single and owned a shoe repair shop simply called *The Village Cobbler*.

One day my dad told me to come with him to Weldon's Auto
Parts; he needed to pick up struts for the Chevy. I sensed that my
stepmother was about to pour wrath upon me for God-knows-what-I-
had-done-or-not done and thought it a good idea to get out of the

house for a spell. It was just the two of us as we turned the corner onto Ivy Lane when we saw Mr. Strathmore outside his house raking leaves. Perry looked up when he heard our car, stopped raking and gazed at us as if staring into the abyss. Abruptly my dad turned to me and said, very matter-of-factly, "Stay away from that man."

"Why?" I asked.

"Just stay away from him."

I could tell by his answer that I was not to ask any more questions. I could only assume that he was a very bad man.

Fourth grade is sort of like hump year for a kid in elementary school. You are not one of the little kids, yet you're definitely not one of the short timers; soon to enter into the world of Junior High. You are in transition, and you find yourself in no man's land—you don't really belong to any group. There are challenges galore, not the least of which is prepuberal purgatory.

I often felt like I was in limbo between two worlds, but one thing that always makes a kid feel better about life is a dog. Every child needs a dog. Period. It was just about this time that I brought Cookie home in a cardboard box. Our family had been dogless for over a year after ol' Jackson had gotten whacked by an Oldsmobile. He was chasing some calico cat and closing in on the filthy, stinkin', feral moggy when he got blindsided. But Tommy Macalister's dog had just had a litter of pups and asked me if I wanted one...for FREE!

Truly, there really isn't anything cuter than a six-week-old puppy and within the litter there was one whelp that seemed segregated from the rest of the group. When I saw that isolated pup, I knew that dog that was meant for me. It takes one to know one. She had a beautiful taffy and white and velvety-soft ears; one ear standing up, the other laying down. The puppies were mongrels; a mix between a German Shorthaired Pointer, a beagle, and some unknown breed; a mutt just like me, but a beautiful, friendly dog, nonetheless. Tommy told me that the dogs were spayed, possibly because his mother threatened him that if he didn't give away all the puppies by the end of the week, they would be euthanized. But I would soon find out that was not the case.

At first, Dasha was pretty upset about me springing a puppy on the family without asking for permission. She had reminded me that it was a rerun of when I had brought home the iguana without permission. However, it did not take long for the entire family to fall head-over-heels in love with the little soft, furry canine, and luckily avoiding punishment, Cookie became a fixture within our household.

I should have said that punishment for bringing the dog home was delayed. Nine months later, having not realized that Cookie had reached her first estrous cycle, the inevitable happened. It was a late autumn morning when I asked my older sister, Olivia, to give me and a few friends a ride to band practice. I was never that interested in playing in the school band; that was Dasha's idea. Football was more my passion. I was a natural at the sport, but I learned early on that if you appeased Dasha and let her see for her own eyes that you were not cut out for something, you had a much better chance at being allowed to shift interests. In any case, my sister Olivia had a baby blue Simca, a square French car that made the Volkswagen Beetle look like a limousine. Olivia grabbed Cookie so she would have company driving home after dropping us off at school.

Large clouds of breath could be seen as my sister and I exhaled into the brisk autumn air. I opened the door for Cookie, and she willingly jumped in, happy to be taking a ride. I rode shotgun and placed the cornet on my lap. I was never quite sure why I ended up trying to play a shrunken trumpet. It never appealed to me, but Dasha wanted clones, not children with varied interests, and since my brother played the cornet, I was going to play the cornet. The drums or guitar would have been more my style, but the drums were outlawed by Dasha due to their repetitive banging and the guitar was not an acceptable instrument for the school band in the 60s and early 70s.

We first picked up Gary Vee (short for Vanderkamp) and his tenor sax and then swung around the corner to pick up Earl Chisum and his sousaphone. Earl wasn't a small boy by any stretch of the imagination and how he, Gary and that piece of twisted tuba-brass fit in the back seat was a positional magnum opus. Maybe that's why Cookie jumped on the back dash. The poor girl seemed a bit agitated and was breathing heavy enough to cause a ring of condensation to build on the back window.

Olivia played with the stick on the column trying to get the Simca in reverse and out of Earl's driveway as Cookie breathed heavier before we turned onto Locust Avenue. It was Gary who first noticed a male mutt trotting down a driveway and towards the car. A short while later another dog came from a back alley and joined the first dog in following Olivia's car. As they turned on to Elm Street two more dogs from opposite sides of the street joined the others to form a posse.

Gary wiped the condensation off the back window with his sweatshirt sleeve and said, "I think Cookie's in heat."

"Oh, she can't be. She's fixed." Olivia answered.

"Well, I'm not a Vet, but Cookie's vulva is swollen and there's a bloody discharge on your vinyl seats," Gary exclaimed, always the first to share his fourth-grade medical mind.

"Yeah," Earl chimed in, "and there's a half dozen horny dogs following your car."

With that, the three of us laughed hysterically while Olivia was mortified and panicking.

"Hurry Olivia," I screamed. "The dogs are gaining on us!"

⏚

The delayed punishment came in the form of a week of grounding. That would not have been a big deal except for the fact that Dasha knew I had plans for that Saturday. Skeeter's father had been given Eagles tickets for that Sunday, and he had invited me to go along with them. Just another disappointment.

⏚

I opened the refrigerator scanning the shelves for something, anything to eat. Nothing looked appealing, so I tore off a leaf of iceberg lettuce, pushed the door shut and grabbed an apple from the bowl that sat on the kitchen table and headed to my room. The lettuce was for Mabel, the apple for me. It had dawned on me that he had not fed the lizard for several days. *That is not good*, I thought.

Entering the room, I was immediately hit with a smell that was a cross between the cemetery pond and dead crayfish. A thick stench that was not going to be covered by a can of Glade. Mabel sat motionless. I grabbed a pencil from my brother's bureau and removed the screen off the top of the aquarium. Holding the point, I touched Mabel's head with the eraser. Nothing. I pushed a little harder. Still, nothing. I prodded the iguana's rib cage, but there was no movement. She was, indeed, dead. What, I wondered, was the life expectancy of an iguana living in an aquarium hardly longer than the length of the reptile's body?

I was pretty upset, but it had nothing to do with the death of my green friend. It had everything to do with the lecture and, perhaps, consequences I would face when Dasha learned of the lizard's demise. The lecture would be on wasting money and the repetitive reminder of *I told you so*. It was time to improvise.

I jumped on my bike and rode to Chollie Mollies with a plastic cup in hand. Following the trail, I rode quickly, doing my best Evel Knievel impression as I lifted my bike into the air whenever I would run over a large stone or root. Parking the bike by a mock orange tree, I began lifting rocks and rotted logs to find some salamanders.

It did not take long before I found a green salamander, appropriately named for its greenish-yellow patches that stood out boldly against the otherwise black body. I watched as the morning air hit the tiny amphibian's body causing it to walk cautiously, slowly as if each foot was lifting off a roll of sticky taffy candy. Not exactly a small iguana, but it would have to do. After collecting five of the little critters, it was back on the bike and quickly to home before anyone got a whiff of the rotting carcass.

I threw open the kitchen door and grabbed an egg out its cradle from the door of the refrigerator. Into Cookie's bowl I cracked the egg open and watched as the dog made quick work of the yoke and clear slimy white. Flying down the hallway and into my room, I placed the salamanders into the aquarium and crumbled the eggshells around the gravel floor. My thinking was that someone would find Mabel dead and deduct that she died giving birth. It sounded plausible to me and, besides, no one in the family exactly excelled in the sciences. Little did I know that if there is no male iguana, the female will lay eggs, but they will not be fertilized. Five eggs were also not normal. They tend to lay between 20 to 60 eggs, but who in the family would know that?

It did not take long before Mabel's adopted family was spotted by Dasha, having been drawn into Cal's room by the fetid odor.

"Tom?" Dasha yelled.

"What's up honey," my father said as he poked his head into my room. "Oh, what is that smell?"

"Cal's lizard."

"What about it?"

"He…she….it had babies!" Dasha cried.

"What? Babies? Oh, my…what in the world? Are you telling me Cal bought a pregnant iguana? And this thing stinks. When was the last time he cleaned this aquarium? Cal!"

I could tell that the discovery had been made. Flying like a startled swallow from its camouflaged nest, I flew down the hallway to his room.

"What's up, Dad?"

"Have you seen this?" my dad asked.

"What? Hey, what's wrong with Mabel? She looks bad."

"I think she's dead. Get this aquarium out of here and bury that thing in the backyard. Now!" My father ordered.

There was not any discipline handed down, partly because everyone but me was relieved that the iguana no longer took residence in the Lloyd household. The salamanders lasted for another month and a half before I decided to take them back to the hollow in Chollie Mollies where I had found them.

"Cal, my friend," Bellamy said, "congratulations on a job well done! I have to hand it to you. You improvised and covered your tracks! That is exactly what I had told you we need to do."

CHAPTER TEN

Summertime: long days, no school, ice cream, warm weather, amusement parks, watermelon, baseball, and picnics—a child's dream that comes true every year.

T he late 60s were a time of strange and wonderful beginnings. The country was changing, my family was changing, and I was changing, albeit, without my consent. My sisters had begun dating and my brother had come into his own as a wonderfully gifted musician. My sense of adventure and discovery made me feel like an experimental jet-fueled craft being tested on the salt-flats. Every day had its own paradoxical reality. It was a time when ice milk, a flavorless substitute for ice *cream*, and a deplorable, inexpensive replacement for butter, was all the craze. The popular ancillary for butter, sold in similar rectangular blocks, was a bit darker in color, but tasted nothing like butter, contrary to the television advertising blitz. It had a foul taste that could not be hidden no matter how much strawberry jam I smothered it with. They called it margarine, but it was really lard that was on an ego trip. Of course, Dasha bought it because it was half the cost of butter. Later, I would discover it was invented by some French guy responding to a challenge by Napoleon to create a substitute for butter to be used for by his armed forces and lower classes of citizens. Figures! No wonder my dad hated the French!

When they were on sale, our family would eat TV dinners when my dad had to work late. Peel back the aluminum foil to find clandestine meat, peas with more wrinkles than my mom-mom, and a cloud of something that was supposed to resemble mashed potatoes, but tasted like heavy cotton. I would put a slab of margarine on it and wait a half an hour for the yellow paste to melt.

Changes in my perspective were also taking place. I may have been immature, but I was also observant, and little got past me. Through my pre-adolescent philosophy of life, I tried to decipher why some adults seemed habitually happy and kind, while others seemed serious to the point of ad nauseam. From a young age I had an innate ability to discern authentic smiles from artificial ones. It was a gift. Sadly, I found that people who were immune to ulterior motives; people who were truly as they appear, were, in fact, unfortunately rare. I found that those individuals were often mistreated and taken advantage of and too often, appeared married to someone unworthy of their pureness. I called these people dandelions, because I always believed dandelions were beautiful and the attractive "weeds" could not care less that people were annoyed with them and wanted their removal. They were going to smile everywhere they popped up. I never could understand why it was so rare to find one dandelion married to another dandelion. My Uncle Neil, Aunt Paula and Aunt Margery were dandelions.

Reverend Markey was no dandelion. There was something off about him, but I could not quite pin it down. Mouche, one of the kids who went to camp with us, did not have a dad. He died at 44 from a heart attack at work. Reverend Markey seemed to take the place of Mouche's dad; his car often seen in front of their house. Mouche pretty much blew off the reverend, but his little brother, Tommy, was not so lucky. What was stranger still was that Mouche's family did not attend our church. Perhaps the minister's interest in Mouche and Tommy was somewhat understandable since they were fatherless, but the reverend also had a keen interest in Choo-Choo. That did not make sense because Choo-Choo had a stepdad, albeit a poor representation of a father. The few times we saw his stepfather he was always ridiculing Choo-Choo.

From a young age, I had the canine-like ability to hear the familiar chime of the ice cream truck when it was still over a mile away. Then again, when someone would blow a dog whistle my eyebrows would rise, and I would cock my head like a vizsla.

It was a fine Saturday summer day, the Queen Anne's Lace and Chickadee were blooming wildly in places where there was but a tablespoon of earth within the cracked pavement. I heard the familiar "Ice Cream" song by Andre Nickatina (which is basically *Turkey in the Straw* without the bass) while the white painted truck was still a long way off. I knew I would have to start early with my sales pitch if I had any chance of securing a dime from my parents. Sometimes, if I was at my cousin's house, or if we had some guests over, there was always a greater chance of being successful, out of sheer peer pressure. My parents certainly did not want to look cheap, but the chances of them splurging for some ice cream were slim. Regardless of the poor odds, I immediately went to Dasha first to hit her up for a dime while she was sewing a skirt for my sister, Audrey. Without missing a stitch, she told me to go ask my father.

"Dad, can I have 10 cents? The ice cream truck is coming."

"I don't hear anything," my dad mumbled while trying to read the *Philadelphia Bulletin*.

"Well, I can hear it. It's coming," I pleaded.

"I think you're hearing something else. Ask me again if it really comes by," my dad said.

The problem with waiting till the truck turned on to our road was that we were the second house from the end of the road, or beginning of the road, depending upon which direction the ice cream truck came. More times than not, it always came down our street where we would be the second house after the turn, so I knew that I had little time to secure the money from one of my parents and catch the truck before it turned the corner. The truck was not going to stop unless kids ran toward it, and no one was going to come a-runnin' till the truck reached Elm Street. I had to make my case now, before it was too late.

"Dad, it's getting closer. Please, can I have ten cents?" Somehow, ten cents sounded like less money than a dime.

"Go ask your mother."

This was not going well. My chances of getting my mouth around a delicious artificially flavored and colored frozen strawberry-shortcake-on-a-stick was dwindling. I thought about whimpering a little, but that would only piss my father off, and then there would be no chance, so I stood there. I stood there when the music got so loud it sounded like the truck was in our living room. I stood there when I could hear that the music had gone from east of our house, to clearly west of our house and I stood there until the chime vanished.

I walked into my bedroom where Bellamy was sitting on my bed.

"That's it! I'm going to find a way to always have my own money!"

"Absolutely!" Agreed Bellamy. "You could do odd jobs around the neighborhood; jobs that grown-ups are too lazy to do."

"I swear that I will always have money saved up so I won't have to ask Dasha and Dad for anything ever again!"

Okay, that may have been a little extreme, but right then I made the conscious decision that I would always have change in my pocket and would not have to rely on others for the simple, but necessary, pleasures in life. I would never have to resort to begging or desperate deal-making. Since I never received an allowance, I would have to come up with creative ways to earn cash, but creativity was never a problem for me. I would rely on my own resources to fulfill the inevitable ice cream deprivation.

On the positive side that day, my step-mom sent me down to Joe's Market for a pound of luncheon meat, thinly sliced sirloin and a dozen Amoroso rolls. The ham would be for lunch sandwiches, but the slice beef and rolls meant it would be a steak sandwich night.

⚄

My parents instilled an almost renowned work ethic upon their children. Work was more than admirable; it was religious, in a cult-like way. You were to be obsessed with it, and a mere eight-hour dose of it per day was simply for slackers. Overtime, you say? You don't have to ask twice. My father's answer would always be "yes," even if there were previous commitments for trivial things like birthdays, ballgames, or Christmas. After all, money does not grow on trees.

I was still too young to get a prestigious job scooping out ice cream at the malt shop, being a lifeguard at the community pool or stocking shelves at Schneider's Hardware store, but I was well-suited for the mundane paper route. I was enamored more with having cash in my pocket than I was having to deliver the news, but at least I was outside (albeit, in *all kinds of weather*). I was basically my own boss and could use my own two-wheel mode of transportation. Even when I was grounded, which was often, I was allowed to fulfill my duties as the sole newspaper carrier in town for the once-a-week *Glenside News*. That one day a week was Thursdays, and it seemed as though Thursdays would always have the worst weather a newspaper boy feared. High humidity and heat, torrential downpours, high winds, and the coldest and snowiest days of winter, but I kept doing it for the money. If I did not dally and pumped the peddles relentlessly, I could finish my rounds in about 90 minutes, weather permitting. One day, while collecting weekly payments from my clientele, I made a titillating discovery.

Several times a year the *Glenside News* would offer their paperboys prizes for opening new accounts. The prizes were always totally cool, like transistor radios, faux leather wallets with a separate zipper compartment for loose chain and even Phillies tickets. Being a natural born salesman, I always opened new accounts and accumulated prizes. Early one Saturday morning, I left the house on an expedition to secure some new accounts. Assuming that everyone was dressed and doing their family chores by 7:30 on Saturday mornings, I flew out the screen door to find new clients.

I was met at the first door by a disheveled man who was not at all happy with being awakened on his day off from work. I quickly apologized and headed to the next house. I would not be dissuaded. No one was home there, and the following house belonged to Perry Strathmore. I had remembered what my father said, to stay away from that man, but a new customer was a new customer, no matter how you looked at it. I grabbed the brass comedy and tragedy mask knocker and let it announce my arrival. Perry Strathmore opened the door dressed in a maroon bathrobe and grey slippers, uncombed hair and holding a cup of coffee.

"Good morning, young man."

"Hello Mr. Strathmore, I'm Calvin Lloyd. I was wondering if you would like to get the *Glenside News* delivered. It's our local weekly newspaper, and it only costs 15 cents a week."

"Only 15 cents? What a bargain!" Mr. Strathmore said with a smile. "Sure. That would be swell. In fact, I'll prepay for the month, because I won't be around at the end of the month. Come on in a minute."

I had that uneasy feeling that I was doing something I should not be doing. I stepped inside the world of the unknown. As Mr. Strathmore turned to go into a back room to retrieve his wallet, I surveyed the living room, which looked more like a museum than a dwelling space.

Orange and white pottery with Grecian warriors cocking javelins and framed paintings of 18th century men and women complete with powdered wigs and cherry-red cheeks festooned the room. There was a floor lamp which was crafted as a palm tree with a monkey climbing three-quarters the way up the base and a maroon patterned Persian runner rug draped over a brass chair. A stuffed ring-necked pheasant stood on top of a bookcase standing watch over the horde of books, mostly old, in faded red, mustard-yellow, green, and black bindings. Two peacock feathers arching themselves out of a very large periwinkle-colored vase stood next to the bookcase. On the dining room table, I noticed a board with a stunning butterfly spread out with small strips of paper strategically placed with tiny pins holding them in place.

"Do you like butterflies?" Perry asked as he returned with his wallet.

"Yeah, I guess so." I said reluctantly. I did like butterflies and moths; in fact, I loved them, but I was afraid of admitting it for fear of being ridiculed as not being masculine.

"This is a spreading board."

Perry saw that my attention was drawn to the rear of his dining room table where I was hypnotized by a spectacularly beautiful butterfly, its wings a dark turquoise with diagonal orange bands.

"It's a Kallima Inachus, commonly called an Orange Oakleaf. It's beautiful, isn't it," Perry asked.

It was, so much so that I was completely transfixed, unable to turn away.

"I've never seen one that looked like that."

"I guess you wouldn't. They are found in the Far East, from India to Japan." And with that, Mr. Strathmore reached across the table handing me a small spreading board, a butterfly net and some pins.

"Here. It is yours."

"Thanks," I said with astonishment and reserved gratitude.

"You will find butterflies wherever there are flowers, including trees that are in bloom, and in open fields. Plants that many people call weeds also flower and attract butterflies. Milkweed, Chickadee, and wild Aster, that many people mistake for a weed, are all butterfly attractants."

"Did you know that Christian tradition views the butterfly as a symbol of resurrection? There's symbolism there. Butterflies appear to transcend the ordinary as they take flight into the sky, higher and higher as if reaching the heavens." Perry knew that my family was devout Christians, because Dasha would try to convert him whenever she would take one of our shoes to Perry's brother's shop to be resoled.

"Really?" I said with an expression of amazement.

Mr. Strathmore gave me the money for the month of newspapers, and I headed home with my gifts. When I got home, I was glad no one was there, as I did not want to explain where I got the spreading board and who gave it to me. I went straight to my room and took out the microscope my older cousin had given me when she went to veterinary school. She had recognized my love for field biology. I was anticipating looking at the butterfly's wings under the microscope. Now all I had to do was catch some.

Turning the spreading board over, I noticed that Mr. Strathmore had written something on the back.

To Calvin, a future lepidopterist,
Never ignore the beauty that surrounds you!
Your friend, Perry Strathmore

I didn't know what a lepidopterist was, so I looked it up in the red jacketed *Webster's Dictionary* that sat on my desk. Just as I had suspected, it said it was a person who studies moths and butterflies. I thought it would be cool to get paid to study these beauties, but I also knew it would never happen. I knew I was too stupid to ever get into college and besides, *I always got Ds in science,*" I reminded myself.

Meeting Perry was different from meeting other adults who would talk in a nursery rhyme rhythm that infants prefer, as if they did not realize that I was no infant. There comes a time when a child comprehends a lot more than the adult realizes, and it always happens much earlier than you might think.

Perry spoke to me, not as if I was inferior, even though, of course, I knew so little and had experienced so much less of life than Perry. Rather he spoke to me in a matter-of-fact kind of way, like, *Hey, want to know something cool?* Or, *I think I know something you would enjoy and I'm going to share it with you.* Whatever it was that Perry had in his communication with me, I liked it...was drawn to it. I didn't feel patronized and believed that Perry actually *enjoyed* my company.

Bellamy walked over and picked up the butterfly net. "Damn! A gift and it isn't even your birthday! That was more than nice of him to do that. Perry is alright!"

I could not help wondering if my dad had gotten it wrong about Perry.

CHAPTER ELEVEN

If you could see within the hearts of those closest to you,
you would turn and run for your life.

There was a knock on the front door, the door only used by people who did not frequent our house. Knowing no one was home, I quickly slid my new possession under my bed and went upstairs to see who it was, assuming it was a solicitor. To my horror, I saw Reverend Markey with that painted smile on his face. Had he not seen me, I would have pretended no one was home. Reluctantly, I opened the door.

"Hello there, Calvin," the reverend said as he entered our living room without an invitation.

"My parents aren't home," I said trying to end the unannounced visit before it began.

"Oh, I know that. I was in the area and thought I would drop by to see how you were doing," he said as he entered the living room and took a seat on the couch.

Now, I'm sorry, but is that weird, or what? *He knew my parents weren't home and he still dropped by? Maybe Dasha told him how messed up I was and that his intervention might help. And maybe not.*

"I'm fine. I was just in the middle of some science homework. I really need to get that finished before dinner," I said, hoping that verbal bug spray would cause the pest to fly away.

"You know, I was pretty good at science. Maybe I could help you with that. What are you studying?"

This is getting worse. Can't he take a hint? Yeah, he was good at science. According to him, he was good at everything (except getting lost when he needed to). I have always been allergic to people who are narcissistic.

Markey strutted around like a sage-grouse at a lek hoping to attract a willing female. I was starting to wonder if it was not a female he was trying to attract.

"Biology," I answered. "That's one part of science I'm good at. I really need to get back to it, but I'll tell my parents you dropped by," I said as I walked toward the door to show the reverend out.

Thankfully, he got up and followed me to the door. Placing his huge mitt on my shoulder, he said, "I hope you know that you can always come to me if you need to talk. If you don't feel comfortable coming to my office, we could go grab a hamburger or something."

"Okay. Thanks," I replied while restraining myself from using my foot to remove him from the premises.

🚲

The next day I saw Hunchback and Muskrat over at Chollie Mollies and told them about the cool spreading board Mr. Strathmore gave him.

"You know Strathmore is queer, don't you?" Muskrat informed.

"What?" I thought Muskrat was jealous of the cool gift and was just being a jerk.

"A faggot. He screws boys instead of girls," he continued.

"My older brother's friends always call him Backdoor Strathmore," Hunchback added as Muskrat threw his head back and laughed so hard that he began to choke.

The thought of me hanging out with a queer made my stomach sick and my head spin. If this got out everybody in town, let alone at school, would think I was a fag. I tolerated a lot from just about everyone, but when it came down to preventing humiliation, another side of me came out. Shame and embarrassment were the things I feared the most. I would do anything to prevent that. I was so insecure and afraid someone would pull back my veneer exposing the fraud underneath.

"Why do you think he's always in his garden pretending to play doctor with his roses?

He's looking for boys to lure into his house, tie them up and mess with their dick and stuff," explained Hunchback.

The premise petrified me. "You're crazy," I said unconvincingly.

"Yeah, he's right, Cal," Muskrat added. "And what about Reverend Markey? He's gotta be a fag."

"He's married," I said.

"That doesn't mean anything," Muskrat interjected. "He's only married so no one know he likes boys, and I mean boys, not guys his age. Why is he always at Choo-Choo's house or Mouche's house. Mouche told me Markey took his kid brother to the roller-skating rink last Friday night. Maybe the rev and Perry are in love!" And with that, Hunchback and Muskrat roared with laughter.

Let's go play wire ball," I suggested, trying to change the subject, knowing that I could never again bring up my association with Perry to my friends...to *anyone*. But this new found information would bother me for days. I knew I could never go over Perry's house again, but I had received kindness and acceptance from Mr. Strathmore. I knew that I had to stay away from this perceived monster, and yet, deep inside, I really did not want to. Mr. Strathmore had opened a whole new world to me; discovery into field biology which captured my attention and interest and besides, he never tried to touch me. Mr. Strathmore, I believed, was a dandelion.

As Muskrat took the pimple ball out of his pocket, he turned to me and hesitated. "Remember what I told you about my dad, that he was acting strangely?"

"Yeah?" I responded.

"Well, now he's working late several nights a week. My mom didn't think that was strange, but he never had to work late before. I'm telling you, something's up."

"You're overreacting," I said in attempt to reassure my friend. "My dad works late lots of nights."

"I can never remember him working nights. Ever! I'm telling you, something's not right. Do you think he has a girlfriend?"

"Your Dad?" Hunchback said with a chuckle. "He's overweight, wears goofy glasses and dresses like it's 1940!"

"Yeah. Maybe you're right," Muskrat said as he tossed the ball high toward the sub-transmission lines that crossed the street from telephone pole to telephone pole.

On Thursday it was raining, which was more than disappointing. It was not only newspaper delivery day; it was collection day. Since I had to take the time to knock on doors anyway, I decided to secure a few new accounts. As I walked down Edge Hill Road, I saw Donna Reagan's house and walked up to the front door and push the doorbell. Donna was my schoolmate, a tall girl with short sandy-blonde hair who often wore plaid skirts and colored knee socks. She was on the quiet side, but friendly enough; a very middling looking girl who would not turn a boy's head, making me think she took after her father rather than her mother. Mrs. Reagan was a goddess among mere mortal women. *Wasn't there a law where a mom should not be better looking than her daughter?*

The door opened, and I gazed upon the most beautiful woman I had ever seen, dressed only in a lovely lavender, silky, shiny, Van Raalte Lace slip, the bustline complete with lace. One of the straps fell carelessly off her shoulder revealing a good percentage of her right breast.

"Can I help you?" asked Mrs. Reagan.

Can you ever!

"Uh, hi Mrs. Reagan. I'm Calvin Lloyd. I go to school with Donna. Would you like to subscribe to the *Glenside News*?"

My biggest fear was getting caught with wandering eyes, but how could I not look? My eyes were drawn away from Mrs. Reagan's lovely face and down at the ripe, firmness of her breasts. The low-cut slip revealed a significant amount of flesh south of her tan line which exposed lighter skin that had not been tanned by the sun. Mesmerized by the half-clad, beautiful woman standing in front of me, I looked up to find that I had been caught red-handed stealing a forbidden glimpse, but the alluring lady responded with a flirtatious smile with one side of her lip raising just a bit, seemingly not the least bit fazed by it.

"Come in here and get out of that horrid weather. How much does it cost?" she asked.

"Fifteen cents a copy," I said as I tried to position myself on the throw rug so I would not create a puddle in her foyer.

"Will you be my delivery boy?" she asked with another seductive smile.

"Yes, I will," I said with enthusiasm.

"Okay then, sign me up."

Ever since that day I became attracted to older women. The sexual maturity of them fascinated me, not to mention Bellamy!

I needed a birch beer float to cool me off, so I walked the short distance to Jack Frost as I conjured various reasons for having to knock on Donna Reagan's door as often as possible. I knew the rain would keep the crowds away from the ice cream stand and that there would be no lines in which to wait. Jack Frost was my little oasis. It was a place I could go by myself and relax without fear that I would be blamed for something and punished.

Arriving at Jack Frost's, I reviewed the menu posted on the board even though I had long-since memorized it. Sundaes were 40 cents, banana splits 60 cents. Bob, the owner of the Taj Mahal of ice cream joints, was a thin, beardless Santa Claus with rose-colored cheeks and a friendly disposition that children were drawn to. Instead of a sack of presents, he delivered banana splits, strawberry sundaes and chocolate dipped soft ice cream cones. Bob was the frozen-custard-chef- extraordinaire; a modern-day Michelangelo who would create edible masterpieces that mesmerized children as they watched him sculp their sweet treat. Bob was kindhearted and would often talk with me. Bob was a dandelion.

Behind the shop was a huge 150-foot ravine which held railroad tracks. Up at street level there were a cluster of wires and cables that extended from one side of the ravine to the other accompanied by a large pipe-like structure roughly five feet in diameter. The local kids would always dare each other to crawl on the pipe from one side to the other knowing well that one little slip would be the last attempt of bravado.

The hot dogs at Jack Frost always looked inviting as they rotated ever so slowly, sweating under the perfectly calculated heat. I knew it must have taken food chemists years to have come up with the perfect cooking temperature for slow roasted wieners. The truth be known, that perfect temperature was 194 degrees...not 193...not 195, but 194 degrees that would slowly heat the middle without causing the hotdog to split down its length. I preferred my rolls straight out of the plastic bag; soft and pliable, and Bob knew that was my preference. I would never have to emphasize that point when ordering. If you got the rolls from the heated drawer, they were crunchy and detracted from the 194. Bob, wanting to keep one of his favorite patrons happy, always kept aside one roll secured in the plastic bag for me.

June had finally arrived and although that meant summer vacation, it also meant final report cards. North Hills Elementary School offered two teachers for every grade, and it seemed as though whatever teacher I hoped to be assigned to in the coming year, I would always end up with the other. For me, the norm would be to receive no A's, perhaps one B, several C's and the remainder of the report card was filled in with D's and F's. My fear was being grounded for the summer and the threat of summer school. None of my siblings had ever received a D. In fact, only 4 Cs ever entered the Lloyd household until I began my schooling. It was not because I didn't *want* to do well or that my poor results were from a lack of trying, but I just seemed to struggle with sitting still and paying attention. My thoughts were like a pin ball bouncing within the glass-top machine, never resting anywhere very long, being tossed about by flippers of ideas and fantasy while always trying to avoid the tilt of people's rejection. Attention deficit hyperactivity disorder (ADHD) was rarely diagnosed in kids back in the 60s and early 70s. We were simply disobedient children who *chose* not to sit still, concentrate, and cooperate. For me, there was a screaming demon within my brain preventing me from focusing in structured environments whenever I was expected to do so.

It was clear to my parents, teachers, and minister that I was simply a troubled kid who willfully misbehaved. I would often make careless mistakes and I lacked attention to details. I would also fail to follow through on instructions, schoolwork, or chores. Not because I wanted to be disobedient, it just came so much more natural to me than the discipline of following through with the assignments. It truly was a case of out of sight, out of mind, and when I failed to complete the work assigned to me, there was hell to pay.

At the beginning of every school year, I was determined to make that year the year I turned things around. However, by the time October arrived I was so far behind in school that any hope of parental praise for my accomplishments was all but gone. The impossibility of sitting still and concentrating was too prevailing. At school, punishment for not paying attention would come in a variety of forms. I would have to stand outside the classroom for an hour, which would only guarantee an "F" on the next quiz on whatever was being taught while I was outside the classroom. Then there was having to stay after class and clean the blackboard and erasers, or the dreaded being told to stand up in class and answer questions from the teacher which I had no ability to answer. More humiliation and embarrassment.

Sometimes I would receive the unconstitutional double jeopardy, which I learned later in high school Civ Ed, was not legal. I would be punished at school for not turning in a paper which would result in cutting ridicule, normally in the form of belittling comments from the teacher communicated in front of the entire class, which was then followed with a detention. A note would then be sent to my parents, or there would be an explanation in the comment section of my report card explaining why the teacher thought I deserved the poor grade. The double jeopardy was that my punishment came from both my teacher and my parents.

It would take something really spellbinding for me to focus long enough to learn and remember schoolbook "facts." What was strange to me was that I could recognize all sixteen of Pennsylvania's common songbirds by ear, but could not memorize the Gettysburg Address. Why is it that we respect someone who is very knowledgeable in one field of interest, but is completely inept in a long list of other subjects, while a child is supposed to excel at every subject dictated to them?

At least this would be the last report card of the school year and at least I would have the next two and a half months off.

CHAPTER TWELVE

Too bad people aren't like dogs; loyal, loving, quick to forgive and only fight in self-defense, or the defense of a loved one.

T he beatings from Dasha continued. She had learned quickly that wooden spoons and even broom handles break too easily when targeting my back or head. Leather belts and belt buckles never break. Most of the marks on my body disappeared within a week, and most of them were where the sun did not shine. Occasionally, the metal buckle would tear my skin. Since I was a rough-and-tumble type of kid, and always had scrapes and bruises from playing aggressively, no one ever questioned the marks Dasha left on my body.

It was a Monday, but a Monday in the summer was like a Saturday during the school year. A day with unbridled freedom and thousands of possibilities. Going outside, the daffodils and tulips gave way to rhododendron and dandelions as temperatures continued to rise. I realized that I was paying more attention to butterflies when I saw a familiar black and orange beauty suddenly appear, only remaining for a few seconds before it disappeared behind some distant brush.

There simply is nothing like summer vacation for an adventurous young boy, and I was no exception. No fear of the reckoning for poor report cards. No homework. No early curfews or lights out at 9 o'clock for bedtime, just opportunities and plenty of free time to make dreams come true.

I had always spearheaded one of the most anticipated events of the summer, the neighborhood go-kart race since I lived on the steepest street in North Hills. And there was another reason. It gave me a realistic chance to excel at...something.

Now, make no mistake, these karts the neighborhood kids made were not those fancy schmancy, pretty-painted symmetrical beauties found in those official soap box derby races kids from rich neighborhoods had. The gang from North Hills made their own karts, with no help from grownups. They were gravity karts made from anything they could find in our garages, basements, or people's trash.

The first day of summer vacation Muskrat and I posted homemade signs on telephone poles announcing that this year's race would be on June 30, giving everyone two weeks to build their karts. The race would begin at the top of Hawthorne Road and the winner would be the first one to arrive at the dead end on Monroe Avenue. Entry fee was a nickel and the winner would receive it all, minus a 25-cent processing and promotion fee that I would pocket. It was assumed that Tommy Kerrigan would be absent from the race since last year he cracked his head open when he hit a large Bitternut Hickory tree in Mr. Kosinski's yard, forcing the doctors to insert a metal plate in his head. From that time on he would whine about how he hated winter, always complaining of headaches whenever it got cold outside.

It was time to begin the scavenger hunt for odds and ends that could be used to create the best homemade go-kart in the whole world. My paper route gave me an advantage, taking me to the far reaches of North Hills, where I could scour around the curbside trash looking for anything that would catch my eye and imagination. Down on Elm Street, Mrs. Bristow was throwing out an old baby carriage which served both as a trailer to gather the rest of my supplies and for the front wheels of my go-kart. It was important to have small wheels in the front and larger ones in the back for optimum acceleration.

A few blocks down the on Hamel Avenue, my eyes widened when I saw that distinctive gold and brown tin in someone's trash. This was my lucky day! A Charles Chips potato chips can, only slightly dented, would serve well for the front hood of my kart, making it look like a train locomotive—*(points for style)*. Mr. Peck at Schneider's hardware store gave me an offcut of plywood and a warped 2 x 4. Turning the corner onto Taft Avenue, I immediately saw an aluminum chair with green and white stripped webbing that someone was getting rid of. The seat itself was basically non-existent since it was missing half the straps. The remaining straps were loose with frayed ends, but the back was in perfect condition, ideal for some comfort while piloting my kart to victory. I also spotted a stained couch pillow with pictures of red, blue and purple peacocks on them and gold tassels outlining its perimeter that would serve well as his cushioned seat. Across town they were building a house and after the workers would go home at five o'clock, I would carefully walk around the perimeter of the house looking for dropped nails. It did not take long before I had myself a pocketful.

I spent the better part of the day constructing an aerodynamic kart with the smaller baby stroller wheels on the front and larger wagon wheels on the back. I weighted the nose of my racer with a cinder block and nailed a couple of 2 x 4s in a triangular pattern so that the front of the kart came to a point. If anyone tried to cut me off during the race, the pointed nose of the kart would cut right through their racer. Using a staple gun, I fastened the peacock cushion to the plywood, giving me a little comfort for the race and used electrical tape to repair a small tear in the cushion. My feet would rest against the extended axel, which is how I would steer the kart. Bellamy reminded me that the year before I had used a clothesline rope fastened to either side of the axle for the steering, which did not end well. The knot on the left side had slid toward the wheel and the friction caused it to break, pushing the kart uncontrollably to the right and head-on into Mr. Proctor's fence, destroying two of his prized hybrid tea heirloom rose bushes. That fiasco ruined any chance of me winning the race. I had learned from my engineering mistakes. I even installed a primitive braking system, a 1 x 3 board a foot and a half long with a single nail attaching to the side of the kart. I attached a thick strip of rubber I picked up from a piece of a tire thrown by a speeding semi's retread as it barreled down Limekiln Pike. I cut a small rectangular piece off the retread and glued it to one end of the 1 x 3 while using the other end as a handle.

By pulling the board towards me, the other end would scrap against the pavement slowing the kart down through friction. None of the other kart entrees had a braking system which had proved costly in previous years.

While I was working on my kart, Choo-Choo had snuck-up behind me to see what I was creating. He had a tendency to be where he shouldn't be and he had a loud mouth. If he knew something, the entire town knew it. A secret was impossible with Choo-Choo.

"What the hell are you doing here? I said as I gave Choo-Choo a good push. "If you tell anyone how I'm building my kart I'll kick your ass!"

"I won't tell anybody, Cal. I was just on my way to Chollie Mollies and saw you working in your garage. Really!"

"You better not. If you're going to Chollie Mollies, go!"

🚲

Another Wednesday night came and with it, the arrival of three stacks of newspapers I would have to deliver the next morning. Since there was no school the next day, I decided to take Cookie along on my route to keep me company. Cookie trotted alongside my bicycle and helped make the chore less dreadful; a friend to share the task with. The houses where tossing the paper onto the front porch was forbidden, Cookie would follow me up the steps as I placed the paper inside the screen door.

The day was going better than expected, when suddenly a car drove up Maple Avenue at a hurried rate of speed. Before I knew it, Cookie darted in front of the car. Screeching brakes could hardly be heard over the pitiful yelps from Cookie; her rear right leg had been crushed, exposing the bone through the bloody flesh. As the car accelerated away with no obvious intention to inspect the dog or to give me comfort, I picked up a baseball-sized stone and threw it as hard as I could clipping the car's sideview window with a crack. The brake lights lit up for only a second, then the car proceeded to the stop sign where it barely slowed as it turned on to Limekiln Pike.

I walked over to Cookie who was whimpering pathetically. As I stroked her head to comfort her, the dog, incensed in excruciating pain, turned and bit me repeatedly on my right hand and wrist. A neighbor, hearing the commotion, had called the police, who arrived in surprisingly short order. The officer gathered the necessary information, put on thick gloves and picked Cookie up and placed her in the back of his police van. I got into the passenger's seat as we drove over to Roslyn Animal Hospital.

The attendant at the door of the veterinary hospital seeing the emergency, ran and got the doctor. Before I knew it, Cookie was in surgery. Asking for my phone number, the officer used the phone at the front desk to call my parents.

The decision had to be made quickly; euthanize or amputate. The vet explained that a dog's front legs are for balance and their back legs are used for speed. He assured my parents that Cookie could live a full and enjoyable life with just three legs. My parents discussed their options and decided, to my surprise, to have the leg amputated, even though it was an unplanned expense.

Cookie was lethargic when she got home, frequently licking her bandaged stub, but she steadily improved and quickly adapted to having just three legs. Within a month's time she improved and within a few weeks, you could hardly notice she had lost the appendage.

After the initial anger expressed by Dasha and my brother, Ted, for having taken Cookie on my paper route, things began to settle down and even though it was not mentioned again. I knew that I would always be blamed for the poor dog's unfortunate fate. But of course, it would have to be me that would cause such a dreadful incident. Who else would have caused such a thoughtless act? But Bellamy understood.

"It was just an accident. It wasn't you who was driving recklessly down Maple Avenue. You would think they would put themselves in your place and see how upset you are over what happened to Cookie. They always act like they've never done anything wrong. Their time will come. A tooth for a tooth!"

Bellamy's encouragement did little to boost my dwindling self-esteem.

🚲

It only took a few days before the racers had completed their karts for the Hawthorne 500, named after the hill the racers would descend. By 9 a.m. the racers began arriving with their 4-wheeled speed craft, that is, all but The Professor, who engineered a 3-wheeler, thinking the friction of four wheels would slow it down. Mouche, a.k.a. The Fly, brought along a can of railroad grease he had found in his garage to slab onto the axles hoping it would add speed to his wheeled-ground-jet, as he called it.

Thanks to Choo-Choo's inability to keep his mouth shut, everyone knew what my kart would look like and all its features. Muskrat brought a race kart which looked like something out of the Beverly Hillbillies, resembling an outhouse on wheels more than a go-kart, and it was definitely top-heavy. He had framed a vertical rectangular box out of used, warped 2 x 4s. Downspouts were nailed horizontally that appeared to be bumper guards. He had "borrowed" some choice wood from his grandfather who was in the process of building a new pigeon loft. He had also taken the landing boards off his grandfather's loft and nailed them to the front of his racer using the trap door as the windshield for his kart.

Boner decided to use the wheels from a shopping kart, however steering would be a serious issue. He would use his shifting weight on a pivoting floorboard to steer his kart figuring the fast-spinning wheels would give him an advantage. Some of the contestants were taking practice runs, but only for a block, down the hill to Locust Road.

Gina Majorino, outfitted in hot pants and a skin-tight white midriff tied tightly around her upper waist, was recruited to wave the green flag to signal the start of the race. Choo-Choo had broken his arm the week before when his bicycle flipped while attempting to jump a wood pile, or so he claimed. At the bottom of the hill, he stood with his one arm in a sling and his good arm holding a homemade checkered flag he had painstakingly created with a white t-shirt and a black magic marker.

"Gentlemen, start your engines," Gina said with a smile that distracted some of the drivers.

"God, I love her! She is so sizzling hot," the Fly whispered to me.

Most of the contestants stood bent over their craft at the starting line, wanting to run as fast as they could and then jump on once the kart had momentum.

Gina gave the countdown. "On your mark, get set...go!"

Early on, there were indications of steering and braking problems, like in years past.

The Fly's coke-bottle glasses fell off and Muskrat ran right over them. The Fly couldn't see two inches in front of him without those glasses and that was evident by his erratic steering. His front right wheel started rubbing against Muskrat's front left which caused sparks to fly. Muskrat tried to push The Fly off the road but with his wheel hopelessly locked to The Fly's wheel he had little time to try and free himself. In one last desperate attempt, Muskrat pulled his steering wheel hard to the right hitting Boner's kart broadside so hard that he tipped it on its side and caused it to slide to a stop in the middle of the road. Meanwhile, The Fly and Muskrat's karts were still attached by two of their front wheels as they headed for the big oak tree in the corner of my yard. Neither could steer and when the karts were a few feet from impact, they both bailed. The latched karts hit the tree squarely sending splintering pieces halfway across the street.

The Professor and Skeeter were right behind me, not gaining on me but holding steady. The Professor's back right wheel was beginning to wobble excessively. When he turned to see what was causing his kart to shake so violently, he saw the tread coming off the wheel. He had no choice but to steer to the side of the road, dropping out of the race.

With that, Hunchback took the lead and was running smoothly with great speed, so much so that it was difficult to keep the kart in the center of the road. He had a kart and a half lead on me, and two on The Freak who had been incognito through the entire race, when disaster struck. Hunchback thought it would be very cool if he had a parachute to slow him down, once he crossed the finish line. He used some corn sacks he had gotten from his cousin who lived out in Lancaster County. By cutting the bags so they laid flat he was able to sew them into a makeshift parachute, fastening it to the back seat of his kart with six strands of box twine. As Hunchback was nearing the finish line, the chute had become loose and, in an instant, flew behind the kart spinning it around to a dead stop as he watched me pass him in a flash and crossing the finish line with both arms raised high in a touchdown pose.

"We won!" screamed Bellamy. "See, you *are* a champion!"

CHAPTER THIRTEEN

The pace of time is an enemy to both young and old. For the youth it moves too slowly; for the elderly, too fast.

After Camp Wackasack, my nickname, "Mayhem," never stuck, unlike the other boy's handles had, that is, except The Fly. We changed his to Mouche, the name his mother called him. I cannot remember exactly why. I was stuck with Cal, something that always bothered me. Not that I disliked the name Cal, but because I always felt that every kid should have a nickname. I *needed* a nickname. Something cool, like Razor or Striker. Heck, even Boner had a cool nickname. Although the first time my parents heard someone calling him Boner, I realized it would be a nickname that could only be used in the absence of grownups. Sundance was already taken, as was Hoss, and it wasn't cool to steal Hollywood nicknames anyway. They had to be original and appropriate. Thankfully, loser or jerk-off never stuck.

Funny, my friends were not all keen on the nicknames that they were stuck with, but at least they had one. Hunchback did not like the nickname he was given, but he didn't like the name Larry much either, thinking Larry was the least of the 3 Stooges. Muskrat thought his nickname was a reference to his looks, which it was, but after camp he had accepted the moniker, and besides, he had more important things on his mind.

By now it was evident that Muskrat's dad *was* hiding a secret. He had always been an argumentative type of guy, seriously critical of anyone who would not measure up to his holier-than-thou measuring stick. He was constantly belittling Muskrat if he ever shed a tear or when he did not perform well on the baseball diamond, the criticism would come in the form of, "Be a man!" That was extremely difficult for a kid who wasn't even old enough to shave, drive or even have pubic hair. Lately, his father had been much nicer to his wife and kids and it was obvious that a change had come over Mr. Zimmerman. It was as if a different man had come home from work. He was a kinder, more considerate husband and father, but for Muskrat, that only confirmed that he was hiding something. He had finally convinced me and Hunchback that, indeed, something smelled rotten on Edge Hill Road. The straw that broke Muskrat's back was when the three boys had spotted Mr. Zimmerman's car parked in the train station parking lot. Muskrat's father always drove to work, he never took the train.

🚲

That Thursday was the first of the month which meant newspaper collection day, or "pay day." It was an unusually windy day with cloudy skies, the type of day that lets you know a front is on its way. It would mean that delivering the newspapers would take three times as long. Bellamy joined me but, of course, other than being company, he really did not help much lugging the papers around town. Knocking on every door to collect 60 cents was what I considered a tedious chore, but it also meant having more cash in my pocket.

"Hey, Bellamy. Do you think if I bought Dasha flowers she'll like me?"

I would often buy Dasha flowers as an expression of my love for her or, more correctly, to get on her good side.

"She would have to, right?" Asked Bellamy. "No one brings her flowers but you."

Bellamy was correct, but it never seemed to have any lasting effect on Dasha. She would be obviously delighted to receive the bouquets I would surprise her with, but it never got me above the bottom rung of the pecking order. You would have thought I would get the hint and stop buying her flowers, but I never did.

After finishing my paper route, I rode down to the edge of Ardsley and went into the flower shop. Mr. Strathmore was putting some fresh roses in the refrigerated display case. He had on skin-tight lime green pants and a Qiana shirt with a bold paisley pattern. He turned around and looked genuinely pleased to see me.

"Well, hello Calvin. How are you this fine day?"

After what my friends had said about him, I was petrified to engage in conversation or nurture a relationship, but Perry had been kind and generous to me and *real* friends were at a premium. It seemed alien to me to have a grown-up be so sincere and nice to me unless my parents were in the same room, or they wanted something from me. The latter made me have my antennae up for anything off kilter. Perry was unlike Reverend Markey, who always seemed *overly* nice to me, which made me feel uncomfortable.

I'll proceed cautiously. At the first sign of anything fishy, I'm out of there.

"Not much, just wanted to get some flowers for my mother," I said, not looking directly at the florist as I walked around the store.

"Now, that's a good son! I have some beautiful gladiolas on sale that just came in. Two dollars a dozen," Mr. Strathmore stated.

"Sure, I'll take 12 of those. Can you mix the red in with the yellow ones?" "Certainement," replied Mr. Strathmore, in a perfect French accent. Perry grabbed some green tissue paper and set it on the counter. Carefully, he selected the gladiolas and gently shook the water from its stems. "Have you used your net to catch any butterflies?"

I had not, at least not yet, but somehow, I did not want to disappoint Perry, especially since he had been so generous with the gifts. "Yeah, but only those white ones with the black spots. I haven't gone down to Chollie Mollies with the net, yet. There is a huge field down there. I think there will be a lot more butterflies down there."

"Chollie Mollies?" asked Perry.

"Penbryn Park. We call it Chollie Mollies. I have no idea why. It's always been called that."

"Oh. Got it, and you can call me Perry. We're not very formal around here. Well, remember, if you want to find butterflies you need to go where there are flowering weeds, plants, or trees. You'll find them all over if you're looking for them."

Perry had tied some ribbon around the bouquet and rang up the sale on the cash register. "That will be two dollars. Would you like to write a note to go with them? They're free."

"Eh, sure," I said, even though I had no idea what I would write. I so desperately wanted to get on my stepmother's good side; to demonstrate in a tangible way that I really was not a bad son. Sure, I was not the student my brother and sisters were, yet I *wanted to be*. I really *wanted* to be a good student and a model citizen. I had such difficulty remaining focused during class or through lengthy readings, but no matter how hard I tried, the goal seemed unobtainable. Reaching into my pocket I pulled out a dollar bill and a fist full of change and counted out two dollars. Picking up the card, I scribbled:

> *To the best Mom in the whole, wide world.*
> *Love, Calvin*

That should surely make her happy, I thought to myself. She'll like me now. None of my other siblings ever gave Dasha flowers.

Like in similar attempts, Dasha was delighted to receive the flowers, but when they died, so did any affection she had for me.

🚲

There is nothing like a good explosion to grab the attention of every red-blooded American boy. The sheer anticipation of the detonation while watching the fuse sparkle as it gets smaller and smaller was enough to have a boy ecstatic. Occasionally, my friends and I were lucky enough to have one of the kids in the neighborhood bring some firecrackers to our local gatherings. Usually, they got some from some cousin who traveled through South Carolina on vacation.

We would pick straws to see who would be giving up their plastic ship model for the good of the group. Ground zero would usually be Floaties pond in Hillside Cemetery, where we would put on a show. Floaties pond was an unlikely place for kids to gravitate to. No one would go there alone, that is, except me. It was the nearest body of water, but it was also an eerie place, a place where danger lurked. A false oasis in a place filled with death. Yet I was drawn to the pond. Safe. Solitary. So many hopes and dreams of mine had already died. A cemetery seemed an appropriate place for me to frequent.

Floaties was the only nearby pond where we could execute our military mission. We would use scotch-tape to secure 3 firecrackers, or one cherry bomb, at mid-ship while, pouring model airplane glue around the ship's perimeter. We would light the ship on fire as one of us pushed the ship out to sea. The fuse would ignite, and it would seem like an eternity, but suddenly a rapid succession of three explosions would scatter pieces of the model as far as 3 feet from the ship. We would watch the vessel slowly sink; the few remaining drops of glue burning on the surface of the water making it seem like the fuel oil from the ship was on fire. The boat never lasted long before it sank, but it was always one of the highlights of the summer. The gang would each chip in a nickel so the kid who lost his boat could get a free sundae at Jack Frost.

Fireworks were illegal in Pennsylvania; in fact, they were not legal in many states, but South Carolina was the nearest place to get any, and that was a good 8-hour drive. Immediately upon entering South Carolina on I-95 you would come across the mother of fireworks stores at a place called South of the Border. My memories of South of the Border were bittersweet.

It had been a hot August day when our family headed to Florida in our aqua blue and white 1958 Chevrolet Brookwood station wagon. The car had a broad grille, quad headlights and my dad referred to it as the "baby Cadillac." The wagon's tail had the signature fan-shaped alcove on both side panels and seating for nine. It was custom for me to sit in the very rear, since I was the youngest. That was fine except it had no air conditioning and heading south on I-95 in August with the heat visibly rising up off the road made the trip more like crossing the Sahara on a camel. Having a crew cut helped a little, but sitting in the very back of the wagon there wasn't much air, unlike the window seats where my sisters sat. My shirt was soaking wet and my thighs would stick to the blue vinyl seats, but that was a small price to pay as I anticipated what was waiting for me in Dillon, South Carolina.

Although the dream of palm trees and white sandy beaches were more than pleasant, my anticipation was to investigate all that South of the Border had to offer. I had heard wonderful stories about South of the Border, and I had been saving the money I had earned by delivering papers and mowing lawns around the neighborhood, and I was going to spend a good amount of that dough on firecrackers, cherry bombs, bottle rockets, M-80s and roman candles.

In the day, South of the Border was a young pyromaniacs dream! It was an island oasis located in the barren sea called I-95 on the North Carolina/South Carolina border at a time when it was illegal to sell or possess fireworks in any other state on the east coast. It was the halfway stop on road trips between the northeast and Florida. You would drive miles and miles through pine forest until suddenly you would begin to see the tacky world of pyrotechnics.

Every kid north of Virginia begged their parents to stop at the fireworks bonanza. But it wasn't like my dad needed the reminder. Corny signs featuring spokesman "Pedro" would pop up every couple of miles which remind the family vacationers that they had X-amount-of-miles till they reached Pedro's fireworks Utopia, whoever Pedro was. Billboards like PEDRO'S WEATHER REPORT—CHILI TODAY HOT TAMALE—SOUTH OF THE BORDER—23 MILES, or YOU'RE ALWAYS A WEINER AT PEDRO'S—SOUTH OF THE BORDER—10 MILES or the one that had a giant sausage on the billboard. That one read YOU NEVER SAUSAGE A THING.

My family had traveled hundreds of miles, having gotten up well before dawn. Off in the distance, as a beacon of tacky tourism, was the colossal sombrero nearly 200 feet high giving plenty of purpose for the hot and weary desert journey. It was Tijuana smack dab on the border between the two Carolinas, except you did not have to worry about being propositioned by prostitutes and the water was safe to drink.

As our car approached the exit, I saw the 97-foot Pedro, which stood adjacent to the Mexico Shop East and the Sombrero Restaurant. I anticipated the joy of driving underneath the legs of the giant man, but to my huge disappointment, the Chevy station wagon drove right past the exit. *Was Dad daydreaming?* "Dad, Dad. You missed the exit!" I screamed as I saw Pedro disappearing in the rear window.

"We don't need gas and you're not getting any fireworks." And that was that.

⅗

My vision of having a motherload of fireworks at my disposal received a second chance that October. My oldest sister, Olivia, was dating a Marine stationed in Parris Island, located in Beaufort, *South Carolina*. I guess the young marine thought it would be a good idea to keep my sister's kid brother happy, because he drove home one weekend and brought back a trunk load of fireworks from South of the Border. My father was not happy about it, but he took the bag of fireworks and *hid* them by placing the box of explosives in the basement rafters, just above his work bench. He could not push them too far in the rafters or they would disappear somewhere between the raised ceiling and the plywood floor of the main floor. It took me all of 15 minutes to discover where they were so strategically placed. The undeniable pink-red sticks of the various rockets were poking out just enough to catch my eye. *Someday, when my parents are not home, we're going to have a whole lot of fun, Bellamy!*

That someday came in the form of a weekday after school. Being grounded for God-knows-what, I was desperate for some entertainment. Bellamy came up with a brilliant idea! I had a neighbor two properties behind my backyard who was an annoying little girl. Her name was Gretel. She was the product of German immigrant parents who escaped Germany prior to World War II. Rumor around the neighborhood was that her father's real name was Adolph but that he changed it to William because of that Nazi thing. Nonetheless, he spoke with a German accent as heavy as cough syrup. He walked with a slight limp and used a wooden cane with a medieval silver-plated dragon head with, what looked like, a black pearl in its mouth that would scare the bejeebers out of me.

Gretel, an only child, would spend countless hours in her backyard everyday caressing and conversing with her pet rabbits. Mr. Ed, I was familiar with, and I really enjoyed Bunny Rabbit on the Captain Kangaroo show, but I knew they were make-believe—for entertainment purposes—simply because naïve kids were watching TV.

Gretel had no idea I was spying on her with my $2 spyglass I had bought at the Howard Johnson's on the Pennsylvania turnpike. She named her rabbits after Pennsylvania politicians. *For god's sake, who ever heard of a rabbit named Milton Shapp?* She would fuss with those rodents as if she was a beautician and they were Princess Grace Kelly of Monaco. Gretel would take her Barbie doll's pink and white banana hair curlers and go to work on those poor four-legged underground muttons.

On this glorious day, while watching Gretel practice her creative cosmetology skills, I got a brilliant idea. Running inside and down the stairs, missing 2 or 3 steps at a time, I pulled a chair next to my father's workbench, climbed on top of his workstation and pulled out a shoe box filled with fireworks. On the top of the open box were 5 bunches of bottle rockets held together with a rubber band. Removing one packet of these little gems, I carefully put the others back in their hiding place. Grabbing a box of stick matches I had stored away in my sock drawer; I went out the kitchen door with the hopes that Gretel would still be out doing her daily routine with her long-eared friends. I was in luck. There she sat on her swing set stroking her prized tick-smorgasbord-walking-hand-muff.

Between my house and the garage was a breezeway that my dad had enclosed. The frame was made of 2 x 4s and was nailed to the concrete floor. There was a little door for Cookie to come in and out on her own discretion, and that would prove to be the perfect launching pad for this novice NASA prodigy. If one of these little rockets could fly from a coke bottle to several hundred feet in the air, then why could not it fly horizontally across the earth's surface for about the length of a football field in just a few seconds, if positioned properly. If I could perfect the launch angle and get good results, the possibilities to use them on Dasha were endless!

I laid one of the bottle rockets on the 2 x 4, lit the stick match off my front tooth and lit the fuse. There is something magical about a fuse. In slow motion the sparks ignite one's anticipation, almost teasing you as it seems to pause; a slight hesitation just before it reaches the explosive device. You never quite know when it is going to explode. Three, two, one, whoosh! We have lift-off!

My calculations did not take into consideration the slight nuisances and variances in my backyard or Mr. Bates' backyard. Our yards were not perfectly flat; there was a slight dip in my backyard and, what seemed to be, insignificant incline in Mr. Bates' backyard, but that small incline made all the difference in the world. The first launch quickly hit the ground, throwing sparks every which way and jerking about like a dragonfly caught in a spider web. *Rats! Back to the drawing board.* My biggest concern was that by the time I would be able to figure out the right geometric calculations, Gretel would retreat into her house.

I needed to position the bottle rocket slightly upward, not so much that it would go skyward, but just enough that it would stay about 10 feet off the ground. I placed a deck of playing cards on the 2 x 4 and was ready for my second launch. I lit the fuse and this time the spark ran quickly to the rocket and, in what seemed to be a second or two, it took off on about a 40-degree angle. Immediately I knew it was positioned too high as I saw the rocket heading straight for Mr. Bate's chimney. Unfortunately, it missed the chimney and exploded on the roof with a bang! I quickly ran for my kitchen and watched for the fallout that was sure to come. Sitting on the kitchen sink, I peered out the window waiting for Mr. Bates to exit his dark house. With each passing minute I felt my luck increasing. No Mr. Bates. He was not home! What an omen for the next launch.

The third time *was* a charm. By removing the deck of cards and using just the 2 x 4 framing, I rested the body of the rocket on the edge of the board with the end of its stick touching the cement floor. The angle appeared to be roughly 25 degrees. I pointed the nose of the rocket for Gretel's rabbit shack. I checked and double-checked the rocket's position, incline, and fuse. All systems go! Breathing through my mouth to dry off my teeth, I struck the match off my front tooth. Crack! I could smell the sweet odor of sulfur as the fuse was ignited. Whoosh! It took off heading directly for Gretel's backyard. I could follow its trajectory by the slight stream of smoke that followed the rocket. The one thing I had no control of was distance, but as luck would have it, just when the rocket reached Gretel's swing set, it exploded. Gretel jumped three feet off the ground and turned around to see a small puff of smoke. Petrified, she ran into her house.

I fell to my knees laughing hysterically as Gretel reappeared in her backyard with her mother. It was clear she was trying to explain what had happened, but her mother wasn't buying any of it. By the time they Gretel had convinced her mother to come outside, the smoke had disappeared and there were no signs of any foul play. Gretel's mother went back inside.

Knowing that her mother might be peering out the back door window, I waited 5 minutes before launching another attack, but that was okay, it gave me time to set-up another rocket. When I thought the coast was clear, I sent another rocket across three backyards. This time it took a bit of a right turn and headed directly over Gretel's head and exploded behind the rabbit pen. Bang! This time I could hear Gretel's scream. Off she ran into the house. Within a few minutes Gretel and her mother came out of the house. I could not hear what her mother was saying, but clearly, she was scolding Gretel for fabricating such an outlandish story. At this point I had peed myself laughing hilariously!

If this worked so well on Gretel, it should work well with Dasha. Perhaps the inexplicable explosions could make her go insane, or at least have my dad think she lost her mind. Maybe he would have her committed. This would take a little more planning.

Over the next several weeks I would revisit the bottle rocket experiment, often inviting Hunchback or Muskrat to experience it. One day the winds had picked up, and since I had yet to take physics in school, I failed to take the squalls into consideration. When I made my calculations as the rocket went well off course, striking Mrs. Bates' bra that was hanging on her clothesline. The rocket made it halfway through the triple E cup and lodged there burning a silver dollar sized whole in the left cup. Thankfully, I never heard any accusations come my way. Sadly, all good things must come to an end as my supply of bottle rockets had run out.

CHAPTER FOURTEEN

It's only in love and in murder that we still remain sincere.
—Friedrich Dürrenmatt

Muskrat continued his clandestine investigation into his father's odd behavior. The day before his mother walked into the kitchen, surprising his father who was on the telephone, so much so that he dropped a glass of water, causing it to shatter across the linoleum floor. When his wife asked who he was on the phone with, he simply said, "No one," but Muskrat was convinced that his dad was cheating on his mother, especially since he had lost over 30 pounds since all of this began. Still, with no concrete evidence, he had nothing but suspicions and conspiracy theories that were only based on surmising.

Muskrat and Mouche asked me to join them at the Saturday matinee to see the movie MASH. There was no sense in asking my parents. I knew what their answer would be. Whenever my friends would go to the Keswick Theatre in nearby Glenside, I was never allowed to join them. The strict, religious upbringing forbade that. My brother, Ted, the chosen one, was able to persuade our stepmother for us to see *Mary Poppins*, and *Funny Girl*, but my cinematic appetite was for *The Good, the Bad and the Ugly* or *Planet of the Apes*. I even had to sneak out of the house to see *Butch Cassidy and the Sundance Kid*.

I thought about going anyway and risk the possibility of being seen by someone who would report back to Dasha, but I squelched that idea. They decided to ask Mouche as my replacement. Hunchback

told me that Mouche said that his little brother, Tommy, had almost
stopped talking. It was if someone had stitched his mouth shut. His
mom was sick with worry, and they were sending him to some shrink
to find out why he went quiet. Mouche said he thought it had
something to do with church because on Sunday mornings Tommy
would scream, kick, and lay on the floor, refusing to get into the car
and go to Sunday School. If it was not church that was scaring him, it
was Reverend Markey.

Instead of the movies, Bellamy suggested that we get up early on
Saturday morning, before the neighborhood kids were up, to tryout
my butterfly net. I knew if I got caught chasing butterflies the
embarrassment and humiliation would be never-ending! Walking
through the woods of Chollie Mollies, covered with a canopy of tall
sugar maple, northern red oak, cherry birch, and black walnut, I felt
the coolness of the morning shade as I weaved down the dirt trail to
an open field. The sun began warming the October chill, drying the
mist that had drenched the field. A bit too early for the late autumn
goldenrod, I quickly spotted several monarchs that had found
abundant nectar on the tall milkweed and spectacular Joe Pye Weed.
Practicing the swooshing of the net with a quick twist of the wrist, I
felt confident I would capture a few of these gorgeous, winged
wanderers.

   With my first try I captured a large male and was surprised at how
easily I had done so. Placing the winged beauty into the pickle jar I
had secured from the neighbor's trash, I went off to find more. I would
have been happy chasing after, and netting, butterflies all morning,
but when I saw the first couple of kids heading down to the ballfield,
I knew I had to hide the net underneath my shirt and head home.
Having a reputation of being a butterfly enthusiast would not be a
good thing, especially when I was striving to be a guy's-guy.

   I took the jar with the butterflies and the spreading board that
Perry had given me and laid it on my desk. While working with the
butterflies I found that I could lose myself in their beauty as an escape

from my otherwise ugly existence. The butterflies were still alive, so I dipped a cotton ball in a bottle of insecticide and gently placed it in the bottom of the jar, just as Perry had instructed me to do. Seconds later there was no movement in the jar. The exquisite beauty and intricate pattern of the insect had me mesmerized as I stood there admiring God's creation. Yet, through the exquisiteness, there was a haunting question which gave me a feeling of melancholy as I contemplated whether I was justified in killing such a beautiful creature for selfish gain. Is it fair to imprison a butterfly, and then euthanize it even when it has a lifespan of a mere 2 weeks? Is it right to kill so you can gaze upon beauty indefinitely as it hangs on your living room wall? If that is acceptable, then why not kill a person who would prevent you from having a beautiful life? What if you were faced with the possibility of humiliation and your reputation ruined? Would that justify killing someone to protect you from emotional harm. Is that not self-defense? I deliberated for some time but could not, or would not, come to a reasonable conclusion, and so I put it out of my mind. So many philosophical questions, so few answers.

The butterflies were dead and ready for mounting. Carefully, I began folding the wings down with forceps using strips of paper and pins. I manipulated the wings perfectly so they were hinged to the body just above the surface of the mounting board. With surgical precision, I cautiously avoided touching the wing surfaces with my fingers so as not to rub off the scales.

"You're a natural at this," suggested Bellamy.

"I am, aren't I," I responded.

A three-hour drive north of my home stood the hamlet of Equinunk, Pennsylvania, a sleepy little town nestled between the Delaware River and the Endless mountains that made North Hills look like a megalopolis. It was a destination of fascination as a place of adventure and perplexing contrasts. It was the location of Aunt Polina's farm which sat on 150 acres and that is where my family was headed this day.

My love for the mountains came from my father, who would take long walks in the woods whenever we were in the Poconos. For me, the woods were a place of escape—a place where I was safe and did not have to answer to anyone. I have always been more comfortable around nature than around people. At Aunt Polina's farm, I could wander in the hills and woods for hours, and no one would care where I had been. The first daffodil that would sprout in the early spring, defiantly ignoring the lingering snow clusters, brought me indescribable joy. The falling acorns, the offspring of the majestic oak, gave me comfort as I would roll the smooth green and yellow nugget between my fingers. I would notice the subtle changes in nature that the rest of the world was oblivious to. I realized that every two to five years there would be an excessive number of acorns that would drop, not knowing that the botanical term for that is "mast years." I would memorize each bird's unique song and would be placed in a state of reverie as my eyes followed the flight of a butterfly.

Aunt Polina was my biological mother's aunt, or, if you prefer, my great aunt. A widow, Aunt Polina stood a mere 4 foot, 5 inches, but looked even smaller as she was hunched over from advanced osteoporosis. She always wore characteristic granny glasses, which Audrey thought were cool and in style, a pale blue apron with embroidered yellow and red flowers around the trim, and she wore her long, grey-white hair in a bun. She was toothless, save for two incisors on the lower plate and one canine in the upper, and she wore black high-top shoes which had been re-soled several times. She was approximately 152 years old and had forgotten her birthdate nearly a decade or two earlier, but what made Aunt Polina memorable was that she lived without electricity, running water or a flush toilet. A spring-fed well was only a few feet from the kitchen door and an outhouse stood about 40 feet behind the wood frame farmhouse.

Aunt Polina would make these delectable muffins stuffed with huckleberries that were growing wild throughout the endless mountains of Pennsylvania. As far as I could tell, huckleberries were small blueberries, just a bit sweeter. When we would visit in the late spring and early summer, she would send me out to pick them before black bear would feast on them. It was easy to know if a bear had beat you to the large bushes because the branches would be bent downward and stripped of fruit.

As my parents were busy discussing something about Aunt Polina, I looked out the window, taking in the change of scenery as the family car left civilization far behind. I understood the term *a simpler life*, but thought, too, that it was misguided as I saw men chopping wood for the winter, being the home-warming fuel of choice, as it came at the right price. The fields were sparsely populated by both men and women bailing hay and old women bent low harvesting green beans and tomatoes for canning. An old man was bent over carrying a bundle of kindling and branches on his back reminiscent of the album cover *Led Zeppelin IV*. There was a poverty that was unlike the poverty I had seen in Philadelphia. Here the people were poor but worked assiduously for their sustenance and survival. The family car passed an abandoned general store, Maggie's Sit n' Eat and a gas station -convenience store, all which were permanently closed. Good ideas gone bad.

My thoughts returned to my great aunt's farm as I gazed out the window at the passing sites. I loved going to the homestead, except for the fact that my parents made me kiss Aunt Polina upon arrival at her house, an obligation which almost made the trip unbearable. A thick cloud of garlic and tooth decay would welcome my lips as I would hesitantly lean over for the obligatory osculation. My great aunt would pinch my cheeks and say something in Ukrainian since Aunt Polina spoke no English. She would smile as Dasha would explain what grade I was in, hobbies I was interested in, and what plans I had after high school. After sitting through the routine pleasantries, I was free to go outside and explore.

On the other side of the gravel driveway was the barn and behind the barn, the chicken coop. The barn was weather-beaten grey with faded red paint intermittently visible on lower portions of the boards and a rusting, silver metal roof would sing whenever it would rain. The chicken coop was approximately 100 feet by 60 feet with wire mesh around the frame and the wooden shelter had a little ramp for the chickens to enter where they would sleep and get relief from the elements. When visiting, Aunt Polina always made sure to tell Dasha to instruct me on shutting the housing door at night to prevent predators from eliminating a chicken or two.

Aunt Polina had three sons; two of them had their challenges. Coy was the youngest. He was a *special* boy; *special* in that he would ride the *little yellow bus* to school. He never made it past the fourth grade. Johnny did a bit better, that is, until he was too large to ride the bus. He was not too old to ride the bus, or too tall, just too *big!* Johnny tipped the scales at well over 400 lbs. When he was entering the 5th grade, he could no longer make it up the three steps of the bus, so he just stopped going to school altogether. Aunt Polina told Dasha that it was all for the better because Johnny could help her around the farm, but Johnny could hardly walk, let alone bale hay, or feed the chickens. Marko was the only *normal* son, if you call normal being consumed with reading and academics, but never using that knowledge outside of their little farm. All of Aunt Polina's sons were older than my parents.

Johnny *never* bathed. I guessed it was because he could not fit into the bathtub, but even if he could, the bathtub was always occupied. From September through April, it was filled with apples from the small orchard that grew on the hill below the chicken coop. There was an awful stench that would linger for a good thirty minutes after Johnny would leave a room making an association with the boy difficult if the visit did not occur outside.

Coy would play with a stuffed groundhog his dad had shot years before and had a habit of repeating words or phrases. Coy's dad was always killing *something*. When Aunt Polina would tell Johnny that he ate too much, Coy would chant, "Johnny eats too much. Johnny eats too much," like a well-trained macaw.

One day Johnny died choking on a pork chop. My great aunt went to a neighboring farm to call Dasha, describing the horrifying story between her fits of Ukrainian hysteria. The best I could understand, Johnny was gnawing on a pork chop when a piece of the bone splintered and got stuck in his throat. Aunt Polina was upstairs when she heard a strange mixture of cackling and retching which she deliberated on a bit too long. By the time she figured out that poor Johnny was choking, it was nearly too late. She found him fallen back on his chair with his eyes wide open. Aunt Polina jumped on Johnny's chest, beating it like a tom-tom, but Johnny just became bluer and bluer and continued his spasms. She tried to remove the bone but, in her attempts, ended up driving it farther down his throat.

It took seven neighbor farmhands to remove Johnny's body from the house, and then they needed a backhoe to place the body on a flatbed to take it to the nearest crematorium, 36 miles away. Aunt Polina told Dasha that the cemetery wanted her to buy three lots to bury him, so she decided cremation was the way to go. Since Aunt Polina was what they call a "shut-in," they told her they would ship the urn via UPS and promised it would arrive on the Saturday following Johnny's death.

Aunt Polina scheduled the memorial service at the farmhouse for that same Saturday. I assume she had no idea that UPS' delivery window was large, because she had not calculated the arrival of Johnny's remains well with the beginning of the service. The extended family, including me and my siblings, were all gathered in the living room and on the porch waiting for Johnny's remains to arrive.

Hours passed, but no Johnny. Dasha was about to suggest that they eat first, then have the memorial service when a UPS truck could be seen kicking up dirt and stones on the gravel road. Coy looked up from his slumber, like a dog from a long midsummer's day nap, and began announcing Johnny's arrival.

"Here's Johnny! Here's Johnny!" repeated Coy, unknowingly doing a fine Ed McMahon imitation.

Death fascinated me, even as a boy.

On the way home from the memorial service, my father took a slight detour and jumped on the Pennsylvania turnpike.

"Dad, I need a bathroom," I pleaded.

"We'll be home in less than an hour."

"That's about 59 minutes longer than I can wait."

As the family Chevy rolled down the interstate, I could see the familiar orange roof with blue spires beckoning the weary traveler, a

Howard Johnson's, the pioneer in comfort food and a selection of 28 flavors of ice cream. I ran awkwardly with a full bladder into the restaurant and was immediately welcomed by the aroma of fried clams.

The bathroom was a primitive sex education lesson for a boy coming-of-age. There was the cologne machine. For a quarter you could get a squirt of your favorite after shave; British Sterling, Brut, English Leather or High Karate. It was clear to me that the cologne was a prerequisite for the second bathroom vending machine, the condom machine. As I stood in front of the urinal releasing the reservoir in my bladder, I was fascinated by the selection the vending machine offered. There was the glow-in-the-dark Pink Panther condom, the lambskin condom for extra sensitivity and the ever-popular French Tickler with ribbed sides and multiple receptacle ends. The French Tickler I had seen before. Somehow Choo-Choo Charlie got his hands on one, filling it up with water so that it looked like a cow's udders. After relieving myself, I got back into the idling car and we headed home.

I was thinking of the Ten Commandments this evening as I was writing this. It is funny, if not appropriate, that as we grow older, as we approach the inevitable end, that our attention is drawn to our past. Even an atheist must wonder if they got it right. If not, they made one hell of a mistake. The specifics of what comes after death is a unanimous contemplation. Judgement for our sins is something we have all become so good at ignoring.

It is curious, that the Ten are wrapped up in two other commandments not included in the stone tablets given to Moses. In Matthew chapter 22, a Pharisee asked Jesus which is the greatest commandment. Jesus answered, "You shall love the Lord your God with all your heart and with all your soul and with all your mind. This is the great and first commandment. And a second is like it: You shall love your neighbor as yourself." In other words, if you love God and you love people you will have kept all the Ten Commandments. In retrospect, I was never particularly good at obedience.

The "Thou shall not kill" thing is another thought-provoking commandment. The State kills with their death sentence. The government kills with their wars. Self-defense has always been an acceptable reason to kill. To me, it was as though killing was okay as long as someone in authority said it was justified.

Even though it had been years since my encounter with Simone at her house, I found myself creating reasons to ride my bike past her house. If I went to Plockies with my friends to pick up some grape balls, I would always make an excuse why we should ride down Ruscombe Avenue, but I always heard the same reason why we could not. "That's the dark side of town." Dark, as in, black people.

My friends were all white, that is, all but Simone, and at this point in my life, I was not sure I could call her a friend. They would use nasty slang when referring to a black person. They would make hurtful jokes about them, not to their face, mind you. I had to wonder if it was hereditary or a learned trait.

One day after church I told my parents I would catch a ride home with Olivia. She had choir practice after church, and I knew it would mean hanging around for an extra hour. By my calculations, the black Baptist church would be letting out about then. The African American church services were at least 3 hours long, but if I could come up with an excuse for us to drive by, I might just catch a glimpse of Simone.

My ploy was to tell Olivia that I had seen a brand new 68' Vette, the only year between 1963 and 1976 that Chevy had not made a Stingray, and I really would like to drive by and see it. Olivia, always easy when it came to my whims, obliged.

As we turned on to Limekiln Pike, I could smell the fried fish coming from Slish's Seafood House. A stout lady in her Sunday clothes was coming out of a restaurant with a large, grease-stained brown paper bag of takeout fish. Driving down the hill towards Edge Hill Firehouse, I saw that my timing was spot on. An older, white-haired black man with a brown suit and purple-flowered tie and in need of a haircut, was standing by the large red doors of the church shaking people's hands. Simone's mother was waiting her turn to thank the reverend as Simone stood next to her dressed in a peach-colored dress with pleats from the waist down. She had white heels on and black stockings. She looked elegant.

I must had been daydreaming because it took me a few seconds to realize that Simone had turned and looked at Olivia's Simca that had come to a stop to allow churchgoers to cross the street. I had no idea what to do so I ducked below the window.

"What are you doing?" Olivia asked.

"Nothing," I replied.

"You always duck under the seat when you see black people?"

"No. I saw somebody I didn't want to see me," I said, hoping it would put an end to the questioning.

"You're a weird kid."

"Yeah, I know."

When we got home, I checked on my butterflies and was delighted to find that they had dried to a flawless position. I had purchased a glass frame and a roll of cotton from the hobby shop in Jenkintown to complete the kaleidoscope of colored entomological art. With scissors in hand, I rolled out the cotton, cutting a piece to the dimensions of the frame. Delicately I positioned the butterflies on the cotton, replaced the back of the frame and secured the metal tabs in place. *What a perfect gift this would be for Simone.*

CHAPTER FIFTEEN

They killed to free themselves from a tyranny of love and care.

—J. G. Ballard

T he murder I mentioned earlier was an ugly thing, as I expect all murders are, but this had that which, to this day, unnerves me. Perhaps because I detest unfounded accusations, or it might have been because the weak and the needy are always easy prey for those in *authority*, or it may have been because I have known who the perp was all these years.

What type of person takes another one's life? Was such an act something they toyed with for years until an acceptable victim presented themselves? I am guessing that most of us do not know anyone who is a murderer, and so delving into a murderer's psyche is impossible.

It was Thursday and it was rainy and windy, which meant I would have to roll each newspaper up with a rubber band, slide it into a plastic bread bag and stick each one on inside a customer's screen door. It would take twice as long to complete my route. The phone rang and Ted yelled from the kitchen that it was for me. It was Muskrat.

"We need to put a tail on my dad and see what he's up to. I've gotta find out what the hell he has been up to. Even my mom thinks something is going on."

"Alright, I'm in. When do you want to do this?" I asked.

"We're going to have to pick a day when we know his normal schedule has changed. There's no sense in following him to work every day. We're going to have to be ready to drop everything, no matter what we're doing, and follow him. We need to catch him in the act."

"Yeah, but he's going to be really pissed off if he finds out we're trailing him," I warned.

"If he's cheating on mom, he'll have more to worry about than the fact we followed him!"

I hung up the phone and finished rolling up the newspapers. I made the rounds in surprisingly less time than I had imagined and stopped by Hunchback's house to see what he was up to. His mother told me him he was at Muskrat's so I headed over there.

I did not want to admit it back then, but Hunchback and Muskrat were best friends. I was the third wheel. I was always the quasi-leader of the pack. I exhibited faux confidence to hide my fear. I had fear of non-acceptance; fear that if someone did really like me, they were probably pretending. Fear that I was, well, peculiar. I have always been life's stranger. Looking back, Hunchback and Muskrat were really not my *friends*, at least not how the dictionary defined the word. I knew the *guidelines;* what I could say and what not to say, so I could be included in their plans. I could never tell them about Simone, Perry, or Bellamy.

I knew exactly what would happen if I told them about my *other* friends. First, I would be ridiculed, something I feared more than Dasha's beatings. Secondly, I would be labeled as a nigger-lover, queer, and a baby. Thirdly, they would never want to hang out with me again, and I would *really* be alienated. Actually, none of the neighborhood guys would want to be my friend.

If I excelled at anything, it was salesmanship. I was a born salesman and often I could convince them both to go along with my ideas, but if it came down to choosing sides, I was out. Bellamy was the friend I had that I could be completely truthful and vulnerable with. I still had to be careful not to let certain parts of me be seen by Simone and Perry. Perry's decision, conscious or not, to let me into his life was not one of sudden declaration, but rather, was a gradual process. His subtle encouragement and lack of criticism was more than attractive to me; it was safe.

"Hello Calvin. How are you today?" Muskrat's mother asked.

"I'm good, Mrs. Zimmerman. Is Bobby home?" I had been mindful to call Muskrat by his given name after making the mistake once and Muskrat's mother made it clear to me that she was not pleased.

"Yes, he's down in the rec room with Larry. Go on down."

"Thanks Mrs. Zimmerman," I said while opening the basement door.

Navigating carefully around Muskrat's kid sister, who was trying to make her *Slinky* walk down the stairs, I heard Muskrat and Hunchback laughing and Curly's n'yuk nyuk before I was halfway down the stairs.

"Yo."

"Yo," they answered in unison.

From the top of the stairs, Mrs. Zimmerman asked, "Calvin, the boys are having a glass of Tang. Would you like one?"

"Yes, please," I answered. Tang was a treat I seldom had at home and, heck, if the astronauts drank it, it had to be good!

The 3 Stooges show ended and the three of us sat around figuring out what to do.

"Let's go over Cal's house and play Nok-Hockey," Hunchback suggested.

"Naw, we only have a half an hour before the 5 o'clock whistle blows, let's play Electric Football," I responded.

They both quickly agreed. Electric Football was a tabletop football game which featured players which moved by the vibrations created by the electro-magnet motor under the metal field. The football was a little piece of felt which was frequently lost and sucked up by the vacuum, and so we would use various replacements including the cotton off a Q-Tip.

"Hey, Hunchback, didn't you say that Keith Steube has a Havahart trap?" I asked.

"Yeah. He got it at one of those second-hand booths at Gilbertsville Farmer's Market."

"Does he use it? Has he caught anything in it?"

"Yeah. The only thing he catches are cats. He caught Mrs. Torintino's cat and she got real pissed off," Hunchback said with a smile of delight on his face.

"Do you think he'd let me borrow it?"

"I guess so. I think his mom said he had to get rid of it. Maybe you could swap it for a couple of baseball cards. He loves collecting cards."

That Saturday I went down to Keith's house, finding him in the driveway throwing a tennis ball against the garage door which left dozens of small round dirt marks scattered in a haphazard pattern below its windows.

"Hey, Keith."

Keith turned around and waved with his mitt. "Hey, Cal. What's up?"

"Nothing. Hunchback told me that you might want to sell your animal trap."

Keith walked over to the dented silver trash can that sat on the curb, lifted the lid and pulled out a medium sized 2-door Havahart trap. "How much you want to give me for it?" Keith asked.

"Nothing," I said. "You were going to throw it away."

"Well, I changed my mind."

"Come on. Don't be a dick."

"You want it? Then let's make a deal."

I did not know Keith very well, but if what Hunchback told me about Keith being an avid baseball card junkie, I had come prepared.

"I'll give you a Don Money and Clay Dalrymple card for it." Not that either player was a Hall-of-Famer, but they were both Phillies and that made them more valuable.

"Throw in a Cookie Rojas," Keith added as he leaned toward me to see what other cards I had in my stack.

"Don't be greedy. Is it a deal or what? These two cards for the trap that you were throwing away anyway."

"Alright."

Keith agreed and the deal was consummated with a creative North Hills handshake. I stopped by home and grabbed a wilted hunk of iceberg lettuce and a pickled herring to use as bait and headed for

Chollie Mollies. Walking down the path to the fork by the large oak tree, I took the left trail and went into the hollow where the mock orange tree stood. At the base of the tree, I set the cage down and gathered leaves and branches to camouflage the trap. After church the next day I planned on seeing if I had caught anything.

🚲

Church ran longer than usual, and Reverend Markey insisted I follow him into his office so he could give me a biology book he picked up at a flea market.

"Here, Calvin. I got this for you since you said biology was your favorite subject." The book looked like it had been dragged through the dissection of a cat; stains covered the pages.

"Gee, thanks Reverend Markey," I said while quickly exiting his office before anymore conversation could develop.

When we got home, I went to my room to get my play clothes on, haphazardly hanging my dress pants on their wooden hanger. I ran into the kitchen, sliding on the linoleum floor and grabbing the phone's handset as I slid past the phone.

"Muskrat, meet me at the mock orange tree in the woods at Chollie Mollies. Let's see what I caught with Keith's trap," I said with unbridled excitement.

"Beat you there," roared Muskrat as he hung up the phone.

Muskrat had gotten to our meeting place before I did, but since he had no idea where exactly where I had planted the trap, he had no other choice but to wait for me.

"What do you think will be in there?" Muskrat asked while I was still coming down the steep path.

"I dunno. Maybe a fox or a raccoon."

"Oh, Cool! I hope it's a raccoon. We can make hats like Davey Crockett," suggested Muskrat.

"Yeah. That would be cool," I said in agreement.

Before we got to the trap, we could hear the metallic shaking of the cage. Both of our eyes got larger than a Rizzo's pizza as we knew that we had caught something.

"There's something definitely in there," I shouted.

It took a few seconds for it to register in our minds what rodent had been caught since we could not see the animal's face. All we saw was a large ball of grey and white hair. The bottom of the beast was all white.

"What the hell is it?" Muskrat asked with an odd look of trepidation and repulsion on his face.

"It's a muskrat," I answered with a laugh. "You of all people should have been able to recognize it."

Muskrat gave me a hard push as he responded. "Screw you."

Just then the animal turned where we could see its long furless tail and a white-haired face exposing its dark set eyes and pointed snout.

"It's actually a possum," I declared.

"That's boss!" cried Muskrat.

"Hey, your cat got hit by a car last year, didn't it?'

"Yeah. By the time we found it, the thing was flat like a frisbee."

"Do you still have the leash and collar?"

"I think so," said Muskrat.

"Go get it." And with that Muskrat was peddling fast as he could up the dirt trail toward his home.

It did not take long for Muskrat to return with the teal-colored collar, which I thought would look great against the light grey hair of the possum, but getting the collar on the sharp-toothed rodent was going to be harder than we expected.

"I'll take a long stick to hold back its head down while you take another stick with the collar looped and try to lasso it over the possum's head," I suggested.

"I've got a better idea," responded Muskrat. "*I'll* take a long stick to hold back its head while *you* take another stick with the collar looped and try to lasso it over the possum's head."

"I'm the one that came up with this plan and I'm the one that caught this possum. You said you wanted to be a part of this, so this is your part."

Reluctantly, Muskrat found a stick and approached the cage. As he opened the side, the possum displayed its nasty teeth.

"Shit! That thing is rabid! I'm not going to reach my hand down there!" Muskrat cried.

"Quit being a pussy. I've got its head pinned down."

"If it's so easy, you do it!"

I could see that Muskrat was getting a little upset and I knew this was a two-man job, so I relented. "Alright then, grab a larger limb. That one with a fork in it. Hold his head down to the ground. Lower!" With a few attempts I was able to get the collar on the possum with the leash fastened on to it.

"Okay, sloooowly lift the stick," I instructed.

At first, the possum did nothing. It just laid there, but suddenly, as quick as a cricket, the thing made an about face and came straight at us. I dropped the leash and the two of us took off through the woods. We had not run far when Muskrat yelled, "I've gotta get the leash back."

"Relax," I said. "I'll get it back."

Walking cautiously back to the Mock Orange tree we stopped when they heard leaves rustling in a straight-line heading away from the tree.

"There it is! Come on," I shouted.

We ran towards the little mound of leaves bobbing along the bottom of the hollow until we saw the leash. Muskrat stepped on the leash as I picked it up by its looped handle. It didn't take us long to realize that I had to hold the possum at arm's length to keep it from biting my ankles, but after a bit I got the hang of it.

"What are you going to do with it," Muskrat asked.

"Keep it as a pet. How cool would that be? Know anyone who has a pet possum?"

Just then we heard the 5 o'clock whistle, that long siren blasting from the fire house instructing all the North Hills kids that it was time to go home for supper.

"Well, I gotta go, Cal. Let me know if your parents let you keep him."

Keep him? The thought never entered my mind that I would have to convince my parents to let me keep the hairy rodent, but I thought that there was a chance my dad could plead my case for me. I was successful in convincing my dad and Dasha to let me keep an iguana and a puppy, but I was not quite sure how I would make out selling a possum to my parents.

Before I got to our driveway, I could smell chicken-a-la-king coming from Dasha's kitchen, a culinary treat my siblings were not fond of, but I liked the creamy banty. If my sisters and brother did not like what was on tonight's menu that meant there would be more of it for me.

I saw my father with his head buried underneath the Chevy's hood. My dad was one of those depression-era, Word War II, the greatest generation guys that could do anything. Carpentry, masonry, electrical tile work, it did not matter, and if he didn't know how to do it, he would read a book on the subject, tackle the project and the end-result was fantastic. I had a pretty good idea that I would never be able to do a fraction of what my dad could.

"Hey, Dad, look what I caught," I said with fervor.

With his head still extended toward the engine block my dad turned his head to see this undoubtedly irritated rodent hissing and baring its razor-sharp teeth.

"Shit!" He yelled as he jerked his head and caught the latch right at his hairline creating a nasty gash. I had never heard my dad curse and had not seen him that angry since I created an anti-snore powder from Ted's chemistry set which I tested on him while was taking a nap, burning the inside of his nostrils. This was not going to be good.

"What in the world are you doing with a possum?"

"I caught it," I said reluctantly.

"And what do you plan to do with it?" This was not going as well as planned. I had to think of something quickly and suggesting they keep it as a pet was not going to work.

"Uh, I don't know." That answer was not what I expected to come out of my mouth.

"Well, I do," my dad said rather sternly. "You're going to set it free, and nowhere near this house. We kept that rooster way too long."

That was a reference to some blue-dyed chicks we received from Aunt Polina one Easter. I have no idea why so someone would dye them. I guess because it was Easter, anyway, all of the chicks died within a month, even though we made a makeshift incubator with a shade-less lamp, that is, all but one that I had named Cletus. It had grown into a nasty rooster with an attitude. It was always a sight to see Cletus run down to the corner of the property to greet my sisters and brother when they got off the school bus. Their schoolmates would slide down the bus windows a begin singing the theme song to the television show, *Green Acres,* and yelling comments about the Lloyds living on the only farm in suburbia North Hills.

My dad put his head back under the hood of the car. "If your mother sees that thing, you'll never see the light of day."

"She's not my mother," I mumbled as I turned and looked back at the possum which had curled its tail. And with that, I hiked back to Chollie Mollies to release my catch.

CHAPTER SIXTEEN

*Youth is the pollen that blows through the sky and does not
ask why.*
— Stephen Vincent Benét

Autumn was my favorite time of year apart from shorter days, returning to school and raking leaves. The problem with raking leaves is that the longevity of a leafless lawn is solely dependent upon your neighbors having raked their leaves as well, a possibility that never occurred. The smell of burning leaves, chilly nights and warm days, football, apple cider, and...mischief night, the informal holiday which always proved to be a lot more fun than Halloween. For a boy who did not need a reason to pull pranks on people, mischief night was a license to do so in grand ways. Bellamy and I would spend countless hours scheming new and creative ways to have fun at an unexpected victim's expense.

At first, Bellamy's ideas were a little too evil. Starting a fire on someone's porch or shooting an arrow through a homeowner's window would have serious consequences if I got caught. I was tempted. The part about *getting caught* was the teaser. I thought I was too smart to get caught, but jail was a decent deterrent.

Mischief night had its origin in England in the late 1700s when some headmaster encouraged pranksters by selecting a play whose last line made a strong suggestion for children to participate in the shenanigans. In North Hills, the youth had a variety of tomfooleries. When still young, they would inherit the traditional pranks from older kids. Those who had a dog (which was just about everyone in town) would volunteer to pick-up the dog droppings, which should have been the first clue to their mothers that the boys were up to no good.

They would take the yard bombs and place them into a brown paper bag and place it on the front doorstep of someone in the neighborhood, normally someone who would accumulate demerit points for being nasty, or, more specifically, those grouches who would not give the kids their ball back if it accidently ended up in their yard. Often these were the same people who would deliberately be oblivious when their dog would leave curb level scourge on other people's lawns. The same people who would never buy any of the things the local kids were forced to pawn off on their neighbors for football camp, marching band trip, or Girl Scouts. Whatever it was the kids were petitioned to sell, these adults would refuse, and rudely so.

Some of these people we would target were simply scary, living in dark houses with a ton of creepy bent trees with limbs that looked like giant arms ready to grab an unexpected kid. The kids would light the bag full of the dog butt truffles on fire and run behind a tree or bush just in time to see their target stomp on the fire to put it out, getting the rusty nuggets all over their feet. Sometimes they would unknowingly go back in the house with their shoes on. Those moments were precious because, inevitably, the boys would wait just a few minutes, till the stink rose in the people's living room, quickly forcing the homeowner back outside where they would remove their shoes on the steps to clean off later. Not exactly an original prank, but one most of us cut our teeth on. If the pranksters were both ambitious and creative, like my gang, they would come up with more devious tricks.

As planned, Hunchback and Muskrat met me at Joe's Market, a local food store that mothers would send their kids to purchase chip steak, lunchmeat, fresh rolls and the like. A hog farmer was hanging several butchered swine by their back feet on a hook as we watched mesmerized. The hogs disappeared inside the market when a butcher in a white coat pushed the large beasts along a metal rail fixed to the ceiling.

"How cool was that?" Asked Hunchback.

"Very!" I replied.

"Ya know, they call that guy the pigman, not just because he bring those pigs to Joe's Market, but cause he looks like a pig. Did you see his flat nose," Muskrat asked.

"You're crazy," Hunchback said as I started laughing.

"No, seriously. My cousin lives in Lansdale and everyone out there calls him the pigman. Says he doesn't talk much. Just walks around town and grunts."

"Whatever," I said. "Let's go inside and get everything we need."

Inside, the market, we emptied our pockets and consolidated the cash to increase our purchasing power. Muskrat had sixty-seven cents with one of the quarters having chewing gum on it. Hunchback had a dollar and four pennies, and I had a crumbled-up dollar and ninety-two cents in change. We were still a little more than a dollar short of what it would cost to get the "supplies" we needed. As if on cue, Choo-Choo came riding up on his hybrid bike that had both a banana seat and ape-hanger handlebars.

I looked at Hunchback and Hunchback looked at Muskrat.

"Oh no, you aren't! We're not taking Choo-Choo with us. We're bound to get caught if he comes with us," Muskrat adamantly stated.

"Look, it's either Choo-Choo or we have to scrap the entire plan," I explained.

"Hey, guys. What's up," asked Choo-Choo as he skidded into a stop.

"What the heck happened to you?" asked Hunchback. "Your lip is swollen like a bee stung it."

"Oh, it's nuthin'. Max got so excited when I brought him his dinner last night that he jumped up and got me in the mouth with his paw."

"I swear, you are the unluckiest kid around. You're always beat-up one way or another."

Choo-Choo simply shrugged his shoulders as Hunchback pushed open the door to the sound of the little bell and went into the market with the rest of us followed close behind. Immediately, I smelled the familiar fragrance of fresh Italian bread as soon as we entered the store. Walking over to the refrigerated food section we grabbed three of the cheap, IGA brand raw biscuits that came in a tube. We weren't going to spend more money on the Pillsbury biscuits. We had just enough money left over to buy a can of Reddi Whip.

Just down the street from Joe's Market was an empty lot that had a few overgrown bushes. Opening the paper bag, I pulled out the doughy biscuits and cracked open the tubes to a "peuwf" sound. Strategically positioned behind a few tall bushes, we armed ourselves with a raw biscuit in each hand as we began to hurl them at cars driving down Jenkintown Road. When a biscuit hit a car, it would instantaneously stick and make a loud PLUMP sound. Brake lights would light up as the drivers tried to figure out what could have possibly happened to their car as hysterical laughter came from behind the bushes.

Having quickly exhausted our dough throwing ammunition, we turned down Maple Avenue heading toward the old Mrs. Kline's Penny Candy Store, which had closed when Mrs. Kline died the year before. Choo-Choo came up with a brilliant idea to visit Mrs. Cacciatore's house. Mrs. Cacciatore was a woman in her mid-seventies with thick milk-bottle glasses and a heavy mustache. She had two Chihuahuas that were more like cats impersonating dogs, which would never stop yapping, and their yammering could be heard at least two or three blocks before you reached her house. When I would arrive at her house to deliver the weekly newspaper, I was repeatedly instructed by Mrs. Cacciatore not to throw the paper on her lawn because the one time I had, the Mexican rats shredded the paper into confetti. I was clearly told to wait at the gate until she came out of the house, down the sidewalk and to the gate, which often took 20 minutes as she walked in slow motion with a walker. She had lived in the states for over fifty years and still couldn't speak more than a dozen words in English.

When we got a block from the old lady's house, I told my fellow desperados, "You've gotta be stone dead quiet. Those stickin', batty-eyed rats have supersonic ears, and if they hear us and start yapping her flood lights will come on and she'll catch us in the act and call the cops."

We sneaked up the sidewalk and reached the gate as Muskrat slowly opened the latch which made a loud metallic clang.

"Shhhhhhh," I whispered.

As he pushed the open the gate, it made a creaking noise loud enough to wake Rip Van Winkle. Immediately, the Mexican chinchillas started yapping and the porch light came on. The four us jockeyed for position best that we could, crouching low behind Mrs. Cacciatore's prize-winning Rosa Meitronis pale pink rose bushes that she cherished almost as much as the cymbal-clapping monkeys she called dogs. The old lady, dressed in in her housecoat with her hair wrapped in small pink curlers, pulled back the curtains and peered outside.

We waited for what seemed to be half the night until the yellow porch light finally went out.

"I've got a freaking thorn in my ass," cried Muskrat.

"You *are* a pain in my ass," laughed Hunchback.

"Come on, guys," I said. "We can't wake up those barking burritos. Let's get to work."

Mrs. Cacciatore had collected dozens of ceramic figurines that she ordained her lawn with. White and pink rabbits, gnomes, frogs, ducks walking in a line, and a miniature 8-point buck were all strategically positioned around her front yard making it look more like a chaotic menagerie than the cute, artful envy of the neighborhood which is what she was seeking. A lawn jockey whose obvious Negro face had been painted pink, obviously as an attempt not to offend any of the radical black militants who had rioted after the Martin Luther King assignation, welcomed us at the fence gate. Creeping around her lawn, we started gathering all of the ornaments we could carry and went a block down the street to Judy Green's house and placed them all over her front yard. We had to make four trips to get all of Mrs. Cacciatore's paraphernalia off her lawn and onto the Judy's yard, but we accomplished our task. Mrs. Cacciatore's front yard was naked and the Greene's looked like a yard sale.

By the time our crew had finished rearranging of lawn fixtures it was well past our curfew, and we needed to head home, but there was one more mischief night prank we wanted to pull off, but, unfortunately, the weather had not cooperated.

🚴

We three amigos waited for an entire week until the weatherman promised that it would rain pitchforks beginning that Thursday night. Just after dinner the three of us met at Muskrat's house. Hunchback had just gotten his driver's permit, but his brother did not want to chaperone while Hunchback taxied his friends around North Hills to play pranks. We would have to trek it on foot. Muskrat grabbed his little brother's jumbo bottle of Mr. Bubble and stuffed it in his jacket as he told his parents that we were heading to Chollie Mollie's to shoot hoops. Instead, we headed to Tommy Carson's house to send a little message.

Tommy had once been a part of our gang. He hung out with us, played and went to school with us and even attended the same church as I did. When he moved to North Hills from somewhere within the five boroughs of New York, City, Hunchback, Muskrat, and I befriended him, and even though he spoke with that funny way that New Yawker's tawk, we made him feel like he belonged. His mother was a nagging old lady who made his father move from city to city because she was never satisfied with any job or promotion he would get. The truth be known, she was embarrassed by his lack of achievement and always thought she had married down.

In any case, when the Hunchback's parents got divorced Tommy wanted nothing to do with him, or any of the guys that hung out with Hunchback. His decision to alienate Hunchback stemmed from his family's belief to *shun* sinners. It was as though his association with the Hunchback would cause his parents to divorce. He treated his former friends like they were lepers, so on this night our motive was to help Tommy *clean up* his act.

The rain was not supposed to start until after midnight, which was perfect for our plan. We crept quietly around Tommy's front yard, each of us holding our weapon of choice, a large bottle of Mr. Bubble. Our thinking was that one bottle would not do much damage, so we bought another bottle at Joe's Market. We poured the bottles of Mr. Bubble all over the front lawn and the driveway, but it seemed anticlimactic because, obviously, nothing happened, but with the weather report promising torrential rain we promised to meet in front of Tommy's before school the next day to see the how many suds would appear. The anticipation was unbearable.

Early the next morning I threw on my favorite blue jeans and my red and white striped polo shirt, half tied my P.F. Flyers and flew down the stairs stepping on every third or fourth step. Grabbing the curved end of the banister I swung 180 degrees and slid into the kitchen while grabbing my denim jacket I had left on a kitchen chair.

"Where do you think you're going young man?" Dasha demanded an answer.

"I promised I'd meet Hunchback and Muskrat so we could walk to school together."

"How many times have I told you not to call Bobby and Larry by those horrible names."

"Aw, they're alright with them, Mom." And then Dasha said those magic words that were sweet music to my ears. "You never brought in the trash cans when you got home from school yesterday, Calvin. It rained so hard last night they're probably overflowing with water. Before you head off to meet your friends, I want you to bring in those cans…and don't forget to put on your rubbers on!"

My mind sprinted. *It rained? Not only did it rain, it rained hard enough to activate the full fury of Mr. Bubble! And what is it with calling those waterproof overshoes, rubbers? Really? The rest of the world calls them galoshes, but Dasha calls them rubbers. She might as well have called them condoms, raincoats, frangers, sheaths, fishnets, love gloves or party hats!*

Muskrat was already at the corner of Elm and Hawthorne—riding around in circles on his Schwinn Lemon Peeler Krate Stingray, the coolest bicycle in town. There were even racing stripes on his banana seat! Hunchback could be seen a few blocks down Elm.

"Hurry up!" yelled Muskrat. "We've gotta get over to Tommy's house before school starts!"

"Look!" Hunchback said as he pointed toward the sky.

A gentle breeze was carrying some bubbles a block from where we were—as we approached the bubbles they would rise, as if climbing stairs, moving six or seven feet above our heads in a parallel plane and then climb a few feet higher with the help of the cool wind.

"Damn, and we're still three blocks away from Tommy's!"

As we got closer to Tommy's house, clouds of bubbles were rolling like sagebrush down Hazel Street, and when we were still a block away what we saw was beyond what any of us could have anticipated...or hoped for. Coming straight down the street was a tsunami of bubbles at least ten feet high, wide enough to cover the entire street and sidewalks.

"Jumping Josephat! Are you kidding me?" I yelled.

Each of us stood there stunned, eyes and mouths equally opened in exaggerated poses.

"Crap! What did you guys do with your empty bottles of Mr. Bubble?" I asked in an interrogating way.

"I chucked mine into an empty trash can on the way home," Muskrat answered.

"What about you, Hunchback?"

Hunchback stood there, head down, staring at his sneakers.

"Oh, no! You didn't?"

"Well, there was still a little left in the bottom and my mother always makes me take a bath on Saturday nights, so I thought it would be cool to try Mr. Bubble."

"You had better go home and get that bottle right now before your parents put 2 and 2 together."

"I'll be late for school."

"What is worse, getting detention for being late to class, or getting hammered big time for the massive suds and taking us down with you? Here, take Muskrat's bike."

"Oh no, he ain't!" insisted Muskrat.

"Come on! We will be grounded through summer vacation if our parents find out. If Hunchback takes your bike, he can get home, destroy the evidence, and still make it to school before the bell rings."

"Aw, alright," Muskrat said hesitantly.

Hunchback did make it to school in time, barely. After school we dropped by the iconic Plockies Penny Candy Store located inside the Texaco Gas Station to buy some grape balls before heading home. The three of us leaned on top of the glass display case until Mr. Nelson asked us to take a step back as he took a white cloth from his back pocket and wiped our fingerprints off the glass. Hunchback bought a packet of Nik-L-Nip which contained five little sweet liquid-filled wax bottles, a packet of Pixie Sticks and some satellite wafers. Muskrat bought a pack of Marlboro and Jolly Viceroy bubble gum cigarettes and a packet of Razzles. I went for a couple of strips of candy buttons and a half dozen grape balls.

We decided to go by Tommy's house to see if the suds had disappeared, but when we arrived, we saw that the mountain of suds had clearly dropped a good 5 or 6 feet, but it was still a spectacle. Maybe that is why we didn't see Tommy at first. We could hear the "swish-swish" of the broom Tommy was using to sweep the clouds of suds off his driveway when Tommy looked up and saw the three of us staring at him with broad smiles. For a second, the three of us just stood there staring. Then, as if on cue, we broke into hysterical laughter.

"You guys are ass-holes," yelled Tommy. "I know you did it!"

How do you let someone know that you will gladly take credit for an incredibly creative hoax without letting them know you did it? We simply walked up Hazel Avenue arm-in-arm smiling smiles of a job well done.

CHAPTER SEVENTEEN

Advise persons never to engage in killing.
—Billy the Kid

I had spent the following weekend up at Aunt Polina's farm to do some archery hunting. I had bagged a doe during rifle season the previous year, but my archery skills had improved, and I wanted to try my luck at more skilled hunting.

Even though Hunchback did not hunt, he had heard stories about my aunt who lived without the modern comforts of the civilized world and wanted to experience it firsthand, so he gave me a ride. I warned him that he might have to clean the chicken coop while I was hunting, but he did not seem to care. We arrived after dinner as the sun was setting over the rolling hills spreading a blanket of orange and yellow across the darkened cornfield. Aunt Polina was fetching a pail of water from the spring as we pulled up to the small farmhouse. I introduced my friend to her, and she was able to repeat Larry's name with a heavy accent.

I took the pail of water from her as we entered the house. A strong odor of mildew and dampness mixed with cabbage hit us we walked into the small dining room. Marko was dragging two stained mattresses down the stairs.

"Hey there, Calvin. Heard you are going to try and get a buck with a bow. If you walk below the apple orchard, you'll see tracks the deer have made. They come up at dusk to steal as many apples they can gorge themselves on. Kill as many as you can," he said with a chuckle. "Sorry, but you two will have to sleep on the floor. We only have two beds."

"No problem, Marko" I said. "This is my friend, Larry. He doesn't hunt, but he was good enough to give me a ride."

"Welcome to our country abode, Larry."

"Thanks, Marko," Larry said, as he tried to take in his surroundings.

I wound up my alarm clock, and we settled in for the evening since there was no tv to watch.

The alarm went off at five o'clock as Hunchback rolled over with a groan. I quickly put on my camouflaged clothes and went outside to retrieve my bow and arrows from Hunchback's car. I sprayed myself with a scent elimination liquid and grabbed my bottle of doe-in-rut estrus deer attractant that I would trickle on a few trees nearby where I would set my tree stand.

Strapping my tree stand to my back, I walked through the orchard and into a wooded area with my flashlight low to the ground. It did not take long for me to see the first buck rub; the bark of a three-year-old ash had been stripped clean at the height of the buck. A good sign. Deer droppings littered the trail and footprints were visible in an area where mud had dried hard. I found a large oak tree that overlooked an open valley and began climbing it with my stand. At about 18 feet up I found a good spot to position my stand and settled in for sunrise.

It did not feel chilly when I was lugging everything through the woods, but now that I had been sitting for a while, I could feel the chill through my jacket. I wanted to pull up the collar on my jacket, but any movement would easily have been seen by a cautious buck. It slowly began to get light, even before the first rays of the sun bounced through the crowded trees. It was then that I saw the first deer, a doe, as she slowly walked into the open area in the valley, her head down, looking for food, and then up again to survey the area. A second doe entered the opening, followed by a third and a fourth. When the rangale had exited the woods and gathered in the valley there was a total of eight deer, but all were doe. At least 15 minutes passed before I saw the girth of a much larger deer guardedly enter the area previously occupied by the doe. His antlers were high and wide, but I could not count the number of points from the hundred or so yards where I was sitting. Isn't that just like a guy to have the girl make sure the coast is clear?

When I saw the first doe enter the woods on my side of the valley, I knew the rest would follow, single file. As they deliberately walked on the path toward my tree stand, I slowly stood and picked up my bow; my breathing becoming heavy. My thin camouflaged mask concealed my breath as I exhaled into the cold air. The lead doe stopped just short of my tree stand and raised her head high and rotated its ears toward me as she stiffed the air. Apparently, my scent was not completely disguised. The others in line stopped and waited for her analysis. After a few minutes she was satisfied and continued walking past my position with the others slowly following her.

My breathing increased in a futile attempt to catch-up with my rapid heartbeat. I knew that I would have the opportunity I had longed for. When the eighth deer entered my space, I drew back my bow before the buck was visible. Within seconds, he appeared. His neck thick and a huge rack that totaled eleven points. My lethal shooting range was 30 yards and I waited till he entered that distance and released the arrow. The buck jumped wildly and ran off to my left into some dense brush.

I was not sure I had hit the deer, but I waited a full 30 minutes before quietly climbing down from the tree. Walking over to the spot where the buck had been, I saw hair and a small pool of blood. A dozen yards farther I found my arrow which was drenched in blood. I began walking in the directions the deer had ran and soon found a blood trail and spots of blood on leaves and thin branches. After walking about 40 yards, I saw the trophy lying in a hollow. I kicked it with my boot to make sure it was dead.

There is a strange sense of power to have a living thing's life in your hands; to have the power to decide whether something lives or dies. To kill or not to kill. It is an opportunity to play God. For me, one who lacked *power* in just about all aspects of my life, this was exhilarating. I was in control of a living thing's destiny. The sense of accomplishment of bagging a trophy buck did not compare to the authority and supremacy I felt.

Hunchback helped me drag the deer back to the farmhouse, and Marko helped us hang it in the barn where I butchered it. I gave Aunt Polina several roasts and steaks and wrapped the remainder to take home.

I had cleared the plates from the supper table when the phone rang. "I'll get it," I announced to anyone listening.

"Cal, it's me," Muskrat said with uneasiness in his voice. "My dad said he had to take care of a few things after dinner. I think we need to follow him."

"But if he takes his car, how are we going to trail him?"

"I called Hunchback. He's on his way to pick you up. I'm walking down to the corner, and he's picking me up there. We'll just wait there until we see his car, and we'll follow him."

Muskrat hadn't finished his sentence when there was a knock on the door. I could hear my stepmother welcoming Larry.

"Hunchback just got here. See you in five," I said as I hung up the phone.

Muskrat was waiting exactly where he said he would be when we pulled up.

"Get in the back," Muskrat said to me. "I need to have a full visual."

I did not argue as he pulled the seat back forward and slid through to the backseat.

We did not have to wait long before we saw Mr. Zimmerman pull out in his Cortex Gold Buick Electra and head down Edge Hill Road. He made a left on to Jenkintown Road, past Joe's Market, and a short distance later pulled into the 19th Hole, a nondescript building of yellow painted stucco and dark tinted windows that was a popular watering hole on the corner of Jenkintown Road and North Hills Avenue. The owner was well-known, not just in the North Hills/Ardsley communities, but throughout the Philadelphia entertainment industry for promoting concerts like Tom Jones, The

Soul Survivors, Blind Faith, and The Young Rascals. The question was, what was Mr. Zimmerman doing at the popular night club?

"Maybe he's picking up chicks here," suggested Hunchback.

"I swear I'll kill him. I'll borrow your father's shotgun and kill him, Cal." Hunchback and I had never heard Muskrat with such venom in his voice.

"And maybe he went in there to have a drink," I suggested. "Does your mom allow alcohol in the house?"

"Just wine and beer."

"Well, there you have it. He wanted a few high balls to let off some steam. That's all," I said in an attempt to bring some reason to the conversation.

"That doesn't explain the weight loss, the new clothes, the whispering phone calls. One of you have to go in there and check out what he's doing."

"Right. We're 16 and there's a bouncer at the door. We'll never get past him and into the bar," Hunchback said as he turned to me in the backseat. "You try, Cal. You can get yourself in anywhere." A bizarre statement that I was the only one of the three of us that looked two years younger than I was.

"Yeah," I responded. "And I can get myself into trouble, and this has trouble spelled all over it." Wanting to live up to the high opinion of my two compatriots and afraid of my warped mentality that if I did not *perform*, I would be minus the only two pseudo-friends I had. Spoken or unspoken peer pressure had a great influence on me. In retrospect, it is somewhat funny that I would succumb to another's suggestion or request to engage in a specific behavior. It is a sign of weakness, which I avoided at all costs. But the fear of not being accepted trumped any logical reasoning.

I quickly began stretching my brain to come up with an idea that would sanction my newly crowned title of being the creative and intrepid point man. "I need a cardboard box," I said looking at my two partners in crime.

"We just bought a Big Wheel for my kid sister. I was supposed to breakdown the box this afternoon, but I got the call from Muskrat,"

Hunchback said with more than a little excitement in his voice. "What are you going to do with it?"

"You'll see. Let's drive over to your house and get it before someone smashes it flat," I said.

By the time we got back to the 19th Hole, more cars had appeared in the parking lot, but Muskrat's father's Buick was still where he had parked it. I closed the lid to the box and walked toward the entrance to the bar with a stride of confidence. The bouncer was a behemoth of a man, standing 6 foot 4 and a girth that blocked the setting sun.

"What have you got there?" he asked me as if he was expecting a delivery.

"Just napkins, stirrers, coasters. You know, the normal stuff," I answered nonchalantly.

"Well, you can't come in the front. I'll have someone open the back door for you."

"Okay," I replied as I walked back down the steps toward the parking lot.

"He got shot down," Hunchback said without taking his eyes off me.

"Wait. You know Cal. He's not one to take no for an answer," Muskrat said with confidence in his voice.

They watched as I walked around the building and disappeared from their vantage point around the back of the taproom. By the time I had reached the back door, it was already cracked open. I opened the door with my foot and saw a woman wearing a tight white midriff and equally tight jeans.

"Do I need to sign for this?" she asked me while looking me over.

"Nope. It's just a backorder. Hey, can I use the bathroom?"

"Make it quick. Kids are not supposed to be in the bar. It's around the pool table and to the right. Underneath the Schaefer Beer sign."

I put down the box, exited the storage room and entered the bar. Not wanting Muskrat's father to recognize me, I pulled my Phillies cap down low over my brow, tilting the bill to hide as much of my face as I could. Turning toward the row of bar chairs, I immediately spotted Mr. Zimmerman pouring a glass of Wild Turkey for a patron from behind the bar. Having seen what I came for, I forgot the bathroom and exited the backdoor. Not wanting to get caught delivering an empty box, I sprinted toward Hunchback's car.

"Let's get out of here. Quick!!!" I directed as I slid into the backseat.

As we were pulling out of the parking lot, Muskrat turned around to me and said, "Well?"

"Your dad is a bartender."

"What?"

"I guess he has a part-time job. He was pouring drinks behind the bar."

"That doesn't make any sense. Why didn't he tell mom? And where does he go during the day when he doesn't go to work? We need to follow him again the next time he ventures off on a day fieldtrip," a confused Muskrat mumbled to himself as much as to the two of us.

🚲

I could hear Cletus crowing even before the sun got out of bed. It would be the last time I would hear his wake-up call. In retrospect, I cannot believe at how naïve I had been. Sometimes I had difficulty grasping the obvious. Like the time our dog Chief, a beautiful boxer, bit a kid who had insistently taunted him by riding his bicycle just beyond the dog's reach. The very next day my dad had to send the dog to "a farm" to live out his days. Yeah, he went to a farm like Roseanne Barr went to finishing school. Cletus was supposed to head back to Aunt Mary's farm but that evening, dinner consisted of broccoli, mashed potatoes, applesauce, and roasted chicken—*very fresh* roasted chicken.

🚲

The next day I headed for Chollie Mollies to meet Muskrat and Hunchback. They got to the Havahart cage before I did and were more animated than usually. "We got another possum!" They yelled.

It's the same one," I said.

"You're crazy," replied Muskrat. "There's gotta be hundreds of possums in these woods. How do you know it's the same one?"

"Look at him. I'd recognize him anywhere. It sure looks like the same one, but we've gotta let it go. I can't bring it home, that's for sure. We have to keep trying till we catch a fox. That will be the ultimate!"

"Yeah!" shouted Hunchback. "Hey, if we put that cat collar on it, we'll know if it's the same one."

"Are you crazy?" Muskrat shouted without taking his eyes off the marsupial. "We had a hell of a time getting a collar on that thing the first time; besides, if the possum never comes back, we've lost the collar and my mom will kill me. She's been really edgy lately. I've been keeping my distance from her. I do not need anything else to set her off. Damn! Look at those teeth!"

Just then I smiled one of my patented smiles. There is more than one way to skin an armadillo! I have got an idea how we can prove whether it's the same possum we keep catching," I said as I jumped on my bicycle. "Wait here. I'll be back in 10 minutes. Find a good stick with a Y in it. We're gonna need it." And with that I was out of the saddle, peddling as fast as I could back home.

"Anybody home?" I yelled as I cased-out the house before deciding how to get that which was crucial to my possum identification plan.

"Me," Ted answered. "I'm going to practice the piano so if you're planning on screwing around, go downstairs."

"I just need to pick something up. I'm going back to Chollie Mollies."

Quietly, I entered my parent's bedroom, a place strictly off-limits, and opened the top drawer to Dasha's dresser, surprised by the large selection of rainbow-colored nail polishes. Who would have thought nail polishes come in so many different colors? After a quick scan of my choices, I decided on coral orange. Closing the drawer, I put the bottle in my pocket and was back on my bike, all in less than 5 minutes. When I arrived back at the trap, Muskrat had found the stick with the Y and was trimming one of its ends with a pen knife to make both sides uniform.

"Whatcha got," Hunchback asked as I pulled out the small glass bottle.

"Nail polish. We're gonna paint his toenails. We'll know for sure if this guy is the same possum we keep catching."

"That's awesome," Muskrat said as he laughed riotously.

I opened the hatch and Muskrat pinned the possum's head down when he came out of the cage. Quickly, I painted all its nails and then set the hairy rodent free.

"Bait the cage and let's come back tomorrow," I said as we watched the possum slip underneath a fallen hemlock.

As I have stated, Dasha always had chores for me to do on Saturdays before there would be any free time. This Saturday was no exception. It was after twelve before I knew it and needed to call Muskrat to discuss another one of my ingenious plans. That is, if we should catch the possum again, but I decided to head over to his house instead. Walking over to a shelf above my desk, I retrieved a book about child psychology entitled *The Aggressive Child*, I had purchased for a dollar at a flea market held in the fire company's parking lot. The book was 3 inches thick, which had been perfect for my purposes. I had hollowed out the inside, leaving the front pages intact, so that I could have a special hiding place for all the secret items in my life. Of course, they had to be smaller items that would fit within the book. A pack of Marlboros, money I had been saving, my favorite pen knife, and a stack of Bazooka bubble gum wrappers I was saving for a free magnet set. For 150 Bazooka wrappers I was promised 2 magnets, 2 metal balls, a wooden dowel, and a magic tricks instruction sheet. I had about 90 wrappers saved and had them secured them with paper clips in lots of ten. I grabbed the pack of cigarettes and placed the book back on the shelf. Upstairs, I could hear Dasha asking my father if he had seen her coral orange nail polish. With that, I headed to Muskrat's.

Muskrat's mother said he and Hunchback were in the family room watching television. When entering the room, I saw they were watching *Wild, Wild West* and drinking Yoo Hoo, so I grabbed a seat without saying anything. That episode was called *"The Night of the Sedgewick Curse"*, a story about a family suffering from rapid aging and the family doctor, trying to find a cure, began kidnapping people with the same malady to test his serum on them. Needless to say, the three of us were riveted to our seats.

When the show ended, I began to share my plan for the expectant rodent capture.

"Guys, if our possum shows up with the painted toenails, let's sell it."

"Sell it," responded Hunchback, "who in their right minds is going to buy a possum?"

"A stupid city person," I answered. "People are always driving down Edge Hill Road when they are coming from Cheltenham or Chestnut Hill. I'm telling you, if we put a sign on the cage that says *Free Cat*, some fool will take the bait."

The three of us fell about laughing and as one of us would stop, the other's laughter just made him laugh again harder.

"Alright, but let's first stop by Plockies for some candy," suggested Hunchback.

As we approached the Texaco gas station that doubled as Plockies Penny Candy Store, a car pulled in and parked next to the gas pumps. A man stepped out of the car and told the attendant to fill it up.

"Cal, how are you?"

To say I was startled would have been a poor choice of words. I was completely drenched in fear. Not to hear my name called unexpectedly, but by who it was that had called my name. When I turned my head, I saw Perry who had stopped to get gas. With a heightened panic washing over me like an august rainstorm, I turned away, ignoring Perry, and quickly opened the door to Plockies and went inside.

"Hey Cal, that queer is calling you," Hunchback said as he grabbed my arm.

"No, he didn't!" I retorted.

"Oh, yes he did!" Muskrat said chiming in. "I think he likes you."

"I deliver the *Glenside News* to his house, you moron! That is how he knows me. Screw him!" I said defensively.

"I think that is exactly what he wants to do to you, Cal. To screw you," laughed Hunchback.

"Very funny. Are you going to buy some candy or are you going to audition for *Laugh-In?*" I responded.

Perry had a look of disappointment on his face as he gave the attendant a sawbuck and got back into his car as he waited for his change.

🚲

The three of us headed over to Chollie Mollie's and headed down the trail to where we had left the trap. We could see grey hairs protruding from the wire mesh and knew they had another catch.

"Look! I told you! It *is* the same possum! Painted toenails don't lie," I yelped.

Muskrat fell to his knees and threw his head back and tried to talk between bouts of laughter. "Let's take it to Edge Hill Road and see if anyone stops for a free pet."

We put the possum in a cardboard box and propped the sign against a large oak that read, FREE CAT as we sat and watched the cars drive by. Reaching into our paper sacks we continued eating tootsie rolls, grape balls, and strawberry licorice waiting for a car to stop and accept the free pet.

An hour and a half past and we were discussing releasing our wild friend, when an AMC Gremlin with New York plates pulled over a good hundred yards past where we were sitting, as if from a delayed reaction. Putting the car in reverse a man with a Yankees cap stopped in front of us and rolled down his window. "Is that cat really for free?"

"Yeah," answered Hunchback. "We are moving and not allowed to take it with us. We're looking for a good home for it."

"That's a weird looking cat," the man said looking into the box. "What kind is it?"

"A Long Nose Vietnamese mouser." I answered. "They're very rare."

"Wow. Okay, I'll take it. Thanks, boys!" The man said as he got out of his car, put the box in the back of his hatchback and drove off.

🚲

It seemed as though Cookie had gotten old without anyone noticing. I knew that she did not chase balls like she once did. She would spend her days lying either in the sun or shade and slowly walking between the two. She had thick, cloudy cataracts over both eyes and money was not going to be spent having them removed. Her movements were restricted to those areas of the house she had memorized. *Thank goodness Dasha never rearranges the furniture.* When she had difficulty standing, Bellamy knew it was time.

"You've gotta do the right thing, Cal. The poor thing is in misery."

She had adapted well to having only three legs, but now she labored with every movement. I looked at Cookie with a plea of forgiveness, knowing that I was to blame for her pain and disfigurement. A plea for forgiveness; a familiar song.

One Saturday morning I insisted that I accompany my dad to the veterinarian's office. When we arrived, I told him that I wanted to take care of the rest; after all, Cookie was my dog.

I slid my arms underneath her warm belly and lifted her slowly. As I cradled her in my arms, she looked up at me, sad-like, as if she knew what was waiting for her on the other side of the paneled door. Thankfully, I felt Bellamy's reassuring hand on my shoulder as I walked up to the counter. A little folded sign was next to a candle which read, *If this candle is lit, someone is saying goodbye to their beloved pet. We ask that you speak softly and with respect during this difficult time.* The candle was not lit.

I knew it was the right thing to do. My thoughts were filled with justification for what I was about to do. I kept telling myself that she could barely walk outside to relieve herself and how she was in pain just trying to stand…and none of that mattered. My mind was like a flip book animation with pictures of Cookie running and playing with me and the times she would snuggle in my lap to take a nap. I was ending a relationship forever. And for a guy who had few *meaningful* relationships, this was no small task. It dawned on me that I had the power to snuff out a life.

"Is this Cookie," the receptionist asked.

"Yeah," I said without taking my eyes off my friend.

"Would you like to say your goodbyes here or do you want to go in the back with her?"

Without hesitation I said, "I'll go back with her." *At least I would be the last person she would see as she drifted off to wherever dogs go when they die.*

As I was escorted into an examining room, I placed Cookie on the table and stroked her head which had become more white than tan. The doctor explained that there would be two injections, the first would be a sedative that would make Cookie extremely relaxed and sleepy before he administered the lethal drug. I was fine with all of that. Cookie was lying on the cold metal examining table as I continued to stroke her forehead and behind her ears. After her eyes closed, it was only a matter of a minute or so and she was gone. Death would soon be a too familiar entity that would define my life.

Once we got home, I jumped on my bike and headed for Simone's. I had been seeing her sparingly, trying to convince myself that she was *just* a friend. I wanted to be with Simone because, other than Bellamy or Perry, she would be someone who would listen and not offer limp sympathies. She would understand. My emotions were conflicted. My dog was one of my true friends. Never criticized me. Always eager to spend time with me. Forgave me before I even asked to be forgiven. *Loved me!*

I had the remarkable ability to compartmentalize, that is, when I wanted to. I was deeply saddened to see Cookie put down and yet I had the calming acceptance that I did the right thing and that my timing was right. The decision was not rushed, and I had not let her suffer from selfish reluctance to keep her alive.

Before I could knock on Simone's door her mother opened the door. She had been sweeping the enclosed porch and had seen me coming up the walk.

"Hello Calvin. I assume you are here to see Simone?"

"Yes, Mrs. Arnett."

Mrs. Arnett turned and yelled toward the stairs. "Simone? Simone, honey! You have a guest."

I could hear Simone's feet before I could see her legs appear from the narrow stairs from the second floor. First, I saw her blue tennis shoes, then her caramel-colored legs. Her pale-yellow shorts came into view, a skinny blue belt and then a blue and yellow stripped pullover top with 4 buttons became visible, the first 3 buttons undone exposing the slightest hint of cleavage. I had forgotten about Cookie.

I had become a superb actor and each day selected who I would become, dependent upon the audience of that moment. There was always a deep-rooted fear of being completely myself; naked and transparent. I was afraid that if I simply reacted to life rather than acting within it, I would never be accepted or loved. This facade met less criticism than my authentic self, and so I learned to evaluate a scene and play the part that best suited that situation. I had become an emotional contortionist, but with Simone I could, surprisingly, be *more* myself.

"Hey there," Simone said with a smile.

"Hey. Are you doing anything?" I asked.

"I was reading a book."

"What were you reading?" I wondered what kind of book intrigued this beautiful creature. Her answer would tell me more of her "inner workings," so I thought.

"*The Left Hand of Darkness*, by Ursula K. Le Guin. It's science-fiction."

I was not a reader back then and had only read one science fiction book, but it was enough to add credibility to the conversation. "I like Ray Bradbury. Ever read *Something Wicked this way Comes?*"

"Oh, yes! That's a great book. I loved how the characters would get younger or older depending upon which direction the merry-go-round went. Have you ever read his *Dandelion Wine*?"

"No." I wanted to talk about something else besides literary preferences since I would only be able to talk intelligibly on that subject for less than a minute.

Simone sensed my short attention span that had already left the conversation and entered another room where she was not. "You would like it. What did you do this morning?"

"I had to put Cookie down." I suddenly realized that Simone had never been to my house. She had never met my parents, my brother or sisters, or my dog, and she probably never would. I was not going to put myself in yet another situation to be ridiculed and criticized. After all, what would they think of my attraction to a *colored* girl? I knew exactly what they would think. I thought there was only one race; the human race.

"I'm so sorry, Cal. Was Cookie your dog?"

"Yeah. She could not stand anymore without shaking uncontrollably. She started peeing in the house. She just got old."

Simone leaned over and kissed me on the cheek. Surprised, I looked into Simone's eyes, cupped my hand beneath her chin and kissed her on her lips. She opened her mouth, and we kissed with desire and purpose. I felt the compression in my pants and placed one hand over my crotch to hide my protuberant reaction. As cool as the November afternoon was, the warmth of Simone's body in my arms was more than I needed to stay sheltered from the cold. I held her face in my hands as I looked at her lovely nut-brown eyes and raven-black hair. I breathed in deeply and caught a trace of her perfume, having the notes of jasmine, freesia, and apple blossom that I always enjoyed whenever I had been close to Simone. I couldn't remember a time when I felt like this, suspended above all that burdened my life, for now all those things seemed mundane.

It seemed as though Simone, unexpectedly, felt validated. She was no longer invisible. She had value because I valued her. I'm guessing she thought that it was funny that that is all it took. I remembered a Pablo Neruda poem she had shared with me and was wondering if she was reciting it in her head as she gazed at me:

I love you without knowing how, or when, or from where. I love you straightforwardly, without complexities or pride; so I love you because I know no other way than this: where I does not exist, nor you, so close that your hand on my chest is my hand, so close that your eyes close as I fall asleep.

If Simone felt validated, I felt that I had found a safe place where I belonged, not so out of place. I had felt safe with Perry, but there was always that issue of his sexuality. Simone was my first true love, my only love. Well, there was Donna Brantley, but she did not count. She was the first girl I had kissed, but we were only six years old, and it was a spontaneous expression of appreciation, not "love." This was different. It felt like a clean undershirt that had just come out of the dryer; it felt warm, and it fit.

Simone turned to me, smiling with her eyes that could not contain her delight. We shared a moment that we could call our own. We did not have to share it with anyone and, in fact, anyone adding to the equation would have detracted from what it was. *Perfect.* We spent the afternoon laughing and sharing intimacies and touching, innocently and honestly. Neither of us wanted the moment to end, but the 5 o'clock whistle abruptly interrupted our reverie and thrusted us back into reality.

"I've got to go," I said matter-of-factly.

"NO!" Simone said as she threw her head back carelessly and laughed. "No, no, a zillion times no!" I looked at Simone and smiled. "I know you must go. Come back to me tomorrow?"

"Of course, I will. And the day after that and the day after that," I said as I stood up, leaned over, kissed her again.

CHAPTER EIGHTEEN

I know many 80-year-old children and 14-year-old adults.

A s I entered high school everything seemed to be changing; however, the war in Vietnam remained constant. I became more interested in the endless war and began thinking of the draft and my ever-diminishing chances of getting into college. Even classmates who had no interest in college were making plans to attend as a deterrent from the draft. Picking up the *Philadelphia Inquirer*, I read about Colonel Ripley and 600 South Vietnamese who were ordered to "hold and die" against 20,000 North Vietnamese soldiers with about 200 tanks, what seemed like an impossible task. The only way to stop the enormous force was to destroy the bridge.

I had been fascinated with the television show *Combat*, that covered the grim lives of a squad of American soldiers fighting the Germans in France during World War II, but this was Vietnam. An increasing number of the American population were protesting the unpopular war and heroes were demonized instead of honored. The perfect kind of war for me, I thought.

The phone rang twice before I picked up the pine-green receiver. "Now!" Muskrat said only the one word and hung up the phone. The three of us had it planned out thoroughly. No wasted time. I grabbed my father's binoculars, part of my responsibilities, told my parents that Hunchback needed help changing the manifold in his car, another pre-planned performance, and headed to the corner where Hunchback and Muskrat would pick me up. I got into the back seat and listened as Muskrat gave his synopsis of the situation.

"Dad said he is taking the day off from work to run some errands. I think he's wise to mom finding out where he goes when he takes a day off and doesn't tell her. She has been calling his office more and more to check on him. Anyway, mom asked him what errands he must run and he said, 'Schneider's Hardware, Pep Boys and a couple of other places.' We'll see about that."

We pulled into the parking lot of Mt. Carmel Church and began debating what Mr. Zimmerman could be up to, but this only added to Muskrat's anxiety. It seemed like an eternity before we saw the Electra passing the church.

"There he is. Follow him," barked Muskrat.

"Aye aye, Captain," answered Hunchback as he offered a sarcastic salute.

We followed the Buick for a short while when it pulled in front of the Schneider's hardware store.

"He said he was going to the hardware store and, guess what? He's at the hardware store," Hunchback said as he appeared to be tiring of the detective game.

"Of course he is at the hardware store. He has to bring something home to cover his lie," responded Muskrat brusquely.

Muskrat's father got out of the car and as he approached the door to the hardware store he dropped his keys, taking three attempts to finally pick them up. Ten minutes later he came out of the store with a bag in his hand, got back into his car, and drove off. My friends and I tailed him, three cars behind, as we followed through Glenside and into the town of Abington. Not much was said between us as we watched our suspect park his car at a building across the street from the hospital. Muskrat's father got out of the car and entered the building.

"What's that sign say?" I asked as while stretching from my position in the back seat to see better.

"I can't see. We're at a bad angle," Muskrat said as he stretched his head out the window.

We became bored having waited for over an hour when it was Hunchback that first saw Muskrat's father come out of the building. Mr. Zimmerman stood there looking up at the sky and looking pensive when an attractive brunette with perfectly shaped legs wearing a white lab coat came outside. Mr. Zimmerman must have known her because they stood there talking for several minutes.

"Do you think she's a nurse?" asked Muskrat.

"Probably," I answered. "She's pretty hot."

Muskrat was about to hit me for my less-than-encouraging comment when we saw his father reach out to woman and give her a hug which he held for, what seemed like, a very lengthy amount of time.

"Bastard!" Muskrat yelled as he opened the car door and ran over to his father.

I reached for Muskrat's shoulder wanting to talk some sense into him, but he was already halfway to where the woman and his father were standing. His father didn't see him until he was a few steps away.

"Larry, what are..."

"What the hell are you doing here and who is she?" Muskrat said as he pointed at the woman without taking his eyes off his father.

"Calm down, Larry. This is not what it looks like. Can we talk about this at home?"

"No, we can't talk about this at home," Muskrat answered in a sing-song tone. "And what it looks like is that you've been sneaking around to meet with...her! We've all known you've got some big secret. It's been pretty obvious with the way you've been acting. Do you think we're stupid? Sneaking off to your underground meetings. Getting a part-time job as a bartender. Changing your appearance my losing weight and growing a beard. No more bullshit! Is this your girlfriend?"

"You have it all wrong, Larry. I wanted to share this with your mom first, but obviously, I need to clear the air. This is Dr. Bradford, my neurologist."

"Neurologist?" Whispered Muskrat as the doctor touched Mr. Zimmerman's shoulder and turned to go back into the building, giving the two some privacy.

"Son, I have ALS, Lou Gehrig's disease. Dr. Bradford has been treating me. I haven't tried to lose weight. It's just been happening. I grew a beard to help hide my drawn look. I took a part-time job just so I can save as much as I can for your mom and you kids before I wouldn't have the energy or coordination to work any longer. I had to quit that bartending job last week because my coordination has become poor and I kept dropping glasses and bottles of booze. I'm sorry, Larry."

🚲

Muskrat's preconceived notions were unfounded. He had believed the worst about his father. Heck, we all did. There are times when those under the suspicion cannot find an acceptable alibi or defense. It has been proven, time and time again, that some law enforcement individuals jump to conclusions and conjure up evidence to support their theory. Prosecutors, too. They *need* to win the case. To hell with the truth and the facts. Gotta put another notch in your belt. I guess the three of us were guilty of that towards Mr. Zimmerman. Even now, I feel ashamed for that.

🚲

As my relationship with Bellamy grew and I became more reliant on my friend's comfort and advice, I knew Bellamy must remain hidden, and yet, any confidence I had, came from the encouragement of Bellamy, and Perry, and yet, somehow, I knew that I would always be an outsider looking in. At least I was becoming better equipped to wrestle with my demons.

After dinner I went to my room since the family television had been commandeered by Ted who was watching *Three's Company*. There would be no Batman for me tonight. Bellamy was waiting for me in my bedroom lounging on the bean bag with his hands clutched behind his head.

"Hey Bellamy. One TV and I never get to watch what I want as long as anyone else is home," I complained.

"Pecking order," responded Bellamy.

"What?" I asked.

"There's a pecking order in every family and you come in last."

"Thanks for that. That sucks."

"Yeah, it…"

I was interrupted by my brother's hysterical laughter as he stood at my bedroom door. I had no idea that Ted had followed me to my room to tell me the tv show was over.

"Cal's got an imaginary friend," Ted howled loud enough for everyone in the house to hear.

"I do not!" I retorted. "I was just talking to myself."

"And answering yourself," Ted said between more bouts of laughter.

I could hear my brother reveal the hysterical news to the rest of the family and listened to the tenor of the five-participant laughter that followed in the same key. My siblings and parents sang to the same melody; they laughed in harmony. I was always off tune, as if having been given the wrong sheet music. They would sway to the right when the music played, me to the left. I sometimes wondered if I had been adopted. Certainly, I could not have come from the same biological parents; I was too different from my brothers and sisters. Life seemed like a private joke that I had not been privy to.

"You should have kicked his ass," Bellamy said with a more than usual callous expression on his face. "Brother or not, you have got to stand up for yourself, Calvin! There is only one way to deal with bullies. You need to have the courage to walk up to them and hit them in the face as hard as you possible can, right between the eyes. That is how you gain their respect. I guarantee, that after you do that once, they will change their tune. They will never pick on you again and, in many cases, they will want to be your friend. Bullies do not *want* a fight. They want to *give* the fight. Do you understand what I'm saying?"

"I guess so," I mumbled.

"You guess so? Stop being a pussy, Calvin. If you cannot start standing up for yourself, I will…out of default," Bellamy said with fury in his voice. "You'll give me no other choice."

My head pivoted backwards with astonishment. I had never heard such antagonism from Bellamy. "You know, you have a triad of clandestine comrades, right?"

"What do you mean?" I asked with a look of bewilderment.

"I'm your secret friend, just like Simone's your secret friend and Perry as well. Have you ever asked yourself why you keep our friendships private? You are in a war with yourself. Part of you, I do believe, actually likes us. Unfortunately, the other part of you is ashamed of us. You need to decide which part of your nature you want to win. That takes courage, Calvin."

Although Bellamy was a calming presence, he also had a retaliatory spirit which could have stemmed from his desire to protect me. It could have also been that my alter ego had had enough of being picked on and kicked when I was already flat on my face.

I pondered what Bellamy had said and knew there was some truth to the accusation, but truth I preferred not to confront. The way I dealt with my various relationships was working just fine…*for me.*

Hunchback and I were determined to distract Muskrat from the reality that his father was slowly deteriorating before his family's eyes. His dad was wilting like a week-old bouquet of flowers, each day displaying a small sign of their inevitable demise. Thankfully, Hunchback's birthday was the perfect diversion.

Hunchback was the first to receive the gift of all gifts, the one gift all the guys in the neighborhood wanted: a Daisy BB gun. The limitless possibilities and hours of pure excitement were guaranteed. Simply shooting soda cans off the back fence would not suffice. I headed for Chollie Mollies with Hunchback and Muskrat. Choo-Choo was to meet us at the edge of the woods with a can of cat food, and he was there waiting for us when we arrived. We invited him to do the dirty work.

Looking at a large bandage on his forearm, Hunchback asked, "What the hell happened to you this time?"

Peeling back the gauze to expose an ugly wound oozing with a yellow puss, Choo-Choo said, "Ahhh, it's nothing. I burned it crawling underneath my stepdad's car retrieving a ball. Got burned by the hot tailpipe."

"I swear, you're a walking emergency room," responded Muskrat with some genuine sympathy.

"I know," responded Choo-Choo sadly. "What are we going to shoot with the gun?" he said, wanting to change the subject.

"A skunk," I said.

I had read in an Argosy magazine that skunks are opportunists, always looking for an easy meal. Although nocturnal, in the springtime, when they have their young and being especially hungry, they will often leave their rocky crag. Choo-Choo had also been instructed to bring a hand can opener as a requirement to be included in the escapade. Making our way to a rock-covered cliff that stood above the hollow, I told Choo-Choo to open the can of Puss n' Boots cat food. Like a choreographed synchronized swimming team, the four of us turned our heads and squinted our eyes.

"That's horrendous!" Muskrat squealed.

"That smells worse than shit!" Added Hunchback.

"That smells like Floaties Pond that time when someone poured some Clorox in it killing a bunch of fish," I said as I held my nose. "But that is exactly what we want. Good job, Choo-Choo."

"Yeah, our house smells like rotten fish for a couple of hours whenever we open a can of this stuff," replied Choo-Choo.

The can was placed a few yards away from the rocks as we sat, sharing a few boxes of Cracker Jacks Choo-Choo had brought along. We didn't have to wait long before we saw a black and white head poke out from amongst the rock pile. Muskrat saw it first.

"Look!"

"Quiet," I whispered. "Give me the gun."

"It's my gun. I get first whack at it," answered Hunchback.

"Alright. We each get one shot. Make sure you pumped the gun ten times, and you have to hit it in the head. If you shoot it in the head, he will not spray us," I assured the others with my less-than-expert knowledge of the Mustelidae species.

The skunk had come completely out of the rock outcrop, twitching its nose in the air. Hunchback, pumped the BB gun, laid on his stomach, aimed and froze.

"What the hell are you waiting for," I asked. "It's not gonna stand there forever. Shoot!" But Hunchback refused to fire the gun. "Give me that thing!"

"I don't want to kill it. Let Muskrat or Choo-Choo get a shot first," Hunchback said.

"Not me," replied Choo-Choo.

"Me, either," added Muskrat.

"I swear, you guys are pussies!" I said.

I took the gun, sat on the ground in the shooting position I had learned at Camp Wackasack, and took aim and fired the gun. Phew! The pellet hit the skunk in the neck and within a few seconds, our nostrils got hit with the robust musk.

"Damn, let's get out of here," Muskrat screamed as he led the four of us through the woods and into a field. Each of us began smelling our clothes.

"We got sprayed! Great! I thought you said it wouldn't spray if it got hit in the head, Moran," Hunchback yelled while grabbing the back of my shirt collar.

"He shot it in the neck!" Choo-Choo said while I pulled away from Hunchback's grasp. "We can't leave it there to suffer. We need to finish him off."

"I'm in a world of shit," Muskrat whispered. "We're supposed to go to Casa Conti's tonight for dinner, and my mom's going to have a conniption. I'm going home."

Choo-Choo fell to the ground laughing hysterically. Casa Conti was a "dressier" restaurant which was a favorite of the older crowd due to their "soft" vegetables; creamed corn, stewed tomatoes, and creamed spinach.

"Screw off, you moron," Muskrat said as he headed toward the path above the ballfields.

Hunchback, Choo-Choo and I headed back into the woods. Before we got to the mock-orange tree, we could hear a rustling in the leaves and the pitiful cry of the skunk.

Pumping it 15 times, I took careful aim and fired. The shot landed just below the striped fiend's left eye dropping it in the leaves.

"Is it dead?" Choo-Choo asked.

"Naw, I think it's still twitching," I answered as I handed Choo-Choo the gun. Finish him off."

The skunk had stopped moving by the time Choo-Choo shot.

"Did you bring the potato sack? I asked Hunchback without turning away from the skunk.

"Yeah, and my mom's going to be pissed when she finds all the potatoes at the bottom of the pantry closet."

"She'll get over it," I replied. "Choo-Choo, go over and pick it up by the tail and stick it in the sack."

"I'm not picking that up. It stinks and it might still be alive."

"Kick it first," suggested Hunchback. "Come on. Don't be a pussy," a favorite line whenever anyone wanted Choo-Choo to do something.

"Alright, but if it bites me, I'm kicking your ass," Choo-Choo mumbled.

Hunchback turned to me and said something about how Choo-Choo could not beat up his grandmother but didn't say it loud enough for him to hear it. He did not want to distract Choo-Choo from his assigned task. Choo-Choo reluctantly placed the skunk into the burlap sack and held it at arm's length.

"Why can't we just leave it here?" asked Coo-Choo. "What are we going to do with it?"

"Yeah, what are we going to do with it?" Hunchback mimicked.

"I have a plan," I said as I led the way out of the woods. "Follow me."

I jumped on my bicycle and started peddling down Edge Hill Road followed by my partners in crime. We turned at Mt. Carmel Church and down to Kenyon Diner.

"Choo-Choo, put the sack in that dumpster on the side of the diner," I said as we watched Choo-Choo quickly obey the order. "Now, we go across the street, sit in the grass and wait."

And wait we did. As cars would pull up to the diner, the occupants would get out of their car and before making it to the front entrance, would turn around and get back in their car and leave. It wasn't long before patrons started exiting the diner, waving their palms in search of fresh air. A heavy-set man with an apron and paper piss-cutter hat came out to investigate the source of the foul odor. Walking behind the diner, the man disappeared for a few minutes, then returned to the front door never having looked in the dumpster.

"This is better than the Saturday matinee," Hunchback howled, followed by his co-patriot's laughter.

The 5 o'clock whistle sounded and the three of us, as if Pavlov's canines, jumped on our bikes and headed to our respective homes.

Dasha yelled something about *feculent,* a word I had never heard before and ordered me to take off my clothes in the breezeway and to head to the bathroom. After explaining that I was walking through Chollie Mollies when I surprised a skunk, I was subjected to a bath of tomato juice, hydrogen peroxide, vinegar, and douche.

CHAPTER NINETEEN

Murder's out of tune,
And sweet revenge grows harsh.
—William Shakespeare

I t took nearly a week before anyone could no longer smell the skunk on me. I had kept my distance from Perry, weighing my interest in the relationship. The more I refrained from going over to see Perry, the more difficult it would be to explain to him why I had alienated myself from my new *friend*. I had no *reason* to go over to see Perry, but the truth is that I had missed him. I stood in front of his door, staring at the comedy-tragedy proscenium mask doorknocker, the verdigris exposing the green pigment in the natural patina from the weathered brass. While contemplating whether or not I should knock, the door suddenly opened.

"Cal! What a pleasant surprise. Come on in. I was just taking these old coke bottles to the garage. I'll be back in a minute."

Entering the house, I was immediately hit with the delicious fragrance of cinnamon. On the kitchen counter was a wooden hot plate and a pan full of warm cinnamon rolls that were twisted like Nautilus shells. I stood over the delectable cinnamon treats when I heard the front door shut.

"Do they smell scrumptious, or what?" asked Perry. Placing a bun on two plates, he handed me a knife and motioned toward a glass butter dish. "Make sure you smother it in butter."

I sat at the kitchen counter and took my first bite. A sweet festivity of decadent pleasure pirouetted within my mouth.

"This is the most incredible thing I've ever eaten," I mumbled with my mouth half full.

"And the butter. It's incredible! So creamy."

"Don't you have butter at home?" asked Perry.

"No. We only have margarine," I replied.

"Ugh! The ugly butter-in-law! That yellow block of artificial lard should be outlawed in all 50 states."

"You're telling me," I said agreeably.

"Hey, have you ever played backgammon?" Perry asked.

"No. Never even heard of it."

"It's a boardgame much older than chess. Chess is only 1,500 years old. Backgammon has been traced back nearly 5,000 years to its origins in Mesopotamia, which is now Iraq. Today, it's a very common game in European coffeehouses. Sit down, I'll teach you to play," Perry said as he pulled a slender wooden box from the bookcase that resembled a briefcase more than a game box.

Perry opened the beautifully ornate board. "One summer, between college semesters, I traveled across eastern Europe playing backgammon for money."

As I listened to Perry explain the rules, I scanned the four sections and the multiple triangles painted on the board. It did not take long before I was hooked; in fact, I won the third game, even though Perry probably let me win.

"You're a fast learner," Perry said as they put the backgammon stones back in the box. "You know, Cal, people actually gravitate to you, but for some reason you seem oblivious to that fact."

I looked up at Perry and simply thought he was blowing sunshine up my skirt, but there was something gnawing in my gut. *Why is it that I am so slow to learn whatever is being taught at school, yet when Perry teaches me something, I pick it up quickly and often excel at it?*

Perry may have been right, but it is so very difficult to see through the smoke when your life is on fire. I think, as a child, I lived under of fog of misconceptions and misconceptions are both dangerous and destructive.

"A fast student? Not really. You should see my report card," I said with a sight chuckle in my voice.

Perry never mentioned what had happened at the Texaco gas station, not that afternoon, not ever. He was darn good at keeping secrets, unlike Choo-Choo. I guess that is what good friends do.

The weather had turned as cold as Dasha's smile and with it came the first frost. No matter how long you live in the north, you are never prepared for the first real cold front. Just a few days ago it had been in the 60s, now there was that sting in my throat whenever I took a deep breath. The temperature was dropping as quickly as my hope for getting good grades in school. The sky promised it would bring snow as soon as the clouds caught up with the wind. The ground was hard and the rhododendron leaves brittle.

Snow really is a beautiful thing. The pre-snow winter with its various shades of grey and brown, absent of foliage and colorful birds and dragonflies and butterflies, waits for the snow to blanket everything with a cleanness. Everything would be beautifully white, at least for a day or two, until the cars and footprints make it dirty. I pity those who must endure an entire year without seeing the white blessing.

I had yet to give Simone the framed butterflies, thinking it was an intimate gift and not wanting to scare her off, but now, now things were different. Grabbing my peacoat and a blue and yellow Beanie cap, I headed down to Simone's house.

When I was a block away from Simone's, Mongrel and his sidekick, Benny spotted me. Mongrel's real name was Matthew Brodzinski, but other than teachers at school, everyone had called him Mongrel, a name he actually preferred. Unfortunately, I had thought it was too cold to ride my bicycle, but now I wished I had. There would be no quick getaway from my nemeses. I tried to hide the frame inside of my coat, but it was too late.

"What ya got there in your coat, Cowgirl?" Mongrel said with a snide chuckle.

"Nothing," I said while quickening my stride.

"Yer lying to me, punk. We saw you sticking nothing down your coat."

I had my hand in the coat pocket to hold the frame against my body, but Mongrel grabbed my elbow and pulled, causing the frame to drop and the glass to shatter on the macadam. All three of us seemed temporarily immobilized, but for different reasons. I was heartbroken, which was quickly followed by a sense of horror. Mongrel and Benny were trying to comprehend what they were looking at. The silence was followed by hysterical laughing, by only two of us.

"Butterflies! Butterflies, Benny! Hey butterfly boy, where are you heading with your butterflies. Are you a faggot?" roared Mongrel.

"You cannot let them find out about Perry," whispered Bellamy. *"Do whatever you have to do!"*

"He has to be," laughed Benny.

"Leave me alone," I said, knowing there was no chance of that happening.

"What a minute. Were you heading to Simone Arnett's place? You had to be! There're only two more houses on this street."

I said nothing.

"Are you a nigger-lover?" screamed Mongrel.

"No!" I yelled. "Are you kidding me? I wouldn't be caught dead with her."

My lie must not have been convincing because before I knew it, Mongrel grabbed the back of my collar and pulled violently causing me to fall backwards smashing my back against the curb. Trying to absorb the agonizing pain in my back, I then felt Mongrel's fist, snapping my head back until it hit the ground. I hardly felt the next two punches as I instinctively curled into a fetal position to prevent any further damage.

"Come on, Benny. Let's leave this Wigger to his pretty butterflies," Mongrel said as he stomped his foot on what was left of the butterflies, making them unrecognizable.

I turned around and headed home, my back sending a throbbing pain down my legs. Every step was like walking through wet sand. There was no sense in going over to Simone's. On the way home from the obliteration of my act of love, I stopped by Perry's house. Perry was just putting a quiche Lorraine into the oven when I lifted the ornate knocker and let it fall upon the door. Looking at the masks, I knew the play I was cast, a tragedy, not a comedy.

"Hello Calvin! Come on in," Perry said with a smile that quickly disappeared. "Dear God, what happened to you?"

"Nothing. I just tripped on the sidewalk. The root of a tree pushed it up, and I wasn't watching where I was going."

Perry wasn't buying what I was selling. "Let me get my first aid kit."

"No. No. Really, I'm fine," I blurted out. The last thing I needed was to come home with bandages on my arm and head. Once my parents saw the condition I was in there would be enough explaining to do.

"Well, let's at least clean up those open wounds," Perry said as he walked back to the bathroom. He returned quickly with some gauze and hydrogen peroxide.

The thing about Perry was that he never pushed. If I did not want to share, he let things be.

"Well, I am glad you dropped by. I just put a quiche in the oven, and I was about to do a little reading," he said as he dabbed the wet gauze on the back of my head. "Nasty cut, but it doesn't look like it needs stiches."

"Hey, I guess all the butterflies have left, now that it's getting cold," I said, trying to change the subject.

"Ahhh, yes. This time of year is always a downer for us lepidopterists; that is, those of us who love butterflies and enjoy raising them at home. Butterflies will not fly when temperatures fall below 55 degrees. Most will leave before the temperatures drop so they can roost in the mountains of Michoacán for the winter.

I know it sounds funny, but I always believed people can be butterflies. There is a special type of person who is a butterfly. I am not referring to the phrase *social butterfly* that I'm sure you've heard.

Not those whose personality is charismatic, and personally gregarious. I'm referring to the person who is emotionally delicate. They are fragile entities, much like the butterfly who is dependent upon the weather. These individuals need the uninterrupted sunshine of another's love. Of course we all need love, but these human butterflies are more sensitive to life's temperature changes and the external heat of a sun that shines from someone who truly loves them. It fuels their muscles used to flap their wings and fly."

I soaked in the words and descriptions my friend had shared as Perry opened the backgammon board and began to place the stones into position.

◴

It is funny how the obvious escapes you, especially when you are young. That was the case with Choo-Choo. It was not so much our naivety, or that we were oblivious to what was happening around us. I think it was more that we *wanted* to believe that our suspicions *couldn't* be true…that evil *couldn't* take residence in North Hills. That was big city stuff. In hindsight, it was all so obvious.

Muskrat and I were walking back from Hunchback's one day when we approached Choo-Choo's home, a two-story white house with a closed-in porch that always seemed to need a coat of paint. Before we got to his driveway, we could hear his stepfather yelling in the backyard. Muskrat and I looked at each other and without either of us saying anything, we began slowly walking up the driveway, stretching our heads around the corner of the house, hoping we could see what the commotion was about. We could hear what his stepdad was saying before we could see him.

"Get down on your hands and knees, you worthless piece of dog shit! I said get down! If I have to make you get on that ground, I promise you you'll never get back up! Get down!"

Petrified, we inched our way up the driveway until we could get a glimpse of the backyard. We were dumbfounded at what we saw. Choo-Choo was on all fours and had a dog collar around his neck. His stepfather was pulling so hard on a leash attached to the collar that Choo-Choo's neck looked like it would snap.

"Now bark, you little turd. Bark!" the man ordered. "Even Max knows how to follow orders He sits when I say sit. He comes when I say come. A damn dog is smarter than you! If you can't obey my rules, I'll start treating you like a dog. Now bark!" he said with another jerk on the leash.

"Woof," responded Choo-Choo sheepishly.

"Again!"

"Woof. Woof."

"Now stay out here until I whistle for you to come in."

Muskrat and I were so frozen in place by the shock of what we saw that we were almost seen by Choo-Choo's stepdad when he turned to walk back to the kitchen door. The broken arm, the black eye, the fat lip, the burn on his arm and all the bruises; Choo-Choo was not clumsy or accident-prone. He was a victim of both physical and emotional abuse that he had desperately tried to hide from all of us.

Choo-Choo's stepfather was a man driven to violence. I knew he was capable of anything. *Anything!* He had Quick Draw McGraw anger, and he had no restraint.

A few weeks later, Choo-Choo had to be taken to the emergency room at Abington hospital with a broken nose and broken orbital socket, which Perry told me was the bone around the eye. He had told the emergency doctor that it happened by being hit in the face by a baseball, but the doctor did not believe it. No one was playing ball in early December. There were three round bruises on his cheek that the doctor suspiciously thought were caused by knuckles. The doctor called the "authorities," but nothing ever happened. Of course not, Choo-Choo's stepfather was a cop. How could a man who was sworn to serve and protect not even protect his wife's son? The man was a blood-sucking parasite, like a tick practicing its domestic skills on the belly of field dog.

I was reminded of the time an off-duty cop was drunk and hit a pedestrian who was crossing Easton Road in nearby Glenside. There was an investigation, but the victim's family was basically told he should not have been crossing the street wearing dark clothing at 2 am. Cops take care of cops, I learned. They are never wrong and, when they are, the fraternity will swear he's not wrong. And my parents wondered why I have a problem with authority.

CHAPTER TWENTY

The seasons know their time and place; people, not so much.

I was dying to share with someone that I had fallen hard for Simone. Isn't that the way love should be? You want to scream from the highest mountain top that you were in love with the most wonderfully, beautiful girl that ever walked the earth? I thought about sharing my feelings for Simone with Perry, but I did not want to discuss intimate matters with him. I could not tell Hunchback or Muskrat about Simone. I was pretty sure they would not make fun of me or say anything bad about her, but I also knew that things would never be the same if I did. They had both said derogatory things about black folk, and the comments they had made about Perry was enough to keep my *special relationships to myself*. Bellamy was right when he told me that the word *friend* is used loosely. People may have thousands of acquaintances, but few have even one true friend. I knew, deep within myself, that Muskrat and Hunchback were not *friends*, but when friends are in short supply, you settle for whatever you can get.

There were so many holes in my life that it looked more like honeycomb than it did a middling teenager's experience. I did poorly in school, and yet I absorbed everything Perry would teach me. I had more secrets than the Pentagon and would only share them on a "need to know" basis, which almost always resulted in sharing them with no one, but Bellamy. I had sorted the areas of my life like a compartmentalized lunchbox, so that my friends, my church life, my girlfriend, my job, would never touch. I contemplated the closest relationships that I had, Perry, Bellamy, and Simone. Each were all people outside the walls of the community that had been built for me.

My peer group was safe. They may not have thought as I did, but they looked like me, talked like me, spoke like me.

To venture out of this protected municipal life was to risk alienation from my peer group. I was not gay or black, yet I never labeled Perry as gay or Simone as black, even though each were. It was inconsequential, and yet I feared turning my back on *my people*; afraid that when the smoke dissipated, I would find myself all alone and rejected by both camps.

But I did have a realistic interpretation of my relationships, thanks to a reality check from Bellamy. No one had ever *really known* me. I would judiciously select which portion of me I would allow any one person to see, so fearful to ever reveal my entire being. Like a sage fly fisherman, I would read the water, cast my line, tucking a hopper at the precise spot the trout lay waiting. I knew when to let more line out, when to reel in and when to swing a soft hackle as the hatch began. Some people earned the right to perceive more of me, but no one could see the leader, let alone the line. If they did, I was convinced they would be spooked and swim away.

It began to be embarrassing delivering newspapers at nearly 15 years old, so I got a job as a short-order cook at a local pub called *Baker Street*. I would cook burgers and strip steaks on the grille and throw frozen fried chicken into a basket which would go into sizzling hot grease. I did just about everything in the restaurant but pour wine and beer. You had to be 21 to do that.

There was a middle-aged waitress named Mora who took a liking to me. In fact, when I went into the restaurant, cold calling, and asking for a job, the manager had said no, but Mora overheard the conversation and said, "Aw, come on, Paulie, hire the kid." And he did.

I worked there several days after school and on the weekends making more money in a few hours than I did in a month delivering newspapers. *Baker Street* would also become the avenue for losing my virginity.

🚲

Hunchback was grounded for a week for getting caught exploring his mother's underwear in the top drawer of her dresser, so Muskrat invited Boner and Mouche to join us for a game of street football, 3 on 3. Thin, with thick coke bottle glasses, Mouche was the prototypical nerd and not overly athletic, but on this occasion, he was invited to fill the void left by Hunchback. We met at the corner of Short Lane and Hamel. Muskrat was already there when I arrived. Mouche was habitually late and while we were waiting, we saw Choo-Choo madly peddling between the wheelies he was popping. No one had seen him since him since Muskrat and I had witnessed his forced canine imitation.

"Who invited him?' Muskrat barked.

"Not me," I answered without taking my eyes off Choo-Choo.

And I think I have it bad. No one deserves the crap that Choo-Choo puts up with. And all he wants from us is to belong. We should be easier on him.

"I swear, Mouche better not have. I'm not playing football with Choo-Choo. You know how he is when he scores a touchdown. He runs for blocks and does that stupid dance of his, and it takes us forever to get the ball back."

Forgetting the, *"We should be easier on him,"* I quickly came up with an idea to lose Choo-Choo. "Look, if he asks what we're doing tell him we're all going to divide up, go in different directions to find returnable bottles, meet back here in an hour to cash in our bottles, then go to Plockies and Jack Frost. Got it?"

"Got it," Muskrat agreed, knowing that Choo-Choo would crawl under anything for 5 cents.

"Hey guys," Choo-Choo said as he skidded his bicycle sideways, leaving a rubber trail on the street.

"Hey, Choo-Choo. Where've you been?"

"I've been grounded for a week, because I got a tattoo at Sailor Eddies down in Philly," he said as he rolled up his sleeve.

Mouche arrived just when we huddled around Choo-Choo as he proudly displayed a

Superman logo on his skinny bicep.

"You should have gotten a Super Chicken tattoo," Mouche said, between bouts of laughter.

"When did you get that?" I asked.

"Last Saturday. My mom and her jerk off husband got real pissed at me. I've been grounded till today, that's why I haven't been around. What are you guys doin'?"

"We're waiting for Boner, then we're going to separate and cover the whole town for bottles to cash in at Joe's Market. Then we'll either go to Plockies or Jack Frost." I explained.

"Ever see that crying Indian on TV? He's cryin' because of all the trash and litter. That's wrong. Can I join you?" Choo-Choo said seeming to plead more than ask.

"Sure," I responded. "Why don't you go down to Floaties pond in the cemetery. Kids are always leaving Coke and Yoo Hoo bottles on the shore. We'll meet you at Joe's in an hour, okay?"

Just then Boner could be seen riding down the steep hill that was named Short Lane.

"Well, go on, Choo-Choo. Remember, Joe's Market in an hour." I wanted Choo-Choo to leave before Boner arrived knowing that he had no idea what was going on.

"Hey, guys. Sorry I'm late," Boner said.

"Hey," I had my back toward Choo-Choo and gave Boner a look of *follow my lead.*

"You take the playground around the school. Muskrat's going to follow Jenkintown Road, Choo-Choo's covering Floaties, and I'll go down to the railroad tracks. Remember, only the bottles that we can cash in. Let's go."

And with that, Choo-Choo was pumping his peddles standing up as he headed for the iron cemetery gate across from the Gulf gas station.

"I thought you were going to call some other guys," Muskrat asked. "We can't play with just the 4 of us."

"You mean the three of you. I forgot that I had to return this library book by today or there's 5 cent fine," explained Mouche.

"Forget it," I said disgustedly. "I'm going home."

On the way back, I decided to stop by Perry's house. When I was only a few blocks away, I spotted Mongrel and his associate before they had seen me. Changing my route, I took a detour, not wanting to be my nemeses' heavy bag. The longer route took me to Perry's front door undetected.

"Calvin, I'm glad to see you! I have a surprise for you! Let me take off these oven mitts." As he walked towards the kitchen my attention was captured by an old sled fastened to the kitchen ceiling, used as rack for copper pots and pans to hang from.

Perry motioned for me to follow him into the dining room. "Just look at this beauty!" I had never seen him so excited as he picked up a small branch from an Omphalea plant. Under the leaves was a greyish mass.

"What is that?" I asked while pointing to the mass. "Is it a cocoon?"

"Ahhhh! Very good, Grasshopper! It is, in fact, not just any cocoon. It just so happens to be the cocoon of a Urania Rhipheus!"

"An Iranian what?" I replied.

"Not Iranian, Urania. A Urania Rhipheus, better known as the Madagascan Sunset Moth, a stunningly beautiful moth. Perhaps the most beautiful moth in the world. More beautiful than many butterflies. I would show you a photo of one, but I do not want to spoil the fun of you seeing it in person when it hatches."

"You mean a real live moth is going to come out of that cocoon?" I asked.

"Yes, in fact, in the next hour or so," answered Perry. "The pupal stage lasts between 17 to 23 days. It took a week for it to be shipped here from Madagascar, and I've had it here for two weeks. I thought it would hatch this week, but just before you knocked on my door, I checked the cocoon, and look!"

I could see that there was slight movement in cocoon. A subtle chipping away from within.

Perry continued to explain. "Within the chrysalis, the old body parts of the caterpillar have undergone a remarkable transformation, called metamorphosis, to become the beautiful moth that will emerge. Tissue, limbs, and organs of this moth have all been changed by now and the pupa is finished. It's still about an hour away from hatching. Would you like some iced tea?"

"Yes, please," I answered as my eyes was transfixed on the cocoon.

The sound of the oven door opening caught my attention and as I turned, I caught the smell of something baking which made my stomach remind me that the cream cheese and jelly sandwich I had devoured hours ago was not going to suffice. Whatever Perry was pulling out of the oven smelled delicious.

"You've got to try one of these as soon as they cool. They are to diiiiiiiiie for." Perry said as he slid a metal spatula across the cookie sheet and placed a cookie on a brown paper sack which had been cut on the seams to lay flat. "They're Persian Saffron Raisin Cookies. I picked up the recipe when I was in Iran."

"You were in Iran?" I was completely fascinated by this refined globetrotter who was introducing me to some of the finer things in life. I was captivated, not only by the museum Perry called his home, but also by the uniqueness of Perry. I had never met anyone like him, and more importantly, Perry treated me with respect, as if we were equals, and with no obvious theatrics.

"Yes. In the Kerman Province about 3 or 4 years ago."

"What is saffron?" I asked.

"Ahhhhh...saffron is the creme de la creme of spices. It is the costliest of all spices by weight. It is derived from the flower of the Crocus sativus. The threads within the flower are collected by hand and dried," Perry explained. "I think the cookies should be cool enough by now. They are always better warm, right out of the oven." Perry took two plates out of the glass cabinet and opened a drawer to get two cloth napkins. He sat the plate in front of me and with a grand smile on his face, waited as I took a bite of the first cookie.

"Oh! Ohhhhh!" I mumbled between bites. "I have never tasted anything like this! They're incredible. I can taste the vanilla and the raisins are awesome. They're so moist and light."

"I'm glad you like them," Perry said with a feeling of pride. "They're my favorite, too. I have an idea. Since we still have some time before the moth hatches, why don't we play Backgammon."

We had finished our first game and had started the second when I jumped out of my seat, startling Perry. Turning to the cocoon I shouted, "It's hatching!"

It was apparent that the hatching was imminent. Slowly, the sunset moth began to emerge. The moth was black with iridescent red, blue and green markings. There was a fringe of white scales on the wing edges. I was astonished at the sight.

"This is so unbelievable! Beautiful!"

Perry and I shared observations and appreciation for the creature until the Fryksdall Mora Grandfather clock began chiming, announcing it was 6 o'clock.

"Shit! Is it 6 o'clock?" I shrieked.

"Yes, it is."

"Man, my parents are going to kill me! I'm supposed to be home 5 or 10 minutes after the 5 o'clock whistle blows."

"Just tell them you were with me, and we were waiting for this rare moth to hatch."

Without thinking, I blurted out "I can't tell them that! I'm not allowed to associate with you." The words were out of my mouth with no way to retrieve them. I realized that I had hurt my friend even though there was a gentle smile on Perry's face.

"Oh. Yes, of course. I understand."

I could tell that he understood. He knew that.

"See ya," I muttered as I sailed through the front door.

"See you," Perry said softly as I pushed open the front door.

I decide not to go directly home. An hour late. Two hours late. It really did not matter. My hope was that the later I got home, Dasha's anger might possibly turn to fear for my welfare. *Maybe.* I rode around on my bike trying to find a place of solace.

When I opened the kitchen door my sisters were finishing the dishes from supper, and Ted came in to happily announce, "You're in a world of shit, you know."

On the way home, I had thought of the choices for an excuse, as to why I missed supper. The truth was not an option. The fact that I had not heard the 5 o'clock whistle was a given, but that had to be accompanied with where I was and what I was doing that caused me to not hear the siren. Saying that I did not hear the whistle was always a lame excuse because the siren was so loud it could be heard easily in the neighboring towns. Nonetheless, it had to be included in the excuse, otherwise my failure to show up at the dinner table would have been deliberate. Mentioning Perry was an impossibility, so my lie had to be believable. There was also the possibility that if I used a friend as an alibi Dasha might just call that friend's parents to confirm my story. That was taking a chance.

"Calvin," Dasha appeared exactly as I had envisioned, irate. "Where were you?"

Not knowing exactly how sound travels, I thought it might be good to include a geographical aberration in my story. "I was catching frogs and tadpoles in the stream behind Jack Frost. You know, in that deep gulley by the railroad tracks. I didn't hear the whistle down there."

"Who were you with?" My stepmother asked as she continued her interrogation.

That was a tough one. I decided to play it safe. "No one. I was going to play football with Muskrat and Mouche, but we didn't have enough guys so I ended up catching frogs." After it came out of my mouth, I thought it really had a tone of authenticity to it, but apparently my wicked stepmother had not bought it.

"I know when you're lying, Calvin! Your hands are too clean to have been down at the stream. Wash up. Your dinner is on the counter…and don't make any plans for tomorrow morning. You're pulling dandelions."

I went into the bathroom and looked into the mirror above the pink sink. The beating I had taken at the hands of Mongrel left a small scar beneath my left eye. I could tell by the royal blue water the Ty-D-Bol disinfectant made in the commode that Dasha had just cleaned the bathroom. I stood above the pool of water, unzipped my fly and watched as the color turned from blue to a bubbly green, with great satisfaction. When I was finished, there was a realization that I had to take a seat. After finishing my business, I pulled the toilet paper off the roll and saw handwriting in ink that read:

BELLAMY WAS HERE

More lame comedy at the hands of my brother.

I went back to the kitchen a few minutes later to find a glass of lukewarm milk, room temperature mixed vegetables and tuna casserole, a dinner I had trouble swallowing even when it was served hot. Mixed vegetables are now called a melody of vegetables. Funny how a name change can change people's perception. Maybe I should change my name.

We were at a time between dog ownership, having had to put Cookie down a few months' past, so feeding my dinner to the dog was not an option. I poured the milk down the kitchen sink and put my dinner in a napkin which went in into my pants pocket which would end up in the toilet. Thankfully, I had a box of Crackerjacks in my desk drawer.

I sat in my bedroom contemplating all that happened that day. Bellamy was there as well but had little to say. Sometimes, just knowing he was there lent comfort to an ever-present uncomfortable environment. My thoughts went dark, in that, my thoughts were not good. I was one who, I can only admit now, had sinful thoughts. Another of the many things I could share with no one…save Bellamy.

🚲

After a breakfast of leftover creamed dried beef, I went into the garage and found the dandelion weeder and a basket and headed to the front yard to start the chore Dasha had assigned me. I knew she would inspect the basket to see if I had gotten the roots. I simply filled the basket with flower heads; the wrath of Dasha would be inevitable. I moved from one pretty yellow, disrespected weed to the next, filling my basket before noon. Dasha inspected the basket, shrugged tentative satisfaction with the work, and then reminded me that she did not believe the frog story and wanted to know where I had been. Normally, when Dasha would not let an alibi go, she either already knew where I had been or had some evidence that I had not been where I said I was. I had no choice but to stick to my story.

I was grounded for a week but was allowed to fulfill my work commitments at *Baker Street*. I loved working at the restaurant and getting a real pay check, that is except for having to pay taxes and smelling like a walking French fry when I got home.

When I was not at *Baker Street*, I spent the week with Bellamy, playing wall ball and throwing horseshoes. The fact that neither Muskrat or Hunchback had called to see why I hadn't surfaced was more proof that I was the third wheel. Bellamy had become my solace. A dwelling where I would be safe, accepted, approved; so was Perry.

After finishing the daily chores, I knew the kids in the neighborhood would be hard to track down by noon, so I decided to catch a few butterflies behind Jack Frost, and then treat myself to a medium soft serve twist. Just behind the wall behind the ice cream shop was a cluster of blooming chickadees that had attracted some eastern tiger swallowtails and a few painted ladies. Making quick work with my net, I had captured three beauties, placed them in a jar and decided I had earned the ice cream. As I sat on the wall enjoying my frozen treat, I looked down the steep embankment to the small stream by the railroad tracks and got an idea. *Why not really catch some tadpoles? After all, the butterfly net would make it easier to commandeer them, and it would lend legitimacy to the story I had told Dasha the night before.*

The embankment behind Jack Frost Ice Cream Stand was steep, and I thought it would be better to slide down on my rear than to risk dropping the net and the jarred butterflies. I made quick progress down to the creek and it did not take long before I spotted several tadpoles swimming in irregular patterns. I chuckled to myself, thinking how they looked like giant versions of sperm I had seen photographs of in my human biology book that we were studying in school.

"They do look like sperm," Bellamy said with a laugh. "Hey, look! There's a paper cup and down by the railroad tracks is a coffee can. Use the cup to scoop up the tadpoles and put them in the coffee can."

Bellamy always had good ideas, and I always seemed to follow them. He always came up with creative solutions to my problems. He had my back and always wanted the best for me.

Commandeering the two containers, I walked over to the creek. Thinking five would be enough, I washed the vanilla shake residue from the inside of the cup and began collecting the larvae, gently dropping them one by one into the cup filled with creek water.

It took me longer than I expected to climb back up the steep bank with my hands full, being especially careful not to drop my new five swimming pets. Making it back to the ice cream stand, I headed home with my butterflies and tadpoles.

As I approached my house, I could hear the beautiful melody of Debussy that my brother was perfecting on our Baldwin upright piano, the music dancing like a butterfly through the open window (we had no air conditioning in those days). I lean toward rock and blues, but there is no replacement for the brilliance of classical music; music which has lasted the ages. It is complex and yet easy for the ears to follow. How I wished I could play like Ted. It seemed as though each of my siblings excelled at something that made my parents proud. Me, not so much.

I went into the garage and found the watering can which I filled up with the garden hose, gently placing the tadpoles into it so they would have a little more room to swim till I secured their more permanent home. They seemed a little shaken from the bicycle ride, but otherwise fine. In the corner of the garage, I found the aquarium underneath a folded tarp, the same one that had housed Mable. I washed it out with the hose and filled the bottom of the aquarium with washed gravel, a multicolored rock, water, and the tadpoles.

I heard Dasha scream with that piercing voice. "Calvin!"

172 G. Bradley Davis

I knew she was still pissed-off about my late arrival for dinner the week before and she her suspicions, but I assumed this time she was infuriated with my new amphibian roommates. I took my time walking to my room where she was waiting.

"What is this?" She asked while holding the spreading board Perry had given me.

"It's a spreading board."

"A what?"

"A spreading board for insect wings to dry in a slightly elevated position." Since she had no idea what it was, I thought I would sound a little intellectual.

"Where did you get it?" She asked.

I was not about to get into a discussion about Perry with the witch. "A friend gave it to me."

Turning the board over to reveal Perry's inscription, she asked, "Is Perry Strathmore that florist who lives down the street?"

"I don't know, is it?"

With that, Dasha slapped me hard and quick across my face. My anger swelled up within me with an intensity I could not contain. As if instinctively, I grabbed both her wrists and pinned her against the wall. Pressing up against her, I looked directly in her eyes and said, "If you ever put even a finger on me from this day on, I will kill you!" And she never did.

CHAPTER TWENTY-ONE

One does not learn how to die by killing others.
—François-René de Chateaubriand

A beautiful dream is rare; the type of dream where impossibilities melt away and desires are fulfilled. I was in such a dream starring Simone when I felt an unwelcome shaking of my arm. I reluctantly opened my eyes to see my father, although it took a few seconds to realize it was he. I was more upset that I was kidnapped from nirvana than I was curious as to why my father was waking me.

"Cal, wake-up."

"What? What time is it?" I mumbled. In my grogginess I saw the light of the streetlamp shine across half of my father's face.

"It's a little past two. Were you with Charlie Cardin at all yesterday?" My father asked.

I could tell by both by the tone in my father's voice and the fact that I was being awakened in the middle of the night that something was wrong. "What? No."

"You didn't see him at all yesterday?" My father wasn't convinced.

"We saw him yesterday afternoon down by the ballfield. He told us he was going to Hillside Cemetery to collect bottles to turn in at Joe's Market," I said, hoping the answer would be sufficient to allow me to go back to sleep. "Why?"

"He's missing. He never made it home last night." And with that, my father left the room. I could hear him repeating my answer to someone he was talking to on the kitchen phone.

⚄

I did not sleep well the remainder of the night and the next morning I felt a melancholy that was difficult for me to explain. Although, never really close to the pain-in-the-neck, Choo-Choo's disappearance had pulled a jalousie over the window of my heart allowing only a sliver of the morning light to creep in. It surprised me that I would be that shaken by the pariah's misfortune. It was as though I knew that something very bad had happened to Choo-Choo.

Choo-Choo deserved better. Better from me. Why is it that when a person who finds themselves on the bottom rung of the social acceptance ladder, when meeting an individual who is surprisingly on a lower rung, they join in the mass ridicule? Wouldn't encouraging and accepting that person make more sense? It is as if they are saying, "At least I'm not as bad off as this poor slob." It is no surprise that a closet alcoholic is the first to criticize a drug addict. Now that Choo-Choo was gone, I felt guilty.

Not feeling like hanging around with Muskrat and Hunchback, I decided to head over to Perry's house. I wanted to clarify my statement about my parents not wanting me to associate with him. I had left him dangling like a party balloon that had been caught on a tree limb. I decided to offer some explanation. Perry deserved that much.

"How are you, Perry?' The type of greeting was not typical of me. A possible sign that I was beginning to *care* more about Perry's life than, perhaps, my own.

"Everything is copacetic," responded Perry with a wide smile.

"About yesterday...my dad forbade me to spend any time with you," I blurted out without any prelude.

Without hesitation, Perry replied, "I understand," and left it at that. Perry did understand. There would have been clusters of people within Philadelphia that accepted homosexuals. There was safety in numbers and there were micro-communities of queers popping up in the city, but in the conservative suburbs? Not a chance. Our relationship would have to be keep secret, at all costs. Plain and simple. I would do anything to keep anyone from knowing Perry was my friend. This would have to be a clandestine relationship if our relationship was to continue. We both knew that.

�🚲

As Muskrat's father continued to deteriorate, Muskrat became more and more withdrawn, not quite sure how to reconcile what he was feeling. After sprinkling some breadcrumbs into the tadpole aquarium, I went over to Muskrat's house to see if I could cheer up my friend, but no one was there so I went over to Simone's. There was no one there either, so I headed home. When I got to my driveway, I saw the evening paper, *The Philadelphia Bulletin* whose slogan was "In Philadelphia, nearly everybody reads The Bulletin." Other than checking the sports section, getting an update on the Vietnam war, and reading the funnies, I had never made reading the paper a very high priority, but ever since Choo-Choo's disappearance, I was obsessed with keeping up with the latest developments in the case.

My curiosity was amplified by outlandish rumors that had been spreading around town like thick strawberry jam on a slice of Dasha's homemade bread. My growing inquisitiveness had me running to the edge of the driveway to retrieve the more official and accurate news. I flew through the breezeway, into the house and slid on a throw rug into the living room, coming to a stop at the base of the couch. I pulled the rubber band off the rolled newspaper but was disappointed once again with more articles of speculation on my friend's disappearance.

I did the few chores Dasha had scribbled on the back of an envelope and left on the kitchen table. I made quick work of the tasks and jumped on my Schwinn (my parents had not let me get my driver's permit, because they thought I was too immature and irresponsible). I headed down to Chernoff's Pharmacy to make a very special purchase. Normally, I would go to Chernoff's for candy bars or a Mother's Day gift, but my mind was on something else I had seen on one of my previous visits.

Entering the drug store, I immediately went to a glass case containing rings and pendants on narrow shelves that automatically rotated. The potential buyer would have about 10 seconds before the shelf moved down and a new shelf appeared. I needed to find the perfect ring to give Simone, to secure our relationship. I *thought* she was mine, but if she accepted and wore a ring that I gave her, it would solidify the bond between us.

I scanned the rings that were on each shelf, ignoring the Timex watches and ID bracelets, and patiently waited for the next shelf to appear. Some had faux diamonds, others faux rubies or emeralds and each sparkled brilliantly under the fluorescent light inside the case. Suddenly, it appeared. The perfect ring; an amethyst with neighboring diamonds on either side; all for the acceptable price of twelve dollars. Sure, the ring would have cost fifty times that in a jewelry store, but Simone would not know the stones were replications. I was delighted when the lady at the counter asked if I would like the ring wrapped. I selected a reflective pink foil paper and watched as the woman expertly curled the ribbon by sliding an open scissor blade quickly across the ribbon.

"She's going to love it," Bellamy said as I put the small box in my pocket, jumped back on my bike and peddled towards Simone's. Knowing the criticism I would receive from adults, I hoped that her mother would not be home as I knocked on the multi-plane door. Unfortunately, as I was peering through one of the small glass windows of the front door, I saw Simone's mother walking toward the door.

"Hello Calvin."

"Hi Mrs. Arnett. Is Simone home?"

"She's in the kitchen doing her homework," she said as she motioned for me to enter.

"Thanks," I said while walking toward the kitchen.

Simone saw me before I entered the kitchen and jumped up and locked her hands around my neck. Apparently, her mother did not mind the display of affection. "Hey, now this is a pleasant surprise."

"Hey. What are you doing?" I asked.

"Studying for a chemistry exam. I need to get those tables memorized."

"Want to go for a walk?" I asked in an attempt to find a better location to give Simone the ring.

"I can't Cal. I have to prepare for this test, and I'm waitressing at the Kenyon diner this evening. Did you hear about Charlie? I'm worried about him."

Crap! Choo-Choo can even ruin a good moment when he's not even here!

"Yeah. That's all anyone is talking about. I can't believe it. Since you can't take a walk, can you at least come outside for a minute? I want to give you something," I said, trying to change the subject.

"What? Sure," Simone said as she opened the kitchen door that led to the side yard. Walking over to the bench swing, she sat down and patted the seat next to her for me to join her.

"What do you want to give me?" Simone said with excitement in her voice. "I love you," I said, reaching deep into my jeans pocket and retrieving the shiny pink box.

"And I love you, Calvin Lloyd! Oooooooh! Did you wrap this?"

"No. I had the store wrap it for me. I'm not very good at wrapping," I confessed.

Suddenly I became nervous as Simone began to unwrap the small box. *Is it too much too soon? Will I scare her off? Will she think it is a cheap imitation and laugh in my face?*

"I love it!" Simone screamed. "It's beautiful," she said as she tried to slide it onto her ring finger. "It's a little small. I'll have to get it sized at the jewelry store. Did you buy it at Sexton's or Rubenstein's Jewelers?"

Now, I had a dilemma. Certainly, Chernoff's would not size a twelve-dollar ring, and I couldn't admit I had bought the ring at a drugstore. I had to think, and quickly.

"I think it is a pinky ring," I suggested. "Try it on your pinky."

Pulling the ring off her ring finger, Simone slid it onto her pinky.

"You're right! It fits perfectly," Simone exclaimed to my great relief. "You are the best Calvin Lloyd! I want to spend the rest of the day with you, but..."

"I know. I understand." I said while hiding my disappointment. "I'll call you tomorrow."

Simone jumped off the swing, gave me a kiss and ran toward the kitchen door, staring at her hand the entire way.

⚄

The news traveled around the neighborhood long before the evening paper was delivered or the 5 o'clock news was broadcast. Choo-Choo's nude body had been by the Floaties pond in the cemetery. There was a photo of Choo-Choo on the front page of the *Philadelphia Bulletin*. The caption read:

Body of Missing North Hills Boy Found.

Picking up the paper, I began to read:

A sixteen-year-old boy, whose body was found in a pond located at Hillside Cemetery, Roslyn, P.A., has been identified as Charles (Charlie) Cardin.

The boy left his home to play with his friends around 12.30 pm on Tuesday, but had never returned. His body, marked with stab wounds and burn marks, was found by a groundskeeper on Thursday morning. An autopsy will be performed tomorrow by Montgomery County Coroner, Jacob Cohen, to determine the cause and time of death.

According to Robert Dalton, Abington Township Homicide Detective, the boy was found without any clothes on, arousing suspicion that he may have been sexually assaulted.

The article went on to say that detectives were focusing their investigation on known sexual deviants living in the North Hills/Glenside area, but what was not yet revealed to the press was that Choo-Choo's tongue had been cut out, most likely a symbolic gesture that the perpetrator wanted to silence his victim, the detectives later thought.

As I have said, Floaties pond was a popular place for catching bluegills and pumpkin bellies. There were also goldfish that had been released by children who had won them in the "ping pong ball in the fishbowl" game at the town fair. It was the location of where the neighborhood kids would blow-up their model ships, and it was also a quiet place couples went to neck. I remembered sending Choo-Choo down to Floaties to retrieve discarded soda bottles. *Did he end up meeting someone he knew?* I rested the paper in my lap. *You mean there are known perverts living in North Hills?*

"Cal," Bellamy whispered. "Let's go outside and throw the football around."

Dasha never mentioned a word to me about my threat and apparently, she had not mentioned anything to my father. He would have had words with me if she had. It almost seemed that she was walking barefoot on broken glass when around me. Dasha had even made Spam, because my dad had to work late. Having spent four years in the marines, my dad swore he would never eat another plate of the military staple, but I loved the salty pork shoulder. That evening everything seemed right in the world.

After dinner I went into my room and walked over to the aquarium to examine the progress my tadpoles had made and the inspection did not disappoint. The back legs started appearing as the tail began shrinking and the body was becoming less oval. Satisfied, I turned off my night lamp and went quickly to sleep.

The summer seemed to be going quickly, as it always had. The milkweed began to wither, and the maple, cherry and birch trees had already begun to change color. I needed things to look forward to, often at the expense of not appreciating the present. I planned a date with Simone but had waited weeks before actually asking her out. Now, I am ashamed to admit this, but I had always worried who might see us out together. The black-white thing was always hanging in the back of my mind like a cobweb on a screen door; it was too sticky and not easy to remove. There was a constant struggle between letting my heart be free and keeping my feelings captive, suppressed from expressing its true desire. But it was her birthday, and I decided to take her to Rizzo's Restaurant *and risk being exposed*. A small step for man…

Unfortunately, I still did not have my driver's license. A few months before the date my parents had decided I could get my permit. I had *borrowed* my brother's dark blue Nova without him knowing it. Ted was home from college for the summer and working the graveyard shift as an orderly at a retirement home, and so he would sleep till mid-afternoon. I saw Ted's car keys on his bureau and decided to take it for a spin. While cruising down Easton Road in nearby Glenside, I was pulled over by a cop for going 50 mph in a 35-mph zone. The result was that I would not get my license till I was seventeen. Simone and I would have to take the train over to Rizzo's.

Simone was waiting on the steps outside her house dressed in Kelly green hip-huggers and a white bodysuit that was as tight as a sailor's knot. I made a concerted effort not to keep looking at Simone's nipples protruding from her top, but they were simply eye-magnets. As we walked towards Ardsley train station, I pointed out a large monarch that seemed to be following us, much to Simone's delight. "Monarchs are also called common tiger, wanderer, and black veined brown," I said in a successful effort to impress Simone.

It was a short train ride to Glenside and just as short of a walk to Rizzo's. As we turned down Glenside Avenue, Simone grabbed my arm and prevented me from stepping in a pile of dog junk. Shortly thereafter, a man dressed in a business suit passed us on the sidewalk. As if orchestrated, both of us stopped and turned our heads to see if the man would notice the mound of turds. We didn't have to wait long to see the man's left foot plant squarely in the pile causing his leg to slide to the point where he could have pulled a groin muscle. Simone and I looked at each other and exploded in hilarity.

We got to Rizzo's just before the 5 o'clock crowd started arriving. By 6 there would be a line of people spilling down the sidewalk for nearly a block. A middle-aged woman with a much-too-tight-for-her-age-or-body waitress uniform brought two glasses of water, looked at Simone, then at me, and back again toward Simone. "What do you want to drink?"

"Two vanilla malts," I answered, knowing what was going on inside the woman's head.

Before either of us could say anything, Simone's stomach began growling a rendition of Tchaikovsky's 1812 Overture. As we turned to look at each other, my stomach joined in, as if on cue. We both had a look of surprise on our faces which only lasted a second or two and was interrupted by more hysterical laughter. People at the other tables stared, but neither Simone or I cared. Why should we? We were part of a fairytale story which we refused to exit from. Why come back to the ugliness and hatred of the "real" world. Our stomach's duet continued until the Italian bread and salad arrived.

Dinner at Rizzo's consisted of veal parmigiana, spaghettoni, garlic bread, house salad and the vanilla malts. The fact that Simone ordered the exact thing that I had ordered gave me more confirmation that our relationship was "meant to be." Things couldn't have been more perfect.

We finished our dinner and left the restaurant. As we walked towards the train station, I felt that the evening was one of those few moments in time and space when all is right with the world. Planets align and moon dust is sprinkled over your head like confetti. The troika of happiness, contentment, and purpose combine to make life as flawless as it can be. I recognized the moment and basked in it. Nothing could ruin the moment; nothing, that is, but Ricky Maddox and his brother Mark.

Ricky was a head taller than the other kids in our class, thanks to his having repeated both the second and fifth grades, and he was always quick to use his size to abuse others. Closely cropped hair, unusually small ears, and darker skin than Simone, Ricky lived to "knock the white" out of any white kid he did not like, and it took little for him to dislike you.

"What do we have here?" Ricky asked as he forced himself between Simone and me, wrapping an arm around each of us. "Are you two going out together?" Ricky threw his head back and began laughing hysterically. "Calvin Lloyd. Do your mommy and daddy know you love some nigger girl?"

I tried to muster the courage to respond with confidence. "Cut it out, Ricky."

"You gonna make me?" Ricky shouted as he pushed me as hard as he could.

I nearly caught my balance, but the shove was so unexpected that I fell backwards and cracked my elbow on the curb. "Simone, baby, come with me and I'll show you what a man can give you," he said as he wrapped his long arms around her waist.

"Go to hell, Ricky, and leave us alone," Simone said as she released herself from his grip.

"Go to hell, Ricky, and leave us alone," Ricky mimicked in a sing-song melody which brought laughter from his brother Mark. "What you doing with this cracker? Ain't a brother good enough for you?"

Ricky grabbed Simone's breast and squeezed hard.

"Ow! You pig! You're hurting me!" Simone shouted while slapping him on his arm.

Even though I knew that the consequences of standing up to Ricky would be painful, I had to try and protect Simone. I charged towards Ricky and lowered my head, grabbed him around the waist and tackled him. It didn't take Ricky long to compose himself, flip himself on top of me and began swinging his fists. The first punch connected with the right side of my nose and cheek. The pain stung high into my forehead. The second punch hit the left side of my jaw and the third cut my lower lip. I felt a warm stream tricked out of my nose. After the first two punches, I did not feel any of the other cuffs that connected. Had it not been for a man coming out of Rizzo's who told Ricky he was calling the cops; I would have suffered much worse.

It was not the beating that bothered me. I was used to that; it was the humiliation. And in front of Simone, no less.

"Are you alright? You're bleeding," Simone said as she opened her purse and grabbed a tissue. "Ricky is such a jerk!"

I had little to say. What was there to say? I had gotten my ass kicked in front of my girlfriend, and I had not landed a punch. There was little conversation on the walk to Ardsley train station, and even less as I accompanied Simone to her house. Dejected, I simply told Simone that I would see her later as I turned and went home.

My dad was in the kitchen when I got home. "What the hell happened to you? What does the other guy look like?"

"He's fine," I mumbled. That was the wrong answer. My father threw the paper down and walked away in disgust.

I had understood what the question meant. Had I inflicted at least as much damage on the other guy as I had received? Not only had I gotten beat up on the street, but it seemed that I had also gotten beat up at home.

I walked down the dark hallway into my room and sat on the floor with my back against the bed. I did not know what part of my body hurt worse. It all did. Bellamy sat next to me and didn't say a word, he just placed his arm around me, and watched as a lonely tear rolled down my cheek.

Courage, or lack of. Where does it come from? Dad fought the Japanese with the 1st Marine Division in Guadalcanal. That took courage. Is courage hereditary? If dad had it, why don't I? The familiar sense of failure and worthlessness overwhelmed me. Would I ever be able to reach deep within myself and do the right thing, no matter what the cost, no matter how difficult, should the time come? I had not that evening and had no idea if I could in the future, but soon I would soon have a tangible opportunity to find out.

CHAPTER TWENTY-TWO

Killing a person's hope is emotional murder.

I felt the cold steel rub up against my legs. The soft clanging of the metal had long since been ignored, for it had been a very long journey. The blood and sweat from past battles had dried, but were still visible through the small gaps in my armor. Somehow, I knew that without the many trials and testing that have come my way, I would never be prepared for the greatest fight to come, yet, how could I know what awaited me?

As I rode to the crest of the hill, my courser stopped, as if instinctively, allowing me to survey the fortress which lay in the valley below. I pulled back my face shield and felt the cool breeze against my hot face. I could smell the sweet perfume of the orange and white wildflowers growing in the meadow just east of where my horse and I stood. The massive ivory beast that stood nearly 20 hands tall had been with me for as long as I can remember. His name was Espoir.

As I gazed upon the castle, I knew the time had come. This was the moment that everything that had happened earlier prepared me for. All the pain…all the battles…all of the perseverance; the victories and the defeats…there was a reason. They had existed only to bring me to this place.

My courage was true, my focus sharp and my mission clear. It would be now that I would gather all my resources for the charge. If I failed, then I would die, but should I be victorious, then my life would forever be changed, well worth the risk. I would then accept the scepter and drink from the silver goblet.

When I reached the fortress, I saw the grand tower where I thought the damsel would be held. After scaling the outside-wall, I entered the courtyard just below the tower. It was from a small, single window that she peered out. Our eyes met at a distance—no words were spoken, but her smile said all I *needed to know. Her eyes seemed familiar, and her gaze was as if she somehow knew how the story would end, and although I believed that I would free this fair maiden from the dungeon that held her captive, it dawned on me that it was she who was freeing me.*

I felt empowered. My weariness was replaced with new strength and a wave of confidence washed over me. I was ready for what lie before me as I entered the heavy wooden door.

The enemies Fear and Self-Doubt swung their swords at me. I stepped aside as they lunged and with a swift backhand brought my sword across their necks. They fell dead. Around the corner appeared Rejection and Humiliation bearing weapons of destruction. The one had a large-link chain with an iron ball and sharp spikes protruding out of it. He swung it towards me but as I ducked, I leaped forward with my sword sinking it deep into his chest. The other guard drew back his bow, but before he could release his deadly arrow, I swung my sword and watched as his head rolled in a bloodstained trail to its rest.

I walked through the cold and damp passageways until I came to a door that had a sliver of light shining from under it. I knew this was where I would find her. Forcing the door open, my heart pounded with anticipation and immediately, I saw her. The light from a small window poured a single narrow beam into the dark chamber and she stood in its light, her beauty illuminated. She ran towards me, my knees too tired to move. Her arms were open and when we embraced my armor mysteriously disintegrated. She kissed me, lifted her head to say…

"Calvin, get up. You're going to be late for school," Dasha yelled from my half-opened bedroom door.

The remainder of the fantasy would have to wait. I envisioned placing Simone on Espoir and riding along the rolling green hills, fording streams and reaching high peaks…and although there was a beautiful sunset, the sun would never go down. Dreams!

I was excited about going over to Simone's, but Dasha had other plans. She announced we would be going to Muncy, PA for the weekend…wherever that was… to take Ted to a special one-week music camp. The chosen one strikes again.

"This weekend?" I tried to hide my look of dismay. I had promised Simone I would spend the day with her and was looking forward to the lunch she said she was going to make special for me. Our relationship was entering another phase, a critical phase, that required me to articulate my feelings, and Saturday was going to be the day to share what was on my mind. "Can I stay home?" I said knowing the answer before Dasha spoke.

"No, you can't stay home," Dasha said very matter-of-factly.

"I've got stuff I need to do. Can I stay with Hunchback?"

"Bobby," she said correcting me once again, "and there's nothing you need to do that's that important."

How does she know what I have to do?

I was told to pack my sister's overnight bag, as I owned no such thing, and to do so in short order. I desperately wanted to call Simone, but every time I went near the phone either my father or Dasha were monopolizing it.

The entire drive home I could think of nothing but Simone. I needed to explain disappearing for three days and breaking my promise of a romantic day and a lunch she had prepared for me. I knew that Jack Frost would be closing, and Sunday was its last open day for the season. As soon as the Chevy pulled into the driveway, I grabbed my sister's red and green, Scotch-plaid bag, tossed it on my bed, and went downstairs to the more private phone in the rec room to call Simone. Instead of ringing, a recording came on the line which stated the number I called had been disconnected. *That's odd.*

I needed to speak with her. I had to explain that parental prerogative had pulled rank, and I was forced to go away for the weekend. I had no say in the matter; it all happened so suddenly, that I had no opportunity to call Simone to let her know. It all sounded so lame. I had to explain in person, and quickly, so I grabbed my bicycle and flew down Hawthorne Road to Simone's house.

When I reached her house, the first thing I saw was the FOR RENT sign in the front yard. That had not been there before. I had a heavy plummeting feeling in my gut. It was like watching a movie you had seen before; one with a sad ending. You know it is coming, but you wish someone had changed the script. I had to be wrong, I hoped I was wrong, but somehow, I knew I was not. I knocked. And I knocked. I rang the doorbell, which I knew did not work. And I knocked again. An elderly woman with white hair that fell to her waist came outside the house next-door in a blue and white housecoat and a lipstick-stained cigarette dangling from her fire engine, red lips. "They moved," she said matter-of-factly.

"What? When?"

"Yesterday. One of those big U-Haul trucks came. They spent the morning loading up and they left. They were nice people. Never gave me a bit of trouble."

"Do you know where they went? Did they leave a phone number?" I tried not to sound desperate, but I knew I was not successful.

"Nope. They wouldn't have left me with anything like that," she said while walking back inside her house and closing the door.

Gone? I sat on the front step and pulled my coat collar high around my neck. I watched as a cold wind blew some late autumn leaves in an imaginary cylinder, around and around. One rebel leaf broke free and my eyes followed it as it ascended high above the telephone wires and beyond the splintered pole. I had a sinking feeling of *what just happened.* I could not reconcile what, if any, options I had. It was like the time I grasped the brass ring on the merry-go-round at Willow Grove Park only to find that all you got was a free ride. It was a sense of utter disappointment. Having flown too close to the sun, the wax melted from my wings. My inevitable fate must be that I would fall out of the sky, plunge into the sea, and drown.

🚲

Everyone remembers their first sexual experience and partner. Unfortunately, I still do. *Baker Street* was an oasis in the middle of my ocean of problems. I was well-liked and the manager would often compliment me on how hard I worked and how well I did my job. He even gave me a raise after only working there a few months.

As I have said, the middle-aged waitress, Mora, took a liking to me. Now, when I say she took a liking to me, I mean *she took a liking to me*. A woman in her late forties with dyed blonde hair and large breasts, she still had much of the beauty that had easily attracted men in her younger years. When no one was looking she would nonchalantly pass me and grab my ass whispering, "Mora needs mora of you," and give me a broad smile while walking away. I really did not mind her flirtations as they fed my prurient interests.

One day, while in the walk-in freezer retrieving some frozen ham steaks, Mora snuck in behind me and, while I was bent over to get the box from the bottom shelf, took a handful of my left butt cheek and said, "Yummy!"

Dropping the box, I put both hands on her waist and said, "It's time for you to back up your words, Mora. Take me home with you after your shift is through, and we'll see if you're just all talk." I think both Mora and I were startled by what came out of my mouth, but she smiled and said, "I may just do that," and walked back to the lunch counter to fill-up the ketchup bottles. I got back to the grille and threw the frozen ham steaks on to the hot griddle like a discus. I tried not to think of that possibilities that could come from being alone with Mora, but I had to keep close to the grille so that no one would see the bulge in my pants.

The lunch rush was over and only a few patrons remained in the dining room when Mora walked up to me and whispered, "Okay. We'll go to my place, and then I'll give you a ride home."

Anticipation is both a wonderful and torturous thing. Visualizing what something would be like; something you fantasized about for years, can drive even a pious man to hard liquor. I was a virgin, and although I had been a bibliophile of borrowed Playboy and Penthouse magazines, I had never been with a girl.

Mora drove an old white Rambler. She lived in a small Cape Cod in northeast Philly. When we entered her house, she threw her keys into a candy dish that sat on a small table next to the front door and said with a smirk on her face, "I'm going to take a shower. Come into my bedroom and make yourself comfortable on the bed."

The bed was neatly made with a pale-yellow bedspread and plenty of canary yellow pillows. I got undressed and laid on her bed, waiting in anticipation for my first copulation. It would not be romantic. It was not making love. It was carnal lust with an older, much-too-willing, lady who wanted her ego stroked.

A short while later she came out of the bathroom with a towel wrapped tightly around her. At the edge of the bed, she let the towel drop to the floor and climbed next to me. We kissed, we had sex, and that was that. Instead of having a feeling of conquest or satisfaction, I was left feeling regret and polluted.

At the end of my junior year, I had accumulated 103 detentions in the 180-day school year. Like every beginning of a school year, I started my senior year determined to play the game and be compliant, which worked through September, but come October the inevitable happened. Detentions. The purpose of detentions was to, one, punish bad behavior and, two, to change that bad behavior. Problem was, I was not mentally, physically, or emotionally able to change my behavior. I wanted to change, badly, but no matter how hard I tried, the results were always the same.

The detentions were mostly the result of daydreaming, talking in class, unfinished homework and being a disruption in class. My first detention of the year came in the second week of October because I fell asleep in Physics class. The teacher, Mr. Renshaw, was a body-builder with massive arms and a half dozen long, wild hairs sporadically spaced on his otherwise bald cranium. Walking over to my desk, he slapped me upside the back of my head so hard that my eyes filled with tears and all I could hear was the ringing in my ears and the faint chuckles from my classmates.

"Lloyd, you pathetic loser, you've got detention! Get out of my class!" Renshaw said as the class broke out in laughter.

Once again, I was made to be the fool. Embarrassment is an emotional rejection that no one enjoys, but for a teenager like me, it was devastating. It erases any popularity points I worked so hard to achieve and even worse, it chipped away at any self-esteem and confidence. Without confidence, a teenager wilts under the desert sun of expected performance and adolescent acceptance. Even the cute goody-goody girls turned to look at me with disapproving eyes. The embarrassment I felt was more than humiliating. Me, the social outcast.

I served the one-hour detention and began the 3-mile trek home. The school buses that ran in the late afternoon were for those participating in sports or extracurricular activities and school clubs, and so I walked the walk that I had done so many times before. It was not the distance that I dreaded, nor the possible punishment that was to be handed down by the Superior Court of Lloyd, it was the self-abasement and disparagement I would self-inflict.

My hatred for Mr. Renshaw boiled over like a pot of stewed tomatoes that burned on a hot stove. I thought of ways I could seek revenge; ways I could inflict physical pain on the pathetic creature. I even thought of hiring a bigger, stronger guy to give him a mula bandha bitchslap, but I knew that would never happen, but I would spend the following days scheming some type of creative retaliation. People like Renshaw never get what they deserve.

When I was approaching my home, I thought about heading over to Perry's place to receive some sympathy, but there would not be enough time before supper. All I needed was for someone to tell me it would be alright. Someone to *insinuate* that I had value. They didn't even have to come out and say it. Bellamy was in my room waiting for me.

"Was it that asshole, Mr. Renshaw?"

"Yeah. I was so bored with his lecture that it lulled me to sleep. The next thing I knew I felt this tremendous pain in the back of my head, and Renshaw calling me a loser and everyone was laughing. We should figure out a way to kill him. I'm not kidding! I hate that some-of-a-bitch!"

"Well," responded Bellamy, "We could come up with something to accomplish that. Ideally, we want to hurt him physically, but maybe embarrassing him in front of the class would be just as good. Let me give that some thought."

Sticks and stones may break my bones, but names will never hurt me. That is wrong, of course. Lips have killed millions of people slowing chipping away at one's self-worth insistently, like waves grinding a stone into sand, slowly, wave by dependable wave.

The next afternoon my father brought a full-grown yellow Labrador Retriever home, much to Dasha's chagrin. Someone he had worked with had to get rid of it because his wife had terrible allergies which were augmented by the dog's long coat. It quickly became apparent that it is, in fact, difficult to teach an old dog a new trick. He was undisciplined and ornery. The name Woody, as previously named by the former owners, bothered my siblings. That is, after I told them that "woody" is slang for an erection, which, of course, I thought was hilarious.

The following day I was back at school staring intently at the number 2 pencil cradled in the grove on the desk, my mind at some distant place too far to hear any of the lecture on stoichiometry my chemistry teacher was explaining in a monotone. It was not until I heard my name, repeated a second time, that I was brought back to reality.

The Vice Principle's secretary, Mrs. Bachman, had come into the classroom and called my name.

"Here," I responded, knowing that although Mrs. Bachman looked and walked like a pigeon, it was improbable that she was the carrier of good news.

"Please follow me. Your presence is requested down at the office."

Something was awry. The Vice Principal was really the school disciplinarian, and you were never summonsed to his office for anything good.

Entering Mr. Latimore's office, the Vice Principle spoke in a surprisingly pleasant tone. "Please, have a seat Calvin," he said as he motioned to a burgundy leather chair that was positioned squarely in front of his desk. He wasted no time getting to the point. "Your teachers had a meeting about you on Tuesday. They are concerned about your behavior. Specifically, your inability to sit still and listen to the teacher and your frequent inappropriate outbursts. We have decided to have you meet with the township psychologist."

Township psychologist? All of my teachers had a meeting to discuss my sanity?

"So, they think I'm crazy?" I asked forcefully.

"No, no, Calvin. It is nothing like that. Your teachers are genuinely concerned about you. They want to help you."

"Sure they do." I mumbled.

🚲

As I had said, I was racking my brain to come up with some type of retaliation against my physics teacher who assaulted me in class. One day, while in the school library, I found myself in front of the rack of periodicals and picked up a copy of National Geographic to see if there were any photos of nude women from some indigenous tribe. While holding the magazine, a subscription card fell onto my lap. That is when the idea hit me, but before I put my plan into action, I needed one critical piece of information.

🚲

When I got home from school, I headed straight to my room. Walking over to the aquarium, I noticed that the tadpoles had developed front legs. Although I had seen Bellamy lying on my bed with his back against the headboard, I sat on the floor with my back toward him knowing that Bellamy was waiting for me to share the latest upsetting news.

"They all think I am crazy. All my teachers got together to discuss me. How did that happen?" I pondered out loud. "Everyone thinks I'm insane; retarded. I am a freakin' reject."

Had I only known that most grownups live in silent fear I would have been able to digest the situation. They are afraid that they will be found out...that they are frauds. Their fears persuade them to act in ways that help shield them from being exposed. I was the product of being a round peg that society keeps trying to fit in a square hole. Most adults simply can't think outside the box. They expect every kid to learn the exact same way, as if they are clones. Just as some people are gifted athletes, others are gifted artists, and still others have a keen mind for analytics, people are all different and they learn differently.

Everyone—*everyone* is afraid of being exposed for being a fraud. We all hide behind some façade. We all have a secret that we would do anything to keep hidden. Not our spouse or closest friend know these secrets. No matter how much we try to bury them, they are there, deep within our minds. They surface and remind us whenever they desire, as if they have their own will.

Jack London and Hemingway, case in point. The two would write grandiose tales glorifying the epitome of what a real man should be, while themselves living an exaggerated lie of being every man's definition of an adventurer. In both cases, the facade was too much to bear, and its weight led each of them to die by their own hands. I am sure that the fact that Ernest Hemingway's mother forcing him to dress in gingham frocks and crocheted bonnets for his first two years did not help.

There are people who abhor the idea of abortion, but when they get pregnant out of wedlock and are facing the horrifying prospect of shame by those they love, they secretly have an abortion. As horrendous the elimination of a fetus is to them, the idea of being alienated and criticized by family and friends is worse. Rejection is an incredibly strong influence—a paradox of sorts; but so is regret.

"Go into the testing with your head up. There is no need to feel ashamed. Answer the questions. Take their tests and do not worry about the results, because what's the worst that can happen? They can kill you but they can't eat you," Bellamy said.

The batteries of tests were scheduled for Thursday, two days away. Although I felt anxious, a feeling of apathy settled my nerves. My greatest fear was that I would be left behind and must repeat 12th grade again. I just wanted out of school. The type of occupation and career I would pursue was still a mystery to me, but I had always been able to earn a dollar, so making a living and survival was never a question.

The testing was supposed to be administered in a conference room next to the cluster of school offices, but because of some last-minute SNAFU, I was to meet the shrink at an office attached to his home, located a block from the hospital. Dasha drove me to my appointment in complete silence. Neither of us had anything to say.

Dasha slowed the car as she looked at the addresses along Woodland Road. Picking up a business card that was on her lap, she announced, "Here it is, 793."

We stopped in front of a two-story brick colonial topped with a Mansard roof. Dasha stayed in the car as I got out and walked toward a carriage house that a sign directed me to. The yard was well manicured with not even a fallen leaf to blemish the immaculate lawn. I rang the doorbell and within seconds the door opened.

"You must be Calvin. I am Doctor Strickland. Please, come in," the man said with a pleasant look on his face.

Doctor? Yeah, that makes sense. Of course, I need a doctor, I am sick!

Dr. Strickland was younger than I expected, perhaps in his late thirties or early forties. His short-cropped, mouse-brown hair was neatly combed, and he sported a painter's brush mustache. He wore blue and white stripped button-down oxford shirt and dark blue slacks. *Boring!*

"Why don't you have a seat over here," the doctor said as he extended his arm as an invitation to sit on a contemporary asparagus-green velvet couch.

While the doc retrieved the "test" I was to take, I surveyed the room to see if I could make any important observations. I ignored the Psychobabble, or pre-test small talk. After a quick scanning of the decorations and relics ornamenting his office, this was my assessment: *The poor doc was putting up a facade. He was probably an orphan with an*

Oedipus complex. He decorated his office with no less than fourteen ceramic, wood and glass giraffes and a China cabinet filled with long neck champagne glasses and other obvious phallic images in an unhealthy, obsessive compulsion of excessive penis worship. Perhaps it is true that those who delve into the field of psychiatry do so with a desire to uncover their own psychiatric disorders.

Throughout the testing, my thoughts kept going to Simone, *where is she? Why hasn't she called? Does she think I deliberately blew her off for that entire weekend I was forced to accompany my brother to band camp?*

The testing was less intrusive than what I had expected, and I found Dr. Strickland tolerable. The entire evaluation took nearly an hour and a half and, of course, I was not told about the results.

CHAPTER TWENTY-THREE

*Killing isn't free. It takes something out of you every time
you do it. You get their life; they get a piece of your soul.
It's always a trade.*
                                        —Paolo Bacigalupi

A s I write this, I have been thinking of all the violence in the
world. Of course, there is so much more of it now than
when Choo-Choo was murdered. With the growing
entitlement mentality that so many people have, could it
simply be a case of "I want it, and if you are not going to give it to me,
I will kill you?" And of course, I am not referring to strictly material
things. The *things* a person wants may be mental, physical, or a
combination of both.

🚲

I made sure I got to physics class before anyone entered the classroom.
I waited outside for the previous class to empty after the bell rang.
Thankfully, there were no stragglers. Quickly, I walked over to Mr.
Renshaw's desk and began rummaging through the drawers looking
for something with my physics' teacher's home address on it. I struck
gold when I saw a letter from the teacher's union addressed to my
teacher in the second drawer. I scribbled down the address in my
notebook and took my seat just as the first students arrived for class. I
had what I needed to implement my plan of revenge.

🚲

There had been nothing new reported about Choo-Choo's murder or the ongoing investigation. Hunchback, Mouche, Muskrat and I had all been questioned by two detectives and there were a lot of police and unmarked detective cars seen around North Hills, which was out of the norm, yet no arrests had been made. Parents were much more attentive to where their children were and with whom. All the neighborhood kids were forbidden to go anywhere near Hillside Cemetery.

🚲

That afternoon Dasha got a call from her sister, Aunt Anastasia, informing her of their hermit brother's surprise visit. Uncle Yaroslav was a wonderfully talented wood sculptor, twice married, twice divorced, and now living as a hermit in the Adirondack wilderness. He once owned a studio in the Greenwich Village section of New York City. Overgrown locks of black and gray hair, crow's feet dancing from his dark eyes and a terrifically thick black mustache made him seem almost as mysterious as he actual was.

My fascination with Uncle Yaroslav was expansive. I loved the man, and yet, I hated the man. He was, to say the least, different from anyone I had ever met. I get different. His lifestyle was one of freedom, unknown by anyone I knew. He had no job, thus, no boss. He had no wife, therefore, no need to compromise with anyone. He was one who could never express himself in word, yet he spoke volumes in wood. It made sense to me why he would retreat into the woods and discount people and civilization.

The area of his two-room cabin where he worked faced east and brought the morning light through the dirty window exposing the wood shavings which covered the wide-planked floor. Women and cervids were his favorite. Impalas with tall and slender legs in various poses were scattered about his cabin along with a slew of smooth curved female nudes. He would visualize his subjects; never using models or photographs. I was busy visualizing the life I wanted to carve out for myself. Whatever we create reflects how we interpret life.

My uncle had a tattoo on his right bicep of a lightning bolt breaking through dark clouds, striking a broken heart and purple rain that poured from the clouds. I had asked about its meaning once, but my uncle only said that it was a long story. I assumed that the story was as long as the man's peculiar life. It was obvious to me that someone, or perhaps *someones* had broken my uncle's heart. Sometimes it is not one person or one thing, but rather a collage of happenstances that cannot help but mesh together to create a weight that is difficult to carry for some sixty-plus years. Something cracks under that kind of pressure. It just happened to be his heart.

Uncle Yaroslav had a romance with bourbon and, when he ventured into town, would win bets in bars by using flies as props. He would catch a fly in the bar and bet fellow drunks he could kill the fly and bring it back to life. A dollar a bet. At first, only three or four dollars would be placed on the bar.

Soon after he arrived at our home, he invited me to the local taproom to observe his scam. He ordered a beer and a shot of whiskey while I was served a coke. After boasting his resurrection claim and gathering a small audience, he asked the bartender, a fifty-something bleached blond with large gravity-yielding breasts and heavy make-up, to bring him a glass of water. Walking over to the fog-glass window, he promptly caught a fly in midair, and returned to his barstool with his buzzing prop in hand. Dropping the fly in the glass of water, he placed his palm on top of the glass, then turned the glass upside down. The fly quickly stopped flapping its wings and succumb to drowning, or so it seemed. By this time, a larger crowd gathered in curiosity behind his bar stool. He retrieved the fly from the glass of water and placed its lifeless body on a napkin upon the bar.

Turning to a half-inebriated patron behind him, he asked the gent to play The Association's *Requiem for the Masses* on the juke box which, without comment, the man obliged. By this time the dollar bills were stacked on the beer-soaked wooden bar. While the juke box was playing the appropriate background music, he motioned for the bartended to bring him a shaker of salt which was sitting at the end of the bar.

The music played as he shook salt on the corpse and waited. This gave Uncle Yaroslav an opportunity to hold court. Where the common housefly is considered a commensal by humans, my uncle would explain that the fly is simply misunderstood. He shared that the fly willingly offered itself to research for the advancement of mankind by aiding in the study of aging and sex determination. He would then begin reciting Aesop's *The Impertinent Insect*, as The Association continued to sing.

The sprinkled salt began to absorb the water and resurrect the fly. In about 30 seconds there was a twitch from the winged dung-eater, then another, and then, abruptly …it flew away. Throwing his head back and laughing, ol' Yaroslav swooped up the pile of money with a cupped hand, got off his stool, took off his sweat-stained hat and bowed to a mumbling, yet amazed, crowd. Yaroslav instantly became known as the Ukrainian Fly God.

A week had passed since my "Let's-see-how-mentally-ill-Cal-really-is" test. Dr. Strickland, my guidance counselor and the township mental health coordinator met with my parents. It was another unexpected day off from work my father had not planned for. The psychologist told my parents that I suffered from hyperkinetic reaction of childhood, a condition that is characterized by restlessness, distractibility, and a short attention span. These deficiencies normally disappear or lessen as a child grows older. In other words, the highly paid township psychologist put a title on what everyone knew were the symptoms I was displaying. ADHD was not a common diagnosis back in the 70s. What he said next stunned my mother and father.

"Cal is a very bright child. Very bright. He has an IQ of 131 which is classified as very superior intelligence. Not genius, but pretty darn close," he said as while closing my file.

Fueled with this information, my parents lit into me when I got home from school that afternoon. They were furious with the results from the testing. If my IQ was below average, I would have a reason for my learning deficiencies, but with an IQ as high as it was, the only explanation for my poor grades had to be laziness and lack of effort.

I felt as though I was damned and expected to be sentenced to a year of hard labor.

Insanity/genius—I am having a hard time distinguishing fact from fiction, reality from fantasy. Thank God I am almost out of here.

⚙

Normally, I dreaded every school morning, but not this specific day. Muskrat had been driving to school ever since he got his license and not having to ride the bus was a better way to start a school day.

My third class was study hall, and I had planned on spending the time in the library, thanks to another brilliant idea Bellamy had. Walking past the rows of books, I went to the periodicals section of the library and scanned over what appeared to be hundreds of magazines. Who would have thought there were so many? *Sports Illustrated, Esquire* and *Time,* I was familiar with, but who ever heard of *Arizona Highways, Harlequin, Desert Magazine, The Libertarian Forum,* or *Pacific Rail News?* I had not, but I was overjoyed by the selection. Calculatingly, I began to tear out every subscription card for each of the magazines. which took me hours. I then filled them out with Mr. Renshaw's hone address marking the "BILL ME LATER" box in each. I was even more delighted to find offers from *Franklin Mint, Time-Life Music Collections, The Bradford Exchange* and many others offering monthly shipments of everything from Norman Rockwell plates, coins with every president imprinted on them, vinyl records with music from each year of the 50s and 60s, and statues of Elvis. I ordered them all for my physics' vilipender. BILL ME LATER, BILL ME LATER, BILL ME LATER.

"I love it!" Bellamy said in a library whisper. "Physical retaliation would have been a bit challenging, but this? Renshaw is a prick, and we are not going to stand for this crap anymore!"

I am guessing that he is still trying to cancel all of those subscriptions. Revenge achieved; satisfaction complete!

CHAPTER TWENTY-FOUR

*Murder is always a mistake. One should never do anything
that one cannot talk about after dinner.*
—Oscar Wilde

T
he next day Muskrat, often moody from the stark reality of
his father's dwindling health, pulled up to my house in his 70
SS Chevelle. I loved that car. Classic body-style, smooth lines,
and one boss engine! Muskrat's brother, David, had come
back from Nam, and they were having a big bash at his house that
evening to which my family was invited. By the time we got to
Muskrat's house, the place was already hopping. David seemed even
taller than his 6-foot 4 frame and his physique was tight. He did not
talk much about the war; in fact, he did not talk much about anything.
He had been noticeably quiet since coming back from southeast Asia.

There were bowls of chips and onion dip, cheese doodles, and
potato stix scattered about on a card tables. Muskrat's dad insisted on
doing the grilling, even though he needed a walker for support as he
leaned over the smokey barbecue. Hamburgers and hot dogs were
sweating on the grill and the grown-ups were sweating on aluminum
webbed lawn chairs. Most of their loud whispering was about Choo-
Choo as they began playing a game of "Who-is-the-likely-perp?"

Mrs. Zimmerman, dressed in tight yellow slacks and a plaid top,
brought out a large sheet cake decorated with the American flag which
highlighted the picnic table which was covered with a red, white, and
blue table cloth. At the end of the table was a large bowl of spaghetti-
type noodles mixed with pieces of hot dogs that were swimming in a
red sauce.

"What in the world is that?" I asked Muskrat.

"Filipino spaghetti. David spent some time in the Philippines when he was on R & R from Nam and got to like the stuff."

"What's in it and what's R & R?"

"Rest and relaxation. You know, partying somewhere without having bullets zipping by your head. Filipino spaghetti is minced hot dog covered in ketchup with thin noodles."

Muskrat's brother had seen the expression on my face which he read like semaphore. "Don't knock it till you tried it," David said as he walked toward a girl with gorgeous strawberry hair.

"Have you tried it?" I asked Muskrat.

"Yeah. It's not as bad as it sounds,"

David was calling all the fathers sir even though he was now a civilian, something my dad enjoyed. I figured it was a habit that was difficult to stop.

Muskrat's dad only lasted an hour and a half before having to go inside. His body was a ghost of what it had been only 14 months earlier. The event was still going on when I left with my parents around 9. As we approached the darkened driveway, the car's headlights raced across the front lawn which, unexpectedly, reflected a dozen little morsels of light, like the star clusters of Pleiades in Taurus. Pieces of aluminum foil Woody had eaten along with the raw hamburger were mixed in the clusters of the dog's droppings, which refracted the headlight back to the car.

"How cool is that?" I said with a sense of glee.

"So cool that you'll be picking up every last piece of that tomorrow morning," my father responded.

🚲

November came and with it, my favorite holiday, Thanksgiving. Cooler weather, a portent of shorter sunlit days and white-covered landscapes. Autumn was a time for Eagles football games, caramel apples and, if just for a day, a hiatus from Dasha's wrath. The entire family sitting around a spread of a picture-perfect turkey deserving of a Norman Rockwell cover on *The Saturday Evening Post*, but the day after was like any other Friday…almost.

With my growing interest in pyrotechnics and an entrepreneurial nature, I decided to create my own fireworks, or explosives, to be exact. The day after Thanksgiving being Black Friday, everyone was out of the house, chasing after highly promoted discounts and sales or running errands.

I rummaged through my father's ammunition box in the basement and found some .306 bullets. Placing a cartridge in the vise on the workbench, I took a pair of needle nose pliers and cautiously pried off the bullet and emptied the primer and powder into an empty 3-inch piece of narrow ABS pipe. Along with it, I added thin pieces of magnesium I had *borrowed* from chemistry class, mostly for aesthetics, knowing that magnesium burns incredibly bright. It would look so much more impressive when the bombs were set off at night. Thanks to an advertisement in the back of a *Popular Science* magazine, I had sent away for a roll of green fuse that is commonly used for model rocketry. Sliding the fuse into the hose that contained a mixture of the explosive chemical compound, saltpeter, sulfur, and charcoal, was the easy part, but I had to find a way to keep the device and its contents tight and compact.

A few days before Thanksgiving, I went to a house that was being constructed and found some knockouts from an electrical box that were scattered on the plywood floor of the partially constructed living room. The partially stamped, quarter-size discs, once removed, allowed electrical wires to pass through the electrical box and were perfect for my use. Going back to my makeshift pyrotechnics' laboratory, I completed my first explosive prototype and was ready to test it.

Throwing on my Eagles sweatshirt, I went outside and walked around the perimeter of the house, trying to find the ideal location for the test. Eyeing the curved section of the white aluminum downspout, I believed I had found a suitable test site. Sliding the explosive device into the downspout, I pulled out a pack of matches advertising Pep Boy's, Manny, Moe, and Jack on the cover. Striking the match, I lit the fuse and ran a safe distance away. The fuse burned evenly and then…nothing. Thinking I had a faulty fuse, I took one step toward the downspout when an enormous explosion occurred sending the curved metal 50 feet in the air and getting the attention of every dog with a 2 mile radius. When the fog of smoke cleared, I retrieved the twisted, blackened and sheared piece of aluminum which was now unrecognizable. The success of my creation surpassed anything I could have anticipated or hoped for.

In the weeks following the explosive test, I produced a dozen and a half of these Black Banana Bombs, as I called them, and began selling them around the neighborhood for $5 a pop. Demand for the BBBs exceeded my ability to produce the devices, mostly due to the limited production hours, when no one was at home, but soon that problem would be solved by unexpected circumstances.

One night, just as we were sitting down to supper, there was a knock at the front door, the door that only strangers went to. My father got up from the table and opened the front door to find an Abington Township Police Officer standing there.

"Good evening, sir. I am Sergeant O'Sullivan with the Abington Police. I'm sorry to interrupt your dinner, but does Calvin Lloyd live here?"

With a feeling of suspenseful dread, my father answered, "Yes?"

"I have a warrant for his arrest. It seems, someone threw an explosive device into the township fire marshal's car and completely destroyed it. We have reason to believe your son was involved. Since Calvin is a minor, if you bring him down to the station right now, I won't take him in my squad car. I will follow you to the station."

Looking at me with a fury equal to the incendiary devices I had created, my dad simply said, "Let's go!"

I felt like I was the hole in the Lloyd dike, causing chaotic water to rush in and no one in the family had a thumb large enough to plug me up. One family turmoil after another. There was always that fear that at any moment the dike would give way and flood our household.

At the station, some clarity of the situation was offered by both Officer O'Sullivan, Juvenile Police Officer, and Deputy Walter Chisholm, Township Fire and Arson Investigator. As Fire and Arson Investigator, Chisholm was part detective, part engineer, part scientist and part law enforcer. I wondered if the Juvenile Police Officer was involved in Choo-Choo's murder investigation. The two men explained to my father...as if I wasn't present...that some type of incendiary device was thrown into the fire marshal's car which was parked in the man's driveway in front of his house. It burned for over an hour before the fire company could put it out.

When my dad asked why they suspected his son of the crime, the officers shared the fact that two teenagers were arrested for setting off a homemade explosive at the intersection of two busy roads. When asked where they got the explosive device the adolescents sang like Barbra Streisand, informing the arresting officers that Calvin Lloyd not only sold, but manufactured the explosives.

My dad turned to me and asked, "Is that true? Did you make these cherry bombs?"

Pausing long enough to formulate an adult response, I said, "First off, they weren't cherry bombs. Secondly, I had nothing to do with what happened to the fire marshal's car. I can't believe anyone would do such a thing, and thirdly, isn't it true that more often than not, someone within the fire department is found to be the culprit? These guys are always pyromaniacs and love to be around fire so much that they pursued, and got, their dream job of working for the fire company."

The response from the three grown-ups was fast and furious and in unison. After the smoke cleared, Officer O'Sullivan told dad that he'd be in touch after the investigation was complete.

🚲

Bellamy tried to put his arm around me to lend some comfort but, welling from my customers ratting me out, I wanted none of it. Walking over to my desk, I saw that Dasha had put two pieces of mail on my blotter. Anytime I received mail it was exciting. *Maybe there would be a letter from Simone.*

The first envelope was from an art school. It contained a drawing of an old salt with a beard and a sailor's cap, smoking a pipe. There was an empty box next to the sketch where you were supposed to draw an exact replica of the sailor and, if drawn well, you would receive a scholarship to their art school. I placed it aside for later. The other envelope had no return address and had something small and hard within it. I tore the envelope open and turned it upside down. Falling to the floor was an amethyst ring with bordering faux diamonds on either side. The ring wasn't the only thing that had dropped. My heart fell and shattered somewhere within me as I searched the envelope for a note, but there was none.

Bellamy followed me as I climbed the stairs from the rec room, walked through the kitchen and out the door to the breezeway. Entering the garage, I searched my father's tool box for a hammer, and after finding one, I placed the ring on the cement floor standing on its end. Bringing the hammer down as hard as I could, the ring exploded, scattering thousands of pieces of tiny violet glass across the garage and rendering the ring into a little undistinguishable metal disc.

The manufacturing of the *Black Banana Bombs* was the last straw for Dasha and Thomas Lloyd. They had run out of options, punishments and appeals for me to conform to their, or at least society's, standards. They decided to consider and certainly threaten me, with the idea of sending me off to Valley Forge Military Academy. They thought that discipline times ten would straighten me out, whatever that meant. *Did they want me to become a clone of my brother and sisters? Did they really want him to be a compliant, non-thinking, mindless zombie who had to be told how to act, what to wear, how to think and what should interest me?*

There is an immunity of adolescence. None of the "crimes" I committed ever resulted in any legal punishment. I thought that rebellion came natural to me, but then again, so did alienation. Alienation that came from not being understood. The only people who "got me" were Bellamy, Perry and Simone, and Simone had given up on me. More than anything else, I thought my parents simply did not understand me. *How could they have had three children who assimilated into their grand scheme of things and one that seemed like someone else's child?* Conformity was not in my DNA. I saw things differently than how the world around me did. I was the prodigal son, the lost sheep, the lost coin.

"You know," Bellamy said, "There is zero chance they'll send you to that military academy. They cannot afford the tuition and even if they had the money, they wouldn't waste it on the one child they think shows the least promise. Any money saved is for Ted." Bellamy never told me anything I did not already know, but sometimes it was just good to hear it from someone else. Confirmation.

I was reminded of Bellamy's comments about my family's pecking order—that I fell dead last—fourth out of four. Some of that had to do with how much honor you brought to the Lloyd name, or, as in my case, how much dishonor and shame you brought upon the family. Desperate times call for desperate measures, as the saying goes, and my parents racked their brains to find a way to get through to their rebellious black sheep. And did they ever come up with a plan—an ingenious one—a plan they were sure would bring me to my senses.

CHAPTER TWENTY-FIVE

*The most loving parents and relatives commit murder with
smiles on their faces. They force us to destroy the person we
really are: a subtle kind of murder.*
                                                    —Jim Morrison

B y the time the summer arrived, my parents determined it was
time to reveal their grand plan to alter my behavior. Having
had three children who were compliant, respectful, and
studious, my parents could not believe their fourth child
could be so different; rebellious, violent, unfocused, and a horrible
student. I was one family emergency after another.

Decades before the television program *Scared Straight*, Dasha and
dad decided to create their own attitude-adjustment-through-culture-
shock which, they hoped, would fashion in their youngest son a
craving to become a model citizen. Their strategy was to send me to
work on a tobacco farm in Lynchburg, South Carolina. I had an aunt
and uncle, not a biological aunt and uncle, but rather, close friends of
Thomas and Dasha who treated us Lloyd kids as their own, prompting
us to call them Aunt Ellen and Uncle Harry. They were originally from
South Carolina, but had come north to find work in the 50s.

Aunt Ellen and Uncle Harry had a nephew who owned a farm
down in South Carolina. My parents thought that by spending a
summer working the tobacco fields side-by-side with black farmhands
I would change my tune and be more biddable. With a snicker, she
gave me the news a week before summer vacation.

"Cal, you are going to South Carolina with Aunt Ellen and Uncle
Harry. They found a job for you working in their nephew Blake's
tobacco farm this summer."

Dasha expected a fight, or at least a reaction of huge disappointment from me knowing I would have to walk away from trying out for the town baseball team and hanging out with my buddies, but I would not give her the satisfaction.

"Great! When do I leave?"

Dasha looked carefully at me and turned towards the kitchen sink. "The Wednesday after school lets out," she said.

🚲

I walked over to Perry's house and knocked on the front door. There was no answer, but as I turned to walk away, I heard Perry's voice.

"I'm in the backyard transplanting some lily of the valley. Come on back."

Perry's backyard was small, but well-manicured. The patio was laid with blue slate stone where several canary-yellow Adirondack chairs, a table and a hammock were positioned with purpose. Clay pottery and potting soil were next to a stool where Perry sat as he continued his transplanting.

"I'm going to South Carolina next week," I mumbled.

"Wow, great! Myrtle Beach?" Perry asked.

"No, to work on a tobacco farm. My mom thinks that will make me into an obedient, intelligent, likable son. I swear, no one likes me. I'm a complete loser."

Perry put down the trowel and looked up at me. He felt the ache that adhered itself to my being. "Do you know what you need?" he asked.

"No, but I'm sure you'll tell me," I replied.

"You need a change in perspective."

"Right. An attitude adjustment. You think you are the first person to tell me that? That's why I'm being exiled to South Carolina. That's old news, Perry," I said while raising my eyes without lifting my head.

"That's not what I said. I said a change in perspective, specifically with how you view yourself. You have an ugly view of yourself and, sometimes, that ugliness is the only side you allow others to see. You are a dead leaf butterfly."

"Dead Leaf butterfly?"

"The dead leaf butterfly is the epitome and perfect example of animal camouflage. The underpart of its wings is dull and brown with irregular patterns and even veins which make it look exactly like an ugly, dead leaf. But the upper part of its wings displays a stunningly beautiful display of striking colors including orange, white, blue, and brown. Cal, you have a beauty that you are showing less and less to people."

Perry's perspective was unlike other adults; looking beyond the obvious, rough, and unattractive shell as he invested the time necessary to decipher a way to pry the shell open and find the pearl that was always there, just hidden from view.

I suffered from a sadness of not knowing that people gravitate to me; that they actually *liked* me. I was oblivious to that truth because the hypocrisy of one's beliefs and their actions did not jive. In retrospect, it was a misunderstanding of Everest proportions, yet one that would motivate me to always have a ready defense; a posture looking to protect myself that had prevented me the opportunity of friendship and joy.

The day before I left for South Carolina, Dasha and dad had received a call from Officer O'Sullivan to inform them that the device that burned the fire marshal's car to the ground was a road flare that someone had tossed in an open window. He also told them that I would not be charged this time for making the homemade bombs, but should I ever get caught with anything that even resembled a sparkler, they would arrest and charge me.

The drive down I-95 was long and I could not get Simone off my mind, nor did I want to. How could I find out where she moved to? A Jimi Hendrix song, *Red House,* kept playing over and over in my head. His baby had moved on, too.

Aunt Ellen and Uncle Harry were the absolute best, but heading to farm work in the brutal heat of South Carolina was not my idea of how to spend the summer. *Maybe it is all for the best. If Simone was still back in North Hills, the time down south would be worse.* To make things worse, when I was not thinking of Simone, Choo-Choo consumed my thoughts. *How would I keep up with the investigation?*

My aunt and uncle never had children of their own, but they treated me like their own, with kindness and generosity. Unlike my adopted aunt and uncle, their nephew Liam, was suspect of northerners and gave an appearance of being annoyed that he had to show a city boy the ropes of tobacco farming. I could only assume he was well-versed in my disruptive nature and the need for straightening this young sapling which had grown crooked, albeit from being trampled upon. What Liam and other grownups did not understand was that this sapling had scarring inside, and although nourishment and fertilizer would aid its growth into a mature tree, and pruning would improve its outward appearance, it would always be damaged internally.

This is where I would spend the summer, working in a tobacco field alongside a couple of dozen African American farmhands. Little did my parents know that working side-by-side with rural black people did not phase me. Liam told me that I would be topping tobacco, the process of manually breaking off the flowering stems, properly called "suckers," which steal nourishment from the valuable tobacco leaves. If topping isn't done, the plants become reproductive seed producing plants instead of a leaf producing cash crop.

I would head out to the tobacco fields, along with the black laborers, early in the morning under the unbearable Carolina sun. Occasionally, we would take 5-minute breaks to drink cool water from the ladle of a wooden pail whenever the horse-drawn wagon would appear. Drinking from the same ladle that African Americans used would have been a deal-breaker for most angry young men from north of the Mason-Dixon Line. I did not think twice about it and besides, working all day with a parched throat in the summer heat without hydration was a much worse alternative. I was acutely aware of my surroundings, and although I kept to myself and had little to say to my co-workers, they treated me with kindness and respect.

The first day of work provided many a life-lesson, not the least was the arrangement for dinnertime. Coming from Pennsylvania, I did not realize that the largest meal of the day in the south was at noon, and that meal was called dinner; supper was the evening meal. The farmer would come with the wagon at noon as the workers jumped on the back bed and headed for the farmhouse.

When we reached the farmhouse, Liam's elderly mother, a small woman with a grey-white ponytail and a large black woman that wore a smile just as large, were bringing the last of the prepared dishes out to the picnic table. Fried chicken, corn bread, collard greens, potato salad, black-eyed peas, fried okra, lemonade and grape Nehi soda filled the picnic table. Soaking wet from sweat, I watched the other workers stand at the table as one of the older men took off his hat and gave the blessing. "Lord, we thank thee for this bountiful feast you have provided for our nourishment. We ask thee to bless this food and nourish our bodies as you bless those who have prepared it. In Jesus name we pray…" and everyone in unison said, "Amen."

I quickly grabbed a seat along with the other workers, more than ready to devour an entire bird by myself. When Liam's mother, a nasty old bird herself, opened the screen door and yelled "Cal, you come on in here. You'll be eating with us," I was more than a bit confused. As I looked at the farmer's mother, over to my co-workers, then back to the lady waiting at the kitchen door, it finally dawned on me what was happening. Bellamy did, too.

Whispering in my ear, Bellamy said, "This may not be a good idea, Cal. You are going to eat in the cool comfort of the white king's dining room when your fellow peasants eat in the heat and humidity."

In short order I declined the old woman's offer, however, it was immediately obvious that I had crossed a line. The expression on her face was both shock and anger. The old farmhand who had just prayed for the meal, gently grabbed me by the shoulder and said, "Now you go on in there, boy. It's alright." A bit naive, I was appalled that Liam and his family would segregate the work crew and place me in a precarious position between the two parties. There was a pecking order on that farm. Thinking of my family dynamics, I knew where I stood in that pecking order; dead last. In a white-boy-sort-of-way, I understood how those black farm hands must have felt.

After dinner the wagon took the work crew back out to the fields. No one had said anything to me about the eating arrangements, but one young man gave me an accusing look of privilege, which was new to me. Privilege? Me? Laughable.

The Carolina sun was somehow more blistering than it had been before they headed back to the farmhouse, if that was possible. Topping the tobacco was not hard work in itself. It simply required taking the flower off the top of the tobacco plant. It was the killing of the horde of different species of worms that repulsed me. There were cutworms, and budworms, and hornworms, and wireworms; some as long as four inches. Liam made it clear to me that if I saw any worms on the plants, and I saw numerous worms, I was to pinch them between my thumb and forefinger. Over the weeks in the fields, I became oblivious to the oozing of the yellowish-green juice and the slight popping sound it would make when squeezed between my fingers.

One day after working in the fields, I sat with my fellow dark-skinned field-hands. They were talking about baseball, some local man's barbecue, and the upcoming harvest as they drank glasses of lemonade and water from the well. I looked out over the perfectly lined rows of tobacco, the leaves moving to the tune of the late day breeze, as a monarch butterfly caught my attention. It danced to some unheard melody as everyone else was oblivious to the orange and black ballerina.

Over time, Liam began to appreciate my hard work and ability to get work done without complaining, and I began to see him in a different light. Prematurely aged by the extended hours of working under the Carolina sun, Liam wore the façade of a clam; being rough on the outside, yet he was soft on the inside, especially when interacting with his children, but he was never quick to show his softer side to me or his other workers.

☙

On the way home from South Carolina, I had convinced my aunt and uncle to stop at South of the Border so I could purchase some fireworks. The carton of L & Ms would not be mentioned. Unlike my first experience passing through the village of Dillon, Uncle Harry pulled into the parking lot of the fireworks mecca and left me alone to make my purchases as he and Aunt Ellen visited the restrooms.

⟎

It was late when we arrived at my house, but Dasha and Dad were sitting in the breezeway watching Johnny Carson on their black and white twelve-inch television. I held the door open for my aunt and uncle and after the four of them did the hugs and handshake thing, Dasha said, "Well, Cal, did you have a nice time?"

Okay. Is it me or was that one of the most sarcastic, bullshit questions you have ever heard?

Yeah, it was a freaking blast, Mom. I love working 12-hour days in a sauna of 100 plus degrees that was hotter than a ten-dollar pistol. It was really fun working with twenty black dudes who looked at me like I was some kind of cheese. My mode of transportation was an old gelding with a sunken saddle and moon blindness that could not trot if its tail was on fire. I spent the better part of two months in this purgatory doing penitence for my inestimable sins. But then there were the evenings where I would spend hours rocking on the porch with rigor-mortis-suffering-old- people who had "that smell of death" while I was a smorgasbord for every mosquito south of the Mason Dixon line. It was swell, Mom.

"It was fine, Mom."

Fine is the word you use when you want to be polite, but really replaces responses less appropriate, like: *It sucked, are you kidding me?*

Changing the subject, I asked, "Has there been any thing new about Choo-Choo?"

"His name was Charlie and no, not really," Dasha's tone had suddenly changed. "There's been something in the paper every couple of days, but nothing that would indicate they are any closer to solving it. What a horrible thing. My heart breaks for that family."

"I'm tired. I'm going to hit the sack. Thanks for everything Aunt Ellen and Uncle Harry," I said as I gave them each a hug.

CHAPTER TWENTY-SIX

Whoever is pregnant with evil
conceives trouble and gives birth to disillusionment.
Whoever digs a hole and scoops it out
falls into the pit they have made.
The trouble they cause recoils on them;
their violence comes down on their own heads.
—Psalm 7: 14-16

I knew Perry's sexual orientation, but I gave him a special exemption from the ridicule directed toward gays that I would participate in with my peers. In the case of my English teacher, who was widely presumed as gay, I would look for opportunities to make snide comments. My motivation was mostly to gain the attention and admiration of my 12th grade classmates and especially a pretty blonde who wore her hair long and as straight as an Amish row of corn.

Halfway through my senior year, I knew I was teetering on a highwire between passing and failing English. I could not commit the time to do the required reading on *Macbeth* and somehow, *Cliff Notes* were not sufficient to get passing grades. My teacher, Mr. Benbow, spoke in a monotone, lectured endlessly on the literary merits of Shakespeare's work standing the test of time and its emotional complexity and concern with truth. His effeminate manners alienated his male students. We nicknamed him Mr. Bend-low, which was unintentionally heard by the teacher on more than one occasion.

I had a particular loathing for Mr. Benbow which was reciprocated by my teacher who despised me and made concerted efforts to make my life miserable by singling me out in class, among other things. Noticing my woolgathering during Benbow's ill-inspired homily on *Macbeth's* act 4, scene 3, Malcolm's questioning of Macduff, he asked me to define some of the characteristics that grant or invalidate the moral legitimacy of absolute power. I sat silently for a minute too long, pondering my response and whether it was worth a detention of two. "Mr. Lloyd, cat got your tongue?"

Without hesitation, I responded, "Isn't proper English, 'Cat *has* your tongue,' Mr. Benbow?"

"Get out of my classroom, you nincompoop! Get out!"

I was not quite sure if the laughter in the classroom was for my witty comment or Mr. Benbow's ridicule, but I was not going to take any chances. I began plotting my retaliation as soon as I walked out of the classroom. *If Bend-low thinks Duncan's, Banquo's, and Macduff's family being murdered by Macbeth was revenge, he ain't seen nothin' yet!*

🚲

Being exiled from class, I went to study hall to kill time before my next class, which was Chemistry. I saw a newspaper that was in disarray lying on the table where two students were both getting their afternoon nap. One of them, with their head on the table and arms crossed in front, had his fingers on top of the paper. I slowly slid the paper from under the sleeping scholar. It was open to the sports section. The '74 Phillies were basically a .500 team, which was better than many previous years. They seemed to be heading in the right direction, but with everything else going on in my life, listening to the games on my transistor radio just wasn't much fun and the sports section of the newspaper became less of an attraction.

Mike Schmidt was still belting homeruns and Steve "Lefty" Carlton and Jim Lonborg were pitching well, but the surrounding cast was not strong. I kept hoping for a Philadelphia pennant, but by midsummer it was clear it would not be this year. It would be the 7th consecutive losing season. That is how I felt about how my year was going; another losing season.

Turning to the front page, I began reading about the war taking place halfway across the globe. Chi Linh Camp had been defended by the 215th Regional Force Company along with two 105 mm howitzers against an attack by the People's Army of Vietnam (PAVN) 7th Division.

I was thankful the war was still going on strong, as I feared it would be over before I reached my eighteenth birthday. I knew my options after high school were limited, at the very least. No college was going to accept me, and I had no craftsman skills. If the war were still going on, I would have an opportunity to demonstrate *real* courage. Perhaps even an opportunity to be a *hero*. Kill or be killed. The year before, I got a punch in my gut when I read about the Paris Agreement Treaty that stated the United States would essentially remove all remaining US Forces, including air and naval forces. U.S. military intervention halted and fighting between the governments of the United States, the Democratic Republic of Vietnam (North Vietnam) and the Republic of Vietnam (South Vietnam) ceased, which concerned me. But thankfully, the ceasefire lasted only a day.

I continued my reading. The two howitzers were quickly damaged, and the ammunition dump destroyed. The PAVN 3rd Battalion, 141st Regiment, with the help of the division's 28th Sapper and 22nd Artillery Battalion overran the base with heavy losses, but the PAVN 7th Division had unimpeded movement along Highway 14 between Chơn Thành and Đồng Xoài.

Turning the page, I almost missed the small article about Choo-Choo. The North Hills community was demanding an arrest as parents became more than nervous. I was stunned to read that the police were investigating Perry for the death of Choo-Choo, calling him *a person of interest,* and the longer I read, the more I saw their investigation was cloaked with the myth of objectivism. They had no other suspects. The fact that a homosexual interacted with Choo-Choo the day before he disappeared was more than enough reason to assume guilt. To hell with justice, to hell with anonymity and confidentiality, and, obviously, to hell with Perry Strathmore. Let's just rush to judgement! Coercion is a very strong drug. An arrest would need to be made, and it needed to be made soon, the article said. The bell rang signaling that it was time to change classes.

In Chemistry class I had a friend named Susan Cummings, an attractive girl with long blonde hair who only wore hip-hugger jeans and t-shirts to school. I would have asked Susan out on a date, but she had been dating Stone DuBois for as long as I could remember. Stone wasn't his given name, he was so named by his friends because, more often than not, he was stoned. Susan and I had become good friends as well as lab partners.

"Hey, Suz, do me a favor?"

"Sure Cal, as long as it's not to take off my blouse in the middle of our lab experiment."

"Great! Will you take it off after we turn in our lab findings?"

"Sure, Cal. For you, anything," she said with a smirk of a smile.

"Here's a dollar. Buy a copy of *Playgirl* and give me the centerfold. You can keep the rest of the magazine. I'm going to pull off a classic on old Bend-low."

"Okay," asked Susan without hesitating. "This ought to be good. I'll bring it to you on Monday."

Muskrat had been incognito ever since his father was put into a long-care facility. I guess that was the proper name, but people called it a nursing home. He was too young to be in there. Everyone else in that place was my grandparent's age. Mr. Zimmerman had become a fraction of the man he had been. Most of his voluntary muscles had become paralyzed, and the muscles of the mouth and throat, and those involved in breathing, become difficult so that eating, speaking, and breathing were compromised.

It was Friday evening, one of only two evenings my parents would let me stay out later with my friends. Muskrat was finally at a point where he needed a distraction, so he and Hunchback decided to hang out at Willow Grove Park Lanes, which boasted being the world's largest bowling alley with 116 lanes, located next to the iconic Willow Grove Park. I only found out that they had gone there after calling Hunchback's house to see if he wanted to do something. When I arrived, Muskrat was bragging about his hot new girlfriend, Tina.

"She let me get to second base, and tomorrow night I'll be sliding into third."

Hunchback decided to give him a reality check. "Ya know, she's going to be as fat as hippo a few years after you marry her?"

"Screw you," Muskrat barked. "You're just jealous."

"No really," Hunchback said. "If you want to see what a girl's going to look like in thirty years, look at her mother. Tina's mother has to walk sideways through a door. She's so fat she wears Orion's belt. It's all that pasta those Italians eat."

"Yeah, well I'm half-Italian and I'm not fat."

"Yes, you are," I added.

When they decided to head over to the billiards hall, I knew it would be another night of girl watching, over-consumption of soda and pizza, and maybe a little bowling. I wasn't into it so I announced I was going to head home and watch my Uncle Yaroslav do some of his wood carving.

"What the hell's wrong with you," asked Muskrat as he looked at me. "You haven't been yourself for months. You in love or something?"

"Yeah, he's hot for sea cow Cleary," Hunchback said as he threw his head back in laughter.

"Screw off," I retorted.

"She's got a face like a French manicure," screamed Muskrat over Hunchback's laughter.

"I'm outta here," I said while turning towards the exit.

"Seriously, Cal, what's been eating you?" asked Muskrat.

"Nothing," I solemnly said.

I had no sooner pushed through the glass double-doors when I realized that leaving at that moment was a terrible mistake. Seeing Mongrel and Benny, I knew I should have stayed with my friends. There was safety in numbers...sometimes.

Perhaps if I did not make eye contact, I would avoid the fury of the half man, half beast. A full head taler than me, Mongrel's entire existence stemmed from his desire to find prey. I was prey. A cold sweat beaded down my spine when I heard Mongrel's hoarse voice.

"Where you heading, Lloyd?"

"Nowhere," I mumbled.

"Nowhere? That is exactly where we're going, right Benny?" Mongrel asked as he turned to the much smaller gargoyle he called his friend.

"Yeah, Mongrel. That is exactly where we were going, nowhere." mimicked Benny with a cackle.

As my nemesis came closer, he put his oversized arm around my neck in a half-head lock, half-neck hug as I struggled to walk straight.

"You have any money?"

"No, I spent it all on skee-ball and a soda," I lied while trying to sound convincing.

"Don't jack rabbit me!" barked Mongrel. "I don't believe you! Give me your money," he said while moving precariously close to my face.

I thought about getting up and running, knowing that I could easily outrun the lummox, but Mongrel had been plotting. I was not his first prey. With surprising quickness, Mongrel pushed me to the ground, grabbed me by both ankles and lifted me vertically off the ground. Loose change trickled out of my pocket and rolled aimlessly on the gravel beneath me. Benny instinctively rummaged through my pockets finding my wallet in short order. Confiscating the 3 dollars that was in the billfold, Benny dropped the wallet at the same time Mongrel dropped me. Hitting my head on the gravel, I felt my neck snap forward as my back slam against the ground.

I thought, perhaps for only a foolish second, that I should call Bellamy to inflict serious pain and suffering on my two adversaries but, obviously, that was ridiculous, and I felt shame for even considering it. Bellamy never made an appearance in public. Of course not. I got up and shook off the parking lot dirt and gravel from my hands, shirt and pants.

A fever of hot rage swept over me that fueled my hateful imagination on how I would cause Mongrel's slow and painful death one day. My emotions teetered between self-loathing and rage, but there had been no avenues for me to express the rage, at least not yet. My frustration kept repeating itself over and over as the rage would build to a level where releasing it would be the natural conclusion, but I would have to stifle it and save it for another time. At this point, the camel's back would take less than a straw to break it.

To hell with Bellamy. I wanted to inflict the anguish and suffering myself. Perhaps trapping him in his car and burning him alive or pushing him off the bridge behind Jack Frost as I listened to Mongrel's scream for 3 or 4 seconds until he reached the train tracks down below would be appropriate vengeance. Maybe by concocting a poisonous powder with the contents of Ted's chemistry set, and slipping it in a soda from Joe's Market, I could, generously, offer Mongrel as a "peace offering." *Yeah, that is what I would do if...*

My neck still hurt the next day when I got out of bed, and I had not slept well, which was why I got out of bed so early. It was Saturday and apparently my parents had decided to sleep in. I threw on a pair of jeans and an Eagles sweatshirt and headed outside to see if the newspaper had any news about Choo-Choo's murder. Brushing my teeth and enjoying the habitual glass of orange juice would have to wait. Rumors had been flying around North Hills like a dry leaf that was at the mercy of a stout autumn wind. Perhaps today I could glean some reliable news. Sliding the rubber band off the rolled up daily, I received updated news aplenty.

> *A 42-year-old North Hills man is under arrest in connection with the death and rape of a teenage boy, Abington Police announced Tuesday.*
>
> *Perry Strathmore was arrested in connection with the death of 16-year-old Charles "Charlie" Cardin. The teenager's body was found by a caretaker at a pond in Hillside cemetery located between Ardsley and Roslyn, approximately 14 miles north of Philadelphia.*

The teen's mother, Judy Cardin, attended the announcement. Afterward, Mrs. Cardin said she was devasted by her loss. "Charlie was a special boy who only wanted to belong. He was naïve; too trusting and imagining everyone was a decent person. He did not deserve this.

The teen's stepfather was shown photos of the victim and identified him after hearing media reports of the discovery of an unidentified boy, according to a police affidavit, which was obtained by Philadelphia television station KYW. The stepfather told authorities Charlie had failed to come home after going outside to Pembryn Park to play ball.

An autopsy stated that "although multiple stab wounds and burn marks litter the victim's body, including his genitals, asphyxiation from sustained pressure was the cause of Cardin's death." The coroner believes Charlies was sexually assaulted. Time of death was between 3 – 5 pm on Tuesday, August 17th. Detective Robert Dalton stated that the time of death was key to the arrest of Strathmore in that the suspect was not at his flower shop and had no alibi.

Strathmore has pleaded not guilty and will be released on $25 thousand bail while he awaits trial for murder. Abington Township District Attorney stated that he will be seeking the death penalty due to the age of the victim and the heinous nature of the crime.

I dropped the paper in my lap. The despair that swept over me was greater than the newspaper ink that covered my hands. *I was with Perry on that Tuesday between 3 and 5. He could not have killed Choo-Choo.* Arrested? Like stepping onto a wad of bubble gum, I just could not shake it off.

Funny, no matter what turmoil is going on in your life, the world continues to turn as if nothing ever happened. People still went to work. Baseball games continued to be played. Doctor's appointments kept, and school still needed to be attended.

On Monday, as promised, Susan gave me a manilla envelope containing the centerfold. Walking into the library, the one place within the high school that had seldom seen my presence, I hid the centerfold Suzie had given me underneath my shirt. A had not been in the book warehouse since my magazine-revenge-project. A mousy-haired woman with cat-eye glasses sat sorting a pile of books looked up at me as her short Chinese counterpart was thumbing through the card catalog, contemplating the relative location of a book by using the Dewey Decimal System. The two librarians were known as Cheech and Chong by the students.

Not wanting to be remembered for asking the librarians for any one book, I walked the aisles of literary choices in search of something very specific. The smell of old paper and leather filled my nostrils and made me feel as if I were in a museum. Finally, next to the newspaper and magazine rack, I found what I had come for, the 1973 Abington High School Yearbook.

Searching the pages, I came to the English Department and found a photo of Mr. Benbow. Pulling the buck knife from my jacket pocket that I began carrying for "protection," I carefully cut out the photo, placed it on the table in front of me and replaced the yearbook. With surgical precision, I cut the face out of the nude model's centerfold and replaced it with the photo of Mr. Benbow.

Sneaking into the classroom before anyone arrived, I pulled down the projector screen and scotch taped the altered centerfold on to the screen, then released the screen so it rolled back up into its frame. Perhaps the only thing I had heard in the previous class was that on Thursday we would be watching a scene from Macbeth, starring Jon Finch.

Susan walked into the classroom seconds later wearing a skin-tight yellow and white stripped body suit, revealing the slightest impression of her nipples that only the most astute observer would have noticed. We were the first two in class, but by the time the bell rung, the remainder of the class had taken their seats, obedient to the schoolmaster's demands.

Mr. Benbow reminded the class that they would be watching a scene from the most recent filming of *Macbeth* and for the students to pay particular attention to Roman Polanski's use of exaggerated pessimism and the ugliness of the character's natures in contrast to their physical beauty. Benbow added that this version of Macbeth is presented in a more realistic style.

With this introduction, Mr. Benbow pulled down the projector screen to reveal the altered naked photo of himself. The classroom erupted in hysterics as Benbow pulled the handle of the screen too abruptly causing it to get jammed. He pulled and pulled, but to no avail, resulting in a sound of thunderous applause and more laughter. Finally, he ripped the photo off the screen and stormed out of the class. I thought, Shakespeare would have loved this story of moral decline.

CHAPTER TWENTY-SEVEN

*Murder in the murderer is no such ruinous thought as
poets and romancers will have it; it does not unsettle him,
or fright him from his ordinary notice of trifles; it is an act
quite easy to be contemplated, but in its sequel, it turns out
to be a horrible jangle and confounding of all relations.*
                                              —Ralph Waldo Emerson

I desperately needed a distraction from Choo-Choo's death and Perry's arrest, and I found it nine miles north of my home. Larger than North Hills, Willow Grove offered more shopping opportunities including a Kiddy City, an all-toy store with everything a kid could want. What made Willow Grove special was the park…the wonderful Willow Grove Amusement Park! The most incredibly perfect park in the whole world!

My Mom-Mom would tell me how John Phillip Sousa would play there every year for the first couple of decades of the century. It really had something for everyone, but what I and every kid in the Delaware Valley loved were the rides! It had the Tilt-a-whirl, Laff in Dark, Fascination, The Alps, the Thunderbolt, and the Tunnel of Love, a favorite ride for teenagers to neck as the small, painted, two-person boat would slip into the darkness which provided temporary privacy. Next to the park was the bowling alley, the scene of my latest beating at the hands of Mongrel. It was a popular evening destination when teenagers did not know what else to do with their sundown spare time, especially on Friday and Saturday nights when there was no shortage of teenage girls and fast cars.

Muskrat was grounded for being caught sticking a potato down the gas tank of his neighbor's car, and Hunchback was visiting his grandparents, so I called Mouche to see if he wanted to head to the park. Mouche not only agreed, but brought both a 6 pack of Ballentine and a joint.

The entrance to the park was strategically located across the street from where the trolley stopped. We could have taken the short train ride from nearby Ardsley station and walk across the street to the park, but that would have meant siphoning money from that which could be spent on rides, games, and food. We decided to ride our bicycles through the 425-acre Hillside cemetery, a huge spread of rolling hills and shaded land littered with tombstones and mausoleums, the same cemetery where Choo-Choo had met his demise. Since it would be dark on our return home, we tied flashlight on to our handlebars for the ride through the fields of death.

The large iron gates were locked at 5:00 pm, which would require one of us to climb the fence to the other side and wait to catch the bikes being passed over the steely bastion. Once on the other side of the fence, we would jump on the bikes and pass some of our favorite spots in the garden of remembrance. First on our route was the grave of MLB Hall of Fame pitcher and Chippewa Indian Charles "Chief" Bender. As was our custom, we would throw imaginary tomahawks toward Chief Bender's grave...out of respect, mind you.

We stopped when we got to Floaties pond, the half-acre body of water with a small bridge where Choo-Choo's body was found. The pond would never again be the place we would take model ships they had built for their maiden voyage; it would, from here on out, be viewed as the water of death. We would no longer draw straws to see who would have to set their ship on fire. But we were getting too old for that kind of stuff anyway.

We sat by the broken slat bridge and drank the beer between drags on the joint and stared at the yellow crime tape that surrounded the spot where Choo-Choo was found.

"Who do you think killed him?" asked Mouche in a solemn tone.

"I don't know. I've been thinking about that ever since it happened," I said without looking up from the water. "I don't know if he met someone he knew, and they thought he was an easy target, or if it was some whack-job who was a transient…some homeless, crazy guy."

"The paper said that they think it was some pervert. He'd have to be to sexually assault him, right?" Apparently, Mouche had not heard about Perry's arrest.

"I don't know about that. Sometimes murderers do stuff to throw off the police. I think it was his stepdad." I replied.

"Muskrat told me you guys saw him beating Choo-Choo up in the backyard."

"Yeah, we did. But he's a cop. You think cops are going to arrest a cop?" I asked.

"Well, they should. What about Reverend Markey. He wouldn't have done it, would he?"

"Who knows. Anything is possible. That guy gives me the creeps."

"Me, too. Let's get out of here," Mouche said as he straddled his bicycle.

We peddled faster when approaching the ghost of Billy Fox. Fox had been a corporal in the 95th Pennsylvania Infantry during the Civil War and recipient of the Congressional Medal of Honor. As far as his ghost is concerned, the story goes that as a private in Company A his troop was the first to enter Petersburg, Virginia, where he bravely assisted in the capture of one of the enemy's guns as well as the flag of the Confederate customhouse. While in Petersburg, he fell in love with a maiden of the South underneath a waning gibbous moon. After making Billy a fine southern dinner, she gave him a lighted torch and asked him to go to the root cellar to fetch some leeks and potatoes. While Billy was in the cellar, the lass slid a heavy board across the latch of the door that extended to the door frame locking Billy in. She quickly retrieved a can of gasoline and poured it down the vent pipe where Billy was holding the torch. When they found poor Billy black and brittle, a potato was clinched in his fist. Legend had it that whenever there is a waning gibbous moon you could hear Billy crying in pain. People were never sure if the crying was from being burned alive or from a broken heart.

That story always fascinated me. I guess all murders do, but some more than others.

We exited the cemetery on the Roslyn side of the cemetery and rode our bikes down Easton Road's sidewalk. While still several blocks from the amusement park, we could see The Alps, the park's signature rollercoaster. Moche tried to navigate between an old black woman wearing an overcoat, (although it was a warm evening,) and a telephone pole, causing her to nearly drop a bag of groceries.

Outside the main gate of the park, we chained our bikes to a speed limit sign. From the vantage point at the entrance, the buildings were all painted pale yellow with a white trim that harmonized with everything else, giving the first impression of being clean and unblemished. Our eyes moved from the various signs promising birch beer, ice cream sodas, and Sno Cones, stopping momentarily at each.

It was one thing to want to see the world's only high-diving zebra or even Charlie Bramble, a real-life alligator wrestler, but that is where my father would draw the line. He would preach to me about the foolishness of throwing away my hard-earned money to watch trained fleas or playing the Milk Bottle Pyramid Game, where "knock-them-all-over-and-win-a-prize," was the promise of the swindler tending the game. The bottom of the pins was always heavily weighted with lead, and the softballs filled with cork to make them lighter than regulation balls.

The prizes were worthless, of course, but they held a magnetic power on every kid, nonetheless. Kewpie dolls, super balls and the always popular stuffed animal were the prizes that lured the youth in. Continued play was encouraged as multiple small prizes could be traded in for a larger prize. The selection of prizes included a poster of Raquel Welch in patriotic bathing suit, Sophia Loren soaking wet on the beach or the inexplicably popular stuffed three-foot Cecil the Seasick Sea Serpent, of Beany and Cecil fame. But that was not what Mouche and I were there to see. The Sideshow was the Holy Grail of forbidden fruit. If my father got wind of this field trip to the dark corridors of human deformity, the consequences would be stiff, but when I quickly weighed the consequences, it was always worth the risk.

There were only a few things that my dad was adamant about. One of those things was clearly the carnival sideshow, or freak show as it came to be known. It was the seedy side of dark entertainment that would put on display anomalies and aberrations of the normal world. My father would say that you never, under any circumstances, find humor or make fun of someone else's misfortunes. His righteous anger would escalate when talking about the show's commercial exploitation of these people. Somehow, he once overheard friends and I talking about wanting to check out the freak show at Willow Grove Park. He made it clear, in no uncertain terms, that the sideshow was off limits. Of course, that just made me want to go all the more.

What mysteries of science are being hidden from me? I wondered. So bizarre and rare were these people that the public science books I was given at school never addressed these biological rarities. What deformities from around the world are there for young minds that continue to question conventional science?

The closest Mouche had ever come to a freak show was his great uncle Ernest who had his ear shot off in the Great War leaving a gaping hole flush up against his head. Fruit flies and gnats would relentlessly torment the old man in the summer as they were drawn to the waxy hole on the side of his head.

But I was fascinated by the life of a carny; life on the road, a small and mysterious fraternity built on "people gawking at you" and suspicion. People would pay to be invited into the freak's living room, but if the tables were ever turned—the thought of the freak sitting in the spectator's living room horrified them. No matter how low on the class ladder the observer was, any sense of pity for the carny was quickly replaced with the *"At least I'm not like this poor slob"* mentality.

As the sun went down in Willow Grove Park, there was an underworld that came to life, and it was beckoning me. It was a world of disturbing and dark truths that the rest of the world would choose to believe did not exist. Here, one could wander about in a mystical world where Fear and Curiosity would give birth to their daughter, Naivety. People did not believe these freaks of nature existed because in their sterile suburban lives, it simply did not fit. It could not be explained away or sanitized with a bottle of Mr. Clean. As the sun disappeared behind the Alps, Mouche and I headed toward the tent city.

The smell of popcorn was replaced by the redolent, yet distinctive, odor of old musty tent canvas and Ben Gay. The evening was warm and still, the type of night that makes one's neck pasty with sweat. The large floodlights were replaced with a string of light bulbs hanging carelessly at the entrance of each tent. The beautifully colorful and intricate signs beckoning visitors to brave the new and mysterious world that lay inside of the dark tents and to have their sense of reality stretched. The freak show drew the inquisitive and scratched that place in each of us that we cannot reach, or that we can reach, but refrain from doing so. My heart beat faster as we walked toward the forbidden, fearing my dad might be right, and wondering if I even wanted to see what was behind the curtain. The sounds of laughter and gawking were drowned out by a beckoning for us adolescents to enter the hootchie-kootchie tent. If time and money allowed, we would end our evening in there, admiring the scantily clad beauties.

The decision needing to be made at that moment was whether we should go into the "Ten-in-One" or be more selective and chose the "Single-O." The "Ten-in-One" offered ten sequential acts under one tent, all for a single admission price. The problem with the "Ten-in-One" was that, for a wannabee Sideshow connoisseur like me, at least half of the ten acts were deemed bogus. The tattooed man, fat lady who was married to the human skeleton, an incredibly thin man, and the various midgets, lacked the exhilaration that some of the other acts offered. What was tempting about the "Ten-in-One, however, was the potential ding, an extra act that was not advertised outside the tent. You did have to pay an additional fee, but the ding was almost always provocative and introduced as not suitable for women and children, though they always took a young boy's dime. After some discussion, Mouche and I decided to go with the Single-O, single attractions that we could select based on our strict criteria.

We paid our nickel and entered the third tent which was thick with smoke that had no avenue for escape from the chain-smoking hawker. In a cage was a boy who was covered with long brown hair, a black shoe-polish-like nose and sharpened teeth, reminiscent of Jo-Jo the dog-faced boy, instilling both fear and pity in the depths of our souls. We had no understanding that the boy suffered from hypertrichosis and as a result, ignorance bred fear. The man who brought us into the tent told a story of how the boy had been found living among wild dogs in a cave deep within the Bialowieza Forest, the last remaining primeval forest in Europe. On cue, the boy would growl, bark, and howl sending sweaty chills down the onlooker's spines. We quickened our pace and left the tent for the relative safety of the evening crowd that was beginning to gather.

The hot August night held the thick fog of cigar smoke between the green canvas tents as we ventured through the forbidden forest of abnormalities. Midget wrestling did not begin till 9 o'clock, so we wandered through maze of tents to find that which we were searching for. We did not exactly *know* what we were looking for, but it's the type of thing that you would know it when you saw it. We dismissed the exhibits for the rubberman and the human pin cushion as we searched for a show worthy of our hard-earned cash, and it did not take long before our patience paid off. We were almost sold on the idea of spending another five cents to see the lobster girl when next to the "hammer and ring the bell" we saw a painted poster of a half-woman, half-man oddity that piqued our interest.

ROBERT-ROBERTA
DOUBLE BODIED
HALF MAN-HALF WOMAN

That is when we heard the man with the stovepipe hat recite his seducing rhetoric. "Boys, you're in for a real treat," the huckster reassured us as he took a nickel from each of us. He continued his opening bally, but honestly, it did not take much for us to be sold. We had never heard the word hermaphrodite, let alone had ever seen one.

Walking into the dark tent was like entering into a bat-infested cave. We were consumed with fear but spurred on by unquenchable curiosity. Passing the huckster's outstretched arm, we could only see a maroon curtain to our left, illumined by a small spotlight.

"Have a seat, young men. I'll be with you in a minute," came a sweet voice from behind the curtain.

Mouche and I were alone among a group of a few dozen folding chairs, and it wasn't long before the curtain opened with two-foot progressions from an unseen person jerking on the cord. There standing sideways was the profile of a middle-aged woman, wearing bright red lipstick and dressed in a cranberry and gold paisley dress.

"Do you like what you see, boys" she asked.

"Uh, yeah, I guess so," Mouche answered.

"What, are you crazy? You *like* this freak," I whispered to Mouche.

"Well, don't get too sweet with me," she responded in a much lower, scratchy voice. And with that she turned 180 degrees to reveal a bearded man with dark slacks, a brown-striped shirt, and a weathered leather vest.

"Shit!" I shouted.

Mouche stood up and opened his mouth, but nothing came out. His eyes were as large as dinner plates as he stood stiff as a week-old hoagie roll. He.... she, turned her entire body so it was facing us to reveal a half-man, half-woman and, to our added surprise, began to undress. "It" undressed down to a pair of short shorts and a Tarzan like top which revealed a hairy man's chest on one side and a well-formed, hairless woman's breast on the other with a star pasty on the nipple. While the two of us remained in a state of shock, she, or he, picked up a mandolin and began to sing:

> You left me in misery
> when you up'd and took my hosiery.
> There's a fight goin' on inside me,
> I don't know who's gonna win,
> There a fight goin' on inside me
> and it's going to end in sin.

"Damn!" cried Mouche.

> *When my lover decided to put me on the shelf,*
> *I ended up making sweet love to myself*

There's a fight goin' on inside me,
I don't know who's gonna win
There's a fight goin' on inside me,
but I'm my next of kin.

As if on cue, we both yelled, "Ohhhhhhhh, shit." I ran to get out of there, turning back just in time to see Roberta pull Mouche close to her breast. Mouche yelled at me, "Get your ass over here."

As I approached the exit, my right foot grabbed the guy-line sending me flying through the air, landing me flat on my face. Before I could get on all fours, Mouche had hurdled over me and quickly exited through the tent flap. It did not take long for me to run past Mouche. We ran past the Two-Headed Cow and the Camel Girl and turned down an alley that led to another tent. We took one step inside. "Hello. Is anyone here?"

There was no response. The tent was lit by a single bulb dangling from the tent post. In the corner was a bed of nails leaning against the wall and to their left was an oak dresser with a half dozen jars of pickled punk, a carnival term for abnormal human fetuses. In one jar was a two-headed hamster and in another twin human fetuses joined together just above the ribcage. Mouche picked it up and turned it toward the light to get a better look.

"Damn!"

"You better put that down, and we need to get out of here!" I whispered.

Mouche put it down at the same moment we heard a voice.

"What the hell are you doing in here!"

We turned to see a man standing in the shadows....

"Uh, nothing."

"Don't jackrabbit me, kids."

We quickly left the tent and went down to the last act in the Freak Show tent village. Shaken, we still had enough money to see the Human Ostrich. A man who would swallow all kinds of outrageous things, like a pair of scissors, razor blades and a broken light bulb, which was a must-see. That would have been freaky enough but, to our surprise, it became a regurgitation act as the objects came back up one at a time.

Mouche wanted to see the three-legged man, but I could not see the point in dropping cash on an extra appendage, so I told Mouche I would meet him in front of Chang and Fang, the Siamese Twin exhibit.

Before I got to the Chinese duo, I saw the banner for Zora, the fortune teller and stopped in front of her tent. My Sunday School scripture memorization of Isaiah 8:19 laid heavy on my amygdala like a brick on a marshmallow, crushing my inclinations. *And when they say to you, "Inquire of the mediums and the necromancers who chirp and mutter," should not a people inquire of their God? Should they inquire of the dead, on behalf of the living?* I thought of another verse from Leviticus that stated something about being cut off from one's people and being unclean, but I could not recall the exact wording. *What people, exactly, would I be cut off from?* I wondered. *I have no people. Is it worth a quarter of my hard-earned money?* The suspense of Perry's trial and the fear of the unknown was enough motivation for me to pull the canvas tent cover back and enter the dark chamber.

It was disturbingly dark, except for a small light directly above a crystal ball that had small bubbles rising within it. I began to question my decision when I was startled by the gypsy who grabbed my hand and led me to a seat in front of the illuminated ball. Tenderly, she put her hand on my shoulder and sat me down while gently removing the clenched twenty-five cent piece I held in my fist. A stream of jasmine perfume lingered behind as she walked around the small table and spoke softly as she faced me. She was younger than I expected; not as old as my mother, yet clearly past forty.

The gypsy was painted with heavy makeup which included black lipstick and wore a long purple scarf tied around her head with the end trailing down halfway her back and a long skirt that came down to her mid-calf which was of many colors. Of eastern European descent, the woman spoke with a heavy accent, but slowly enough so I could understand.

"You are troubled, my son," she whispered with an aura of mystique.

I said nothing.

"The crystal ball detects anguish within you which is causing static which prevents me from seeing your future clearly. Let me see your palm, my dear one," the mitt-reader whispered.

The gypsy took my hand and explored my palm with her long index finger when suddenly I heard a sound from somewhere behind her. Fearing that we were not alone, I squinted to see something moving on a floor lamp. It did not take long for me to identify the squirrel monkey dressed in little green suit jacket and a straw hat as it moved into the light and sat on a stool next to me.

"You are a friend of misfortune. There's trouble that is brewing like a typhon that rises from the sea. Escape is not that easy when there is nothing to hide behind. My child, it is only going to get worse. You need to avoid this friend, or you will drink the same poison that made him ill. There is no cure for him, but there is for you, *if…. you keep a safe distance between you and him.*"

I massaged her words and knew she must be giving me the credence to refrain from testifying as Perry's alibi. Looking back at the monkey, I saw that it was masturbating while smiling it's crooked and dark-stained teeth.

"Don't mind, Mihai," she said as she viewed the disturbed look on my face. "He only strokes himself to get an erection. He does not spill his seed." It was clearly time for me to leave.

Again, I remained quiet. I have always been suspect of mystics. The question has always been, what percentage of these sorcerers are nothing but swindlers and what percent actually believe what they are doing? Or, perhaps, have some kind of power to *tell fortune or fate?* My concern was, if this woman did possess some kind of supernatural power, was it satanic?

The woman's facial expression suddenly changed. "You have betrayed a friend. *That* is what this is about. Yes, you have betrayed someone. No. There are two people you have betrayed! You must leave at once!"

And leave, I did. Mouche was waiting by the entrance to the Siamese Twins, clearly disappointed by the three-legged man when I walked up to him.

"Let's get out of here."

As we were walking out of the Freak Show tent with our heads turned away from the direction we were walking, I walked smack dab into some woman's chest, knocking her over.

"I'm so sorry, ma'am," I said while bending over to help the lady up. It was then that I felt a horrible pit in my stomach. The woman I had knocked over was Mrs. Sharp, the piano teacher who taught my sisters and brother, and who just happened to live next door to Mouche.

"Donald Garnier, do your parents allow you to go into that House of Sin?"

"Uh, I don't know," Mouche responded, knowing that before he would get home his mother and father would know he had ventured into the dark underworld of freaks. What I feared was that they would phone my parents. If so, I was screwed.

"Well, I'm sure they wouldn't approve," the woman said.

"Yeah. I guess you're right. We didn't see nothing. We won't do that again," Mouche said, trying to defuse the situation.

"Anything." Mrs. Sharp corrected.

"What?"

"Anything. The correct word is anything. You didn't see anything."

"Exactly!" Mouche said as we walked away.

Before leaving the park, I wanted to stop by one game of chance and spend my last fifty cents. "Shoot the Star" was a game where you are handed a Tommy Gun replica, one similar to the guns the 1920s gangster would pull out of a violin case; this one shooting BBs. That alone made the game worthwhile. The object of the game was simple, shoot the one-inch red star completely out of the small piece of paper hanging on a line with the help of a clothespin. If any red remains on the card, you lose. If successful, you win the prize of your choice, including a black & white TV, a set of walkie talkies or, what I had my eyes set on; a magenta-colored Rupp minibike! I was an excellent shot with a BB gun, so I thought my odds were significantly better at this game than the others the park offered.

I placed my two quarters on the counter and chose one of the guns that looked as though the barrel was straight. Being an excellent marksman, I figured I had a better than 50-50 shot at winning the mini bike. Instead of holding the trigger down and having all 100 BBs exhausted in 6 or 7 seconds, my strategy was to fire only a few pellets at a time in a circle, carefully eliminating any red that was visible. my focus was as keen as a heron stalking a frog, and as I began shooting, the star began disappearing. By the time the last BB left the barrel of the Tommy Gun, there was no red visible on the white paper! Exuberant, I screamed, "I did it! I won the minibike!"

"Unbelievable!" Mouche chimed in. "You did it, Cal!"

"Not so fast, Cowboy," the carny said as he interrupted the celebration. Taking the paper off the line he turned it over to reveal a small hanging chad of red paper.

"But there's not a spec of red on the front of the paper. The game is to shoot the red star off the front of the paper, and I did that," I argued.

"Look kid, I didn't say the front of the paper. The sign says to shoot all of the red star out. You didn't do that, now scram."

"You're a lying, cheating piece of monkey shit," I responded. Turning around at people who began to gather at the sound of the commotion, I said, "Folks, steer clear of this game. This Communist Carny reneged on my prize! Don't waste your money. He'll rip you off!"

As people turned to walk away from the booth, the carny lifted the end of the counter to come over to the front where we were standing. "Why you little creep," he yelled while reaching for me.

"Let's get out of here," screamed Mouche as he ran for the exit. I was only a step behind him.

Exiting the park, we walked over to where our bikes were. As Mouche was unlocking the chain, he turned to me and said, "You got screwed."

"I know I did. Pisses me off. I won the minibike. How cool would that have been?"

"Very! answered Mouche.

CHAPTER TWENTY-EIGHT

*It's harder to kill people. The empathy is so much stronger
that the mind must invent new reasons. But, if we can
somehow link it to our own survival, the mind will make
the devious twists and turns necessary to rationalize it.
We're very good at that. Prejudice is a disease created by
the acceptance of ignorance, the fear of the unknown and the
hatred of God.*

—Jean M. Auel

W ord of my adventure to the sideshow had reached Dasha before I got home, and this time my dad had decided on my sentence. I knew it was more about how he detested people taking advantage of those who had an abnormality; however, I did not feel like I was taking advantage of anyone. I paid the asking price, and I figured that no one forced them to participate in that line business. Punishment from my father amounted to being grounded for a week, and his disappointment in me. The latter was much worse than not hanging out with the guys.

Obedience was a God-given commandment, but I always seemed to learn better the hard way. Disobedience brought discovery, and discovery, knowledge, but, of course, you never had control over that which you learned. You *can* control what you learn by asking questions or by reading a book you select on a desired subject, but what you learn from ignoring instruction from one with a hidden agenda is uncertain. It can be enlightening or problematic. Sometimes, you really do not want to know the truth. Falsehood is often more palatable.

I walked into the kitchen where Audrey had just finished warming up a can of Campbell's alphabet soup. She was home from grad school for a few weeks. As I sat down to my bowl, I stared at the steam rising as my mind was fixed on Perry, not hearing my sister ask me if I wanted some saltines.

"What's the matter with you," she asked.

"Nothing," I mumbled.

"Are you grounded again?"

"Aren't I always grounded?"

"What did you do this time?"

"I went out and had a good time. You know, that's against the rules. I'm not allowed to have a good time," I responded.

I never heard what Audrey said next. She was busy trying to spell words with her alphabets while I devoured the floating letters, fearing they would spell *disaster*.

That Perry-thing was bothering me. *Surely, they would figure out that it could not have been him. Geez, Perry did not have a mean bone in his body. They would release him any day now, wouldn't they?* A deep sense of dread passed over me like a cool, wet wash cloth. *What if Perry told the police that he had an alibi… that I had been with him most of the afternoon? What will I do? I would have to deny it. I cannot, I will not, admit to having a friendship with Perry. Afterall, everyone would think I was queer. Who would believe that we had a platonic, normal relationship? No one! Damn, Perry. Why did he have to put me in this spot?*

No matter where I went in town, the talk was about Perry's arrest, and the public consensus was that Perry was guilty. His soft, friendly demeanor was simply a façade that he used to lure the poor boy to his death. Choo-Choo's murder was the biggest tragedy to ever transpire in our parochial village. Other than Jacob Rainer, who had shot his wife's lover while the adulterer was still on top of his wife, North Hills had never experienced a murder. This was even bigger than when Randi Lopez took off for the Bahamas with her high school English teacher. That court trial was a circus, but the one to come would make that look like Romper Room.

My mind began forming justification for not coming to my friend's defense; rationalizing why I could not come forward. *Even if they went to trial, they would never find him guilty… would they?*

It was obvious that the police and D.A. knew that Perry was a homosexual. That alone would be enough to convince an antiseptic, suburban jury that Perry was more than capable of any number of sexual deviances. Even murder was conceivable since there would be an obvious motive; the need to cover up the assumed sexual assault.

After my latest detention, I walked to the nearly deserted east wing of the school where my locker was located. After retrieving my notebook and a paperback copy of *Lord of the Flies*, required reading, I walked down the long hallway and pushed the heavy metal double-doors and heard them slam behind me. I had not taken two steps outside when the cool Autumn breeze reminded me that I had forgotten my jacket. I went to the door, but it was locked. *It figures. I cannot do anything right!* Stepping aside to the tall glass window I cupped my hands and looked inside pressing my nose hard against the glass. There was no one there, so banging on the door was worthless. I would have to walk clear around the other side of the school where the gymnasium was located to find an open door. I felt fortunate to find the door by the pool entrance unlocked, perhaps my luck today was changing, I thought as I headed back to the southside corridor toward my locker.

My fingers made short work of the combination lock and I opened the locker, grabbed my jacket, and headed for the nearest door. As I approached the exit, I faintly heard someone talking at a distance, a mere whisper. It was a girl's voice that sounded vaguely familiar, but it was the familiarity of the girl's perfume that brought awareness; having notes of jasmine, freesia, and apple blossom.

As I got closer, my eyes widened. I knew who that voice and perfume belonged to. Who is she talking to? I deliberately walked even quieter, so I could sneak up and ease drop on the conversation. Positioning myself adjacent to the blue glass pane across the hall, I could see Simone's reflection in the glass. I could not decipher exactly what I was feeling, whether I was angry or elated.

"...and they said they were my friends. What is wrong with me? Really? What the hell's wrong with me." There was a short moment of silence, and then the voice continued. "Oh, stop it! You always say that, and I know you're just trying to make me feel better. Is it too much to have just one friend? One?"

There was no answer to Simone's question. I pressed my shoulder against the wall and got as close to the corner as I could without being seen.

"I hate it here. I want to leave this place, but that is a dream, isn't it? If I really wanted to get out of here, I would need money, and I don't have zip."

I could not resist. I had to see who it was she was speaking to. I slid my face up to the crease in the wall and allowed my left eye to peek around the corner. Simone. Just as beautiful even with a frown on her face. She was sitting on the steps and ...there was no one else. Unpredictably, I completely understood. Simone was a dandelion.

"How about that?" Bellamy whispered, having just appeared. "Maybe I could have a special relationship with her imaginary friend," he continued with a chuckle.

"Should I let her know that I heard her conversation? Me, more than anyone in the entire world, got it. I could tell her that I truly understood what the world never would."

"Yup," responded Bellamy, "but will she be devastatingly embarrassed?

I walked back the way I came, about a third the way down the hallway. Then, turned around and made enough noise with my sneakers so Simone would realize that someone was approaching. Deliberately pushing the toe of my sneakers into the tiled floor, a squeaking sound announced my arrival.

"Simone?"

"Baby!" She said as she jumped off the step and put her outstretched hands around my neck.

"I thought you moved." I said with a somewhat raised voice. "What the hell? You could not call me? Write me a letter? You didn't even have the decency to tell me you were going to move?" I regretted the words before they even had a chance to pierce Simone's heart. I *did* want her to hurt as much as I had been. My conflicting emotions were a battle between complete delight to have been reunited with Simone and anger fueled by rejection and abandonment.

"I didn't know we were going to move. My Mom lost her job when they closed the Sears catalog store, and she couldn't afford the rent, so we moved in with my aunt in Crestmont. She did not want me to worry, so she never told me until the day we moved. And I did call you, a million times!" Simone's voice had changed, unveiling an anger. "Your mother always answered and said she would tell you that I called, that is until the last time I called. That time she said that you instructed her to tell me that you had a girlfriend, and to never call again. Besides, the Friday and Saturday before we moved, you never came by, like you promised. Remember?"

I did remember. Like Simone, that had not been my fault. My parents had kidnapped me for that stupid surprise trip to Muncy to take my brother to music camp. I remembered how I tried to slip away to call her and when I finally had, there was only an operator's recording that the line had been disconnected.

"My parents forced me to go with them to take my brother to some music camp in the middle of nowhere."

I opened the heavy door and held it for Simone. I walked over to the small-roofed area where students boarded their bus after school. Simone followed. Standing there, I gazed out to the parking lot.

"That is not true. What my mom told you is a lie! I don't know why she told you that. I did not have a girlfriend and I certainly didn't tell her that I didn't want to talk to you. The complete opposite is true. That weekend, I did try calling you, but the phone was never free and by the time I got back home and called, all I got was a message saying the number was disconnected. You were gone." There was no response from Simone. It was as if she was weighing the legitimacy of the explanation to see if the scales would tip toward fallacies or truth. "Are you alright?" I asked.

"I am now that you're here. I was just upset because a group of girls that I thought were my friends decided to head over to Carvel's for ice cream. I assumed I was invited, but they said there wasn't room for me in Anita's car, even though there were only four of them. I swear I never seem to fit in."

"Fit in? I'm the one that doesn't fit in. I don't conform. Never have. You've always had plenty of friends at school."

"You haven't seen me in over a year. How would you know who my friends are? What you think you understand, you don't, Calvin! Let me tell you about not fitting in. I'm adopted. My teenage mother deserted me when I was born. Who the hell knows where my father is or who he was, for that matter? Every click in this school *accepts* me in some superficial way, but when it comes down to being a friend, when it's not beneficial to them, I don't exist. The blacks at school refer to me as Mrs. Uncle Tom, Betty Crocker, or School Girl and the whites use me as their token to appease their consciences."

I felt myself at a crossroads that needed a decision. *Should I simply get up and walk away without another word, reciprocating the pain and confusion I had felt when Simone had moved without warning, or should I take her into my arms and tell her how incomplete I had felt without her. Do I really need this on top of everything else that is going on in my life. Do I even have time for her?*

It started to rain. Not the type of rain that would accompany dark clouds and a sense of loss, but rather a steady drizzle through some lingering sunshine that I hoped would wash the dirt from the memory of unacceptance and inadequacy. The kind of rain that makes things clean. I didn't have to make that decision.

Not knowing what my response would be, she took a chance and leaped at me, locking her hands behind my neck and kissing me with delight. I responded, somewhat reluctantly at first by placing only one hand on her waist, but I could not resist her touch. Relenting, I wrapped my hands around her freely. I relaxed the embrace, holding her by her shoulders, and looked fixedly at her face and kissed her again. I had missed Simone terribly. A plethora of maturity, both physical and emotional, created a beautiful change in Simone from the last time I had seen her. What was once a natural prettiness of a middle school girl had morphed into the exquisiteness of a young lady. I was transported to my earlier dream where she was a fair maiden and I, the knight in shining armor.

She could not contain her smile and glee. That smile would have lighted the darkest of ocean storms, and it was exactly what I had longed for as I had become lost in one such gale. Simone was the beacon of light that brought me safely to shore. There was always something about my relationship with her that was covert, at least back then when I was dating her. It was a forbidden love that was so enticing. It seemed as though everything was more attractive when I wasn't supposed to have it.

Unannounced, Simone ran toward the parking lot with her arms outstretched as if she was welcoming the rain, trying to dance between the rain drops without getting wet. Her hair glistened as raindrops fell upon it, and she laughed as she threw her head back, lighthearted, and mirthful, as if to say that everything was going to be alright.

I, however, felt a happy kind of sad. I wanted everything to be alright, but I knew better. I knew that even Simone could not fix the situation with Perry, only I could do that, and the trepidation of the situation prevented me from truly enjoying the moment. My fear of coming forward as Perry's alibi dampened everything, my happiness, my contentment, my purpose, my hope.

🚲

The following morning was beyond beautiful, with a hint of a warm breeze, and large puffy clouds. It was the type of day that could just about make you forget about all your troubles. To make the day even better, as if that was possible, word had spread around town of Mongrel's arrest on assault charges. Sometimes three 7's come up at the same time on a slot machine. An argument over a parking spot at Willow Grove Bowling Lanes ended with some poor guy in a coma at Abington Hospital. Mongrel had spent the weekend in jail but was released on bail.

Bellamy had given me a brilliant idea. I jumped on my Schwinn and peddled over to Hillside Cemetery to find new burial sites. I had gotten my driver's license but access to the family car did not happen frequently. Being in the cemetery alone was more than eerie, and I knew I had to make quick work of my idea before a caretaker, or a burial took place in this necropolis. Before I could do that which I came to the cemetery to do, I needed to go by Floaties Pond to see the scene of the crime once again. The yellow police crime tape that had quarantined a large portion from the wooden slat bridge to the large sycamore was sagging, as if to say that the murder was old news. I walked over to where Choo-Choo drew his last breath and stood there with thoughts rushing through me like water through a dike. A fear overcame me that I had only felt once before.

I heard a car approaching and quickly jumped back on my bike and continued my original search. It was not long till I saw a rectangular patch of fresh brown and red dirt. Letting my bicycle fall on the soft grass, I walked over to the heap of fresh flowers. Gladiolas were too funeral-like, but there were plenty of chrysanthemums, daisies, and carnations. Taking out my pen knife, I cut a selection of flowers and assembled them into a bouquet.

Crestmont was a small black community that overlooked Willow Grove Park. Simone had given me directions and when I approached her house, I saw she was outside, anticipating my arrival. She wore purple hip-huggers as tight as a Chinese finger trap and her skin-tight body suit accentuated her small but flawlessly shaped breasts.

"Here, these are for you," I said while extending my clenched hand of flowers.

"They are absolutely beautiful! You are the absolute best, Calvin Lloyd," Simone said with a brightest of smiles. "My mom is at my aunt's house. She will not be home till 5 at the earliest." Simone said as she took my hand and directed me into the house. "Let's go to my room."

Immediately, my mind began racing as to the possibilities. Alone with Simone? *Dreams do come true!* I thought as she led me by the hand up the wooden stairs to the second floor.

Simone's room was bright, with two large windows trimmed with sky-blue drapes which faced the street below. The hardwood floor was partly covered by an oval rug the shade of cornflower. An Earth, Wind and Fire poster was mounted above the single bed which was unmade.

Simone slid in an 8-track tape of *The Stylistics* into the Montgomery Ward stereo, setting the mood which needed little help. *You are Everything* flowed out of the stereo as she sat on the bed, pulling me close to her and began kissing as if to devour me. Our lips and tongues impulsively danced together and as we rolled one way and then another, our clothes became cumbersome. Simone wore a flowered turquois bra, and she turned on to her side to allow me to unfasten it. I cupped her breasts and held them, stroked them deftly as if they were fragile. Simone's nipples responded to my touch as my body responded to hers. Simone's breathe quickened as she felt my hands glide down the hollow of her back.

We were novices at love making, and our innocence had no discomfiture as we taught each other what felt pleasurable while the stereo serenaded us. The intensity of the moment was beyond mere verbal expressions or cliches, and yet it was over much faster than either of us had expected. Making love with Simone was everything my earlier "Mrs. Robinson" experience was not. I looked tenderly at her serene contentment and gently ran the back of my hand down her taffeta-soft cheek. We ignored the 8-track's mechanical click as it switched programs, and Simone rested her head on my chest as we both fell into a deep, contented slumber.

We were awakened by the sound of Simone's mother tossing her keys into the glass bowl on the Centeno accent cabinet that stood by the front door.

"Shit, my mom's home! Get dressed!"

"Simone? Honey? I'm home, Baby," came a voice from down below.

"Hi Mom. I'll be down in a minute," yelled Simone, with hopes of delaying her mother's inevitable trip upstairs; however, Simone's hope was short-lived.

"Don't bother, I have to put these bags in my bedroom. Went shopping with Aunt Rhonda."

I was already opening the window to Simone's bedroom while trying to get my second leg into my jeans. I was out of the window quickly but soon realized getting to the ground would be a challenge, the distance was just a bit too far to land safely. I thought of hanging off the gutter, then dropping to the ground and rolling, but I feared the gutter would give way. I shimmied myself along the eave of the roof and slid my buttocks towards the downspout. Reminiscent of climbing the rope in gym class, I grabbed the downspout and began my descent.

All was going well until two of the rusted brackets gave way and the top of the downspout gave way. As if in slow motion, it made its way toward the ground like a felled tree,

forcing me to let go of the downspout. I hit the ground and felt my ankle turn as I rolled across the grass. A moan came from my mouth as I laid there withering in pain. Not wanting to hear an ultimatum from Simone's mother, I struggled to my feet and hobbled toward the neighbor's bushes.

Inside the house Simone's mother had heard the downspout release from its perch but thought the sound came from within the house.

"What was that noise?" Mrs. Arnett asked with a quizzical look on her face.

"What sound?" responded Simone.

"Girl, are you telling me you didn't hear that? It sounded like the Titanic hitting an iceberg."

"Oh, yeah, I heard that. I thought it was those old water pipes. Where did you go shopping?" Simone said trying to steer the conversation away from the obvious.

"Gimbels," answered Mrs. Arnett as she leaned over the kitchen sink to look out the window. "I do believe the rain spout fell off the house. That was the sound I heard. Unh unh," she said as she slowly shook her head from side to side. "Must have been that hard rain we got last night."

CHAPTER TWENTY-NINE

*Prejudice is a disease created by the acceptance of ignorance,
the fear of the unknown, and the hatred of God.*

A
t Sunday's church service, Reverend Markey had preached on 1 Corinthians chapter 13, the love chapter. He often spoke about love. The sermon kept repeating in my head as I tried to settle on some elusive level ground. *Love is patient, love is kind. It does not envy, it does not boast, it is not proud. It does not dishonor others, it is not self-seeking, it is not easily angered, it keeps no record of wrongs. Love does not delight in evil but rejoices with the truth. It always protects, always trusts, always hopes, always perseveres.*

I saw the implication this scripture had on my relationship with Simone. *It doesn't delight in evil...it's not self-seeking...it is not easily angered.* I felt the coward in me take control of my mind like aliens had done to a man in a recent episode of Rod Serling's *Twilight Zone*. If I truly loved Simone, I would push aside my cowardness and stand-up to the inevitable ugly remarks. *It always protects, always trusts, always hopes, always perseveres.* If I truly loved her, I would not care what people said about me dating a black girl, and I would protect her from all the consequences of my decision. *If* I truly loved her, I would share with her the truth about my careworn dilemma about testifying at Perry's upcoming trial. *If...if...*

On the way home from church, my father said he needed to stop for gas. I suggested we go to the Texaco station so I could spend five cents on some grape balls at Plockies, but I knew that he would dismiss that idea. My parents always filled up at the Sinclair station; their gas was two cents a gallon cheaper and they gave away S & H green stamps. *Too bad I can't redeem them for a new life; a carefree life somewhere Simone and I can live alone.*

Ever since our midsummer's night *faire l'amour,* Simone and I were consumed with when and where our next dalliance would occur. Finding an appropriate location that was private, yet romantic, was difficult for the amorous couple we had become. I had considered Hillside Cemetery since it was quiet and there were plenty of spots we could be hidden from view, but I was not sure how Simone would react to making love in a boneyard… no pun intended. New housing construction was another, but the idea of one of us getting a splinter in the ass axed that idea. The quandary would preoccupy my mind for the majority of my waking, and non-awake, moments that Perry's trial did not occupy.

The next day, before I headed to the bus stop, I checked the small metal box which, twice a week, would contain three bottles of milk left by the invisible milkman. Apparently, he would come in the wee hours of the morning. Each time I checked the metal box, I hoped to find at least one bottle of rich, chocolate moo juice, but to no avail. Just the white stuff. I even tried to use my flair of persuasion and salesmanship on my stepmother. I told her that I had read that chocolate milk is more nutritious than its white cousin, delivering 11 grams of protein and double the carbohydrate content, ideal for the muscles of growing youth. She quickly obliterated my pitch with a short retort that it cost more. I figured that Dasha did not believe I had read it anywhere since my reading habits were basically nonexistent; *Spy vs. Spy* in *Mad* magazine, did not count.

As I rode the bus to school, I stared out the window contemplating my masculinity, or lack of, and what it would take for me to assimilate into being *a man.* I struggled with what should have been my loyalty as a friend to Simone and Perry, and my insecure reluctance to do the difficult thing. There was a constant bickering in my mind, like the iconic angel on one shoulder and the demon on the other. I hoped it was simply a case of teenage cowardice that I would soon outgrow, but the demons were too familiar and I had often yielded to their lure.

My first class of the morning was English. Ever since my *Playgirl* centerfold escapade, Mr. Benbow would always have a scowl on his face whenever he looked at me. We were still studying Shakespeare, to which I responded with condescension, that is until we came to Sonnet 130. Unexpectedly, Shakespeare had captured the essence of my heart. I had to look up some of the words the celebrated poet used, so I could fully comprehend its meaning, and when I did, I wondered if Shakespeare had not fallen in love with a dark-skinned princess as well.

If snow be white, why then her breasts are dun. Her beasts are dun? What in the world does that even mean? Webster described dun as brownish gray. "Yes!" I thought. If snow is white, then her breasts are a brownish gray. *If hairs be wires, black wires grow on her head.* "Yes! Yes! Of course," I thought with exhilaration. I became thrilled with the discovery that one of Britain's greatest authors was in love with a lady from the dark continent! And 400 years before I did!

I had memorized the entire sonnet and kept repeating the last few lines:

> *I grant I never saw a goddess go;*
> *My mistress, when she walks, treads on the ground:*
> *And yet, by heaven, I think my love as rare*
> *As any she belied with false compare.*

This validation of my relationship with Simone by the classic English author of an interracial love affair was further reinforced when I brought home *Diamond Girl,* the most recent album by *Seals and Crofts*. I had bought it the day before at Woolworth's 5 & Dime. I did not have the time to open the album the day before, let alone play it. Looking at the photograph of the pop stars, I slid my thumb nail across the plastic film so I could open the album. The album jacket opened like a book and inside were photographs of both Dan Seals and Dash Crofts with their wives. To my amazement, I saw that Dan Seals was married to a black woman.

Scandalous, I thought, but then I was reminded of the courage that love can generate. Maybe 1974 had ushered in a social awakening that the turbulent 60s never could. Maybe, just maybe, my relationship with Simone would be accepted by my family, but any chance of fanning the flame of hope was quickly extinguished. I knew better than that. Those kinds of thoughts were more those I would live in my dreams late at night, but those dreams had recently tried to morph into reality so that I had difficulty differentiating between the two.

I slipped the vinyl disc onto the Radio Shack Realistic turntable and listened to track one; the album title song, *Diamond girl*.

Another exhausting day of school had come to a close, another day that made me feel like I was doing time in prison. I had even began crossing off the days till graduation by drawing tally marks on the small bulletin board in my bedroom. The magic number would be 180, the number of days in a school year. I preferred counting up the number of school days rather than counting down to graduation. Again, my mindset was that I was doing time, serving a sentence.

Hunchback and Muskrat were waiting for me when I left the school building.

"What do you wanna do?" asked Hunchback.

"I don't know. I don't feel like anything," I responded.

"I'm gonna go see Tina," Muskrat announced.

"Didn't you see her last night?" I asked.

"Yep."

"Did you get a little trim?"

"I'm getting all I want," Muskrat said with a smile as he turned and gave a halfhearted wave while walking away.

"I'm going home," I said. "I'll catch you tomorrow."

My thoughts regarding Perry's predicament continued when I got home and were only interrupted by my stepmother who was calling me to the kitchen. Dasha told me to set the table for dinner, and I was mindful to position the silverware in their proper sequence; folded paper napkin to the left of the plate, knife with teeth facing toward the plate was on the right, with the spoon on its far outside shoulder. Dasha, with her back to me and facing the sink, nonchalantly mentioned that Simone had called.

"That colored friend of yours called the other day. What's her name, Sarina?"

"Simone," I responded. I Felt the anger rise within my being, but not wanting to get into an argument with Dasha over her habitual reluctance to tell me when Simone would call.

"What?"

"Simone. Her name is Simone, Mom," I barked.

"Well, whatever. I heard her mother was arrested for driving drunk. Apparently, she hit a utility pole while under the influence."

"Where did you hear that from? And why didn't you tell me she called?"

"Seems it slipped my mind. Why are you so upset? Do you like her, Calvin?"

My heart sank as thoughts raced from unanswerable questions to a dreaded hypothetical answer. *This cannot be true, but Dasha never spoke this badly about anyone, did she? I remembered what Hunchback had said about Muskrat's girlfriend, Tina. If you want to know what a girl is going to be like thirty years from now, look at her mother. I wonder if that applied to a woman's character as well as how she will look. Does the apple fall far from the tree? But her mother isn't her biological mother, so that theory does not apply, does it? I should have known it was too good to be true.*

"You can't keep things like that a secret in a small town, Calvin," Dasha counseled. "If you don't have high morals, then you can expect a life full of problems and heartache." There was no winning this conversation. I retreated into the depth of the bilge—that dark area of the rec room where light could not find its way, and sat on the cool, hard tiled floor. Picking up the moss green telephone receiver from the wall, I dialed Simone. No answer.

"I'm sorry. I am truly sorry." I recognized Bellamy's voice, but did not turn around to acknowledge him. "You never know, do you? Everyone's got secrets. Wonder what Simone's are?"

"What the hell are you taking about, Bellamy? Simone hasn't ditched me," I interrupted with a good bit of anger.

"Really?" Bellamy responded, sprinkling a little doubt for me to breathe in. "Have you considered that Simone is toying with you? You see, unfortunately, the vast amount of people in this world view love as a tool to acquire a "feel-good" sensation. A sensation like a drug, or sex, which is fun, while it lasts. To them, love is simply a means to an end, not the journey itself. That is why it doesn't last for them. It has no substance. That which has no foundation cannot stand when the winds blow, and Cal, they always blow, sooner or later. Remember this, my friend. Love is not a feeling…it is an action. Feelings are temporary. Do not give up. Never settle for second best."

I looked up at Bellamy and knew, somehow, that he was speaking the truth, but I asked, "You talk like Simone deliberately tried to hurt me when she moved. It was not her decision to move, and she tried calling me. If that bitch in the kitchen would have told me she had called, we would have never broken up. Why are you attacking Simone?"

For the first time, I began to wonder if I had become a modern day Neville Chamberlain, having had misguided trust toward Bellamy. I started questioning Bellamy's motives. Something did not seem right, but I could not put my finger on exactly what it was, or maybe it was nothing. I lay on my bed and stared at the late afternoon shadows of the oak tree outside my bedroom window. The tree limb was elongated across the bedroom ceiling looking like the outstretched arm of that Grim Reaper, ready to pluck me out of my bed and throw me into oblivion.

Ten years earlier the shadow would have filled me with fear, but now I gazed at it as if a premonition of what was to come. My thoughts wandered to something Mr. Benbow had talked about that week, specifically, Alfred Lord Tennyson. He was best-known for saying "'tis better to have loved and lost than never to have loved at all." *This guy is an idiot! You don't get hurt if you don't love.*

I toyed with the paradox in my mind. *Would I rather have loved and been loved by Simone and now live without her love, or have never been known and loved by her?* The aching of my heart was only matched by the torment of my mind. *I had regret and self-humiliation for not standing up to those boys who harassed Simone. I felt anger towards Dasha, who clearly didn't approve of our relationship, and falsely judged Simone's mother. It was the constant "what ifs" that haunted me. What if we stayed together and got married? What if we ran away together? What if, what if, what if?*

🚲

The change of seasons could not keep up with the speed by which my life was changing. Physically, I had gone through a two-and-a-half-inch growth spurt in less than a year. My vellus hair that had rapidly multiplied was removed by occasional shaving. My perspective on life was being challenged daily, as well as the seriousness of the consequences that would inevitably surface if I were to be Perry's alibi. They were all moving at warp speed.

The end of the school year brought finals, but by this point my academic career was over. All I cared about was passing, which was not guaranteed. I thought that even if my grades were below the threshold of passing, my teachers would probably make sure I would graduate, so that I would leave and never come back. Having Calvin Lloyd for another school year petrified all my teachers.

It seemed that my suspicions were correct as I was told that I did, in fact, qualify for graduation. But I had a bigger problem than graduating. The senior prom was only a few weeks away, and I had not asked Simone to be my date. That would present a multitude of problems. Photos taken at Simone's house would be fine. Photos at my house, well, need I say more? I was *expected* to attend the prom. All of my siblings had. It was all my friends were talking about. Nearly everyone went to the prom, even if it was with a friend and not someone they were dating. Simone had even hinted that she and her mom went to Strawbridge's department store, and she had bought a beautiful dress that she was just dying to wear *somewhere special.*

🚲

There are rare moments in life when you walk into a room and you know, instinctively, that something is awry. No one has to say anything, you just know. That was the first sign that something was not right; the second was that when I entered the kitchen, everyone stopped talking. My dad and Dasha were there, but so were Mr. and Mrs. Pollard, a couple from church, and Mrs. Zimmerman.

My mind raced like a Pontiac Trans Am with a 455 under the hood, trying to think of what I could have done to piss off this many people. Before I had enough time to narrow that field down, my father broke the silence.

"Cal, come into my bedroom. I need to ask you something."

Oh, crap! Whatever I did, it must be bad. Real bad!

My dad closed the bedroom door behind us. My heart felt like Gregory Hines was tap dancing on it.

"Sit down, Cal." I sat on the edge of my parent's bed as my dad stood directly in front of me.

"Cal, I am going to ask you a serious question, and I want the truth. You are not in trouble, no matter what your answer is. I want you to know that. You will not be punished." The tap dancing slowed down. This changed everything. "Has Reverend Markey ever touched you inappropriately?"

"What? No!" I blurted out.

"He never asked you to undress or tried to kiss you or touch your penis. Anything like that?"

"Hell, no," I relied, knowing that I should have never inserted the "hell" part. "I would have punched him in the face! Why?"

My father stood there, obviously pondering whether to let me in on the secret everyone but I knew. "There have been several accusations against Reverend Markey from parents of several boys. He may have been involved in some terrible things."

Okay, vague, but I more than got the picture.

The next day, Dasha told me that Uncle Yaroslavl's health was failing and that it would mean the world to him if I went to pay him a visit. Translated, she meant, "I don't want to visit that insane brother of mine, but someone should, so, to appease my conscience, I'm making you go." Reluctantly, I went.

My uncle had spent the last sixteen months in a nursing home on Edge Hill Road for the senile as his overall physical and mental health had quickly declined. A man who had spent the majority of his last fifty years outside in the mountains, found himself confined to a walk-in closet they called a bedroom.

The nursing home was a building that, although not that old, had the feeling of a much older structure. Built in the late 60s with dark yellow bricks, the windows were dark and stained with rust from the downspouts. I walked up the ramp to the front door which opened automatically. Immediately, I was hit with the stench of nonenal. To me, it smelled like week old urine that had dried in the sun.

A large black woman in a white uniform sat behind the front desk.

"Hello, may I help you?" she asked with a pleasant tone.

"Yes. I'm looking for Mr. Uvorvykishki."

"Who?"

Fearing the last name was confusing, I tried another approach. "My uncle Yaroslavl."

"Oh, Super Fly," the lady said with the largest of smiles and an unrestrained laugh.

"Yeah, well, Curtis Mayfield he ain't," I said with a dead pan face.

"He's in the rec hall, second door on your right," the woman said while raising her eyebrows. "But he may not recognize you, baby."

I decided not to ask the obvious question and walked down the beige and white tiled, antiseptic hallway into the dark rec hall. Entering the poorly lit room, I perused over the fog of depression and despair. An Asian man was playing checkers by himself while arguing at his imaginary opponent that "You can't double jump on a different diagonal! No! No, you cannot!"

A woman with nylons rolled up to just below the knees sat with her legs spread wide open and her dress pulled up to expose her left thigh that she was scratching. She looked hopefully at me. "Danny? Did you come back for me, Danny? I've been waiting for you, Danny. Are we going to the dance?"

Like someone who had been hit in the head by a foul ball, I found it hard to look away. Scanning the remaining residents in the room, I didn't recognize my uncle at first. His hair had been cut shorter than I had ever seen it and combed back to where it began to curl behind his neck. Surprisingly, it still had some of the dark gray I remembered. Uncle Yaroslavl's beard was longer and unkept.

"Hi, Uncle Yaroslavl. How are you?"

My uncle looked up, but straight through me, as if I was cellophane. There was no confusion on his face, as if he was trying to figure out who this person was, just complete obliviousness. I sat down on the ottoman in front of him and drew a deep breath, which I quickly regretted. A strong union of Ben Gay meets day old urine burned the back of my nostrils and caused me to dry-heave. Lifting his head to look at me, Uncle Yaroslavl spoke.

"My balls dangle so low that I need a rake to scratch them."

"Yeah, well, sorry about that," I responded, but my uncle had already lowered his chin to his chest.

I got up and walked over to the magazine rack that stood near the entrance of the room. I was trying to decide whether to grab the *Sports Illustrated* or the *Argosy* magazine which had a picture of Bruno Sammartino on the front cover. When I saw Perry's picture on the front page of the *Philadelphia Inquirer*, I picked the paper up instead and began to read the article.

Most of the article had been regurgitated news reworded in an article to keep, what had become an old story, alive until the long-awaited trial began, but there was something new in this write-up. It appears Perry had hired Choo-Choo to rake his leaves, but the reporter, Cynthia Gomes, changed her reporting to an editorial when she added that witnesses had said that Perry asked Charlie to do the work, so he could lure the boy onto his property. I could hear Sergeant Joe Friday in my mind; "Just the facts, ma'am."

I made sure no one was looking as I carefully tore the article from the newspaper and placed it in my pocket. I still have those newspaper articles, cut, and saved, the corners curling and the scotch tape now yellowing.

When I looked up, I saw my uncle who was now grabbing at flying insects that were not there. Of course, he was.

🚲

I knew that if I headed straight home Dasha would give me a hard time for such a short visit with my uncle, so I decided to ride my bike over to Simone's and see what her demeaner was like. Rather than ask her about her mother's arrest, I would let Simone volunteer the information. When I arrived at her house, Simone was sweeping the front porch. As soon as she saw me, she dropped the broom and ran down the cement steps to greet me.

"What a pleasant surprise," she said with convincing cheerfulness. "I didn't know you were dropping by."

"I didn't either," I replied. "My mom made me visit my crazy uncle in that nursing home up on Edge Hill Road. I feel like I need a shower. A half an hour in there is like a month and a half. It was brutal! I needed a sweet reprise of you."

"Sweet reprise. Look at you," Simone said jokingly. "You sound like a poet. Are you a poet, baby?"

I felt a little embarrassed and wished I had not used the phrase, but it had come out so quickly I had no opportunity to lasso the words before they galloped from my lips.

"Hey, let me finish sweeping the porch, and then let's go for a walk," suggested Simone. "I bet you have something to ask me."

Here it is! The time has finally come. The prom question and a walk. Ugh!

The last time I made a public appearance with Simone it did not end well. I had already heard some talk around town that I was dating a black girl. Even though Simone had moved several towns north of our community, I figured that is how Dasha got wind of it. North Hills was a small bedroom community where most of the fathers worked in Philly, and the mothers were housewives. It was difficult, if not impossible, to walk a few blocks without bumping into someone, or at the very least, be seen by someone who knows you as they sat on their porch or worked in their yard. This day seemed to be pretty quiet around the neighborhood so, reluctantly, I agreed to take the walk with Simone.

Simone emptied the dustpan in a plastic trash can and told me she would be right back, as she needed to wash her hands. My fear of being exposed as Simone's boyfriend reared its ugly head, and I could feel it chewing deep within my gut.

"Okay, you ready?" Simone asked.

As we walked down the steps, Simone grabbed my hand. That fear within my gut multiplied tenfold. If I pulled my hand away, it would be a clear sign to Simone that she had mistaken where our relationship was and where it was headed. But on the flipside, if I should be seen holding hands with a black girl, well, I would have a lot of explaining to do. I decided to take my chances and keep my hand clasped in hers; after all, who knew me in Crestmont? If I could shorten the walk and escape being seen, all would be fine.

"Well, are you going to ask me or not?"

"What"" I said knowing well what the question was.

"Are you going to ask me to the prom?"

I really want to, Simone. More than you know, but I can't. I just can't.

"I can't dance," I said knowing the answer would not suffice.

"I'll teach you, baby," she said with hope in her eyes.

"Proms are lame. I really don't want to go."

"Calvin, this is a special event. Something I've been looking forward to all year. I really want to go. You'll do it for me, won't you?"

"No. I can't," I said, knowing that I shouldn't have included the second two words.

"Can't? What do you mean, you can't?" Simone said with an unusually angry tone. "Is it the black white thing you have a problem with?"

"No. Of course not."

"Fine. Then we are going," she said matter-of-factly.

"I am not going. Don't bring it up again," I said, knowing I just sealed my fate.

"Calvin, you are a huge disappointment," Simone said with tears rolling down her cheeks. "No need to explain. I understand. Oh, do I understand."

Turning around, she ran back to her house. My reluctance to take Simone to the prom was fueled by a necessity to choose self-preservation over her. I knew I had failed the test once again, cowering by putting my needs before the needs of the girl I said I loved. I stood watching Simone rush into her house and with her, the relationship I valued the most. I had been careless with her love.

This was bound to happen. She was too good for me. What was I thinking that I, a pearly white boy, could ever have had a long-lasting relationship with a colored girl. What a joke! What was I thinking? I was so afraid of anyone catching us together that IF we ever had real love and got married, I probably would not even have the stones to invite anyone to the wedding. I am a loser! I am ugly! I am stupid! I am worthless! I am a disappointment!

CHAPTER THIRTY

The first thing we do, let's kill all the lawyers.
"King Henry VI, Part 2"
—William Shakespeare

W ith a graduating class of over a thousand, each student was given four tickets to ensure there was enough room for every student's family to get a seat in the stands at the football field where the ceremony would be held. The "brighter" students were asking around for extra tickets, and I saw an opportunity to make a buck, so I sold my 4 tickets for five dollars apiece.

I did not attend graduation, nor the celebratory parties I had been invited to. There was little to celebrate when finishing 997th in a class of 1013. The only celebration I could muster was seeing high school in my rearview mirror. No college applications went out. No rejection letters came in. As far as my future was concerned, those decisions would need to be delayed until the Perry-thing was resolved.

Even Bellamy could not shake the depressed state I was in. Nothing was going well in my life...obviously. My mandate for survival had proven stronger than the love I had for Simone. The fact that I had carelessly *caused* the breakup with Simone haunted me, but that haunting had lots of company in that crowded room within my bodily-residence. The funny, or not so funny, thing was that word had leaked out and swept around town like the plague that Simone had been my girlfriend. Even Hunchback and Muskrat questioned me about dating a black girl. I accepted the fact that I would no longer be asked to join them in reindeer games.

I guess I got used to being by myself; entertaining myself. It made sense that Bellamy and I would find each other. There is a nothingness that comes from abandonment. It is an emptiness that leaves a void, a black vacuum. The difficulty in moving beyond such a state is that you are left with nothing, no tools to build a bridge to a better place. And so, you are banished to some uninhabited island dependent upon someone to sail by and, possibly, with a little luck, see the coconuts on your beach that spell S.O.S. But who was left to sail by? Both Simone and Perry's boats were in drydock, thanks to me.

I had noticed that things around me were changing, and not necessarily for the better. The situation at church was a mess. Reverend Markey denied the accusations, but he resigned, and the church had hired an interim clergy, a follower of Markey from Kansas, or Nebraska, or someplace out there. The church was split over believing, or not believing, that the good reverend had been a pedophile, causing a large group of Markey-defenders to leave the church, but other changes were happening around me as well.

Even the mundane things around town had changed. I heard that a 7-Eleven store was opening next door to the firehouse. Unfortunately, it was also located across the street from Plockies penny candy store. The unexplained excitement of having a 7-Eleven in the small hamlet of North Hills had the neighborhood kids flocking to the bright red and green sign to purchase the store's calling card, Slurpees, the juvenile gossip being what the new flavors of the week were. It did not take long after the 7-Eleven opened that Plockies closed its doors for good. Not a big deal in the universe of things going on around me, but it was representative of how everything in my life was dying. It is an odd thing to see your youth ebbing away.

The terms of Perry's bail were that he could not come within 1000 feet of any childcare facility, school, public park, church, recreation facility, playground, skating rink, neighborhood center, gymnasium, or school bus stop, and was to have no contact with minors. Adding to the avalanche of commiserations that had buried him alive, Perry had been delivering a floral arrangement to a grandmother who was celebrating her eightieth birthday when the next-door neighbor spotted him knocking at the elderly woman's door. It just so happened that this neighbor was hosting a Cub Scout Meeting in her house at that very moment. She promptly called the police, and they responded by escorting Perry out of his floral store in handcuffs. The judge stated that the conditions of his bail were broken, and now bail would be denied both for the safety of the public and for the safety of the accused. He was to be held at the county jail awaiting trial. Fear, shame, desperation, and terror brawled within me for governance.

Perry was certainly not the "prison" type. I feared for his survival. I knew he would be easy prey for the prison-yard hierarchy and could be both physically and sexually abused. Six months after his arrest, I was introduced to Perry's cellmate, Bobby McCoo, by Hunchback. It just so happened that Bobby was Hunchback's second cousin. Bobby had done a short stint in the joint for check forgery. He told me what Perry's first day in jail was like. As I recall, it went something like this:

Perry got off the grey painted prison bus and entered the holding room, a cold, painted cinder block room in the same grey measuring 30 x 20. He got in line with ten other men, most who were no strangers to the bastille. Two guards were tasked with preparing the men for incarceration. The younger of the two did not say a word, observing the ordeal. The other guard was a middle-aged man who looked like he could have been handing out textbooks to first year college students. It was routine for him. His mundane existence made his cadence robot-like.

"Empty your pockets of all personal belongings and place them in the manilla envelope," the guard said as he handed out the envelopes. Most of the men did so instinctively as if they were asked to zip up their fly, but clearly Perry stood out like a priest in a disco.

The man behind Perry in line was shuffling his feet trying to stay warm. Sensing Perry was a newbie, he whispered in Perry's ear.

"CO Moretti is a faggot. Here comes the fun part."

"Line up and take off all your clothes," the guard ordered in a monotone voice. The other ten other men did so mechanically, as if Pavlov's inmates. Perry watched as the other men stood nude in front of the strange guards, hesitating for just a minute.

"Are you hard of hearing, sweetheart?" questioned the guard. "Get your damn clothes off…now!"

A convict bent overturned to another inmate in a similar position and mumbled, "From what I've heard, Strathmore shouldn't feel nervous at all undressing in front of a group of men." The two men laughed.

"You find this funny, asshole?" the older guard hollered. "Spread them, girls."

In almost perfect unison the men bent over and spread their butt-cheeks, allowing the guards to inspect them for contraband. Perry quickly followed suit. Clear plastic bags were then handed out, and the men put their street clothes into them as they were handed their prison attire. Perry looked at the orange jump suit with the letters MCCF printed on the back and as he put the clothing on, realized it was at least a size too large,

"Welcome to Montgomery County Correctional Facility."

Perry kept his mouth shut. One at a time each man was escorted to his cell. As Perry walked the cell block corridor, cat calls and whistles were directed at him by the jailed inmates. He noticed that everything was in a cage, even the clock on the wall, as if it was hanging in a gym and needed a cage to prevent a ball from inadvertently striking and breaking it.

Perry's cellmate was a short, thick man in his 20s, with light brown hair cut in a shag.

"Yo. I'm Bobby. What are you in for?"

Perry was more than relieved to see who he'd be rooming with, having seen the alternatives who mostly looked vicious and aggressive. He assumed that his cellmate had not yet heard the cellblock gossip about his arrest.

"Murder, but I didn't do it. I don't belong in here," answered Perry.

"Yeah, everybody in here is innocent," Bobby said with a chuckle. "Who did you not murder?"

"No, I am serious. I have no idea why I was arrested in the first place." Perry didn't want to reveal his sexual orientation, nor answer who it was he was supposed to have killed, especially in this place, but nothing is a secret for very long on a cell block. Some of men had known of Perry's imminent arrival a day before he appeared. He feared that as soon as the entire cell block found out the details of his case, he would be in danger of being beaten, raped or even worse. News of a high-profile inmate traveled through the jail faster than prune juice through an old lady's body.

"Okay. Whatever," Bobby said as he laid back on his rack. "You've got the top bunk."

Perry took his sheets, pillow case and blanket and laid them on the mattress as he surveyed his six by eight-foot home. There was not much too survey. The walls were cinderblock, and Perry could not discern whether the walls were painted a pale yellow or if they had turned that color due to age. He opened the small plastic bag which contained a toothbrush which was half the size of the one he had at home, a small tube of toothpaste, a bar of soap and a roll of toilet paper, what would be his earthly possessions for, at least, until his trial was over.

As the days passed, I tried not to think of Perry, but that was like ignoring that place in your mouth that you had inadvertently bit. I would go through stretches where I was able to wipe the thought of Perry and his predicament out of my mind, but inevitably, something would spark a memory or experience, and I was forced to contemplate the ugly truth. I did have thoughts about visiting Perry in jail, but I never did for two reasons. First, for the same reason I did not come forward as an alibi witness; I was afraid someone would associate me with Perry. Second, I could not look into Perry's face with him knowing I had refused to testify that we were together at the time the murder was committed.

Back in North Hills, the upcoming trial was all that anyone spoke about. It did not matter if you were in Joe's Market, Chernoff's Pharmacy, or any of the three gas stations in town, someone would bring up the murder and how they hoped Perry got what was coming to him. Down at the local taproom, the smoke-filled talk was about the queer who had molested the simple kid that everyone in town knew and what these half- inebriated men would do to the creep if they could get their hands on him. Castration was a popular suggestion.

The months leading up to the trial seemed to go quickly, for everyone but Perry. His attorney, Tim Larsen agreed to a lie detector test, believing in his client's innocence, and Perry passed the test with ease. Although the polygraph results would not be admissible at trial due to their unreliability, Larsen was hoping to mention the results in passing while cross examining the witnesses. Objections by the prosecution would be moot once the jury had heard the results of the test.

Perry's lawyer, Tim Larsen, a successful Philadelphia attorney who had represented many gay men and women, was best known for a civil suit brought against the city. Two of Mayor Rizzo's policemen had brutally beat Robert Stizler, a gay man, for parading down 9th Street Italian Market with nothing on but a pair of leopard print bikini underwear, and a yellow boa. Intoxicated, the cops dragged Stizler by his shoulder-length hair down to Washington Avenue where they kicked and beat him with billy-clubs, targeting hinged joints and nerve clusters till he was unconscious. The city eventually settled out of court in excess of a million dollars. Having a gay lawyer represent him, Perry felt as relaxed as he possibly could, knowing his life was teetering like a stack of children's books.

Attorney Larsen had tried to receive a change of venue, arguing that Perry could not and would not receive a fair trial in Montgomery County, but the motion was denied. During voir dire, the opposing counsel objected to any prospective jurors that had any family member that was gay or lesbian. Larsen, being gay himself, had a feeling that some of the potential jurors may have, in-fact, had a relative or friend who was gay by carefully observing their body language as they answered the question. *Better to deny any association than to have others know that homosexuality lurked a little too close to home.* At the completion of voir dire, the jury consisted of seven men and five women. Two of the men and one woman were African American, one woman was Hispanic, and the remainder were white.

The wait for the trial to begin was a lesson in patience. It was evident that the long-awaited spectacle was what all of Montgomery County, if not the entire state of Pennsylvania, had been anxious for, if only to see *justice* served. The anticipation, amplified by months of newspaper articles reaching for any interesting angles, even if a bit exaggerated, had finally arrived.

The trial began on the second Wednesday of October in Norristown, the county seat. It was a gorgeous autumn day with bright sunshine illuminating the splashes of red, orange and yellow that the oak and maple trees provided as they formed an umbrella that lined the streets of the small city. The air was filled with the natural fragrances of damp, moss-covered bark, and the faint aroma of burning leaves whose ashes floated aimlessly in the air. The trifecta of the trial, Simone, and my unknown future were all like heavy soot that covered my emotions.

I had hoped to take the train from Ardsley station to Norristown, but SEPTA did not have any direct lines. That meant I would have had to go to center city Philadelphia and then back out to the western suburbs, so I decided to ride my bicycle the thirteen miles. No matter what, I had to be there for the beginning of the trial. The trip took longer than expected, because I had to stop twice to ask for directions, but I arrived at the courthouse well before the trial began, knowing that getting a seat would not be easy.

The courthouse was built in the mid-1800s and stood with six large, majestic columns and a dome that was added at the turn of the century. An institution representing justice and impartiality, *in a perfect world,* but the distance between neutrality and reality was as far as the war in Nam was from Park Avenue. Lady Justice's allegorical personification of moral vigor was as flawed as her blindfold had slipped below her eyes allowing a glimpse of *guilty until proven innocent* to blemish Perry's reality. So much for the sixth amendment to the Constitution.

Stopping at the front desk, I asked the guard at the podium where the Strathmore trial was being held.

"Courtroom five," responded the guard as he pointed to a hallway that was to his right.

Hurrying down the large hallway, I looked at the numbers on each door, until I came to the large carved wood door with the number five above it. Pushing it open, I entered the courtroom, taking one of the few remaining seats.

The courtroom's public gallery had quickly filled up as a queue of people jockeyed for the opportunity to get a seat for the show. A crowd also gathered outside the courthouse for news they would receive from friends who would update them during the few breaks the judge would give throughout the day. Reporters from *The Philadelphia Bulletin, Philadelphia Inquirer, Glenside News,* and *The Gay Dealer* were present in the gallery as an attractive redhead courtroom sketch artist had her pad of vellum paper on her lap.

The room was aged, with high ceilings, three large windows and plenty of dark, polished wood that looked rich and impressive. The room was larger than the ones I had seen on the *Perry Mason* episodes that Dasha watched. As I surveyed the courtroom while waiting in anticipation for the trial to begin, I noticed Perry's brother sitting directly behind the defendant. I had never spoken to the man and knew next to nothing about him, other than the fact that he dressed normally, much less flamboyant than Perry. I also saw Mongrel and his mentee, Benny, sitting in the next to the last row. *Why were they here?*

Attorney Larsen entered the courtroom with Perry, dressed in a double-breasted suit made from paisley brocade, complimented with a maroon and gold bow tie. Larsen had asked Perry not to dress in a flamboyant style and to embrace *understatement* so as not to antagonize the jury and their prejudices. Perry agreed, however, neither of them had informed those who would attend the hearing. An assemblage of the Philadelphia gay community gathered in the courtroom to offer moral support and to make certain the trial was free from the public's prejudice and prejudgment. Before the judge entered the courtroom to begin the trial, Perry was approached by his mignons, who scandalized the spectators by their effeminate manners. Exactly what Larsen was afraid of.

The Assistant District Attorney, Robert Fitzpatrick, was a man in his mid-50s; short and stout with blue eyes and dark receding hair that was slicked back with Brylcreem. He was replete with a WC Fields-ish nose that was perpetually red so one could not tell if it was caused by rosacea or his habitual drinking. Long days in court had made him a sugarholic, as his body craved the sweetness he received from his vodka martinis. His protruding belly had been the victim of a regular breakfast diet of Tastykake butterscotch krimpets and coffee with 3 sugars with half and half, which made him a borderline diabetic. Having the state behind him to prop up his spineless posture, Fitzpatrick's arrogance filled the courtroom like smoke in a flue-closed cabin.

The ADA strutted around the courtroom barking accusations and showboating reminiscent of the sideshow huckster at Willow Grove Park. His opening statement painted a picture of Perry as a quiet local businessman with dark secrets...secrets which, he warned, were repugnant and would likely seem unnerving and dirty to the well-sanitized jurors. He described the charges against Perry, and they were as sordid as they come.

"Perry Strathmore is being tried for oral copulation with a minor, forced oral copulation of a minor, forcible penetration with a foreign object, rape and murder. We will be seeking the death penalty in this case."

There was no reaction from Perry, who apparently, had played the scenario repeatedly in his mind so that he would not succumb to emotional outbursts. It was important to him to act like a sensible, calm individual, one that any of the jurors would feel comfortable with.

As the Assistant District attorney spoke, Perry glanced at a window just beyond the ADA's head. I followed his line of vision and saw a Monarch butterfly dancing in a carefree manner, as if improvising its flight pattern as it moved along. It must had been dawdling, as most butterflies left Pennsylvania a few weeks before due to a lack of nectar sources. The sun illuminated its orange wings, laced with black lines, and bordered with white dots. As the traumatic courtroom drama played out, I could see that the butterfly gave Perry an indescribable peace.

ADA Fitzpatrick had an ability to talk endlessly without saying anything. Without an original thought, sounds came from his mouth like a mockingbird that chirps out a dozen stolen songs from other birds. It was not until he began describing Perry's frequent visits after dark to Philadelphia that I began listening in earnest.

"Mr. Strathmore had secrets. Many secrets. Ladies and gentlemen of the jury, you're about to hear a side of Mr. Strathmore that he doesn't want you to hear. Several times a week, Mr. Strathmore would drive to Philadelphia late in the evenings. Not all that unusual for a single man to frequent bars in the city of brotherly love, but, ladies and gentlemen, that is exactly what he would search for…*brotherly* love. Mr. Strathmore did not go just anywhere in Philadelphia. No! He would explore the area around Chestnut, Pine, Juniper, and 11th Streets best known as "The Gayborhood."

Tim Larsen's objection could hardly be heard over the chatter that erupted in the gallery. The judge had to bang his gavel four times as he raised his voice.

"Order in the court! The gallery will remain silent during these proceedings! Objection overruled."

The prosecutor continued. "If Philadelphia's Gayborhood is strange and foreign to you, let me explain. This area within Washington Square is a large concentration of small business, restaurants, services, and bars that are very friendly to the gay community and by "gay" I'm not referring to people who are happy or who are full of mirth. I am specifically referring to those who are prone to decadence and promiscuity. This lifestyle is an abomination!"

"Objection, your Honor," Mr. Larsen shouted once again over the gallery that had become disorderly causing the judge to caution them that the next time he had to warn them, he would clear the courtroom of all spectators. "Your Honor, I strongly object! The prosecution has repeatedly used derogatory language that exhibits bias and prejudice based on my client's sexual orientation."

"Ah ha! So, you admit the suspect is queer!" shrieked ADA Fitzpatrick.

"That's it," shouted the judge. "I want to see both of you in my chambers…now!"

Ten minutes later the three men came back into the courtroom. ADA Fitzpatrick continued. "Your Honor, I apologize to Attorney Larsen and to Mr. Strathmore." Turning to the jury, the prosecutor continued.

"Within this red-light district of Philadelphia are bathhouses. What exactly are these bathhouses, you may be wondering? The bathhouses are quite frankly a place where homos perform and discuss sexual acts in secrecy behind closed doors. That is their sole purpose and why they exist."

"Your Honor," interrupted the defense, "Your instructions to the Mr. Fitzpatrick have fallen on deaf ears. The term homo is derogatory and insulting, and there has been no proof that Mr. Strathmore is gay."

"Objection sustained. Mr. Fitzpatrick, I'm warning you for the last time. You will refrain from any slang or improper terms referring to the defendant."

"I apologize, your Honor." Once again, the ADA continued. "Although our investigation revealed that Mr. Strathmore was a regular patron of several of these bathhouses, his favorite seemed to be *Drucker's Bellevue Health Baths and Saunas* located on the 4th floor of the Hale Building at 100 South Juniper Street. Ladies and gentlemen, I cannot describe the depravity and self-indulgence that goes on in these immoral houses. Our evidence will show that over the past few years, the defendant's field trips to these houses of ill repute became more and more frequent. When he could not fill his insatiable appetite for illicit sex, he preyed upon a neighborhood boy, raping, and then killing him, so he could eliminate his only witness. He did not want Charlie to tell anyone how he solicited sex from an underaged boy and so, symbolically, after murdering the boy, he cut off his tongue. The tongue was never found. Mr. Strathmore probably kept it as a souvenir."

The gallery of spectators gasped as the press had not been informed of the dismemberment. The ADA proceeded to pass out photographs of the badly abused body.

"The defendant has no alibi. He has no one to confirm his whereabouts for the afternoon of the murder. Not one."

🚲

According to the conversation I had with Mr. Larsen after the trial, Perry did not need his attorney to tell him that the first day had not gone well. The conversation went something like this:

"You need an alibi," Larsen explained. "You had told the police that you were at home the afternoon the murder happened, but you have not been forthcoming about the details of that afternoon. We have gone over this before, Perry, but I need to ask you again, were you really at home?"

"I was," Perry responded softly.

"Can anyone collaborate that? Were you alone?" asked his attorney.

"No, I wasn't alone."

"Great! That is not what you said the first time I asked you that question. The person you were with can present evidence that they were with you on the afternoon of the crime. Your friend can testify that you were not at the scene of the crime. Perry, an alibi defense is based on witness testimony and if the witness is the credible, we have an excellent chance of having you acquitted. Is your friend credible?"

"Very," muttered Perry.

"And honest?"

Perry hesitated, as if pondering how exactly to answer the question. "With me he is."

"Then what is the problem. Tell me who your friend is, and we will get him to testify."

"I can't."

"What do you mean you can't. This is your life you are talking about," insisted Larsen.

"I think he's afraid to come forward," Perry said while staring at Larsen's briefcase.

"Is your friend still in the closet? Is he married and afraid to come out?" asked Larsen.

"No, it's nothing like that. I think he is afraid for others to know we were friends. We were platonic friends. He's straight. We had a true, pure, and honest relationship. There were no ulterior motives. Neither of us wanted anything from the each other. We both simply needed a friend. It was an unlikely friendship but one cut from outside our circle of acquaintances. The normal formalities and prerequisites that traditionally precede any peer relationship were not obligatory. We were two lonely people who needed acceptance outside our peer group."

Attorney Larsen contemplated what Perry had said. "Let me at least talk to him. Maybe I can convince him to come forward. Perry, if he truly is your friend, he will see how imperative his testimony is. He may be your only hope."

"He'll come forward if he wants to. I do not want anyone pressuring him," responded Perry, knowing that even if I did come forward to testify, my age would raise doubt in the jurors' minds of his innocence.

Larson leaned forward and touched Perry's hand. "Perry, I did not want to bring this up now, but they are offering a plea deal. Second degree murder. Twenty-five years to life, but the death penalty would be taken off the table, and you could be paroled in possibly ten years. I think it's a good deal."

"Good deal? No!" Perry said sternly. "No plea deals! I am innocent, and I will never admit to something I didn't do! If they execute me, so be it! Maybe one day the truth will come out."

"It's a matter of betrayal. Perry, this person is no friend of yours. A friend in need is a friend…"

"Indeed," interrupted Perry. "Enough!"

CHAPTER THIRTY-ONE

I think everyone should go crazy at least once in their life. I don't think you've truly lived until you've thought about killing yourself.

—Pete Wentz

B efore I turned my bicycle on to Hawthorne Road, I could smell the unmistakable odor of cabbage cooking. Had I been on Pine Avenue I would have thought corned beef and cabbage was on the menu at Sean Donahue's house, but as I was a few houses away from my house, it could only mean that we were having halupki for dinner. I still hate the smell of cabbage, but I love the Ukrainian dish of rice, beef, and pork encased in cabbage and yet, this night it would not matter what Dasha was serving for dinner. As I opened the kitchen door, supper was just being served at the table. "Calvin, wash your hands and come to the table," my stepmother said.

"I'm not hungry," I said as I headed to his room.

"You're not hungry? Are you sick?" asked Dasha.

"No. I'm fine."

"Well, do not come into the kitchen later looking for something to eat and don't forget that you have a few chores to do tomorrow," Dasha said as I left the kitchen.

There was no one else I could pawn the ever-increasing list of chores off to. My siblings had all grown wings and left the Lloyd nest, leaving me to do all the household tasks. I grabbed the newspaper sitting on the living room couch and headed to my room, jumped on the bed, and stared at the ceiling till the shadows became indistinguishable from the evening darkness. I turned on the lamp next to the bed and began reading about where things were at in Vietnam.

President Nixon assured South Vietnam's President Nguyen Van Thieu that any violation of the peace settlement that Secretary of State Kissinger and Le Duc Tho had agreed upon would result in a recommitment of B-52s to combat. President Thieu rejected the settlement, being adamant that he would never accept any settlement which left North Vietnamese forces in South Vietnam.

In a different article I understood that President Nixon was facing his own war at home. Congress had become reluctant to escalate the conflict, and the Watergate scandal was gaining speed. Economic restraints also joined the offensive on the President. As I continued reading, the article stated that the five men that were arrested for breaking into the Democratic National Committee headquarters at the Watergate hotel had no alibi.

No alibi. Perry had no alibi, I thought. Motivated by self-preservation, I knew that I could not, would not, testify. *Why me? Why did I have to be Perry's only hope? Why did Perry have to be queer?* So many questions, but there was only one question that haunted me. Could I somehow find the courage to testify?

Courage. That was the real question, wasn't it? Where does it come from and what does it look like? Is it instinctive, hereditary, or a learned trait? There are no text books that teach the art of courage. Is it simple reacting to a given situation with selflessness and a disregard for one's own consequences? Is it as drastic as running into enemy fire while dragging a wounded comrade to safety, or can it be as subtle as taking the witness stand to give true testimony for an innocent person with no regard for what others may say about me? If one cannot have the courage to disregard what others think of them, would they ever have the courage to run into a barrage of fire to save another man's life? We are who we are today because of the choices we made yesterday.

I was taught to always be honest, to always tell the truth. But here I faced a conundrum. The people who taught me the importance of being trustworthy would be the same people who would question my relationship with Perry. I had been self-taught in the art of avoiding rejection and ridicule, not that I was immune to it. The blindness that comes from self-justification was the fuel I had used to energize questions that I already had answers to. *Not coming forward is not the same as lying, is it?*

🚲

The trial was the biggest news that hit North Hills in decades. In fact, the entire Abington Township was following the case, which meant that *if* I were to testify, every kid that I knew would find out about my relationship with Perry. They would never believe our relationship was platonic. People prefer to believe the worst about others. It would be just like what happened to Mrs. Evans who lived less than a block from us. She was accused of cheating on her husband. The newspapers never reported that dirty laundry, but every soul in town heard about it. She was called awful names like *harlot* and the grownups kept talking about some book and a scarlet letter written by a guy named Hawthorne, whom I assumed my street was named after. Later on, it came out that she had taken a part-time job babysitting, something her controlling husband forbade, in order to help her family meet their rising financial obligations. There *was* a legitimate reason for her sneaking out at night, but the false allegations had been laid, like unmovable bricks that had been cemented in place.

I looked down from the ceiling to see Bellamy sitting on the bean bag and wished he was Simone instead. I did not know whether I had spoken my thoughts out loud, or if I was simply daydreaming, not that it mattered. Obviously, Bellamy knew my thoughts.

"What are you going to do?" Bellamy asked.

"I don't know. Why should I take the risk when Perry may be acquitted?"

"He may be acquitted, but what if he's not? Do you really want to take that chance? His life is literally in your hands."

"Thanks! Don't you think I know that?" Bellamy did not sound very convincing.

My fear was consuming my entire being. Again and again, I thought of *truth,* that I had always been taught that telling the truth was non-negotiable. But my situation was more complex than that. I was not lying; I just was not providing the truth that would greatly benefit another person. The obvious consequences of saying that I was with Perry that day were enormous. I would be the laughingstock of the entire high school and neighborhood and they, and perhaps my family, would alienate me. *But high school is over, and I will probably never see those people again. Would I?* Contradictions conflicted with reality. It simply was too great a risk.

Bellamy moved closer to me. "Decisions. This one is a lot harder than whether you should order chocolate or strawberry at Jack Frost, or whether or not you should steal second base."

"No shit," I mumbled.

What I did not understand then is that life is all about three or four, maybe a half dozen decisions that *will* alter your life. These decisions are so crucial that they will decide what direction your life takes. Certainly, the person you marry and what career path you want to pursue are two of those decisions, but there are always a few unexpected ones. Whether or not I should have testified was one of them. Make the wrong decision and it will haunt you for the remainder of your life. Make the right one and it can cause pain and grief in the short run, but you will have peace for the rest of your life. *Do not choose poorly.*

Bellamy continued to encourage me, but he never told me what to do. He looked fixedly into my eyes and began retelling a story I faintly recalled. I could not remember where, exactly, I had heard it.

"Let me tell you a story. There once was a young lion lost in the jungle. He walked in the sweltering tropical heat day after day trying to find water. Finally, when it seemed like he would perish from dehydration, he came upon a fork in the road. One of the paths was nearly hidden by overgrown brush; trees and large rocks were scattered on the path. The second path was clear of brush and appeared to be smooth and so the lion chose the easier path.

He had not walked far when suddenly he stepped into a hanging snare employing a counterweight on a tree which lifted both the noose and the lion high into the air. The lion hung by his foot upside down for quite a long time, but from that vantage point the lion could see that the overgrown path led to a crystal-clear pond of blue water. Calvin, never mistake a clear view for an easy journey."

I could not recall Aesop having ever told that story, but I did understand that it conveyed a moral which I really did not need any illustration for. I knew well what my dilemma was. I was being sucked down the rabbit hole. It was a dark, ominous cloud with deep-seated eyes of a feared detestation that I had come to know too well. The fear of making yet another bad choice was crouching like a chilling gargoyle, pointing its accusing finger of failure, depression, and a lack of value. It was a measuring stick bought at the five and dime store called *Adult Expectation* which reminded me that I came up short, like the measuring stick at Willow Grove Park that determined if you were tall enough to go on the rides all the others kids were on. I was always just a little short.

"You know," Bellamy said while interrupting my kaleidoscope of thoughts, "on second thought, I think you must let this one go. There is nothing you can do. Strathmore is a big boy. and he's got Larson by his side. They will figure it out. Let things be."

The reality of being a coward, failing to step up and do what was right, not caring about the consequences that would inevitably surface from doing the difficult, but right thing, consumed me. A wave of depression drenched me. *What kind of friend am I if I am not there when Perry needed me most? A friend in need is....*

Leaving my bedroom, I went down to the rec room. Walking over to my father's gun rack hanging over the fireplace, I reached up for the JC Higgins 12-gauge double-barrel shotgun, the same one I had taken to Aunt Polina's to hunt pheasant and rabbit. I entered the back room which contained my father's tools and workbench as well as the washer and dryer and a pantry of shelves storing canned goods. I knew that my father had the ammo in a wooden box concealed in the rafters above his workbench, the same hiding place I had found the bottle rockets. I pulled a chair over to the workbench and stood on it. I could just about reach the wooden ammo box. A ruler on the workbench helped me slide the box off the rafter. I was surprised at the weight of the box as I caught it before it hit the floor. The lid opened and .306 and shotgun shells scatter over the cement floor. I jumped off the chair and, on my hands and knees, began gathering the shells and putting them back into the box.

Having returned the shells to their wooden coffin, I kept one in my clenched left hand and returned to the rec room and sat in the overstuffed chair. Furniture that made it to the paneled basement was too shabby to make a presentation upstairs. I sat in the chair and felt my backside fall lower in the sagging seat due to the worn foam in the cushion.

I pondered my existence. *Who would grieve, who would miss me?* There is a place that I dreaded, yet a place I felt I had to be. A place that I *wanted* to be, that is, in a warped kind of way—a place called pain. It is warm and familiar and the only place I knew to be welcoming. My agony opened that lock box where past pains were meticulously kept. They never really go away, they are just saved for the next time heartache pays a visit, the accumulation of which makes each future occurrence a little bit more painful. It always leaves a residue like an empty glass of milk. Oh, the glass may be empty, but there is never a doubt what had been in there. It is like pushing a bruise.

I possessed a haunting fear. I dreaded that I would never die, that I would be forced to live in this world forever. As if in some type of warped humor, God removes morality from me and makes me live in this horror show for eternity. Once was more than enough for me, thank you very much!

I placed the barrel of the shotgun in my mouth and extended my arm as far as it would go to see if I could reach the trigger. I could. Sliding my thumb against the top lever that caused the break-action, I slid one shell into the first chamber.

The accusation was always the same. *Coward. How could the son of a marine who battled the Japanese in godforsaken Guadalcanal be so gutless?* I feared that when a critical time came, and it had come, I would reach into a cavern void of courage. I longed for the opportunity to prove to the world that I had moxie, but I was petrified of the same opportunity. A paradox of wills.

The barrel of the gun remained in my mouth, the metallic taste of death strong upon my palate, my finger gently caressing the trigger.

CHAPTER THIRTY-TWO

All who are lost do not necessarily want to be found.

I had no idea how long the barrel had been in my mouth, only that the gun was getting heavier. I lowered the shotgun and rested it in my lap. The taste of metal and failure lingered in my mouth as I lowered my head and wept. *I cannot even do that right.*

Sometimes I think I am crazy. Okay, often I think I am crazy. There, I said it! Not going "postal" crazy, going out and killing a bunch of people. I guess I would have to have a very good reason to take someone's life. Crazy like, not "normal." But what the hell is normal? If society is normal, I have no desire to be normal. I have finally embraced my individualism…it only took me some sixty plus years. I feel at peace with who I am, but I continue to feel like an outsider. Someone standing in the snow while observing through a living room window the world dining on Christmas goose and Chardonnay. It's in my genes, you know. My Aunt Olena went crazy. My uncle Yaroslav joined her. All from the same gene pool, the Ukrainian bloodline. I am not insinuating that Ukrainians have a greater number of insane people. Lord knows, every ethnicity has their fair share.

I guess I had always known that I would not testify. It is a strange game you play, perhaps to appease your conscience. You convince yourself that you really did struggle desperately with what to do. *I was* disappointed in myself, and that disappointment fueled my self-deprecation and anger which manifested itself in my growing anger towards others. I loathed myself and wanted everyone to join in. I picked up the phone to call Simone, stopping short of dialing. *Am I beyond anyone's reach to be loved. Is it even possible for a severely wounded heart to love or be loved? Am I damaged beyond repair and is the best I can expect a mundane and/or sexual relationship with someone to ease the pain?*

I began disappearing for days at a time, sleeping in parked cars, waking up early to slip out of the vehicle before the owner would head to work in the morning. That is, until one day I overslept. I was awakened in the wee hours by the sound and jarring of the car door being slammed shut. Thankfully, it was still dark outside. Startled and scared, I quietly slid to the floor of the back seat, lying on my back with my knees bent just enough for them to rest upon the bump from the drive shaft. When the driver reached his place of employment twenty minutes later, I decided to wait nearly an hour before slipping out the door. I knew I was in Cheltenham, a town sitting on the border of Philadelphia, by the trolly stop, a shopping center, and a cluster of stores lining Ogontz Avenue. Farther down the street there was a nightclub, a Crown fried chicken joint and a barbershop with its signature rotating red, white, and blue rotating pole, but the pole wasn't rotating, it was too early. Crossing the busy street, I hitchhiked north and got a ride from a man in a box truck.

It did not take me long to realize that new house construction would be a safer place to rest my weary head rather than parked cars. To this day, whenever I smell the fragrance of fresh cut pine, I immediately associate it with those memories. But those memories also include abandonment, isolation, and loneliness. There is a core need in all of us to be loved, especially when we need it most. It is criminal not to be loved. It is painful not to be loved.

The next night I found a new home that had been framed and the electric and plumbing installed. Entering it, I found a corner away from the streetlights and wrapped a patchwork blanket I had salvaged from someone's trash tightly around my shoulders as I listened to the rain hitting the tar paper the builders had nailed earlier that day. The sound was oddly comforting, like the sound of popping bubble wrap. I knew that the builders would be putting the asbestos shingles on the roof early the next day, and I was mindful that I needed to be out of there at the first sign of dawn.

�🚲

I did not sleep well on the hard floor, so vacating the house before the builders arrived was not a problem. I headed home to take a shower. As soon as I closed the door, Dasha entered the kitchen.

"Where in the world…" I extended my hand out as a stop sign. She said no more. Making my appearance at home after a two-day absence, I found my parents concerned and scared rather than angry.

I needed to get away to clear my head. Anywhere but North Hills. I thought Aunt Polina's farm would be the perfect spot to do just that. Only three hours away, yet thousands of miles from my problems. Taking the opportunity while they were vulnerable, I asked my dad if I could borrow his car to spend the weekend at Aunt Polina's and do some pheasant hunting and, to my surprise, he said yes. I knew that meant cleaning the chicken coop for my aunt, but that was a small price to pay to get reinvigorated.

Aunt Polina spoke only Ukrainian but her son, Dasha's cousin Marko, spoke perfect English. Marko received an all-expenses paid amusement ride to Girard College, an independent college preparatory five-day boarding school located on a sprawling and beautiful 43-acre campus in Philadelphia. A professional student at heart, Marko excelled, and although he received several scholarships to reputable universities, he returned home to the farm as Aunt Polina's umbilical cord had stretched as far as it could, barely reaching Girard College.

Marko was a confirmed bachelor who became nothing more than a well-educated chicken tender. If you call owning a hundred birds farming, then Marko was a farmer. He spent his days putzing around the farm, but not really accomplishing much. He would stay up late at night spending hours with his shortwave radio talking with people from the Ukraine and the western fringe of the Soviet Union. He would explain that the reflection characteristics of the ionosphere are better at night, and therefore reception and transmission were much better than during the daylight hours. That would explain the inexplicable; that a farmer could sleep till noon. My father suspected

Marko of espionage for the Commies, but that would have required minimal travel, and Marko simply never left the farm.

Cousin Marko avoided the war by complaining he was the eldest child, specifically, the only son of a widowed farmer and he was the only one able to physically run the farm. Apparently, it worked because the only action Marco saw was when he would shoot the occasional racoon that would stage an attack on his henhouse, looking for a cheap dinner of Chicken Cordon Bleu. Why he never got a job and felt he was entitled to government welfare was another question altogether.

That next morning was beyond beautiful as I walked through the apple grove with my father's JC Higgins Double-Trigger Side-by-Side 12-gauge shotgun. The same gun I had almost eaten. My senses were keen, and I was acutely aware of everything around me. The apples were just beginning to turn from green to a blush of red, like a young girl's cheeks when told by an adoring boy who thinks she is the most beautiful thing in the whole, immense world. I watched as a robin finished his carnivorous breakfast, the end of the worm protruding from its beak, as I weaved through the grove, rambling between rows of trees like I belonged there. For a boy that never seemed to belong anywhere, the simplicity of nature always seemed comfortable to me. I have always felt most at home in the fields, forests, and mountains.

Beyond the grove was a large field of hay. Soon the neighbor who leased the land would do the second cutting of the summer, when the hay was tall and dry. They would sell it as animal fodder. I watched as each stem bent in unison with the wind like a choir bowing to applause. The early morning dew clung to the seed head as the sun reflected off each droplet making the field look like a million diamonds and making me feel as though I was king of the bounty. For only a moment I had forgotten my troubles and lived in this moment of bliss.

A rabbit jumped up in the high grass just to my left. Instinctively, I lifted the shotgun to my shoulder and aimed. Leading the rabbit perfectly, I was sure to make the kill when, slowly, I lowered the gun and watched the game slide safely within some brush. There would be no killing today.

I walked over the crest of the hill and found a fallen tree to sit upon. Looking down into the valley, I saw a pond and watched as three mallards circled its edge and gracefully glided to the water. Simone would have loved this spot, I thought to myself.

I looked out upon the mountain filled with Eastern Hemlock as far as the eye could see. Little did I know that 50 years later 80% of Pennsylvania's state tree would be eliminated by the non-native invasive hemlock woolly adelgid. There has always been death where something that does not belong is introduced into an unsolicited environment.

My stomach began to growl as I walked back to the little farmhouse. Aunt Polina would be cooking breakfast and expecting me back soon. Passing the outhouse, I nearly lost my appetite from the stench, but as I came upon the springhouse, I could smell onions cooking. Thick slices of scrapple, eggs and perogies with onion were frying on the cast iron stove. Aunt Polina shouted something in Ukrainian and motioned for me to wash my hands outside at the well where a bar of homemade soap sat next to the hand pump.

Having cleaned my hands, I walked into the tiny kitchen and watched as Aunt Polina poured a glass of goat's milk and placed it in front of me. It would be Aunt Polina and me for breakfast. Cousin Marko was sleeping off a late night of meaningful conversation with someone he had never met and who lived some 4,900 miles away.

After breakfast I headed out to the chicken coop without being asked, grabbed a rake, shovel, and wheel barrel, and began the task of cleaning the chicken commune. I made sure to close and latch the flimsy door, having learned the hard way that you do that first, and very quickly. Once I had taken the time to lean the tools against the fence before securing the door to the coop and a half dozen hens saw their opportunity at freedom and made a run for it. Aunt Polina had seen it from the kitchen window and ran after them with a broom in her hand cursing me in Ukrainian.

I was not in the henhouse for more than a few minutes when a big ol' cock came cautiously strutting toward me. He lifted one paw at a time and holding it in the air for what seemed to be at least a minute or two. Clearly, this was the top cockerel, being unequivocally larger than the rest of the brood. The rooster had a mean look in his eye as he extended his neck in obvious intimidation. Calculatedly, the bird puffed up his feathers, clucked, then crowed loudly, and aggressively approached me. I got the impression that this nasty cock was not fond of me. The cock would run to my left and then to my right, never taking its eyes off of me. The rooster flapped his wings and started dancing in a tight circle. This is not going to be an easy job, I thought.

Having survived the few pecks I received on my shins, I thanked Aunt Polina with gestures, a kiss and a hug, and drove up the gravel road. The short retreat did not do what I had hoped it would. Perry was on my mind and haunting my conscience. Nothing seemed to work as a distraction. Well, almost nothing.

On the way home my stomach began that *Oh no!* feeling one gets when something you ate wants to get the heck out of your body…quickly. Whatever it was had proceeded from the vomit stage and was now screaming inside the walls of my intestines, begging for an exit. I could not decide if it was the goat's milk or the scrapple that was in rebellion, but it really did not matter what the culprit was, I needed to find a bathroom, and fast. Thankfully, I saw the familiar dinosaur sign indicating that I was approaching a Sinclair gas station. Never had I been more enamored with wanting to be a paleontologist.

Knowing I had the green apple quick step, I headed straight to the restroom, which, regrettably, was locked. Hurriedly, I went to the counter inside the station, interrupted the attendant who was giving change to an elderly lady and begged for the bathroom key. The attendant, sensing that I had the backdoor trot and not wanting to have to clean up the liquid stool all over his grease-stained floor, quickly handed me the key which was attached to a large piece of wood by a brass-colored chain. The elderly lady had beaten me to the oasis and was trying the handle to the only restroom the gas station had, when I pushed her aside, unlocked the door and took a seat. The lady, upset by the rude actions by the clearly bad-mannered teenager, waited outside the door preparing to give me more than a "piece" of her mind. However, upon hearing the explosion of anal blasts and clatter, she thought better of it and, at a remarkable pace, got in her car and drove away.

Monday morning arrived earlier than usual, or at least that is how I perceived it. The trial was to resume at 9 a.m. that morning, but I could not get the previous day's news out of my mind. The Sunday newspaper had a large section dedicated to the trial, and it had me worried that Perry was beginning to be tried by the press. *Tried and convicted.* Back then we believed that everything the press wrote was factual. Today we know better.

I came to understand the evil power of accusations. Something does not have to be true to have a long-term, destructive and cancerous effect. It does not take long for the accusation to be caressed in the public's mind, where it is nurtured and fed until it gives birth to some warped edifice of "truth." The sad and sobering truth, I realized, is that people prefer to believe the bad rather than the good. Dirty laundry. It is bad news that people tune in to hear. That is what sells newspapers; the power of accusation. Guilty until proven innocent, and even when *proven* innocent, the strong concrete foundation of assumed guilt is so strong that a shadow of doubt always lingers in people's minds.

Muskrat had decided to take a day off from his job at Joe's Market and join me at the trial, albeit for a different reason. One of Muskrat's favorite movies was *To Kill a Mockingbird.* Ever since he first saw the flick, and he had seen it seven times, he wanted to become a lawyer and emulate Atticus Finch. He saw this as an opportunity to observe a real murder case that was too good to pass up. He also wanted a diversion from watching his father slowly deteriorate before his family's eyes. He picked me up in his Lucerne blue 70 GTO, a possession more precious to him than his girlfriend, Tina. By the time we found a free parking space, four blocks from the courthouse, the trial had already begun. Luckily, we found the last two seats in the gallery.

The prosecutor talked endlessly layering each piece of circumstantial "evidence" upon the last. I listened carefully to the ADA's rhetoric feeling more and more confident that Perry would be acquitted due to the weak case that was being presented. There would be no need for me to come forward with Perry's alibi.

It had been a little over a month since I had last seen Simone when I found out that she had begun dating the star running back on the high school football team. *But of course, she has! Serves me right!*

I mentally critiqued my new competition by visualizing Simone kissing him. He had an athletic build and a perfectly shaped afro. *He is taller, stronger and better looking than me. What the hell does she see in him?* The comical thought made me laugh out loud. *Just like my Uncle Ernie.* My uncle would buy a new Cadillac every year, and I felt that I had been traded in for a newer, shiner model. After all, who wants to be seen in last year's model.

I went home and immediately went down to my dark and damp bedroom. I turned on the Realistic stereo and listened to the first song that came on WIFI, the local pop radio station. The Chi-Lites began singing *Have You Seen Her?*

"How could so much go so wrong so quickly," I thought. "I should go get Simone back." But I knew I simply did not have the fight in me. It seemed as though my heart had been sucked out my chest, as if I no longer had one.

Bellamy had been on my bed, laying on his side. "To hell with her. You don't need her." I was taken back by Bellamy's harsh response. It was not Simone's fault; it was my culpability. I had discounted her. I had painted a masterpiece for her. A painting of a safe, respected, loving relationship, but when the paint dried, nothing was left but a counterfeit relationship. One based on my conscious fear of failure to comply with social norms and that others would never view me as highly as they had before. The comical thing was that people did not view me very highly. I was kidding myself. Thanks to my actions, Simone went from feeling she could dance on the petals of a sunflower to feeling like a rusted sardine can. The questions she would have for me had no answer. She was left to fill-in the answers for a test she never studied for. There is no way to receive a passing grade in that scenario.

"Come on, let's play wall ball," suggested Bellamy.

Wall ball was Bellamy's favorite game. He liked it because the two of us could play alone. It did not need more than one…or two to play. I knew he was trying to distract me from the Perry-Simone dark cloud, but I had no desire to play. Not only had Perry's trial taken any desire to have any fun, but Bellamy's rude attitude towards Simone eliminated any chance of me wanting to be with him.

I needed to be alone, and I knew the perfect place. Floaties, the cemetery pond, was always my haven. A safe place among the shade of the black alders, hedge maples and sycamores. Bellamy was not invited.

As I was approaching the pond, I saw a car parked just off the road. I got of my bike and walked it slowly to get a better look. It was Choo-Choo's stepfather. He was inside the yellow police tape and was putting something in his pocket. With a quick pace, he walked back to his car and drove away in the opposite direction from where I was standing.

I propped my bicycle against my favorite tree, an old and large sycamore with its bark peeling off in large chunks. I took a seat on the bridge, my feet dangling above the still water. *Why was he at the pond? Returning to the scene of the crime? Possibly, it was nothing more than curiosity, but why would he even care? He had no regard for Choo-Choo.*

Two eastern painted turtles sat as if frozen on a half-submerged limb that had taken a swan dive from its elevated home months before. I watched as a grey catbird landed on a stump and offered its repertoire of sounds, from meowing to confirm its name, to whistles and then chirps. I spanned the perimeter of the pond spotting frogs who mistakenly believed they were camouflaged.

Everything was linked together out there, the pond, the fish, the birds, the trees, the turtles, the frogs, the snakes, the lily pads. One needed the other for survival. But the circle of life that was present at the pond also included death, of course, but not only the obvious gravestones and above ground tombs that resembled a sarcophagus. The dried skeletal remains of a fish that a racoon had enjoyed for a predawn meal was lying at the edge of the pond. A sparrow that, at first, appeared intact, was the centerpiece for a congregation of ants. It was probably the victim of an herbicide the cemetery groundskeeper had spread to keep the field of death alive and green. The aesthetics of a mirage, masking what it kills, only so it can provide the gravestone visitor subliminal beauty while mourning.

🚲

Mr. Larsen sat with Perry explaining how he was going to continue presenting their case for the upcoming day. Instead of concentrating on Perry's innocence, he thought it best to show the jury that the prosecution literally had no proof. He would take each argument that the prosecution had made and, step-by-step, show how that argument had either no evidence to support it or that it was simply irrelevant. He felt strongly that he could discredit several of the state's witnesses as well, beginning with the lead detective.

"Perry, I want you to listen very carefully to what I'm about to say. I think we have a strong case. In fact, this case should have already been dismissed. But that the fact that it has not is the point I'm trying to make. We are fighting an invisible enemy; one that can be identified, but not seen, and it's nearly impossible to fight an invisible foe. You are accused of a heinous crime. You are fighting both prejudice in the jurors' minds as well as preconceptions about homosexuals. *They think that because you are a homosexual that you are also a pedophile.* Their perception of homosexuality is that it is a perversion that is prevalent in impulsive men. To think that a gay man would then sexually assault and murder a teenage boy is not that far of a jump. You need to know that.

You are the accused. You are suffering enormously from the stigma created by a dozen intolerant and ignorant people who have tremendous power to decide your fate. You have been under a lifelong suspicion long before Charlie Cardin was murdered.

You need one solid piece of evidence for the jury to not be able to get out of their minds. Perry, I know I sound like a broken record but, you need an alibi. We are down to the two-minute warning. We are desperate. We need your friend to come forward."

As if he had not heard one word that his attorney just spoken, Perry changed the subject and asked, "Do you think I should take the stand?"

"No, Perry, that seldom goes well," answered Larsen.

"They need to see that I am not a monster. Someone needs to expound to the jury who exactly I am. That I could never have hurt that boy. They need to see me as a person who cares for the youth of this town. I am a respected business owner. I have always supported this town. A few years ago, when they did not have the funds needed for that year's Little League, who was it that donated the money so they could buy uniforms and equipment? It was me."

"Yes," responded Larsen, "and they would not allow your flower shop to be printed on the uniforms. Sure, they took your money, but they did not acknowledge you. Look Perry, the simple truth is that there is a deep-rooted prejudice against gay people. I am alienated by other lawyers because I am gay. When the members of the Union League found out I was gay, my membership was terminated. The other men at our table would not speak to me and Mort Dexter, the Real Estate mogul, was livid when he found out. I thought he was a friend, but he has not spoken to me since."

Perry looked aimlessly beyond Larsen. "At this point, what choice do we have? What harm can it do? I realize that we are rolling the dice, but if I do not testify, we will certainly lose the case."

Looking off and pondering the choices, Larsen reluctantly agreed. "Unfortunately, you may be right. Okay, let's spend some time preparing you for the inevitably difficult cross examination."

CHAPTER THIRTY-THREE

History has proven that "Majority Rules" is dangerous,
simply because the majority is senseless.

M y second wife would tell me that I am an introvert who expresses himself as an extravert, which is to say, I can be quite gregarious in a crowd of people. But I prefer to be by myself. I am not sure if that is the result of years of disappointments from others, if not disappointment in myself. I do find it curious that I hated my loneliness as a child, and yet now, embrace it. My first wife would tell me that no one could ever love me enough, and my third wife simply said I was insane. Perhaps all three were correct. All I know is that my desire for self-isolation became more than attractive as I went through this stage in my life and even more so as I got older. The combination of events and experiences back then caused withdrawal, and I began to retreat from the masses.

Perry entered the courtroom dressed in a cream-colored dickey and a beige corduroy jacket. His appearance was tired, and his face drawn. Clearly the trial was having a draining effect on the gentleman florist.

"I'd like to call Dr. Jacob Cohen to the stand," Mr. Larsen stated.

After being sworn in, the tall, balding man with a comb-over took the seat in the witness stand. The doctor wore a poorly fitted gray suitcoat and a white shirt that, apparently, he had forgotten to put the collar stays in as the collar points were curling up. Mr. Larsen began his questioning.

"Dr. Cohen, would you please state your occupation?"

"I'm the First Deputy Coroner of Montgomery County. I am also acting pathologist for the county until Dr. Nicholas returns from a short leave of absence due to a health issue."

"And what is your responsibility as First Deputy Coroner?" Larsen asked.

"To deliver high quality professional forensic and laboratory services to the citizens of Montgomery County," responded Dr. Cohen.

"And in a murder case, what else might that entail?"

"To establish the cause and manner of death."

"Were you able to determine the time of death?"

"Between four and six o'clock the day before the body was found."

"How accurate is your analysis of the time of death, doctor? Could it, say, have happened at 3 o'clock? 7 o'clock?"

The coroner clearly was becoming increasingly uncomfortable with the questioning. "That is possible. The time of death is an approximation."

Attorney Larsen walked back to his table and looked at some notes he had written on a yellow legal pad. From his table he looked up and asked, "Did you determine that Charlie Cardin was sexually molested?"

"Yes, I did," answered Dr. Cohen.

"What made you come to that conclusion, doctor?"

"Semen found on the victim's body."

"Was any semen found in the victim's anus or mouth, doctor?"

"Well, no," the coroner reluctantly replied.

"Where was this semen found?"

"On the boy's pants," Dr. Cohen responded.

"Couldn't that have come from the victim having masturbated at some point prior to his death?"

There was no response from the coroner who was pondering the question as if he had never thought of that possibility.

"Doctor Cohen, I ask you again. Couldn't that semen have come from the victim himself and isn't it true there was no evidence of a sexual assault?"

In a softer tone, the doctor answered, "I suppose so, but...."

"Just yes or no, Doctor Cohen. Was there any evidence of anal penetration on the victim?"

"It was inconclusive."

"Inconclusive? Wouldn't that be easy to ascertain, doctor?" Larsen asked as he walked closer to the witness stand.

"The victim had been in the water for at least twelve hours. He had goose flesh. Decomposition changes advance more slowly in the water, primarily due to cooler temperatures and the anaerobic environment. Once a body is removed from the water, putrefaction will likely be accelerated."

"That's all fascinating, doctor, but I don't presume any of our jurors have a medical degree. Just to clarify, the *goose flesh*, as you call it, is a marked wrinkling of the skin and eventual sloughing of skin, also known as *washerwoman changes*.

"Correct," responded the doctor.

"Doesn't that *goose flesh* make it impossible to tell whether or not any penetration had taken place?"

"The anaerobic nature of decomposition for a submerged corpse may result in adipocere formation, a unique process that results from incomplete transformation of lipids by bacteria."

Pushing the doctor for a concise response, Larsen, placing his hand on the edge of the witness box, asked, "Please answer simply yes, or no. Could you tell, with certainty, that Charles Cardin was sexually assaulted?

"Not with 100% certainty."

"In fact, establishing sexual assault and even the cause of death is difficult enough without adding the postmortem changes that naturally take place. So, we have absolutely no evidence or proof that Charlie Cardin was sexually assaulted. Was it you who gave the press the misinformation that the Charlie Cardin was sexually assaulted?" Larsen asked with a bit of anger in his voice.

"Objection, argumentative," barked the ADA, the words coming out of his mouth before he stood.

"Objection overruled," stated the judge. "I'd like to hear where this fabrication of the truth came from."

"I don't remember," answer Dr. Cohen.

"In fact, it did come from your office, doctor. Wasn't it the Assistant Deputy Coroner, John Tyson who provided those lies to the press, and wasn't it a friend of his, a reporter from the *Philadelphia Inquirer*, that helped him shape this web of lies?"

"Objection!" shouted ADA Fitzpatrick. "Hearsay and argumentative!"

"Withdrawn," responded Mr. Larsen. "I have one more question for you, Dr. Cohen. Is it not true that many of the bruises found on Charlie Cardin's body were old injuries that occurred days or even a week before his death?"

"Yes," answered the doctor.

Mr. Larsen paused, as if thinking how exactly to proceed with the coroner's agreement. "An accurate interpretation of bruising at necropsy is essential to understanding how a victim was injured. This helps the pathologist in a reliable reconstruction of the events leading to his death and whether there were older injuries consistent with being habitually abused, say at home, by a parent?"

"Objection, your honor," the ADA repeated.

"I have no further questions. Your witness."

ADA Fitzpatrick briskly walked close to the witness stand and asked, "Doctor, have you ever performed an autopsy on a body that was submerged in the water?"

"Yes, at least a dozen times," answered the Dr. Cohen.

"And haven't you received praise from your colleagues on the work and conclusions you documented in several of these cases?"

"That is true."

"No further questions, your honor." Larsen stood and stated, "The defense would like to recall Detective Jorge Herrera to the stand." After the judge reminded the detective that he was he still under oath, Mr. Larsen began his questioning. "Detective, you were the lead investigator in this case, were you not?"

"I was," answered Detective Herrera.

"What was it about my client that made him a suspect?"

"He was the last person who saw the victim alive," answered Detective Herrera.

"How did you determine that?" asked Mr. Larsen.

"We found a note in the victim's pocket written by Mr. Strathmore."

"Could the note have been written and received on a day other than the day Charlie was murdered?"

"It could have been, but we assumed the victim wasn't wearing the same pair of shorts two days in a row," responded Herrera.

"You *assumed?* As a detective, do you make it a habit to make assumptions?"

"Objection!" barked the ADA.

"I'll reword, your Honor. Detective Herrera, isn't it dangerous to make assumptions in an investigation? Can't that lead to false conclusions?"

"It can," agreed the detective. "However, in this case it didn't. Your client admitted to writing the note. He lied about when he wrote it, and he lied about which day it was that Charlie Cardin raked his leaves."

Attorney Larsen continued to remove the detective's confident and arrogant outer layer to the real person beneath the façade, like an apple peeled back to reveal its flesh.

"How do you know he lied about what day Charlie did the work for Mr. Strathmore?"

"His neighbor, Mrs. Buettner, said she saw Charlie Cardon in Mr. Strathmore's yard the same day he was murdered."

"Didn't she say it was either that Wednesday or Thursday, she couldn't remember?" asked Perry's lawyer.

"I don't recall," answered the detective.

Attorney Larsen walked back to his table and picked up a yellow legal pad, looked at it briefly, then tossed it on the table. His head hung low, as if pondering whether he should state what was on his mind. He decided to.

"Detective, is it not true that you have a hatred for homosexuals, and you are repulsed by the idea of intimate contact with a member of the same sex?"

"Excuse me, your honor, objection on the grounds of irrelevance." Mr. Fitzpatrick said as he got up from his chair.

"Which part of the statement was irrelevant?' asked the judge.

"The detective's personal opinion on homosexuality is irrelevant. Mr. Herrera is not the one on trial here."

Mr. Larsen took a few steps toward the judge and responded. "Your honor, I am attempting to expose the detective's paranoia and bias towards homosexuals in general and my client specifically. This bias led to the hasty arrest of my client which led to the district attorney's office charging him with this murder. The District Attorney was the one who opened the door regarding my client's sexuality."

"So, he did. Objection sustained, but Mr. Larsen, you better tread lightly," the judge said.

Mr. Larsen nodded his head to the judge; acknowledging that he understood. "Let me reword the question. Mr. Herrera, do you believe all homosexuals are pedophiles?"

"Not all," answered the detective.

"Do you believe *most* homosexuals are pedophiles?"

Detective Herrera did not hesitate to answer the question. "It's been proven that a lot of homosexuals *are* pedophiles."

"Really," responded Larsen with a louder tone. "And what legitimate statistics do you have to back-up that preposterous statement?"

"I can't remember where I read it."

"You cannot remember, because it's not so. Detective, this is an article written by the University of Pennsylvania Psychology Department based on seven years of research. Would you please read the highlighted section?"

Detective Herrera glanced over the article Mr. Larsen handed him before beginning to read it out loud. "The conclusion of this study shows there is no evidence that gay men or lesbians are any more likely than heterosexuals to molest children than heterosexual individuals. In fact, research proves that the vast majority of child molesters target children in their circle of family and friends, and the majority are men married to women." The detective took off his glasses and looked up with a look of defeat.

"Detective, Dr. Cohen testified that Charlie's tongue had been removed. Did anyone ever find the tongue?"

"Not that I know of."

"Wouldn't you, as lead detective, know if it had been found?"

"Sure," the detective answered.

"So, the tongue was never found at the defendant's house when a thorough search was conducted by your detectives?"

"No, it wasn't."

After the trial I had spoken to Mr. Larsen and he told me that the tongue had been mailed to the detective's office in an empty box of Good & Plenty. What we did not know was *when* exactly it was delivered. One thing is for sure, Perry could not have mailed it.

"Thank you, detective. I have no further questions for this witness."

ADA Fitzpatrick stood and said, "I have one question for this witness. Detective Herrera, was the relationship between Mr. Strathmore and Charlie Cardin known to anyone else?"

"Not that we could gather," responded the detective.

"If no one knew of this relationship, wouldn't you say that Mr. Strathmore would do anything, even murder Charlie, to keep their relationship secret."

"Objection!" called Mr. Larsen, "That's a leading question requiring a conclusion."

"I'll withdrawal the question," responded the ADA.

My mind was running sprints through the lanes of thoughts as I tried to segregate them and concentrate on only one. For some reason, my thoughts came to Choo-Choo's tattoo. *Charlie. If only you could have put on your Superman cape and flown away from your assailant or, better yet, had beat him up.*

🚲

The following day, Mr. Larsen called Perry to the stand as planned. He asked questions which were intended to bring credibility to his client's integrity. He illuminated Perry's generosity towards the community. Specifically, that he had no prior arrests, not even a parking ticket, and his flower shop had provided flowers free of charge for a funeral of an elderly gentleman in the community whose family had no money to purchase them on their own.

I looked at Perry sitting on the witness stand, thinking how he should not be up there on display. *Perry is my friend. There, I said it. He was the only one who really tried to understand me without wanting anything in return. He saw something in me that others had not. He never talked about his sexuality to me. Why would he?*

When the cross examination came, it came with despicable bias and false assumptions and, the ADA saved the best for last.

"Mr. Strathmore, I would like you to take a look at this torn envelope with Charlie's name on it. Is this your handwriting?"

"Yes," answered Perry.

"Now open the envelope and tell the court, was that note also written by you?"

"Yes, it was," Answered Perry

"Please read it out loud."

"Charlie, I am grateful for the job you did for me. You are a beautiful young man. Please never forget that!"

Whispering and chatter from the gallery filled the court room. The judge banged his gravel and demanded order be restored to the courtroom. ADA Fitzpatrick leaned over the banister and looked closely at Perry.

"Mr. Strathmore, what were you referring to when you said you were grateful for what Charlie did for you?"

Perry turned from the prosecutor and looked directly at me, not with an accusatory look, but one of sympathy. Thinking that it was impossible for me heart to sink and lower, I pondered whether Perry could see through me and understand that I lacked the courage to live an authentic life. Most people do lack that ability, of course, but my lack of authenticity was going to suffocate Perry.

"For the good job he did raking my leaves. He was a boy who lacked confidence and approval. I was simply trying to encourage him. He needed a friend, that's all." Perry's words fell limp on the banister that stood in front of the witness chair.

"A friend? A friend? And why does a grown man want to be friends with a teenage boy?" the prosecutor asked.

"Objection!" Perry's attorney shouted. "The prosecution is being argumentative."

"Sustained," the judge responded. "The jury will disregard the last question."

Muskrat leaned over to me and whispered, "Strathmore's screwed."

"I'll withdrawal the question." responded Fitzpatrick, "Is beautiful an adjective that a grown man uses to describe a boy?"

"Like I already said, Charlie was insecure and felt unwanted. He may have been a little slow, but he did not need to be constantly reminded of it. At home, at school, by the neighborhood kids. I believe that if someone starts hearing compliments and positive reinforcement, they eventually begin to *believe* it." It appeared as though Perry felt like one of his butterflies pinned to a spreading board.

"I'm glad to see that you are a self-educated psychologist as well as a florist, Mr. Strathmore."

"Objection!" Shouted Mr. Larsen. "The question is sarcastic and argumentative."

"Withdrawn, your Honor. I have no further questions for this witness," the prosecutor said as he walked back to his chair.

The judge looked at his watch then proclaimed the court was adjourned until Monday morning at 9:30, when closing arguments would be heard.

🚲

After the prosecution regurgitated the inferred evidence and their clumsy attempt to "connect-the-dots" with the evidence they did have, it was Attorney Larsen's opportunity to give his closing arguments for the defense.

"Ladies and gentlemen, thank you for your service and sacrifice in this case. Circumstantial evidence, bias, false information that had been leaked to the press are all you have heard from the prosecution. The prosecution had the burden of proof, a burden they still possess. They still have this burden because nothing at all has been proven by them during this entire trial. They certainly have not proved beyond a shadow of a doubt that my client did anything wrong, let alone murder Charles Cardin. The Abington Police Department and the county District Attorney's office never pursued leads or questioned any suspects other than Perry Strathmore. They never considered the victim's stepfather, who had frequently abused the young man. Charlie Cardin's pastor, although not arrested yet, resigned his position due to allegations of improper contact with young boys. Both individuals should have been viable suspects, but the police decided Mr. Strathmore was guilty long before this trial began and by doing so, never performed a thorough investigation. Shame on them!"

And what about Mongrel, I mused? He was arrested for assault and had a reputation for beating up neighborhood kids.

Mr. Larsen continued. "The district attorney has not proven that Perry Strathmore murdered Charlie Cardin. He proved that Mr. Strathmere is a homosexual and that is not what he's on trial for. He will gladly plead guilty to the charge of homosexuality. What a horrible offense! The prosecution has done an atrocious injustice to this man. Do you find homosexuality to be a sin and an abomination under your eyes? Fine, but so is bearing false witness and punishing an innocent man. They are sins, as well, ladies and gentlemen.

You are charged with the responsibility to find the defendant guilty *only if* there is proof beyond a shadow of a doubt. Ladies and gentlemen, there was not only a shadow of a doubt that Mr. Strathmore never hurt Charlie Cardin, but there is also an eclipse of doubt causing a darkness to fall upon this courtroom. Bring just sunshine into this courtroom and make a statement that this charade of a case and the false accusations brought against my client, will not be tolerated. With courage, find Mr. Strathmore not guilty. Make a statement here today that regardless of a person's skin color, ethnicity, or even sexual orientation, they deserve decency, fairness and the pursuit of happiness. Thank you."

Yes…courage.

The jury never heard about a similar murder that had taken place a few days earlier in Lansdale, a semi-rural town 12 miles northwest of North Hills. The local newspaper in the North Penn area reported that a young boy, labeled as *retarded*, had been sexually assaulted and strangled. The body had been found in a farm pond. There were too many similarities to Choo-Choo's murder for the connection to be ignored. A hog farmer, the same one who had been delivering butchered hogs to Joe's Market, had been arrested and was sitting in the same jailhouse Perry was in. But the jury had been in deliberations at the time of the arrest and never heard about this case. No one brought up the name of Reverend Markey. Choo-Choo's stepfather was briefly questioned and released. His alibi? He had been in his patrol car with his partner.

The next day a large crowd had gathered outside the courthouse anxiously waiting the much-anticipated verdict. Those who had been lucky enough to secure a seat in the courtroom had arrived at sunrise and formed a line outside the building.

The jury had deliberated for only three hours when they were ushered into the courtroom. I knew Perry's stomach resembled a ride down Philadelphia's pot-hole-riddled Front Street. It appeared that he had not slept at all. Perry looked pensive as he stared out at the window to see if the Monarch had returned. It had, but its appearance was weathered. With wings closed, it slowly walked up the wired glass, glass which had a grid of thin metal wire embedded within it, but the butterfly seemed lethargic. Within minutes, the Monarch started to deflate, and its chrysalises began to turn dark brown and pupate.

"All rise." stated the Bailiff in a sturdy tone. "The District Court of the State of Pennsylvania is now in session. The Honorable Judge Hoskins presiding."

"Please be seated," the judge said.

The jury foreman walked deliberately to the Bailiff and handed him the verdict, who then gave it to the judge. The judge read the verdict and returned it to the bailiff who then gave back to the Jury Foreman to read to the Court.

"Have you reached a verdict?" asked the judge.

"Yes, your honor," answered the foreman.

"Will the defendant please stand?" Looking at the jury the judge continued. "What say you?"

"We the jury, in the case of The State of Pennsylvania versus Perry Strathmore, find the defendant *guilty* of the charge of first-degree murder."

A choir of applause flowed from the gallery. Perry made no visible reaction to the verdict as his eyes were transfixed on the butterfly which was dangling by one fragile leg that was still attached to the window. He never heard the judge thank the jury for their service, nor announce that the sentencing phase of the trial would take place the following week. He did not hear the judge adjourn the court as he was led by two sheriffs out of the courtroom. He never felt his attorney's arm around his shoulders, nor him saying that they would appeal. He heard the nothingness that accompanies the injustice of being tried for who you are rather than what you did or *did not do.* Perry had become just another victim of the ignorance and prejudice that comes from a preconceived fallacy and fear of the unknown.

CHAPTER THIRTY-FOUR

There is no such thing as common sense. There is only rare sense.

Muskrat and I left the courthouse from the rear entrance and got into his car.

"You wanna do anything?" Muskrat asked.

"No. I'm beat," I said, trying to give some kind of excuse why I did not feel like talking and had no desire to be in anyone's company. "Just drop me off at home. I'll see you tomorrow."

After I got home, I went into the garage and grabbed my bicycle and rode aimlessly. I found a park bench near the Glenside Library and sat down. There was no one within sight. I sat emotionless and watched a panting dog lift his leg to pee on an azalea bush. After what seemed like a very long time, I jumped on my sunset orange Schwinn Super Sport and headed home in bemusement, the words banging repeatedly against the walls of my mind...*guilty!*

I did not notice the neon ice cream cone that was perched above Jack Frost and had not seen the canary yellow De Tomaso Pantera, my favorite car at the time, parked at the Kenyon diner. I also failed to see the UPS truck that nearly hit me as I crossed Limekiln Pike that was heavy with traffic. I peddled imprecisely in a fog.

Guilty! The verdict came as no surprise to many, yet it took me off guard, leaving me with a perplexity of emotions. I had convinced myself that Perry would undoubtedly be acquitted. I had failed my friend; I had failed myself. The demon of cowardice had won, but I knew that it would never stop harassing me unless I made some drastic changes and started doing what I knew should have done all along.

The sad truth is, when one places themselves in a situation which would expose their inner secrets, most will choose the cowardly way out. People who have disdain for abortion will often have one themselves when discovering they are pregnant, rather than face the rejection and criticism of loved ones. A person will join along with those who criticize and ridicule a person, or will remain silent, rather than opposing the group and defending the individual being attacked. Safety in numbers? No one likes to be the Lone Ranger. Truth is, most people are cowards.

I could not quiet my thoughts. There were dozens of times in the past when I assumed I had reached the lowest place possible, but now I found myself at a new cellar. It seemed like someone had opened the trap door at the floor of a bottomless pit. I had no one to share my grief with. Hell, no one knew all the intricate details of the situation, so how could they empathize? There was no one to purge the pain that rotted deep in my soul. No one who could comfort me. As so many times before, no one to understand me, that is, except Bellamy, and I had become increasingly distant from him. I was beginning to question both his empathy and his authenticity. The more I questioned Bellamy's existence, the less Bellamy had come around.

Bellamy was so much apart of me, so much so, that I had difficulty distinguishing him from me. He always appeared wiser than me, more confident that I was. He increasingly encouraged me to act on my impulses; impulses that I had always stifled. He wanted me to *react* to situations. He told me that by withholding my desired reactions to things, I was becoming anxious, and it was chiseling away at my already low self-esteem. He was right. It was time to act.

I knew what I had to do, and I was now willing to proceed, but I needed to determine how I would do it. I had feared that when a critical time came, and I knew it would come, that I would reach into a cavern void of courage and that is exactly what happened. I longed for the opportunity to prove I had a backbone, but was still petrified of that same opportunity. A paradox of wills...and I had failed. *Not again! This is where things change, beginning now!*

Like the lion in *The Wizard of Oz*, I believed that my fear made me inadequate, but that fictious lion was, in fact, brave; he simply doubted himself. I certainly lacked that kind of confidence. I was still searching for that moment when I would be brave. I needed to start anew. A new life, a new location and environment where my history was unknown to others. College was not an option given my low high school GPA. I knew there was only one option: the military.

I was torn between joining the valiant ground troops of the Marines or enlisting in the Navy and becoming a River Rat in Nam, the only men in the history of the Navy authorized to wear the black beret. These men patrolled the brown water of the Mekong River Delta and the numerous distributaries in southwest Vietnam. These were the men who fought the Viet Cong, who used thick vegetation along the water to their advantage. There would be no place for me to hide. Kill or be killed. *That is where I could prove I was a man.*

Four or five blocks before I reached Hawthorne Road, I saw a few bicycles propped up against a large Maple tree. Approaching the street corner, I saw it was my nemesis, Mongrel and his faithful sidekick, Benny. As I slowed to make my turn on to Hawthorne, I caught a blurry glimpse of the rock Mongrel had thrown, perfectly leading the bicycle. Before I could react, I felt the sting on the right-side of my knee as the stone cut deep against my flesh. As if instinctively, I swung my injured leg over the crossbar and balanced myself on one pedal as the bike glided to a stop.

Laying my bike on the grass at the corner of the intersection, I walked briskly toward the now laughing Mongrel. Without hesitation, I threw a right hook as hard as I could, landing squarely into Mongrel's nose, shattering it. Sensing the danger I was in, I followed with a vicious uppercut, dropping my tormentor on his back. With blurry eyes from the tears caused by the broken nose, a stunned Mongrel placed his hands behind him in an attempt to get up and gather himself. Before he had a chance to, I dove on to his chest, unleashing a rapid series of jabs to Mongrel's bloody face that were fueled by a lifetime of built-up anger. The self-hate, the repeated failures, the disappointments, and the numerous ridicules joined forces to create a right cross with incredible knockout power.

A dumbfounded Benny, finally realizing that his mentor needed help, pulled me by my shoulders and freed the large bully, but

Mongrel's face was bloodied and his confidence had been traumatized. Once Mongrel got to his knees, I began kicking hard into the beast's ribs until I was utterly exhausted.

"Get up, you piece of dog shit! Get up," I yelled.

After a few minutes when it was clear that there was no fight left in Mongrel, I got back on my Super Sport and slowly pedaled home.

The house was reverently quiet when I got home. Olivia had gotten married to a softball-playing engineer. Audrey was in Europe working on her Masters' in romantic languages, and Ted was beginning his junior year at university. Woody had walked into the kitchen from his nap under the dining room table, shook, and walked next to me waiting for the customary massage.

"You're not going to see me here much longer," I said to Woody while continuing to rub his neck. "I've gotta get out of here. I'd take you with me, buddy, but you wouldn't be happy where I'm going. I'm not sure I'll be happy there either, but at least no one will know me."

I was still feeling the anger simmering within me, but I was more than ready to put that person I was to death and start anew.

Walking into my room, I glanced over at the aquarium. The tadpoles had disappeared and in their place were a half dozen frogs. I scooped each one up with my hands and placed them gently into an empty shoebox that had a half dozen ventilation holes I had punched through with a pencil. Securing the lid with masking tape, I grabbed my bicycle and headed to Hillside Cemetery.

Riding the curvy roads within the graveyard, I approached Floaties Pond, laid the bicycle down, and sat on the bank. A remnant of yellow crime tape was still wrapped around a large sycamore. I opened the shoebox and watched as one by one the frogs hopped over to edge of the pond and disappeared under the water. I leaned against the tree, much of its mottled bark had flaked off in large irregular masses exposing gray and greenish-white areas that made the tree look hauntingly beautiful.

I threw a stone into the pond, watching the ripples run away, just like I was planning to do. Run away from all of this, but not before I finished the task I had been avoiding. Staring at the water, I contemplated the obvious. I had depleted my arsenal of arguments for not coming forward as Perry's alibi. Now I had no choice. An innocent man would be executed or spend the rest of his life in prison. I would go tomorrow to see Mr. Larsen in person.

🚲

Over the phone, Larsen was ecstatic and told me there would be some standard questions I would need to answer and some papers to sign. He said that this changed everything and would most likely lead to having Perry released on bail, and there would be a motion for a new trial. He did not ask the obvious questions as to why I had waited to come forward. I assumed he did not want to do anything to scare me off, but the tone in his voice clearly displayed his excitement and delight with my decision. It was too late for him to go and tell Perry the good news that evening, but he said he would go to see him first thing in the morning, as soon as the county jail allowed visitors.

Perry will forgive me for taking so long to come forward. He will understand. That is the type of guy he is. I will be his savior. He will think he was born again. I know he will be over-the-moon happy, and it will be because of me! I had been working on convincing myself that Perry's reaction would not be undesirable. That just is not who Perry was. I also knew it was time to step-up and begin this long-neglected transformation into becoming that which I had so longed to be, but there was something I had to do before I went to see Perry's attorney. I needed an exit strategy after testifying.

I had been teetering on the balance beam between an innocent juvenile life of blissful ignorance—a life absent of consequences—and the life of adult maturity, one where every decision has consequences—a life that requires sensibility and responsibility. *When I was a child, I spoke as a child, I understood as a child, I thought as a child; but when I became a man, I put away childish things.*

I rode my bike down Jenkintown Road and turned on to Keswick Avenue, located in the heart of Glenside. I passed the Keswick Cycle Shop where I had purchased the Schwinn Super Sport and stopped in front of the Recruiting Station, securing my bike with a chain by locking it to a parking meter. *Life is all about decisions. Life is about three or four, maybe as many as a half dozen decisions that will drastically alter your life, depending upon how you choose.*

I only had one decision to make: was I going to enlist in the Navy or the Marines. The Marines would probably be a fast track to seeing action in Nam. The few times I had mentioned my thoughts of entering the Corp, my father, having survived four horrid years in the Pacific Islands during the Great War, strongly tried to persuade me against the Marines and for the Navy. Afterall, the conflict in Vietnam was still alive despite media reports that it was winding down.

Walking into the building, I had made up my mind to enlist in the Marine Corp, but when I looked at the recruiter's desk for the Corps, it was empty. "Corporal Shaw had to leave for the day," a sailor in navy blue and white crackerjacks said from his desk that was facing the marine's desk. "Why not join the Navy and see the world?"

Was it large enough to disappear in and reinvent one's self?

"Where do I sign?" I asked.

CHAPTER THIRTY-FIVE

This is the law: blood spilt upon the ground cries out for more.

—Aeschylus

I could feel the months of stress evaporate from my life like rain drops on a hot windshield. I would come to Perry's rescue, and it would be *me* who set Perry free. *Better late than never, right?* I would be in Great Lakes Training Facility—far away from the inevitable innuendos and sarcastic remarks by the time the folks in North Hills heard the news of my relationship with Perry, but I really didn't care much what they thought of me anymore.

Having scheduled an early morning meeting with Mr. Larsen to share my decision to come forward on Perry's behalf, I left the house before my parents had gotten out of bed. I knew that the attorney would ask me why I had waited so long, and I was prepared for that. As far as I was concerned, Larsen should be grateful that I had the courage and decency to right a wrong. That should be all that mattered.

Larsen's office was a few short blocks from the courthouse, a converted white spacious home from the glory days of Norristown. I walked up the wide steps and opened the double-wide green door and immediately, to my right, was a receptionist who appeared to have been crying.

"Hi. I'm Calvin Lloyd. I have an appointment with Mr. Larsen."

The lady stood up, wiped her nose with a tissue and walked toward a set of doors. "Mr. Larsen is expecting you," she said as she opened the door.

Tim Larsen stood up from behind his desk and motioned to the oversized chair facing him. "Hello Calvin, please have a seat."

Without hesitation, I began explaining how Perry could not have murdered Choo-Choo, because I had been with Perry all afternoon till nearly 6 o'clock and shared the embarrassing reasons why I had not come forward during the trial. "Mr. Larsen, I'll do anything you tell me to do just so that we can get Perry out of jail."

Expressionless, Larsen leaned forward placing his palms upon his desk and looked directly into my eyes. "Calvin, Perry was found dead in his cell this morning. He hanged himself."

I sat there trying to comprehend the words that lingered in the air like smoke on a still August night. I said nothing, for there was nothing to say. It is a sobering thing to be exposed to an unexpected scenario after thinking you have solved an insoluble problem. "I believe this note was written to you," Larsen said as he handed me an unopened envelope with the lone letter C written on its face.

I do not remember getting up and leaving Larsen's office, but I do remember that the sun was bright and steam was rising from the streets after a brief shower had washed the filth from the city. Yet, there was the stench that remained from which the legal process brings. Trash was piled high, waiting for the garbage-eating trucks to devour it and make the city clean again, but I knew that this town could never be sanitized. The rats that wandered those streets wore 3-piece suits and worked at the courthouse looking for cheese. They would never feel comfortable traversing their way through the heaps of debris that littered the streets.

Sitting on the park bench that was sparsely shaded by a wide maple that had lost most its leaves, I opened the enveloped and unfolded a narrow piece of paper.

C,

If one cannot step into the light for fear they will be exposed, is this reason alone to lose another's friendship? Not my friendship, I assure you.

Always remember that one must be truthful with oneself, before they can ever be truthful with others.

Forever your friend,

P

🚲

Bellamy droned on for an hour or more even though I hardly heard a word, but I clearly remember him saying, "I told you that I would never let anyone take advantage of you again. I would take matters into my own hands if I had to, and I had to. I could no longer sit idly by and see you coward...."

"What do you mean?" I mumbled.

"Your entire life you've been getting your ass kicked, and I don't just mean physically. People have treated you like dog shit that they scrap off the bottom of your shoes! No one treats you with respect, so you have to stand-up and demand it! If people do stupid stuff that's going to cause you grief, you have to stop them!"

I looked deeply into Bellamy's eyes. They seemed darker. Harsher. The brightness was gone. "Why did you do it, Bellamy? Why did you have to kill Choo-Choo? Were you jealous of my relationship with Perry? Were you?"

"You are pitiful," Bellamy said as he looked at me with disgust; as if he hated me for my accusation; or maybe for my ability to transfer my blame to him. "You don't get it, do you? I had to. Choo-Choo was walking past Perry's place when you were leaving his house that day. You never even noticed him, because he was walking his bike up the hill and your vision was blocked by a parked car. He knew that Perry was queer. All the kids know that. When he saw you coming out of

Perry's house, I guess you became guilty by association. He was going to tell everyone. You know how he is. *He has always told everyone everything!* I lured him to the cemetery promising him that I had a girl for him who wanted to get laid. Choo-Choo was so simple. I tried to talk some sense into him, but he kept saying over and over 'That man kisses boys and licks their dicks. I'm telling your friends.' Cal, I had to. Oh, and that coroner got the time of death wrong by an hour. We had left Perry's house at six, remember? You didn't get home until after eight."

Bellamy was a murderer. A murderer! But he only killed Choo-Choo to protect me. Wouldn't any true friend do that? He took risks. He acted, when I could not, all so that my reputation would not be completely destroyed. I turned my back on Bellamy, and he was gone.

EPILOGUE

I first killed an ant with a magnifying glass. Years later, a
sparrow with a slingshot. Then, I progressed to killing a
deer with a rifle. Now I prefer
killing man.

J ust about everyone has forgotten about Choo-Choo's murder by now. There are only a handful of people living in North Hills who were there when it all happened. Time tends to do that. But I reminisce a lot.

I once was called for jury duty on a murder case. How funny is that? I was selected as the foreperson and did an incredible job...if I say so myself...of convincing the other eleven jurors to convict the defendant. During the sentencing phase, we were split on whether to give him a death sentence. Again, by my gift of persuasion, or manipulation, I did just that. He was executed just a few years ago. I was obsessed with finding the man guilty and allowing the state to snuff out his life, not because he was guilty, I thought he had a good reason to kill the person, but rather that he was so pathetically stupid for getting caught. If you are going to commit a crime, do it by yourself, or have an imaginary friend do it. Most people arrested and convicted had a co-conspirator rat them out, often to receive a plea deal. Believe me, your mother would testify against you to keep herself out of jail. There is no honor among thieves.

I find it interesting that people's opinion of others suddenly improves when that person dies. I guess you should not speak ill of the deceased. Those who elevated Choo-Choo to some elite status when he was dead were the same people who viewed him as a nuisance and with little value when he was alive.

For what purpose can a civilized society justify the taking of another's life? That is the question, isn't it? War? State sanctioned punishment? Self-defense? Ah, yes! To defend oneself from harm. But I ask you, why should self-defense be limited to physical harm? Is not one's emotional and mental health just as important than their physical health? I would argue that it may be *more* important. You can live with physical limitations, but you can never *live* with deep emotional injuries. Not really. I believed that I killed Choo-Choo in self-defense.

The truth is often hard to swallow. You may argue that if Bellamy murdered Choo-Choo that, in fact, it was really me. I will not deny that accusation, but at the time it was much more palatable to believe it was Bellamy. My hands were clean. Blame fell on Bellamy. Trust me, it was a much better way to live. Those who would have ridiculed me for having Bellamy as a friend lack the advantage I held. Bellamy willingly took that which I preferred not to handle. That is what I would call a prefect relationship!

All these years later, you should know, I do feel the weight of guilt, but you may wonder whether that guilt accompanies having regrets. Not really. I did go to Perry's attorney's office to offer an alibi, didn't I? Considering the time all of this took place, the prevailing environment in which I lived—that which influenced me and what I had experienced—what other options did I have? I ask you this: Was there any other way this could have turned out? I am not sure there was. You may wonder why I made sure Choo-Choo's body was found naked. Well, I certainly did not sexually abuse the kid. My thoughts were that the police would think some child molester was the culprit— maybe Pastor Markey. On the other hand, I would have much rather had Choo-Choo's stepfather been convicted of the murder. Not being convicted of the crimes he *did* commit, but being convicted of a crime he *did not*. Now that would have been poetic justice!

So, why have I decided to share this lengthy confession with you? Why, indeed. After so many years, I could have let things lie, and I would have, but even now, after all these years, Perry deserves his name and reputation to be cleared. I do not like unfinished business. Never have. And I do believe in God and sooner or later I am going to face Him. Sooner, it turns out. You see, I am now sitting on death row. I have been given a death sentence; the execution date about three months from now. This judgment was not handed down by the State, mind you. It is a sentence that cancer has given me. Terminal, the doctors say.

I had given my lawyer a manilla envelope with instructions not to open it until my death. Within the envelope is this confessional story on a thumb drive, along with a few documents. This is kind of my last will and testament.

I cannot remember who it was that said, once a man dips his hands in another man's blood, he will always have the desire to do it again, or that it is easier the second time. Well, whoever it was, they were correct.

ACKNOWLEDGEMENTS

This book is truly a "life-work," not that it has taken me 66+ years to write it, but that many of the stories are, in some shape or form, an experience I had growing up. That is not to say that this body is not fiction, because it certainly is, and with any fiction work, I have greatly exaggerated or invented much of what is written. North Hills, Pennsylvania is an actual town located in the suburbs of Philadelphia, where I grew up. It is a wonderful town, and I have many good memories growing up there. My description of it in this book is not accurate.

I did, in fact, have an imaginary friend when I was young. Thank you, Jock-a-Conti, for being a good friend when I needed one!

Virtually all books are influenced by other books and people who have crossed the author's path, and Bellamy is no exception. There are several people who have contributed greatly to this book, and I am extremely grateful for each of them.

Special thanks to my editor, Kevin Smith, who is also an author of several books and, more importantly, a great friend. His insight, thoughtful criticism, and suggestions helped make this book a much better read. His encouragement spurred me on and my endless questions were always received with patience and kindness.

The story about Coy and Johnny was inspired by a story my friend, Gary Slish, had told me years ago. Gary is a wonderful storyteller in his own right.

To my four children and three grandchildren, thank you. You will never know how much I am blessed to have all of you in my life.

Love and gratitude to my wife, Carolyn who has listened to my life stories endlessly. I do not know anyone who reads more than she does, averaging a book a week. Both her extensive reading and her experience as a high school English teacher gave me invaluable advice. Her encouragement and love gave me what I needed to cross the finish line.

To all the friends, relatives, and acquaintances, and to the "gang" from North Hills, a heartfelt thank you!

My publisher, Steve Himes at Telemachus Press, patiently answered my numerous questions about how best to present the book to you, my readers. My daughter, Bayley Ramos, was wonderful to work with in creating the front and back covers, even with me changing my mind countless times. Their help made this book more aesthetically pleasing.

AUTHOR'S BIO

Before turning to fiction, G. Bradley Davis was the CEO of Apex Packaging Solutions, and earned a BA in Communications from Temple University and a Master of Arts in Theological Studies from Bethel University. Bellamy is his second book; his first work of fiction. An avid fisherman, he also enjoys playing golf, softball and pickleball.

He is the father of four children and three grandchildren and currently lives on Marco Island with his wife and a vizsla named, Clark, where he is working on his next book.

Visit the author website: www.GBradleyDavis.com

Made in United States
Orlando, FL
10 January 2024

42357560R00200